SEA OF TRANQUILLITY

Also by Paul Russell

Fiction

War Against the Animals
The Coming Storm
Boys of Life
The Salt Point

Nonfiction

*The Gay 100: A Ranking of the Most Influential Gay Men
and Lesbians, Past and Present*

SEA OF TRANQUILLITY

Paul Russell

St. Martin's Griffin ✹ New York

www.stmartins.com

This novel makes use of information found in the following sources: *First on the Moon* by Neil Armstrong, Edwin E. Aldrin, Jr., Michael Collins, with Gene Farmer and Dora Jane Hamblin (William S. Konecky Associates); *Return to Earth* by Edwin E. Aldrin, Jr., and Wayne Warga (Random House); *The Voyages of Apollo* by Richard S. Lewis (Times Books); and Francis X. Clines and John Noble Wilford in *The New York Times*.

Library of Congress Cataloging-in-Publication Data

Russell, Paul Elliot.
   Sea of tranquillity / by Paul Russell.—1st. St. Martin's ed.
     p. cm.
   ISBN 0-312-30372-6
    1. Gay men—Fiction. 2. Astronauts—Fiction. 3. Parents of gays—Fiction.
  4. AIDS (Disease)—Patients—Fiction. I. Title.

   PS3568.U7684 S4 2002
   813'.54—dc21
                                           2002068130

First published in the United States by Dutton, a division of Penguin Books USA Inc.

First St. Martin's Griffin Edition: August 2003

10 9 8 7 6 5 4 3 2 1

For Michael

who patiently endured
my nights in the attic

ACKNOWLEDGMENTS

I wish to thank Harvey Klinger, my agent, and Matthew Carnicelli, my editor, for their consistently sound advice; the National Endowment for the Arts, for a Creative Writers Fellowship, which enabled me to complete this work; my cherished companions of Turkey, Matthew Aquilone and Linda Reilly; trusted readers Tom Heacox and Ann Imbrie; also Daisy, Sugar Baby, Spike, and the late and much-lamented Chickpea—antic interlopers from the 10th dimension all.

Book of the thousand and one dreams; shadow play of night sweats and nocturnal emissions; calendar of spent days; rumor-chronicle of voyages lunar and sublunary; the secret history of a plague as told by a dying American prince to his father the astronaut: in the name of God, the compassionate, the merciful.

PART ONE

PART ONE

HOUSTON, 1970

There's the time Allen comes home from a week's survival training in Panama to find Joan sprawled in bed with an empty bottle of vodka and a pistol—his old Air Force–issue Colt. It's lain untouched in the dresser drawer for years.

He's more surprised than alarmed, and Joan isn't so much pointing the pistol as using it to randomly punctuate her rapid, oblivious monologue. He's heard her talking since the instant he walked in the back door. His first thought: she's rehearsing some play for the community theater that takes so much of her time. But he knows, even before he's stepped into the darkened bedroom to catch her at it, how wrong he is.

"Joan," he says. "What on earth?"

"Sorry," she tells him, laying down both the pistol and the vodka bottle, one to either side of her, with exaggerated care. "I seem to have lost track of time."

Disheveled in her housecoat, amid rumpled sheets and strewn pillows, one hand resting lightly on the pistol, the other on the empty bottle, she's sheepish. She lies there and refuses to look at him. He glides quickly to the bed and pounces on the pistol, which, without any struggle, she relinquishes from her grip.

"It's not loaded," she assures him—but he checks the clip, racks the slide just to be sure. A single bullet pops out onto the carpet. Reaching down, still not quite believing, he picks it up and shows it to her.

3

Joan takes a careful look and closes her eyes. Allen sticks the pistol in the waistband of his trousers and clenches the bullet tightly in his fist.

He asks, "Have you gone totally berserk on me?"

"Take a good look," she says. "This is a binge. Nearly anything can happen."

"No," he tells her. He slides the bullet into his pocket, out of harm's way. "This is just a really unconscionable thing to be doing to yourself."

"Unconscionable." The word makes her laugh out loud, an abrupt explosion that trails off into a belch.

"Joan." He speaks her name forcefully, as if to reclaim this woman he's clearly never known in all their sixteen years of marriage. In the bedroom's half light, reeking of sweat, drunkenness, slumber—she might as well be anybody.

"Where's Jonathan?" he asks.

She moves to pick up the vodka bottle, but he stops her. He holds her wrist tightly.

"You should know," she says, her words blurred, "I think our son is a homosexual."

Allen blinks hard three or four times.

"Be quiet," he commands sharply.

"You want to know," she continues, "or just pretend I didn't say it?"

"Joan," he says, "don't talk to me like this. I don't want to hear anything."

Drunkenness makes her grand and vague. "What he's up to," she tells him, "where he is right now, for example, I have no idea. I never know where he is anymore."

Then turning her face away from him, into the pillow, she bursts into sobs. "Don't get angry with me," she says fiercely, her voice muffled. "Don't you dare."

But he isn't angry with her. He never gets angry with people, just with bad luck. And up till now, he and Joan have been the luckiest people alive.

This is a test, he thinks. Another contingency, another procedure. NASA's famous for its procedures. But it isn't, he knows, a test. For once it's just life, and there's no test, no procedure on the books for that. The slow burn starts under his heart, flushes its way into the open.

Suddenly he can't stand to be in the room with Joan another instant. He releases her from his grip and bolts for the door. But her sobs, as he stalks the rooms of the house, somehow follow him—acoustic fluke of heating vents, echo space between the walls. *His* house—and yet, away as he is for weeks at a time, he's never spent enough time here to feel at home: not in the living room with its lifeless furniture Joan's kept pristine over the years for company, not in the formal dining room where they never eat. Only the kitchen has any kind of warmth. Filtered by the thinning shade outdoors, October light slants through the windows, fills the breakfast nook, where on ordinary mornings he'll have coffee, a quick glance at the newspaper before heading out to whatever city the week's training takes him; or a late-night pizza, some beers, just himself and Joan in bleary reunion after long days apart.

His circuit carries him out into the hallway and up the stairs. He hasn't been up here in weeks, he realizes, maybe months. No reason, really. Jonathan's bedroom is here, a guest room, a bathroom at the end of the hall. Narrow stairs lead up to the big attic Allen's always thought of finishing as a study, but of course there's never any time. At Jonathan's door he pauses, listening. No sound—the boy's out—but still he knocks once before barging in.

In there is another world. Garish posters cover the walls: rock stars, a lunar map, blue-skinned Hindu gods. Desktop, bed, floor: everywhere littered with *things*. The strong smell of incense assaults him. Joan's words, that he's held in check for several minutes, flood over him and he winces to fight them back. A little speech for later gathers in his head: *I don't want this house going up in flames, mister, just because you think it's hip to burn incense in your room.*

If he could just say that to Jonathan and be done with it, let everything else slide by.

It's hard to know where to step. Scattered about the room among discarded clothes, school books, and sneakers lie various odd souvenirs Jonathan's scavenged over the years: geodes, old green-glass insulators, dried seed pods, a bright orange rabbit's foot.

A blue lava lamp percolates grotesquely in the corner.

Carefully Allen picks his way over to a nightstand beside Jonathan's bed. A cone of incense there has burned completely to ash, yet it remains intact, its shape fragile but perfect. Gingerly, afraid of jarring something invisible, he sits down on the unmade bed and wonders where on earth Jonathan came up with jet-black sheets, of all the crazy things.

Over the dresser Jonathan's hung a large color photograph of Michelangelo's statue of David. Only he's doctored it: where a fig leaf should be, he's pasted a cutout of ruby-red lips. Boldly parted, those lips leer at Allen. A tongue lolls obscenely between them.

And only hours ago, Allen thinks, I rode the dawn in from Florida in a T-33. Everything was fine and clear. I never suspected a thing.

Jonathan's room is definitely a fire hazard. Beyond that, it's simply a hazard. Allen's stare keeps returning, squeamishly, to the poster of the David statue and those lips, that long dangerous tongue.

He gives up. Abandoning his house for the cool refuge of the garage he takes several deep breaths: he likes it here, the musty, masculine smell of gasoline and grass clippings, clutter of old bicycles, a trampoline set, a seldom-used fiberglass canoe.

Pulling the pistol from his waistband, he hefts its sober weight in his hand. A single bullet in the slide, now safely in his pocket. He fingers it there among loose change. "Goddamn it, Joan," he says aloud. He stows the Colt in a box, underneath old *National Geographics* Joan insisted they save for Jonathan to help him in his school projects, something that to Allen's knowledge has never happened.

Next to the Ford Galaxy family car, his white Corvette gleams. His only indulgence, a richly deserved reward after the Gemini mission. And Joan has always hated sports cars. The day he brought it home she stood on the front steps, arms crossed, and refused to come out to the driveway to admire it. Now he flees in its safety along the suburban streets of Nassau Bay and out to the interstate. Saturday morning, and the fabled Houston traffic is light. A faint tang of smog hazes the air. On this side of the city the recent boom of suburban development fades quickly, till soon he's in open country beyond the city limits. Interstate 45 angles a clear run south toward Galveston and the coast: straight as an arrow and practically deserted. He floors the accelerator, savors the bracing spurt of speed. He can see ahead to the horizon. The flat land blurs past, telephone poles tick by. Beyond the curve of earth, clouds flower over the Gulf of Mexico, cumulonimbus, majestic formations. Their shadows fall over water far from land. He loves clouds, he can watch them for hours, their slow surprising evolution.

What shocks, even shames him, he realizes, is that he never noticed anything. That's the truly unconscionable thing: how he didn't see it coming. Not till it's all hit full force and he knows—ace fighter pilot he might once have been, seven kills to his credit over the brilliant skies of Korea, MIG Alley all the way up to Suey Ho—no matter how skillfully he might try to evade it, his family has cracked, shattered, fallen in a fiery rain of debris completely out from under him.

Later in the afternoon he calls Frank.

"I need a drink," he says. "Want to invite me over for a drink?"

The best and worst that can be said about Frank is that he's always ready for a drink. A flight planner, Frank dreamed up the notion of centering the Apollo program star charts around the plane of the ecliptic instead of the lunar equator. In his way he's brilliant, indispensable. Allen's known him for years. It was Frank who alerted him to the supercheap mortgages NASA employees were getting in Nassau Bay. Their houses went up at the same time, next door to each other, and are nearly identical colonial two-stories. They barbecue together, he swims in Frank's pool. Their wives belong to the wives' club, act in the local theater together.

"So what are we celebrating?" Frank asks once they're armed with martinis and settled in lawn chairs by the swimming pool.

"How about a little navigation trouble?" Allen jokes, but regrets it as soon as he says it.

Frank settles comfortably into his chair. He's a little man, wiry and balding, with a broad Alabama accent. "Cryptic," he observes.

"Yeah, well," Allen says. He feels the sickness underneath his heart again and backs off. "Terrific martini."

"The secret is dry, dry, dry," Frank says. "Half a drop of vermouth. Less, if you can manage. Personally, I recommend opening your vermouth, taking a deep sniff of it, then breathing it out slowly over the gin. That, to my mind, is all the vermouth you need. A whisper."

Allen doesn't mind that he's heard the secret of Frank's martinis a dozen times before. Frank explains it with such gusto.

"You're not here to talk about martinis," Frank observes.

Allen hates this. He wants to be flying airplanes. He wants to be in Baltimore doing underwater simulation, or in Panama learning to sur-

7

vive on iguana meat. He wants to be weightless for thirty seconds in a falling 707.

He takes a deep breath and plunges into the free-fall of confession. "I consider you my friend," he says.

It puts Frank subtly on alert. "Likewise," he acknowledges.

Allen loses heart almost immediately. "I need to talk to somebody in confidence," he admits.

"Certainly."

"Total confidence," he stresses.

"Total confidence," Frank says.

Allen pauses. Two huge sycamores shade all of Frank's backyard and half of Allen's. Fall has begun to yellow their leaves. The afternoon is mild, humid. A couple of leaves float on the surface of the pool. From this vantage, Allen's house looks entirely reasonable; it gives away nothing of its discontents.

He expels a long breath.

"I can't do it," he says. "Sorry."

They sit in embarrassed silence. He can't believe she'd actually loaded the pistol. A surge of fear rushes from somewhere deep in his bowels. He rubs the pad of his right thumb with the side of his forefinger, a secret insistent motion that in times of stress usually calms him.

And it does seem to calm him. He takes in the ordinary, stabilizing things: a con trail high in the clear sky, the dapple of shade and sun on the grass, the serene blue of Frank's swimming pool. From a neighboring yard comes the steady drone of a lawn mower. He and Frank both watch as a young black man pushes around an old machine with giant spoked wheels.

Frank breaks the silence between them. "Enterprising fellow," he notes.

It's William, who does any number of lawns in the neighborhood. Though not the Clouds's lawn—mowing is Jonathan's chore.

"Last mow of the season," Allen speculates in order to drive Joan's hateful words, newly resurgent, out of his mind.

William's battered green pickup truck can be seen parked along the street most every day in summer.

"Sometimes, you know," Frank says, "you just need the opportunity to talk, and it serves the same function as actually talking."

Allen's not sure what he even wanted to say to Frank in the first

8

place. Suddenly, despite all their years together, the good times, they don't seem friends at all, just strangers thrown together for the ride. He can't believe he was about to confide anything in anybody.

He taps the side of his glass. "I should finish this and go back over to the house."

"Everything's okay down at the Cape? Walt and Mike are fine?"

But Allen's already retreated to safety. "Dandy," he says. Still, he remembers again how that bullet surprised him, popping out of the slide like it did—and he almost didn't check the slide, since the clip was empty.

"You seem a little, I don't know, shaken up this afternoon," Frank comments.

"And I'm unshakeable," Allen says with a laugh, his finger working nonstop and in secret against his thumb.

Sometimes the best course of action is simply no action. He decides to make dinner: salmon croquettes, a favorite from way back that his mother used to make, and one of the few things he ever cooks, since Joan does the cooking. He empties a can of salmon, chops an onion, spends a long time shaping and reshaping the patties before coating them in bread crumbs. A man cooking by himself, in a brightly lit kitchen, a meal from his childhood: for an instant, he finds himself blinking back tears. He never cries, not in thirty years. The sizzle of Crisco in the frying pan soothes him.

He stands at the foot of the stairs and takes a deep breath.

"Jonathan," he calls, and his son appears at the top of the stairs.

"Hey," Jonathan says. He leans against the stair rail, hands in his pockets, a thin boy with hair that should have been cut months ago. He's wearing one of those garish tie-dyed T-shirts he always seems to have on these days: this one, all shades of purple and lavender, features in its central medallion a moon with a human eye staring from it. Disconcerted, Allen averts his gaze.

"Want some dinner?" he asks. His heart hammers in his chest.

"Sure," Jonathan says. "Love some." There's a lilt to that voice that Allen's heard since Jonathan was a child, but now it sets him strangely on edge.

"Then come get it," he says sharply—a reprimand, but for what he's not sure. Jonathan, mercifully, doesn't seem to hear the shift in tone. He gives a thumbs up signal and disappears back to his room while Allen, wiping from his brow a film of sweat that's suddenly precipitated from nowhere, goes to the downstairs bedroom and knocks on the door. "Joan?" he says softly. It's completely dark in the room, and he can just make out her sleeping form. She's been up, she's laid a wet washcloth over her eyes like she does on those rare, rare occasions when she's hung over after some bit of festivity.

In the kitchen, Jonathan's seated himself at the table. "Mmm," he says. "Croquettes. What made you cook these up?"

Allen won't look at his son. His face flushes.

"I got this craving," he tells him, hyper-aware of everything he's saying, careful not to sound in any way strange. "Flying out here, I was thinking about salmon croquettes."

In recent months, even years, they've not been much on conversation. He sees how far, without his consciously remarking it, they've drifted apart. They eat in an amicable enough silence, though Allen focuses so much attention on the croquettes on his plate that he's surprised they don't levitate.

"Dad," Jonathan says. "You're sweating."

It nearly makes him jump.

"Hot stove," he says, wiping his brow.

"So where's Mom?"

He thinks he's going to explode. All he wants is for this to stop, but it doesn't stop.

"Your mother's not feeling well," he says.

"I figured," Jonathan admits. "She gets too many headaches these days."

This is when the conversation should occur—Allen sees the moment so clearly, the words he should somehow say, but he doesn't say them, and with each second the opportunity recedes, until a minute has passed and it is very far away.

He's not even going to try.

"I love salmon croquettes," Jonathan says. "I really do. It's so cool you made them."

Allen forces himself to watch as Jonathan cuts them into little pieces, the way he always does with his food. Closing his eyes, he savors each bite as if oblivious to everything else in the world.

There was the time he came so close to dying. 1951, fighter training, and that fall day, confident and a little bored, he'd decided to experiment with a double Immelmann. It was a stunt the instructors didn't exactly encourage, but everybody did it anyway. His plane that morning was a T-28—too slow, really, for a speed stunt, so he pushed it into a steep dive to build velocity, nothing he hadn't done dozens of times. At the top of the first double loop he pulled up, then decided he'd go for another one. He commenced that second dive and the next thing he knew he was drowsily waking up from a delicious nap. A propeller was spinning in front of him. One more instant and he realized he was aimed straight at the ground. He wasn't so much alarmed as quietly astonished—a calm feeling (he hadn't even remembered he was flying) that expanded all through him till he was enveloped in its radiant embrace. While in the meantime, completely apart from the leisurely pace of his brain, his hands urgently worked the controls.

At just under a thousand feet he pulled out. And that was it. At no point did he have any sense of danger or panic—only that astonishment. Then afterward, skimming low over Texas brush country, a tingling in his extremities, some residual electricity that danced along his nerve endings to tell him he was alive. Cumulative gravity forces, a gray-out: any number of pilots had bought the farm, as they said, on that one.

The whole thing couldn't have taken twenty seconds from start to finish.

He's washing dishes when Joan makes her appearance. She's made herself presentable—slacks, a blouse—but he can see the dishevelment still in her eyes, the tight lines around her mouth. That blouse, embroidered with colorful cactuses. He remembers the very afternoon she bought it, a Woolworth's in Las Vegas. He was stationed at Nellis then. Every detail's so clear. They bought the blouse and a goldfish they carried home in a plastic bag half full of water, and when the time came to move four months later they solemnly flushed the fish down the toilet. Nearly sixteen years: he's been inside her body, thrilling moments of nearly incomprehensible joy. She's carried his child, stayed loyally beside him through the long haul: tactical flight alerts; Edwards, where she could watch his X-100 exploits from their little house high in the

11

hills; danger wakes with the other astronaut wives; press conferences on the front lawn; one raucous weekend at the LBJ ranch after the Gemini flight. And all these years she's managed to preserve her secret miseries intact, away from him, festering till they had no recourse but to burst.

"Hon," he says gently, trying to pack every kind of sympathy into that single word, "how're you feeling?" Desperately thinking, Say fine, and we'll both forget everything like it never happened.

Joan, for her part, says, "Fabulous," the word hard-edged but still vastly reassuring and then, as he's catching a skipped heartbeat: "I'm not going to live here anymore, Al."

It surges through him, spreading out to the farthest reaches of himself along paths and byways he never even knew were there. "This house?" he says stupidly.

She lights one of her cigarettes and takes a long, reflective puff—a woman (he's never seen it so clearly about her before) who's been worn down, lost her looks through long years of battle.

"No," she exhales along with the smoke. "Not this house. This whole thing. You have to let me go."

She says it so simply—those years at the community theater, her voice is calm and rehearsed. All he can manage is a small disbelieving laugh.

"Just like that?"

"If you only knew," she says.

"What about NASA?" It's exactly the wrong thing to ask, and he tries to backtrack the instant the words have left his mouth. "What about us? Everything we have together?"

"You'll survive," Joan says.

"We'll survive together," he reassures her. But he's trembling all over. "Like we've always done," he says. "We'll be brave in this."

But she just shakes her head.

"Please, Joan," he says. "Let's sit down. This is way too fast."

"Actually," she says, "it feels like it's taken forever."

Before he even knows what he's doing—he's never done anything like this—he's at her feet, on his knees. His arms circle round her calves as if he's tackling her, bringing her down, but he doesn't bring her down. He just kneels and clasps her. He muffles his sobs in the smooth fabric of her slacks.

"This can be as awful as you want it to be," she tells him. The calm in her voice terrifies him: a resolve she hasn't so much rehearsed as, after all these years, finally discovered.

He can't help it. The sickness under his heart surges into his throat, and before he can choke it back he's vomiting the mess of his salmon croquettes on her slacks, her shoes, the linoleum floor.

A SECRET HISTORY OF FLIGHT

Such a good girl, Allen.

When I was fourteen years old I stood on the low bluff of the shallow river outside Armistice and watched three white boys beat up a black boy. I came there by accident—a bicycle path I used to follow home in the afternoons from piano practice—and I stood there, high up on the eroded bank, mesmerized as, quite methodically, they beat him senseless and then continued to beat him for some time after that. Boys older than me, sweet unruly sixteen or seventeen. The black boy my age. One of them glanced up to where I stood and our eyes met, locked, the way years later your eyes and mine would lock, Allen, that first time, only this time there was no love, there was nothing, just a dull blankness between us, a complete lack of everything. I made no move, and neither for the longest time did he, till he resumed kicking the now motionless form of the black boy lying face down on the sand, all the time looking up at me and kicking, kicking away with a listlessness that was like despair. Till I remounted my bicycle and rode on.

Fled.

The other two boys never once saw me. I knew them—the white boys, not the black one, whom I'd never seen, and I presume he lived because nothing was ever said in Armistice about that afternoon on the riverbank, not a word, and so I presume that somehow, bloodied and bruised, a kidney knocked adrift, some ribs, a nose, a cheekbone broken, he quietly survived and may even be alive somewhere today, knocking

14

back a drink or beating up his wife, or maybe he is a saint living some-where in Africa.

I never told on those boys. Never uttered a word. As the one boy who locked eyes with mine must, somehow, have known from the first instant, because he never raised the alarm, never said a word, hardly even faltered in the grim task he was carrying out. We were in this together.

My whole life, I see now, I've moved from one complicity to the next with scarcely a word of protest.

Shy girl, too, never happier than when alone with the piano in my grandmother's front parlor playing the old waltz *Für Elise* for hours at a stretch, haunted by something so sad and lost in that melody. Even at ten years old I could hear it as I moved through that music again and again, trying to squeeze from those simple notes whatever could sound so sad and lost. But again and again it eluded me—though the years held me up, practice and determination, till late adolescence found me learning, painfully, with barely measurable progress from one winter afternoon to the next, *The Art of the Fugue*. Its rigors and won-ders, that glorious discipline of hands and fingers.

Or listening with such longing to Wanda Landowska on those scratchy 78's speed like lightning through a dark thicket of notes, flash of illumination so brilliant it lit up a whole world. The swoony rush as Rubenstein played Tchaikovsky, Rachmaninoff's moody vistas, Horo-witz sharpening the knife on a piano arrangement of Petrushka.

Hidden from prying eyes, among the ferns, on ancient Turkish car-pets moth-eaten but still magic, I danced. Dim light fell past heavy curtains amid immense dark furniture and the smell of lavender my grandmother gave me sprigs of from the garden, to crush in the palms of my hands.

With what ardor I accompanied the choir of the Armistice Episcopal Church on Sundays, or better yet performed duet interludes with the organist, a young graduate of the Oberlin Conservatory.

In all our moving here and there on an air force salary: We'll get you a piano, you promised, but we never did till Houston, when you presented yourself a Corvette and me, with belated and tender apolo-gies—to the most patient gal in the galaxy, was what you actually said—

15

a brand new Sohmer upright, a fine make of instrument, excellent action and a warm, solid tone. But by then it was too painful a reminder, my hands gone all rigid and unpracticed, and I never played. I'd moved on, as they say, to other things.

Till I knew you, I never had a drink. Never a one. Social drinking, you called it. Lubrication. Oil the gears.

You were right.

Practically frictionless some days, I make myself remember. Bitberg, the old Luftwaffe Officer's club we and half a dozen other air force families called home: bedroom the size of a closet, no living room, only that cavernous common room downstairs with its bar, its leather chairs. Jonathan skittering around, demented two-year-old, pouring sand out of the ashtrays every chance he got. And that wasn't the half of it. Some excess electrical charge in his little body even then, something precocious and haywire that I hid from you because I thought, selfishly, I could protect it. Even nurture it, if there was a way.

Whatever *it* was.

And you, in the meantime, on flight alert every four days: ready to be in the air in fifteen minutes, you and your F-100 and your tactical nuclear weapons. Thirty-sixth Fighter Day Wing. Then the Russians invaded Hungary, you were moved to the front lines at Fürstenfeld-bruck, and those of us who stayed behind were issued evacuation plans.

I think that was the beginning, those evacuation plans. A glass of wine in the morning while I perused, with a growing sense of surreality, the road maps they gave us. By the time you finished your mission, Germany would either be occupied or annihilated, so while you flew on to bases in Turkey, we, the hapless flotsam and jetsam of the oper-ation, were to load our children into cars and drive in a convoy to Marseilles where ships would be waiting to evacuate us.

Eyes on the road, ladies, and watch out for stray thermonuclear ex-plosions.

We kept food on hand, a suitcase packed, an extra container of gasoline in the trunk of the car. We drilled every other day.

All that time spent waiting, waiting. Nuclear jitters, a whole world jumpy for years. I thought it would be better when you were back, when the crisis faded, but there was always the next crisis, real or imagined,

Cuba or Berlin, to keep you shuttling from one base to the next. Two-week stint here, monthlong there, and then when you were home it was nonstop party, it had to be. Reckless nights and hungover days, pilots and wives alike down in the common room, no getting away from it and no reason to, either, unless you'd drawn the lot to keep watch over everybody's kids that night. All those theme parties we spent our anxious watches planning: toga parties and harem parties and the ever popular coon parties (blackface required). It's a wonder any of you ever managed to get those jets in the air at all. Or that any marriage there survived.

I'm telling you these things because sometimes, Allen, I think I barely remember them myself.

I barely remember, for instance, our sojourn in Naples—a fifth-year wedding anniversary of sorts—when we took a taxi out to Lake Avernus to look for the cave that is the traditional entrance to hell. One of your buddies had confirmed it was a must-see, and since our whole stay in that benighted city had been one short-change after another as far as you were concerned—the lousy hotel breakfasts, the outrageous taxi fares, the disappointment of Herculaneum which, for some reason, we had chosen to visit instead of Pompeii—we set out on our odd quest. It was late when we started, and soon dusk came on, a great lavender swarm of light, a sky suddenly filled with bats. Our young guide threw pebbles in the air to attract them. Unaccountably confused after his repeated assurances that he knew his way to the cave, he led us along a narrow, deserted road—more a dirt track than anything else—till we found our way blocked by a parked car. As we moved to skirt the car, we suddenly noticed it was rocking back and forth on its springs, and that two half-naked bodies inside were grappling with each other in passionate abandon.

Regretfully acknowledging that our quest had come to nothing—*Ah*, remarked our guide with a laugh, *perhaps here is the true entrance to hell.* And we laughed too, though uncomfortably. Apologetic, he insisted on taking us instead to his family's dubious-looking osteria, itself occupying a small cavern in the side of a hill. As his mother brought out plates of steaming mussels floating in blood-red diavolo sauce—was it too late in the season, I wondered, for shellfish?—and his father poured us tumblers of dark homemade wine, at last you were pleased, even exultant: our day had ended up with an adventure of sorts after all. Relax, you told me, and enjoy. But I could only think of that couple in the backseat of the car, their own desperately achieved enjoyment of each other on the road to hell.

A month later our piss was dark as Guinness Stout. The doctor diagnosed infectious hepatitis. Jonathan went immediately on a program of prophylactic gamma globulin and we spent the next three months in a hospital in New Jersey. It was the wine, or the shellfish. Filthy country, you raged. We should have known.

Jonathan cried ceaselessly, your parents complained from Ohio. They couldn't find a way to calm him. Four and a half years old, so hoarse he could barely speak. He ran wild, pulled books off shelves, tossed cushions from the sofa. He bloodied his forehead by beating it against the braided rug in the front room every time they left him alone.

They drove him all the way to New Jersey so he could see we hadn't been taken away and burned. That was his fear, your parents said, that we'd been taken away and burned. We were waiting for him in wheelchairs in the lobby. He stood there in the door, a rigid, terrified little boy. Then he let out a yelp. He ran to me, burrowing his head in my lap and humming with a joy so urgent I have never gotten over my terror at being the recipient of it.

All those afternoons in our California cabin listening to music, playing one LP after the other, "Lonesome Valley" and "Ten Thousand Miles" and "Midnight Rambler," smoking cigarettes one after the other, taking a nip from the vodka in the liquor cabinet or opening a bottle of wine at ten in the morning because I could have it finished and a nap besides before you got home and you'd never know. Waiting for you to come home, knowing that one day you never would come home. I could see everything from that cabin perched in the hills: the B-52 piggybacking your test plane into the sky, then the release, the trail and sonic boom you left across the sky, and it seemed unbelievable to me that you were up there flying at four thousand miles an hour and I was down here feet firmly planted on the earth in our little garden. Remember the garden I made there, where everything seemed to bloom, every flower

I stuck in the ground blossoming like magic, colors everywhere? I never had the heart to garden after that.

You could say I lost God somewhere over that desert past Edwards Air Force Base. I prayed and prayed, and one day I couldn't pray any more, and that was the day I dared your plane to fall from the sky. I remember standing there in the garden of that little house and saying, not aloud, because I didn't have the courage to talk aloud to myself in those days, but to myself: God, whoever or whatever You are, if Your hands are holding that plane aloft at this instant, then let it drop, let it fall. But nothing happened. You flew on, and when you landed, I could see the little cloud of dust the X-100 kicked up on the desert runway and I knew you were safe, and also that there was no God. There was nothing, just the accident of your plane holding together for ten minutes, fifteen, but no guarantee, nothing but the raw operation of chance and luck, and I would be witness to everything.

You dreamed in your golden youth of flight, that childhood dream where you hovered a few feet above the earth, able to control with your breathing the various dynamics of your levitation, a calm, peaceful dream; and later when you grew up you flew to your heart's desire. I dreamed of flight too, and fifteen years later I've finally gone and fled. Not to my heart's desire but to here, Minerva, Tennessee, site of old confirmed disasters, in whose singular obscurity—this is a promise, Allen, a promise—I fully intend to disappear.

THE PREACHER'S SON

That spring of 1971—the spring I first laid eyes on Jonathan—I used to sneak out of my parents' house every Friday and Saturday night. The whole family was usually in bed by ten-thirty, so sometime after midnight I'd open my bedroom window, let myself out onto the carport roof, ease across its gentle slope and then clamber down the woodpile. I'd been doing it for several weeks, living the life of a criminal, miserable and ecstatic with myself, making my way through backyards and vacant lots to the All-Nite Travelers Bar & Grill. Next to the bus station, it was a greasy little haunt with a few tables, a jukebox, and on weekend nights a crowd of fifteen or twenty kids, some high school, some from the local college, there to dance till two, three, four in the morning.

Around one the New York City–Los Angeles Express bus pulled in for a forty-five-minute rest stop, and the tables in the grill would fill up with bleary-eyed travelers having a coffee or a beer. George, the manager, a burly Greek with tattoos and a mustache, would try to talk them into a world-famous Minerva Hot Wiener, seldom with any success.

They'd watch us dancing, sip their coffee, then file back to the waiting bus. And sometimes I'd follow, drawn out to stand in the cool air, watching the bus's dark windows, imagining the people inside, places they were going, Memphis, Little Rock, Amarillo, Albuquerque. I'd looked at maps, memorized the route, the cities, and I'd rehearse to myself the names of those places I'd never been—till the bus sighed shut its doors, and with a shudder pulled out into the night.

I felt, with those buses, the way I felt in the fall when a V of geese or endless rivers of starlings bled across the sky. The sense of far places, destinations.

Then I'd go back inside to the dancing.

One night there was a new face in that room where I'd come to know all the other faces. I went to high school with a number of them, though by day we never spoke. It was a secret we'd wordlessly agreed to share: how on weekends we danced together empty-eyed, loose-bodied, with enormous concentration. Passing in the halls of Minerva Central High we'd nod, go our separate ways. We must have known, even as kids, how separate ways was, peculiarly, what we were all about.

In retrospect it seems stylized, a ritual we'd evolved without being in the least aware of it. Each person had an unvarying place. Some danced by the door where it was cooler, others by the bar with its stools where three or four older men sat, silent and watching, night after night. The new kid took up his position by the dull glow of the jukebox. There was something vaguely shocking about him, a girlishness that was also boyishness. Long chestnut hair spilled past his shoulders. His face was fine and delicate. At first glimpse I actually thought he was a girl, then only in the next instant did I know he was a boy. But there was some gap left between first and second impression. He wore billowy white pants, a tie-dyed T-shirt, a necklace of plastic beads. I could have sworn he was wearing mascara.

That first time I laid eyes on him he made me extremely uneasy. In some secret way he was exactly the person I'd always wanted to be.

My parents were missionaries in Africa for five years before I was born—in Tanganyika, before it became Tanzania. What they seemed to carry away from the experience, more than anything else, was a deep distrust of the world, a sense of its lurking dangers, which they did their best to instill in me. There was an invisible barrier around our property, they told me when I was small, and I was never to venture beyond without being accompanied by one of them. Outside that barrier, anything could happen.

As if to reinforce the warning, a police car used to lie in wait in a neighbor's driveway. Several times an afternoon, unsuspecting motorists who whisked too quickly down our quiet street brought the police to life. Lights flashing, siren rising in dreadful alarm, they'd give chase. Shielded from harm by the invisible barrier, I'd stand in the front yard and watch. But I never could get it out of my head that the police were really there not to catch speeders but to enforce the barrier—whether to keep the world from me or me from the world, I never knew. But I did know, without any doubt, that the instant I left the front yard, they'd be sure to nab me.

Even when I got older and the barrier was no longer in force, the idea stayed with me.

"A filthy place," my mother used to say about Africa. "You can't even imagine the filth." Unpeeled fruit and vegetables were dangerous, the meat infested more often than not, whole villages had gone blind from river water. Even soft drinks bottled in Africa were suspect because of possible contamination at the plant.

More dangerous than any of it, though, was the African night. They never got used to it. A watchman named Juma hired himself out to my parents to patrol the compound. Wearing a black ski mask even in summer, and armed with a spear—such a fright to look at, my mother remembered—he'd make the rounds till morning. Then, as my parents sipped coffee on the veranda, he'd tell them terrible tales, a severed head discovered underneath a table in a restaurant, charred human thigh bones lying in a ditch outside of town.

"I can't even begin to tell you," he would say.

My father always thought Juma was teasing them, but my mother never had a sense of humor. And she claimed never to be able to forget a word anybody ever said to her.

My father, in his way, had loved Africa—or at least loved the work he did there. He loved addressing crowds from the back of a flatbed truck parked in an open field. He loved baptising men and women in the river. It was my mother, in the meantime, who'd had to dial in the day-to-day details: she was the one who had to be firm with the servants, had to scold and fret and bargain and upbraid. "The help in that place," she used to say, "wouldn't know how to burn a house down without the proper supervision." She was the one who, in her first few weeks in Morogoro, had to fend off the hard-drinking European women who would drop by with a pitcher of cocktails at ten in the morning. The Mormon missionaries who lived in a compound down the road, of whom my mother was suspicious for other reasons, were the only friends she could rely on when my father was out in the field with his flatbed truck and loudspeaker.

When she found out she was pregnant with me, my mother said to my father, "That's it. We've done our work. I am not going to carry my child in a place like this." It was a story she repeated to me many times. "You were conceived in a dark place," she would say, "but thank God in heaven you weren't born there."

As a child I grew up with the sense that my mother loved me unconditionally, but that my father was sorely inconvenienced by my existence. It was my birth, after all, that had called him back from his epochal work abroad to minister to the Baptist population of Minerva, Tennessee. In Africa, it was clear, he had been a great man, a healer and leader, and if his stature in America was unfairly diminished, I shared responsibility in that. In my fantasies I saw myself as rehabilitating his mission: sweeping aside my mother's sickly qualms, I would one day return with him to Africa, an invincible father and son soul-saving team, and the two of us would sweep the continent with our heartfelt preaching and outstretched hands. When I was seven and eight and nine, such was the perfect future that beckoned.

In reality, I was forlornly aware that my father paid me little mind, and I was desperate to gain his respect. Taking it on myself to memorize great swatches of the Bible, I'd interrupt him in his study, where he was formulating Sunday's sermon, to impress him with my stumbling recitation. "Yes, yes," he'd say. "Very good. But remember—even the devil can quote scripture." Crestfallen, I'd renew my efforts, once proudly presenting him with a quite gruesome picture of the crucifixion I'd painted on a piece of cardboard. He studied it for a minute, and then pronounced that it looked awfully Catholic, a mysterious term I intuitively knew meant nothing good.

To supplement his meager preacher's income, my father sold vacuum cleaners on the side—the Vacu-Lux, a Philippine-made brand whose unique feature was an attachment called a body ash siphon. In my younger years, till my role was eventually superseded by my little brothers, I'd often accompany him after school as he went door to door. More often than not, my alleged thirst for a drink of water or need to visit the toilet gained us entry into otherwise impenetrable households. Once past the front door, my father could usually convince his suspicious clients to accept an on-the-spot demo. I listened entranced as, modulating into his most irresistible voice, he described the function of the body ash siphon: "The human body," he'd explain, "is always shedding its skin. The dead layers slough off, invisible to the naked eye. But collect enough together and you've got body ash. What's body ash? It's a scum of dead flesh, and it settles in the crevices of your sofas, your armchairs, most of all it's smeared into the very texture of your bedding, your sheets and your mattress and the bedclothes you sleep in. You don't realize it, but you're covered every day with a thin film of death. And every night when you lie down in bed next to your husband or your wife, you're lying down in a smear of dead, sloughed-off flesh.

"Many of the tribes I ministered to when I was in Africa had a saying: 'The body is excrement.' Pardon the expression, but think about it. Think what an old dead body really is. And that's what we're carrying around with us every day of our lives. So I'd say to them, 'you're right.' And they were, in a simple way. We are excrement, and we live among it. But while the physical body that eats and drinks, that sits in chairs and sleeps in beds is doomed to rot and decay, to come to resemble that excrement which it always has been, the spiritual body that is in Jesus Christ endures unblemished and incorrupt forever."

I admired intensely how selling vacuum cleaners and saving souls could dovetail so neatly and effectively. And the body ash siphon was invariably impressive in demonstration. Attaching the siphon, my father would go to work on a sofa, a bed, whatever seemed appropriate. When he emptied the filter, he shook out a sediment of gray oily ash.

The Minerva school system was impressed enough to buy a fleet of six, and I remember whenever I'd stay after school for music lessons, I could hear the whirr of Vacu-Luxes as the maids scoured the classrooms and corridors, siphoning up all the body ash our febrile young bodies had shed over the course of the day. The woods behind the football field were littered with piles of the stuff where the maids had discarded it.

"God sees everything," my father was fond of saying, and to me that statement clearly implied that my father likewise saw everything. Never was his possession of powers of insight far beyond the ordinary more clear to me than the time when he was away on crusade for a couple of weeks, and a stray white cat showed up at our back door. "Let that animal alone and it'll go away," my mother confidently predicted, but before we knew it, the skinny little animal had adopted us. It was my fault: I fed it surreptitiously.

My mother had grown up on a farm, and the experience had instilled in her a general loathing for animals. Chickens and roosters were the worst—she told us how they used to peck at her bare feet whenever she stepped out into the front yard. And when her grandmother wrung their necks, they ran headless, spurting blood, in circles before collapsing in a flurry of wings. "Like a chicken with its head cut off"—my mother shivered even to hear that phrase. Greedy, filthy things, she called them. And she'd never gotten over the time in adolescence when she'd caught the family's dog nuzzling a fragrant heap of carrion with what seemed like ecstatic abandon. "I can hardly eat a bologna sandwich," my mother would say, "if I have to think where it comes from."

I was inclined to take after my mother in that respect. One of the virtues of the New Jerusalem would be no animals. Certainly none dead by the side of the road. Nevertheless, with what I can only call perversity, I continued to slip kitchen scraps to our scrawny stray. I knew it was probably diseased, liable to scratch or bite if I got too close. But I'd stand at the screen door, vigilant lest I be caught in this betrayal of my mother and common sense, and watch it devour the bits of food I'd left for it. I liked its greediness.

One day as I sat on the front steps, it leapt into my lap. The surprise paralyzed me. I held motionless with fastidious revulsion as it settled itself down and began to purr. What happened next was even more surprising: its warm weight instantly gave me an erection. I was ten, and I think that must have been my first-ever conscious experience of an erection. Instinctively I knew it was a perturbing, even shameful development. I didn't touch the cat—I just let it knead its claws in my jeans, all the while purring contentedly.

When my father returned home at the end of the week he took one look at the cat and announced to us, "She's pregnant."

"Good grief," said my mother. "That's all we need around here."

What with one thing and another, though, nothing was done about the cat, and a few days later it disappeared—only to reappear in about

25

a week, more gaunt than ever and ravenously hungry. When the kittens had grown large enough to emerge from hiding and gambol about on the lawn, the front porch, underfoot, my mother announced, in the wounded tones she sometimes adopted with us, that she had had enough.

I suppose, looking back on it now, it was a major domestic crisis. Whatever my mother's discontents, they only ever manifested themselves in trivial ways. She exiled herself to the bedroom, threatening not to come out until something was done. So that same afternoon my father enlisted me to help round up the kittens and their mother, and put them in the trunk of the car—a protracted procedure, since the animals, especially the mother, didn't intend to stay in the trunk. But finally they were all in, and the trunk slammed shut. I felt a sense of keen satisfaction that we were ending this once and for all.

We drove out into the country accompanied by the kittens' terrified mews and their mother's unearthly moans. It was hardly bearable, but we bore it bravely, my father and I. I watched him, looking with his beard like any Old Testament prophet, as he drove with grim determination. We turned off onto a sparsely settled road. Equidistant between two poor-looking houses—the kind of run-down houses blacks lived in—we stopped, and my father announced that this was fine. There was a ditch that ran along the side of the road, and I realized I had been here before: we had come here back in the spring to unload an old washing machine.

When my father opened the trunk, the white cat leapt out and disappeared into the weeds. One by one my father lifted the cringing kittens and tossed them lightly in the direction their mother had fled.

"Are they going to be all right?" I asked him dubiously. They seemed so tiny, he'd flung them away so carelessly.

"I wouldn't worry," he assured me. "They're cats. They'll be just fine. They'll find their way over to one of those houses or another."

I admired my father for solving that episode with such dispatch, for knowing so clearly what to do, and also for knowing, as I was sure he did, that I had been secretly responsible for this mess in the first place. He hadn't had to utter a word, but I knew he knew. A complicated world lay between the two of us. Our secret complicity. And, I remember, I despised my mother just then. Her weakness, her manipulative ways.

I think, in retrospect, I must have wanted my father to love me the way we ordinary humans want to be loved by God in heaven.

When I was fourteen I began to suffer painful swellings in my groin, tender lumps that appeared right at the base of my penis and lasted several excruciating days before disappearing as mysteriously as they'd arrived. Each time I was sure I was dying, and each time I foreswore forever the furtive pleasures I was sure had led to this. For months I kept those episodes secret, till the pain from one swollen lump drove me to reveal my affliction to my parents. It was night; I'd been lying in bed for an hour unable to do anything except concentrate on my imminent mortality. I came downstairs and stood in the hall, in my pajamas, for half an hour, debating whether to creep back upstairs and suffer my body's guilty revenge for my abuse of it, or to reveal this terrible thing.

"I have a problem," I announced abruptly, barging into the room where they sat, my mother on the sofa, my father in his recliner, in front of the television.

They looked startled.

"I have this sore place," I went on. "Down here."

My father was gruff. "Well, let's see," he said. I was acutely conscious that my parents had never seen me since I'd grown pubic hair down there, and the shame was topped only by my certainty that I was dying. I walked over to the recliner and opened my pajama bottoms. The air was cool on my exposed flesh. My father put his finger on the swelling, probing me where my penis was rooted in my body. His touch, palpable and arousing, sent a shiver all through me.

"That's a bad boil," he said. "It must hurt like the devil."

"It just started hurting tonight," I lied.

"Well, we better lance it for you."

My mother had craned forward to see. "You make sure and wash down there, don't you?" she asked with a distinct tone of anxiety.

"It doesn't have anything to do with cleaning yourself," my father assured her.

I was in a trance, unaware of anything except the blessed relief that this wasn't a tumor—or worse, some easily recognizable sign of my depravity.

27

My father led me into the bathroom and had me sit on the toilet seat while he rummaged in the closet for a needle, some matches to sterilize with, telling my mother, as she hovered in the doorway, "Give us some room. You go sit in the den and I'll call you when it's over."

"This is going to stick some," he told me, "but then you're going to feel so much better."

And it did stick. A white pus oozed out, foul-smelling, rot and death itself, followed by a copious flow of blood. A woozy blackness rose up in front of my eyes and I heard my father telling me to put my head down, then to go ahead and lie on the floor.

The cold tiles against my back woke me up.

"Whew, that stuff really stinks," my father kept saying as he handed me wads of Kleenex to stanch the flow.

And finally it stopped.

"You making out all right in there?" my mother called in from the den.

"Just fine," said my father, then observed to me: "You look mighty peaked. But that probably offered you some relief."

"I'll say," was about all I could manage. I lay on that ice cold floor, naked from the waist down, and looked up at him towering over me, powerful, solicitous, my father. It's the most intimate, in its peculiar way, we ever were with one another.

That first midnight I opened my bedroom window and torturously inched my way across the roof, I remembered that incident with my father. It was something I hadn't thought about in a long time, but it came back to me as I eased myself down onto the woodpile and then clambered safely to the ground. All those secrets locked up for so long inside my body.

I'd planned my escape for weeks: or I should say, the moment had been planning itself, held festering inside me till sooner or later it would have to break loose. It astounds me, in retrospect, that I had the nerve. In everything else I lived a life with no seams. In school I was the model student—perfectly behaved, responsible, obedient. In my father's church I was a youth leader, famous for my recitations of scripture. At Christmas I played "O Holy Night" solo on the French horn for the carols service. The invisible barrier held me safely in check on all sides.

I'd known for some time that the Travelers was a place where a few of the kids at school went to dance. Never having set foot there, I can't say why I came to feel with such certainty that I had to go. I only knew it was somehow vitally important to me. I remember marking its location once, when I went to the bus station with my mother. As the missionary whose bus we'd met chattered on about the talk she was going to give to the women's prayer group, I peered intently into the bar's dark open doorway but was able to see nothing.

For weeks after, the idea of the Travelers tantalized me. At night I lay in bed tense with rumors I'd heard: unspecified, evaded things. No one ever knew anything precise. No one ever actually knew anybody who went there. We just knew there were people who did.

Nothing is ever going to happen to me, I'd told myself as a child, pacing back and forth on my parents' front lawn, watched over by the police car in the driveway up the street. At sixteen I was still pacing. After homework I found myself studying the run of roof beyond my bedroom window, the drop to the woodpile, the scramble down to earth. I dared myself, night after night, feeling sicker and more trapped every night that passed.

Then one night I simply bolted out of bed, threw on my clothes, and went to the window. I can't even remember the actual process of getting to the ground. I was just there, transported as if by some magic to the dark lawn, looking up at my window that gaped wide for all the world to see. Then I started running. I cut across lawns, took shortcuts through the bushes. Dogs barked, I think, but I didn't hear them. At every turn I imagined the police cars of my childhood waiting, dark and unmarked, to pounce.

From our house to the bus station was a fifteen-minute walk. Taking it at a sprint, before I knew it I was there. It was one o'clock in the morning, a Saturday night in early March. A bus had just pulled into the station, and a few people were straggling into the Travelers next door. I mingled with them, a traveler passing through myself. Inside, a jukebox was playing, the lights were dim, there were about twenty indistinct figures dancing in the back of the room.

That first night I was so tense I stayed less than two minutes. But I'd seen enough. It was there, it existed, and somehow I knew. I raced through the empty streets euphoric, unafraid. Half an hour after my escape I was back in bed as if it never had happened.

Unable to sleep, I masturbated. I lay rigid with the covers pushed down mid-thigh and ran my fingers lightly as possible along the shaft of my penis. With forefinger and thumb I slowly massaged myself, never using my whole fist because even that quiet friction, I was sure, would start some subtle rhythm in the bed inaudible to me but amplified through the floor of my room, the heating ducts and wallboards, to my parents' room downstairs. The sound of my footsteps on the carport roof, the thump as I tumbled across the windowsill wouldn't have wakened a soul. But the rasp of two fingers along the taut skin of my penis would be enough to jar my parents into supernatural alertness in their bed one floor beneath me in the house that, henceforth, could never be my home.

Dancing had never been allowed in our church, and watching the long-haired boy at the Travelers dance I suddenly knew why, and also that I had always been, from the very first, on the side of dancers.

For five weeks in April and early May he held me in a kind of spell. Then he stopped coming. I looked and looked for him but he didn't come back. I'd seen him in all about six times.

School let out, the deep trough of summer opened up: my two brothers and I were bundled off, as we had been for the past several years, to a church camp in Alabama—the Jesus Camp, on whose board of directors my father served. Twice a summer he came to the camp and preached on the missions to Africa, though he hadn't been back there himself since 1956. Despite the fact that his color slides were starting to fade, he was inspirational, and we three Voegli boys got free tuition as well as an odd sort of prestige.

Our mornings at the camp were spent in Bible school, our afternoons in organized activities like visiting the Evergreen Rest Home and reading to the old people interned there. An ever-vigilant resident counselor led us in prayers and hymn-singing before lights out at ten. We slept eight to a cabin, in bunkbeds that creaked with every move. There was practically no chance to masturbate.

My body gave itself over to wet dreams. I'd dream of the dancing boy from the Travelers and go hollow with loneliness. When I'd wake, sticky and shameful with seed, I'd purge him from my thoughts as the impossibility he was.

In the middle of the summer my two younger brothers, thirteen at the time, finally persuaded my reluctant father to baptise them. Like everything else, they decided they wanted to do it together.

Keith and Kevin were twins. They both had the same red hair and pale freckled skin, but Keith was tall and slim while Kevin was short and favored my mother.

Despite that difference, they were spookily close in personality. I felt outnumbered by them, outflanked. We went our separate ways. They were always getting bones broken in whatever sport they'd decided to hurl themselves into that particular season. And they were extremely fervent about being Baptists; they took it with a seriousness that was unsettling. To most observers, I undoubtedly appeared to take it the same way.

They'd been wanting to get baptised for about a year, but my father was wary. It was extremely important, he explained to them, as he'd explained to me a couple of years earlier, to understand fully what they were doing, and why they were doing it, and what it meant. Baptists, he said proudly, didn't force children to be baptised. That's what made them different from both Catholics and other Protestants. Baptists, my father said, took baptism seriously; that's why we called ourselves Baptists. We were the only denomination who believed in total immersion baptism.

When you buried somebody, my father would argue from the pulpit, you didn't just sprinkle a little dirt over their head and call them buried. You put them all the way under the ground. And the same with baptism, which was the death of the old spirit and the birth of the new. You didn't sprinkle a little water over the head and call somebody baptised. You had to put them all the way under. Anybody who didn't understand that didn't understand baptism, and if you didn't understand baptism then you didn't understand what Jesus Christ was all about.

When he talked like that, he could be very impressive.

There was a lake on the Jesus Camp premises, and my brothers thought it would be a terrific spot to get baptised. But my father said no. The reason was a Mrs. Filbert, who'd been brought to the Lord at my father's first visit to the camp at the end of June, and had waited till his second visit because she wanted to be baptised by him and him alone. And she was terrified that there were snakes in the lake. So they had it in the sanctuary of the Jesus Camp.

The baptismal pool was just behind the pulpit, a narrow pool about four feet deep and ten feet long, with a glass front so you could see below the water level. Behind it hung a heavy curtain on which had been embroidered a scene of the river Jordan. Everybody called it the Jordan curtain, and behind it was a little changing room.

Three steps led up to the baptismal pool, and then three steps down into the water.

That Sunday morning, Keith and Kevin were baptised first—in that order, since that had been the order of their first birth. It went without a hitch. Keith disappeared behind the curtain to change while Kevin was being baptised, and then Kevin went to change while Mrs. Filbert descended into the pool for her turn. She was a very large lady, and my father put her under with an enormous wake that sent water over the edge. She came up spluttering, with a look of complete astonishment on her face. Whether it was what she expected or not I have no idea.

As she made her way up the water-splashed steps out of the pool, she suddenly slipped. She went crashing back on top of my father, who'd been waiting to climb out behind her, and at the same time she reached out in a panic to steady herself. What her hand found was the Jordan curtain, which she pulled right off its curtain rings and into the water on top of both her and my father.

Kevin had just stepped out of his wet clothes, and when he turned around to see what the commotion was about he found himself, stark naked, facing about three hundred startled campers and churchgoers. He glanced down at himself, picked up a folding chair to try to hide behind, saw that wasn't going to work, and in a single magnificent leap dove right into the pool, on top of my father and Mrs. Filbert who were just managing to extricate themselves from the Jordan curtain.

Of course everyone there laughed—the campers uproariously, shouting encouragement to Kevin, to my father; the regular churchgoers in embarrassment or anxiety or God knows what. I laughed most of all—uncontrollable, hysteric, gagging and hacking till I collected stares of undisguised consternation. But that panicked laughter was the only safety I could think to hide myself inside of.

Such was the summer of my desperation.

UNDERWATER

Six months, and the whole episode has become completely unreal. Life, for a terrible moment fractured, resumes its unblemished sheen. He is not, he tells himself, terribly lonely. Not lonely at all. Nearly every day he still does what he loves best, which is flying machines. The house is empty; he chooses more often than not to stay in Florida for the weekends, but that only means he's better rested for the next week of training. And training accelerates. He's been named to a moon mission scheduled for the spring of 1972.

If anything, what happened was a stark warning from whatever fates might be watching over him. He's never particularly believed in God, or disbelieved for that matter, but he has had, for years, the vague notion that he's being watched over. If he calls them "fates," it's for lack of a better word. But he feels he's been severely chastened by them, whoever they are, though he's not exactly sure why.

He has no doubt that the time will come when he will find out.

With his schedule what it is, he hasn't seen Frank to talk to him in ages. On an April afternoon they sit in the pale spring shade of the sycamores and drink martinis.

"I love these trees," Allen says. "Magnificent trees."

"Pain in the butt," Frank says. "I should cut them down. They drop their leaves right in my pool. Besides, they're way too big for the property. Some storm's going to come along some night and knock them right over. Shallow roots. I have my investment in my house to think about. Or they could fall on your property. You could sue me."

"I'd never sue," Allen says. "I wouldn't even think of it."

"You say that now. Can I have it in writing? Just joking, of course. You know what I hate most?"

"No, what?"

"The damn birds. They roost up there, shit all over my car."

Frank keeps his red '65 Mustang in mint condition. A cloth shroud covers the car except on Sundays, when he tinkers with it or takes it out on the road. Still, he complains the acids in bird droppings leech through the cloth and spot the paint.

"You should build a garage," Allen says. "It's crazy your house doesn't have a garage."

"I should cut down those trees is what I should do. . . . So Joan took the kid?"

The change of topic catches Allen off guard, and before he quite realizes it he's said yes.

"Well, don't blame yourself," Frank says. "You already work just about the most high-stress job on this planet without worrying yourself sick over this stuff too. It's not the end of the world."

Just the end of *my* little world, Allen wants to say but doesn't, not because it would sound self-pitying, but because he senses it's not, in fact, true. His world is flying, and flying is precisely what, unencumbered, he's still doing. In one version of the events he's constantly rehearsing in his wounded conscience, Joan and Jonathan have opted to bow out gracefully rather than risk entangling him unnecessarily in their various wreckages. In other versions, though, it's been an outright attempt at sabotage.

"It frustrates me," Allen tells Frank. "I mean, she knew I was a pilot when she married me. We talked about it. What did she expect?"

"It's hard," Frank agrees. "Ask not what your country can do for you."

"I told her, I want a family, but I can't do it all. I'm going to have to be away. And there's always the possibility that something's going to happen. The unfair burden would have to fall on her. She said she knew all that. She said she was ready for it. I guess I thought it was all settled, and it wasn't settled at all. But after sixteen years, she didn't give me a chance to fix what was wrong. She just flicked the switch. That was that. Sixteen years of married life down the tubes."

34

He's aware, even as he speaks, of some other version of events that lurks perhaps too deep inside him to retrieve. But he has glimpses.

"Like I say," Frank tells him, "you can't afford to blame yourself. How's the kid? What's the story with him? Are you getting soaked for payments?"

Allen hears the question, but his mind's suddenly jumped the rails. "You know," he says, "when I was a kid I built this mouse cage."

"What are you talking about?" Frank asks him, but Allen knows that's not a simple question. He signals Frank to listen.

"I was always building stuff like that," he says, "but I swear this one was a masterpiece. Different levels and tunnels and all that. My mother went and bought me a gerbil, and not a week went by before that gerbil had babies. Squirmy little things, but I was so excited. I remember I made this special compartment in the cage, filled it up with straw. I was crazy about those little babies."

"Tell me when the punch line comes," says Frank, but what Frank thinks doesn't matter. Allen hasn't thought of this in years.

"I came home from school," he remembers aloud, "and when I went into my bedroom to look in the cage I couldn't find the little babies. Then when I looked closer I saw the mother was eating them. One after the other—she just gobbled them up. She was on the last one. She'd bitten its head off."

He can see that Frank's looking at him with some small amount of concern. He laughs, in part to reassure Frank, but it's a laugh that's too nervous by far, and it shows in Frank's expression. It's peculiar—the air's very still, quiet. It's as if the sycamores are bending down breathlessly to catch his every word.

"You know," he says, "if I'd been there even a minute earlier I could've saved them. But I wasn't there. I remember I let out this screech—my mother came rushing into the room, she must've thought . . . Lord knows what she must've thought. But after that I just kept replaying in my head how I walked home from school that afternoon. Every little detail. What I'd done. Everywhere I dawdled. There was this girl Anne I liked. I talked to her for the longest time. I was teasing her about how she'd covered her schoolbooks in wax paper instead of brown paper bag paper like the rest of us, though I thought it was terrific she'd done that. Out of the ordinary, which she was. But if I hadn't have done that, if I'd walked on a little faster. But no matter how many times I replayed all that in my head, nothing changed."

There's complete silence between them. Frank's still looking at him with unabashed concern. Studying him. He shifts in his chair and says to Allen, "Well. So now you're going to tell me what all that means?"

"You tell me," Allen says. "I don't know what anything means. Jonathan wanted to stay here in Houston, you know, with me. With his Dad. Not have to transfer schools, disrupt his routine. That kind of thing. But what could I do? I'm never here. I can't have a sixteen-year-old running around the house with nobody here. Think what trouble he could get in—I could get in, for that matter. So he went to Tennessee with his mother, which I think he was not at all happy about."

"It's hard," Frank says soothingly. His reassuring tone is vaguely irksome to Allen, though he understands how Frank thinks it's his job right now, in the conversation, to be reassuring.

"If I'd really wanted him—I mean, more than anything else—I could've fought like hell to keep him, Frank. I would've got custody, just between you and me. *That*'s the hard part. I made the conscious decision to cut him loose. What do you think of that?"

"I think it was an impossible situation," Frank assures him. "You made a damn hard decision, but you stuck with it. I think that's the best anybody could do."

"What worries me most, if I can be honest with you: this kind of mess does not sit well with NASA. That's been made very clear."

"We have these impossible standards," says Frank. "We all know a wife and kids can be anybody's Achilles' heel."

"Still, it was one of the things we knew from the word go, how we were expected to behave. Wife and kids too."

"Did you cheat on your wife?" Frank asks bluntly.

"Absolutely not."

"Then there you have it. Nothing to worry about. You're not going to see your name in print that way. Now my advice to you is, you're going to the moon. Don't think another thought except that. You were put on earth to do that one thing, and there's a lot of us depending on you to do it. Think how you feel about Joan bailing out on you. Do you want to let us down like that? Think about it that way."

Allen nods grimly and lets the wisdom, which it undoubtedly is, sink in. It comes to him, what to say next, and he says it with a certain degree of sincerity. "I just want to thank you and Sally," he says. "It's been a really long winter, but you've been there for me in this, and I appreciate it."

Frank and Sally's swim party, a month later, tilts heavily toward Mission Control. The only other astronaut is Pete Leitner, who's assigned backup for Allen's mission, and with whom Allen trains at the Cape five days a week.

"Long time no see," Pete says. Then he whispers, "The secret is, they let us go home on the weekends, but it's all part of the simulation. Social training. What to do if you get invited to a party while you're on the moon."

Allen likes Pete, though he can never stop thinking of Pete as his shadow. Any kind of mishap, it's Pete who'll replace him—and Allen's too aware how many careers, his own included, have advanced because of capsule fires, T-38 crashes, random sports car smashups.

"I know all these people," Allen says, "except that one, over there."

A young woman with long, tan legs suns herself on a lounge chair she's pulled out into the yard, away from the pool, free of the mottled shade of the sycamores.

"Janine," Pete identifies her. "Remarkable lady. She's been to hell and back and just look at her."

"I don't follow."

"Last year. I-45. That truly horrendous accident."

Allen never seems to have time to read the papers.

"Police chasing some black dude who stole a car," Pete elaborates. "Plowed into Janine's husband instead. Bringing the kids home from a birthday party, no less."

"She wasn't in the car," Allen says.

"Nobody came out of that car alive. Were you on some other planet that you never heard about it?"

But Allen doesn't remember; though looking at her gives him a strange thrill. Her suffering sets her apart. He thinks he can see, in her face, some beautiful sadness sharply etched there.

He doesn't know why he longs so much, all of a sudden, to meet her. He wouldn't have any idea what to say.

But after a couple of Frank's martinis, he works up his nerve. She

37

hasn't moved, except to pull her chair a few feet further ahead of the encroaching shade. There's some kind of space around her: he can feel it. She shades her eyes as she looks up at him. He's trim, fit as can be, but he still feels awkward standing in nothing but his baggy bathing suit. Despite his famous grin and his crew cut, beautiful women intimidate him.

"Enjoying the sun?" he asks.

"I'm baking," she tells him. "But I need my ultraviolet quotient. I was getting all shriveled from being in the water too long. Frank and Sally've got a terrific pool."

"You like to swim?"

"Swim, water ski, scuba dive. I was a mermaid in some other life. What were you?"

Stumped, he answers the first thing that comes into his head.

"A wheelbarrow," he says.

It makes her laugh. She tilts back her head and closes her eyes. His gaze makes a quick, discreet circuit of her body. His eyes are all over her in that instant, finished before she opens her eyes to study. "Best answer I ever heard," she says. "Sounds like some fairy tale. Did you ever see 'Rocky and Bullwinkle'? Those cracked fairy tales they used to have. The mermaid and the wheelbarrow."

He doesn't entirely follow, but he can sense his foolishness has somehow, magically, turned to gold. On an impulse he stretches out his hand and she takes it. "Come swim with me," he says. He helps her up. "There's no excuse not to be swimming on a day like today."

Frank and Sally's pool *is* terrific. They dive into its blue underwater world. Everyone else is eating, so they're alone down there, and Al's not a wheelbarrow at all. When they break the surface together laughing, the sight of barbecue-devouring couples jars them, and they dive instinctively back into their dream. Usually when he's underwater it's in a tank with other guys in cumbersome space suits. Technicians monitor them with notepads. Cameras record the whole thing for playback. But this is silent and secret. He reaches out to hold Janine's waist with both hands, allows her to slip from him, her body gliding sleekly between his hands; catches her again, she allows herself to be caught, he allows her to escape so he can reach for her once more. Up for air, clinging to the side of the pool, they look at one another seriously. There's a question in her eyes, and all at once he's embarrassed at this underwater game of tag they've played. The way they've touched. It's incredible.

"Come on," he says, hoisting himself up out of the water, onto the pool's wet rim. "All the food's going to be gone, and I, for one"—he lunges once again toward that image that's brought him all this—"have got a wheelbarrow's appetite."

Restless in the bungalow that serves as crew quarters at the Cape, he drives to the nearby Luna Lounge. It's a hangout for NASA types that he seldom frequents. Tonight's Sunday, the place nearly deserted. He sits at the bar and nurses a double scotch and thinks about Nora Brittain. He hasn't thought about her much in the last five years, and he realizes, vaguely, that he's only thinking about her now as a way of thinking, obliquely, about Joan.

Nora and Joan had been close, the way astronaut's wives are close. And he'd been pals with Chuck. They'd all four flown to Mexico City for a weekend once, and Chuck had taken him out fishing in the Gulf once or twice. He had a boat down in Galveston. At the time Chuck was prime crew for Gemini 9, and Allen was assigned backup crew for Gemini 10. That meant, through the vagaries of scheduling, that Allen would be prime crew for Gemini 13. The problem was, the program was only slated through Gemini 12, which meant he wouldn't fly. A bitter disappointment, but he'd almost certainly be near the top of the list for the Apollo flights, maybe even Apollo 1.

He was in his office one raw February afternoon when the news came through: the T-38 carrying the two Gemini 9 astronauts had crashed in St. Louis. Allen had been in a meeting with them only that morning. They were flying up to inspect their capsule at the Grumman assembly building. By some fluke, while making a second landing attempt in a sudden snow squall the wing of their plane clipped the roof of the Grumman building. "Killed instantly," as they say—though of course it's never literally true.

For a full minute he sat motionless, staring out the window. The gray Texas sky was lowering itself down, degree by degree, onto the flat landscape. He felt nothing. Only the presence of the sky, his old friend and archenemy. Then he picked up the phone and told Joan what had happened. All she said—no other words were necessary—was "I'll meet you there."

A cold rain was starting to fall as he drove the short distance home. In the kitchen of the Brittain's house, looking distraught, a drink already in hand, sat Joan, and Frank and Sally, and the minister from the Brittain's church. Frank was on the phone, trying to track down Nora, but she was nowhere to be found. They waited, the weather got worse, the radio predicted sleet and freezing rain. Finally Nora's car pulled up in the driveway. She came in carrying a sack of groceries in each arm. The instant she saw them sitting there, her face went rigid. Then she said in a calm voice, unearthly calm, "Thank you all for coming." He was the one she looked at—straight at him, a look he'll never forget, though he's tried. Loss, utter devastation—and rage. Rage for him alone. She held him there for one awful instant as Frank relieved her of the grocery bags she'd utterly forgotten. Then she turned and walked quietly into her bedroom and shut the door.

Two days later Allen learned he'd been moved to Gemini 9 backup, which meant he'd fly, after all, on the last mission of the program.

It's late when he leaves the Luna Lounge and gets back to the crew bungalow, but he calls Texas anyway. Though it's an hour earlier there, Janine's gone to bed. She sounds groggy.

"Next weekend," he says. "I'd love to see you."

"Isn't it awfully late?" she asks him.

"It's never too late."

"It's two thirty in the morning here," she tells him.

He hadn't realized. He's drunker than he thought.

"Next weekend," he says again. "My place, next door to Frank and Sally's. Seven thirty."

The next day he's not a hundred percent convinced he ever made that call. Certainly he shambles through training with a hangover that calls existence itself into some kind of question. And the next weekend, as he wheels his cart through the supermarket, buying fat steaks, fresh gulf shrimp, and corn on the cob, it seems entirely possible she won't show up, that he's hallucinated the whole episode from start to finish. Either he's crazy, he tells himself, or he's not, and this is one way to find out.

Seven thirty passes, then eight. She's late, she's not coming. He starts the grill anyway, an act of faith that might be just the thing to encourage her arrival if it turns out the fates are for some reason hesitating.

The door bell's soothing chime nearly makes him jump out of his skin.

"Traffic was heavy through town," she explains.

"You should've taken the interstate," he tells her, then kicks himself.

And he'd wondered what they'd say when they saw each other again. But she puts him instantly at ease. "Show me around," she says. "I love to see how other people live."

"I feel more camped out here than living," he apologizes. "But look around. I want to get these steaks on."

"Let me guess," she tells him when she's completed her circuit. "Yours is the exotic bedroom upstairs."

He laughs, though he feels mildly compromised. He thinks of that room as off limits.

"My son," he says. "He lives with his mother, but he wanted to keep his room here. I wasn't about to try to clean that mess up."

"Well." She looks for a word. "Groovy." She says it slyly, and it makes him laugh, though nervously. He doesn't want Jonathan—or Joan, for that matter—hanging around for the course of the evening.

They feel incredibly distant, ghosts from another life: vivid, but ghosts nonetheless.

"I opened some wine," he says, "and the chow's ready. Is it okay if we eat in the kitchen? The dining room's all formal, and I hate that. You should know right off: I'm not your formal kind of guy."

She laughs. "And I'm not your formal kind of girl," she says. "A little old-fashioned, maybe, but definitely not formal."

He eats heartily while she picks at her food, cuts it up in little pieces: shrimp that's overcooked, steak that's just right. He could live off steak, three meals a day. Steak and eggs. He sees her, when she thinks he's not looking, use a fingernail to unwedge a piece of corn kernel from between her front teeth. Afterward, they sit together in the old glider out on the patio and finish off the wine.

"Yay," she says. "My parents had one of these on their front porch. I haven't sat in a glider in years."

It's a piece of furniture Joan picked up. Personally, he never cared for it, but she didn't want it when she left—she didn't want much of anything—so here it stayed. And now it's had its purpose after all.

"You have an accent," he tells her.

41

"Mississippi," she acknowledges. "Biloxi. I grew up there, this wonderful old house with miles of porches. Right on the Gulf. The breezes went all through it. Every window had these big gauze curtains that used to go sailing out in the breeze. Hurricane Camille wiped that house off the face of the earth. I was going to go back to see the damage, but my parents said, Don't, it'll only break your heart. So I never did, and they bulldozed it, and now there's nothing left to see."

She doesn't say whether it was before or after she lost her family. She had a son and a daughter, five and seven years old. It's a subject she doesn't mention, doesn't even allude to. He hates himself for mentioning the interstate.

"I can guess how you feel," he tells her, treading gently, wanting to allude and not to allude. He knows what he's really talking about, and wonders if she does too. He hopes so, but gently, gently. "My folks always lived in the same house," he goes on. "No place else ever feels like home . . . it's just where I happen to be living at the moment."

"But we're always trying to make a home, aren't we? Isn't that what we're always trying to do on this planet? And up there, too? Do you get back often?"

It takes him by surprise. "Not too often," he says, realizing it's been years since he was in Ohio. "Too busy, I guess." Even as he says it he feels old reasons, mostly uncomfortable, nudge their way toward the surface. Changing the subject, he points to the western sky.

"First star out tonight," he announces.

"I thought that was Venus. A planet."

"You're absolutely right. But you're supposed to make a wish on it anyway."

Janine doesn't take him up, however, doesn't even seem to have heard him. "I didn't have any idea who you were," she confesses. "When I said that joke about how I used to be a mermaid, why didn't you just tell me then you were an astronaut?"

"I've always had this aversion," he says. "Talking about it. Anyway, you managed to find out."

"Aversion," she says. "Don't be silly. You should feel proud."

"I don't care for that," he says. "Really I don't. I'm just a flyer. It's the way I've always considered myself. Just a very, very lucky one. I could be an airline pilot for all the difference it makes."

"I don't believe you," she says, "but I'll pretend to. So you always knew you wanted to fly?"

"I always knew. I used to read everything I could get my hands on. Memorized airplane specs, performances. Saved every penny that came my way for lessons."

"I can't believe I'm sitting next to a man who's been in space. You know what I heard about you?"

He can't imagine.

"I heard you fell asleep during lift-off."

"Who told you that?"

"Your friend Pete."

"Well, it's not quite true," Allen says. "I did doze off, but it was only during countdown. Actually, in a hold during countdown. I was exhausted, and my suit was warm and comfortable, and before I knew it, hey, I was out like a log."

"Amazing," she says. "I love the idea of space travel, but I can't even get on an airplane without getting a panic attack. I can just barely manage to drive a car."

That's different, he almost says, but instead he tells her, "There's nothing to be scared of on an airplane."

"I know, but I can't help it. Does that disappoint you about me?"

"Why should it?"

But it does, in some way he can't put his finger on. He likes her, though, for having second guessed him on that one. It reassures him about her.

"Were you ever scared?" she asks.

He shakes his head. "I can honestly say no. You train so much for a mission, it's like doing it in your sleep. That's the whole idea: no surprises. Now, over in Korea, there were the surprises. But I got back from Gemini and I had to literally sit down and ask myself, now did I really do all that? It's bizarre. But to this day, I can barely remember it. All I remember is being sleepy all the time. I could hardly stay awake up there."

"There wasn't anything that surprised you?" She sounds disappointed, and he racks his brain trying to think of something to say.

"I remember just one thing," he says. "It was kind of odd. When I was doing my EVA, my walk, during the night pass when I was supposed to be resting, I noticed this strange thing. I have this habit when I'm not doing anything: I rub my thumb with my finger. Just this nervous tic, I guess. But I looked down and noticed, where I was rubbing, my glove had started to glow. Just right where I was rubbing. So during the next night pass, I tried it again and the same thing happened. It wasn't dangerous, not like I could light myself on fire that way or anything. But it was odd. Just to have some part of yourself glowing like that."

"That's the kind of story I was hoping to hear," she says, and leans in closer to him. "Things you never read in the papers."

"Then how's this?" he tells her. "One guy, and I won't say who it is because you might meet him one day, he even swore, scout's honor, he saw a glove float by the window of the capsule."

"No kidding?"

His fingers walk up the ridge of her spine, and he can feel her shiver.

"That's what he said. I guess we'll never know."

These things do nothing for him. They're exaggerations of otherwise only mildly interesting phenomena, but he's learned other people like to hear them, so from time to time he's happy to oblige.

They sit in contented silence. Janine has her scoop on outer space and he, for the moment, has Janine. Dusk, that has settled in the sycamores, pours down like a flood across the patio where they are. Bats are out in its current, and swallows. It's time to say what he really wants to say, and he takes a deep breath.

She speaks just as he opens his mouth. "I'm getting mosquito bites," she says. "Sorry. What were you going to say?"

"I heard about what happened," he says awkwardly. "I'm very sorry." He's been waiting all evening. It had seemed, in the lingering pause between them, the time to say it. He hesitates, then goes on. "When I was test piloting at Edwards, we used to have a saying we all believed in. It was our credo. 'The future belongs to the brave.' "

She reaches for his hand and squeezes it. He loves her touch.

"Thank you," she says.

It's just a moment, a small acknowledgment of something. But he feels glad he said those words. He never trusts himself.

"Frank and Sally told me you had some problems of your own."

"Nothing compared to what you've been through," he says. "Nothing. It's embarrassing even to put it in the same category."

"I heard she walked out on you. Took your son. That must've hurt."

"Joan wasn't brave," he says. "God love her, but she wasn't brave."

Janine smiles at him, a smile so sad it's heartbreaking. "I think that woman probably had a whole lot of courage," she says with such assurance that he's momentarily taken aback. "It's just that being brave's not enough, sometimes."

"You seem to know all about Joan."

"I think I do," Janine tells him. "I think I know what kind of a woman she must have been. I think women know certain things about each other that men don't."

"She didn't give me a clue," Allen says furiously. "She just left."

"This was very recent," Janine says. "I can tell."

This time when she squeezes his hand, she lets her hand rest there against his, palm to palm, a momentary unexpected communion of sympathy from a fellow sufferer in the fires of life.

Later, when he walks her to her car, he leans close and says, "I think I ought to kiss you goodnight." It's the logical next step, and he realizes, as he does so, that she's maybe an inch taller than he is. His height has always been a blessing and a curse. But the kiss is delicious. He hasn't kissed this way in years.

Then she's gone, tooting her horn twice in farewell as her taillights disappear down the dark street. He feels his system pumped full of something he can't rid himself of. It's not so simple as adrenaline. It's not even the messy itch of desire.

He feels aimless, utterly adrift in his life. He's forty years old this summer. Not old, but no longer setting out on the adventure either. He's been in a mild panic ever since Joan left him, an internal distraction invisible to everyone else but putting him, and the things he does, in jeopardy.

He can't fly to the moon like this. He'd resign rather than try.

NASA's old strict policy makes perfect sense to him: to do nothing in one's personal life that will affect professional capability in any way. Frank's been wrong on that one. Only someone who's out of sync with the rule, as Allen feels himself now to be, can fully understand its importance.

Unable to sleep, he puts on the old plaid bathrobe Joan made for him years ago. The house at night is immense, ten times its size by day. Often he'll stay in Florida for the weekend rather than make the pointless trek back to occupy its emptiness for a couple restless nights a week.

It's not the house, of course. He can be happy anywhere, never happier than in that cabin where he and Joan lived in the hills above Edwards. It didn't even have running water. Joan used to bathe Jonathan in a tub in the garden, surrounded by rosebushes and oleander. We have each other, they used to say. But what did that mean, exactly, to have each other?

The moon's up. It floats, pale and mottled, just above the silhouette of the sycamores in Frank's yard. Looking at it, he feels nothing. It's a dead chunk of rock in the sky. He'll be there one day. He'll stand there. It's just unimaginable, though, in a way that does no good to even try to imagine. Trying to imagine is not his job, anyway.

He never really thought about the moon as a kid, or the stars. What he thought about all the time was flying. He even dreamed of flying: the recurrent dream of his boyhood, where he floated above the earth, calm, able to control with his breathing his movements, his height above the ground. Except just for an instant an odd sensation passes over him, something he barely remembers. He stands there on the lawn, struck by it, and then it's gone. But he doesn't move. He remains there staring at the moon, at the great branches of the sycamores, and there's something so familiar about the moment he can almost taste it.

Then, whatever it was, it recedes. He waits for it to return, but it doesn't, not even a glimmer. He stands there feeling absolutely lost for the longest time, then regretfully turns to go back inside.

His bowels are bothering him. He's been constipated for a week. Sometimes it helps to get the stomach acid going, to loosen himself up inside. Sitting on the toilet, he tries to make himself nervous by thinking of what it will be like to go to the moon. But he doesn't get scared or excited. He just starts thinking about checklists. All he feels is tired.

Get this mission out of the way, then there's the rest of his life.

And then what?

He thinks of swimming with Janine in Frank's pool, how underwater they were different people with each other. For the space of a few minutes, in that filtered blue light, how they slid in and out of each other's arms, just for that second, touching, so nimble and out of this world.

They click, as the saying goes, but in their case it's no idle turn of phrase. Rather it describes perfectly the way he feels. Something precise and mechanical, that he's always admired in certain simple yet essential tools—a gasman's copper-pipe flarer, for example. With it, the task's a synch; without, impossible.

A perfect fit of two people, he tells himself. Simple yet essential. Of that—sitting there, pants around his ankles, in agony on the toilet—he's never been more desperately certain.

The desperate certainty opens up his bowels. He grimaces, then the delicious sensation of relief floods through him.

A PROPOSAL

The Coach House Restaurant, after mushroom-smothered filet mignon, baked potato, a bottle of expensive French wine whose quality he knows he can't appreciate and suspects Janine can't either. But it's the thought that counts. He pulls a piece of paper from his wallet, unfolds it, spreads it on the tablecloth so they both can see.

Systems briefings and lectures, 300 hours
Spacecraft testing, 370 hours
Simulations on lunar modules, lunar landing research vehicles, command and service modules, 680 hours
Operational briefings, 270 hours
Mission equipment development, 350 hours
Flying check rides and personal travel in T-33 and T-38 jets, 200 hours
Flying helicopters, 40 hours
Miscellaneous: planetarium visits, egress training (Gulf of Mexico), procedures development, survival training (Panama, Utah), physical training, weightless training, experiments, lectures, suit fittings, photographic training, ??? hours

He notices how Janine moves her lips as she reads silently to herself. It seemed like a good idea. He's wanted to be completely honest. Now he has to resist the temptation to snatch the paper from her hand. Instead, he says, "That's for last year. 1970. My life, like it or not."

Janine folds up the paper and hands it back to him.

"You don't have to give me an accounting," she says. The look on her face is impossible to read, but he thinks he detects some kind of amusement there. Maybe it's best to turn it all into a joke. But there's something earnest in her face, too, that stops him.

Restlessly he shifts forward in his seat. "This piece of paper," he explains, "is why I'm not married anymore. It's why I lost my wife and my kid."

An invisible current seems to carry her closer to him, though physically she doesn't move. But they've launched into some new territory with each other. He can feel it, and apparently she can too. That they both realize it at the same moment astonishes him. He hasn't expected anything like this. In his experience, people are never together. It's thrilling. He's thought about what he might say, and now he lurches ahead with it.

"I consider marriage to be people helping each other. It would be great if we could do life on our own. Self-sufficiency and all that. But we can't. I can't. I've found that out, never more so than in the last nine months. All those things on that sheet of paper, I couldn't do those without a team. I've done a lot of thinking on that point. Life's teamwork. Do you see what I'm saying?"

She doesn't say anything. Her lips are parted like she's going to say something but she doesn't. She hangs back for the longest time. He can't stand it. He moves his hand across the table and covers hers. Her nails are painted. Joan never painted her nails.

"You're asking me to marry you," Janine says, "and we practically just met."

He doesn't trust himself to say anything more, so he nods. No doubt she can see the sweat he's broken out in. He resists the panicked urge to say she's got it all wrong.

She slides her hand out from underneath his, leans back in her chair, and folds her arms. Then she laughs that wide generous laugh she has.

And it had been going so well, like it never does between two people. As always, he's the fool.

"You're asking me to marry you," she repeats.

"You sound, um, discombobulated," he says.

Joan would have snorted at him for using that word.

"Allen," Janine says, her voice serious, and once again, marvelously, he can feel how perfectly near they are to each other—though they've both, protectively, sat back in their seats. "Honey," she says. "You don't understand. This is a dream come true. It's just so fast."

He feels her words like a wave. For a minute he's swept out of himself, out into some illimitable sea of possibility. Then he's more sober.

There's one more thing to say. He's thought about it; there's no need to say it, but he wants to. Wants to get it out in the open where it won't lurk.

"My whole life," he confesses uneasily, "I've had these spells. Episodes, I guess you could say."

She looks at him with a polite, blank look.

"It's hard to explain," he goes on. "Like some kind of déjà vu." Once spoken, his qualms feel ridiculous. "Really," he admits, "it's nothing."

"Not like epilepsy?" she says.

"No," he laughs, shaking his head. "Nothing in the world like epilepsy. It's a completely minor thing. Some little twitch in the brain."

There are things he's never admitted to NASA.

"Anyway," he finishes with a smile he can feel is a little forced, "you have to be sort of crazy to do what I do."

"Crazy," she tells him, "but cool as a cucumber. The kind of guy who falls asleep on top of a rocket."

"That's me," he says.

She looks at him across the table. He can't take his eyes off her: smart, pretty, and this lady's going to be his wife.

That night as they lie together for the first time, in his bed, in his house that finally, in some way, really is his house, Janine has her own confession: "I haven't been with a soul since Bill died. Not a soul."

With the exception of a single drunken, abortive night down at the Cape, Allen's able to say the same about himself since Joan. And that escapade was so farcical, so unreal, he's relieved, now, to be able to consider it as never having happened.

"We're starting over," she says. "The both of us. We have our whole lives ahead of us."

"Mmm," he agrees. Drowsiness fills him with its warm steady state. Her head rests against his shoulder. Their thighs touch. She felt so familiar to him earlier, and yet everything was an unfolding surprise. He can count on the fingers of only slightly more than one hand the women he's slept with since he lost his virginity to a Mexican prostitute back in—when was it?—1949. High school sophomore interested in the air force, on a trip to Fort Bliss. From there to here.

"You know what?" Janine says.

Drifting peacefully, peacefully. Toward slumber. How he loves women, their bodies, the secret places they enclose.

"What?" he murmurs.

She raises up on her elbow to face him, though in the dark they can barely see each other.

"I want to have children with you," she says. Her voice, suddenly, is passionate. "Raise a family," she says.

His heart practically stops in his chest.

She must be able to hear the sudden deafening silence because she says, "We never talked about a family, did we? I guess we never had time."

"It's all happened so fast," he says.

"Well, I want a family with you," she tells him, a little more boldly than before. "Maybe this is a good start." She reaches down and touches her hand to his slumbering penis.

They didn't use protection. It never would have occurred to him—he hasn't used protection in decades. Now her words stop him dead. They seize him with terror.

"Janine," he says. It's more of a groan than anything else. His heart's not only resumed its pace, it's now pounding like mad. He feels so stupid he wants to die.

"Janine," he says. "Oh, honey."

It's from so far back—how had he managed to forget? He considers the possibility of not telling her. Talking to his doctor, faking confusion, consternation, somehow getting away with it down through the years of their worsening life together till death finally parts them.

It's not something he can get away with.

"You don't want any more children," she guesses. She flings herself back on the mattress beside him and lies crushed and inert.

"I'm just so stupid," he says. "How can you ever forgive me? It's not that at all."

He can feel how she's come alert. There's tension like a bad electrical storm between them. Where they touched and touched only minutes ago, poking and rubbing and caressing, now it feels impossible, they're total strangers together in his bed.

51

"I never tried to tell you any of this," he says. "Jesus, this is so awful. It's not like I forgot, it's like I misplaced it somewhere, and in the rush of everything it got left behind. See, I have to think about so many things, my mind's not where it should be."

"Al, what are you trying to tell me?" Her voice now gone hollow, matter of fact. Possibly beyond caring.

He can only groan again under the weight of his stupidity. He told her about his episodes, inconsequential flickers, and in the meantime this, *this* he managed somehow, incomprehensibly, to let slip his feckless mind.

He tells her: "Joan and I, we tried to have one more child. After Jonathan. She wanted a girl, and I wanted a girl too, or a boy. Both at the same time. It didn't matter to me. I'd have been happy with twins. I was an only child, so I wanted a big family."

He pauses, and Janine's hand somehow finds his and holds on tight. The gesture touches him like nothing else. He clings to her hand.

"Joan got very sick," he goes on, his voice measuring itself for him now. "An ectopic pregnancy is what they called it. She had a miscarriage and nearly died, Janine. And that happened a second time, and the doctor told her, If you get pregnant again, you'll die. He said it just like that, no if's, and's, or but's. And he took me aside and said, It's up to you, buddy. You go and get her pregnant again and it's on your hands."

"You can't have children anymore," Janine says, but Allen hardly hears her. Now that he's started his story, he's going to finish it.

"Tell me what I should do, I told the doctor, and he said, I think you should have a vasectomy. I think that's the safest alternative. You know what a vasectomy is? he asked, because back then they weren't all that common. But I knew. Then he said, You should know it's not reversible.

"I told him I knew that too. I have a kid, I told him. I have a beautiful boy and I'm thankful. You need to make sure, he said. And I told him I was sure. It was that, or never be a husband to my wife again without being afraid I was taking her life in my hands, and I couldn't live with that. Do you understand? It was so hard to foresee the future back then. That was in 1960, 1961. Janine, are you following me?"

"I'm already there," she says. She continues to hold on tightly to his hand. He feels they've come untethered from everything except one another, and are racing headlong into some unstoppable blackness.

"I can never, never make this up to you. I don't know why I didn't tell you right off the bat."

"It's not something you just go and say on the first date," she tells him. "Still, you went and forgot it. At least tonight you forgot it."

"It was like I was holding my breath hoping for something that I never thought would happen to me," he says.

She starts to sob. He's never heard anything that had less to do with him. He won't roll over and hold her; he can tell she wouldn't want that—and besides, he's too afraid to, way too clear and not clear at all about the things she must be crying for. He only goes on holding her hand, and she makes no move to slip hers from his. Without this tenuous contact, he's quite certain, they're both lost without a trace.

He wonders how he could be so selfish.

No matter how much attention he pays, things slip by him. It's what damned him in his old life, and now it reaches out to take hold of his new one as well. That old phrase comes over him again: "personal life." Such an odd, elusive thing. It's what one's supposed to want, a personal life. And yet what they never tell you is how distracting it is, how demanding. It isn't that other people are selfish, it's just that they're complicated. You never mesh with anyone because you never meet them on anything like common ground.

He's had his ideal: marriage as team work. But it turns out to be more dark and desperate than that. It takes place at night, never out in the open. The underside is where it lives and feeds.

"You can let me go," he says, referring not so much to the grip they continue, hand clasped to hand, as everything else. "If you want to," he says, "I understand." It's the only thing, besides taking back the six weeks they've had together, that he feels he has to offer.

"I don't walk out," she tells him. Her voice becomes small, brave, and he can hear the magnitude of the defeat he's handed her. Or not even him: rather, that terrible thing, Life.

"I make the best of things," Janine says, still holding on tightly. "It's who I am."

Picking up Jonathan at the airport, Allen's wary. His son bounds through the departure gate wearing mirrored sunglasses. For an instant

Allen doesn't recognize him, but the tie-dyed T-shirt gives him away. He wears tight white pants, black motorcycle boots, a knapsack slung over one shoulder. His brown hair is way too long. He looks like some kind of a freak.

"Hey Dad," he says, hugging Allen and planting a wet kiss on his cheek, a childish habit he's never outgrown.

"Hey," Allen tells him, pushing him away playfully, "let's not overdo it."

Jonathan slaps himself lightly. "That was such a bad plane ride," he says. "But you wouldn't believe who I was sitting next to. Al Green's mother. She kept praying the whole way. The stewardess had to tell her to stop, because she was making the other passengers nervous. You know, you really look like life's agreeing with you."

"Well, you look—scruffy," Allen has to say. "Who's Al Green?"

Jonathan grins, then sticks out his tongue. "You're right. I'm pure scruff."

Allen winces. Those awful lips and tongue pasted on the crotch of the *David* statue in Jonathan's room. And he thinks his son is wearing some kind of cologne.

Jonathan rubs his hands together vigorously. "Hey Dad, you know, it's so cool to be here," he says. "I'm so excited. I nearly had diarrhea I was so excited. Just kidding. Yeow!" He does a little dance right there in the airport corridor, sticks one fist briefly in the air.

Allen has no idea what he's going to do with this kid. He hasn't seen him in three months, so he's arranged to take the week off. He just had no idea he'd feel so awkward. He's forgotten how ebullient Jonathan can be, how wearying. A memory comes back: Jonathan standing beside his chair, ten or eleven, reciting in a singsong voice, "Sea of Tranquillity, Sea of Storms, Sea of Fertility, Sea of Vapors.

"Sea of Spasms," he chirped. "Sea of Dizziness, Sea of Diarrhea."

"Yeah, sure," Allen told him.

"On the dark side," Jonathan said, "where we can't see."

He'd made a map, complete with crayoned seas and craters.

"Great," Allen said. "Very nice."

"You can help me make a globe. I'll make the globe and you can draw in the craters. I'll tell you where they go."

"Don't knock yourself out," Allen told him.

"New moon, crescent moon, waxing gibbous, full moon, waning gibbous, the old moon in the new moon's arms," Jonathan chanted. "Hey Daddy?"

"What?"

"What's gibbous?"

"Hunchbacked." Allen raised a shoulder, grinned hideously, like Quasimodo in that movie that had terrified Jonathan, inexplicably, for weeks. "I'm the Hunchback of Houston. Now leave me alone or I'll get you. Go help your mother in the kitchen."

Jonathan had shrieked.

Allen wonders when, exactly, he stopped knowing his son. It wasn't a conscious decision, and yet at some point he let him go. Gave him over, exhausted, to Joan.

And then he came home to find that everything had fallen apart, and there was Joan lying in bed and drunkenly naming their son, spitting out the word as if it were some bitter seed. He felt no surprise, only a numb confirmation.

How, then, had he known?

He used to see couples who had a retarded or disabled child and feel pity for them, a sense of their shame. No one would say it openly, but everyone knew some secret flaw in them had been cruelly exposed.

I don't like my son, he tells himself regretfully. I can't force myself to like him.

"So, how's your mother?" he asks warily, once they're in the car and on the interstate home.

"Alcoholic," Jonathan says, all at once, blunt as a bullet. "Very alcoholic."

Allen's heart drops out from under him. "What's that supposed to mean?" he says sharply.

Jonathan flicks him a smile so like Joan's that it makes him wince. Brilliant, artificial. Grotesque.

"Actually, Dad, that's exactly what she told me to tell you. Word for word. I have an alcoholic mother. I live with her."

Suddenly Allen's furious. In his blind haste to extricate himself, he's been all too eager to accept Joan's promise that a binge was only a binge. "What do you know about any of that stuff?" he shouts at Jonathan. "Jesus Christ." But then instantly he's cautious. "Forget it," he says. He can hear his tone adjust itself. "You don't have to answer that."

Jonathan puts both hands on the dashboard, lowers his head to rest there. "Then I won't," he says. "I'm the one who has to deal with it, right?"

This is some kind of cry for help from a kid who wants out of there. I can't believe what I've done to you, Allen wants to say to him, but he won't say it. He won't say it because he knows, difficult as it was, he's done exactly what he had to do. Even Frank has said as much.

He hates how easy it was. How he was sure, in some unformulatable way, Jonathan and his mother were in cahoots—though for what purpose he never, in the eerily calm progress of divorce and custody, figured out.

They ride on in silence, the Gulf highway carrying them south toward the Space Center and Nassau Bay. Their exchange has made Jonathan fidget. He writhes in his seat. He raps on the dashboard with his knuckles, a frenetic rhythm.

"Calm down," Allen says. "You're making me nervous."

"Sorry, Dad. I'm just so excited, you know, to be home."

The word jars.

"And I have friends here," Jonathan goes on, "that I can't wait to see. I don't have friends in Tennessee."

Allen has to look over at him. The boy sits in profile, staring raptly ahead as the skyscrapers of the city loom magically from the plain. There's a whole life going on inside that head he doesn't have a clue about.

After a few minutes Jonathan resumes his erratic dashboard drumming, though more quietly. Allen is about to tell him to stop, but by that time they're nearly to the house, and he decides not to say anything at all.

"Same old house, same old everything," Jonathan says as they turn into the driveway. He pounds the dashboard one last time. "Same old 'vette, huh Dad?"

Allen shuts off the engine and turns to his son. He feels so awkward.

"There's somebody here, Jonathan, that I, um, want you to meet."

THE ASTRONAUT'S SON

He's always showing up next door in a broken-down pickup to mow the lawns up and down the street. Not ours, because Dad dictates that's my job, but practically everybody else's.

This is last summer.

I don't know who he is because black men never come in our neighborhood, only maids. But I love how he hauls the mower out of the back of his pickup, hefts it around like it's nothing. Sets it on the grass and tugs at the starter cord. I love the dark spot of sweat on the back of his T-shirt, and how he wipes his brow with a handkerchief from the back pocket of his trousers. Man, do I want to be that handkerchief. I'll get the mower out whenever I see him doing the MacLean's lawn next door. I'll wave and he'll wave back, our two mowers moving back and forth in a kind of rhythm, sometimes close, sometimes at the far end of the properties, and that goes on half the summer till one day I call over, When you're done you want some iced tea? With the racket of the mower he can't hear, so he shuts it off and comes over. He's shy at first but then he says sure. I get the pitcher Mom keeps in the fridge, and when I come back outside he's got his shirt off and is using it to daub the sweat from himself. William, he says his name is. Bill. I can't take my eyes off him.

Black men, the way they look and smell, the special way they hold themselves.

The MacLeans aren't home, and since Bill's cutting their grass for them I say we should take a swim. We don't have a pool but they let me swim in theirs all the time—they're nice that way. Bill says, I don't have no bathing trunks on me. That's what he calls them, bathing trunks. I tell him we can swim in our underwear, I do it all the time. It's not true, but it works with him. He does this little dance when he steps out of his jeans. His white jockeys have a yellow pee stain on the crotch. He's sweaty all over, he just shines in the sun. Man, I have to say, him in his underwear and me in my underwear, but all he says is, You sure this is cool? One hundred percent cool, I tell him. He holds his nose and cannonballs into the water with a huge splash. Then he swims the length of the pool, butterfly. His strokes are big and strong, very methodical. I just sit on the side with my legs dangling in the water and watch and it takes my breath away. When he comes up for air I call over, You swim a lot? I guess he doesn't want to be yelling, because he swims back to where I'm sitting on the side of the pool and says down at Corpus Christi in the ocean with his cousins. I get this immediate picture of him and his cousins: beautiful strapping men out past the waves where the ocean gets calm and comes at you in long slow swells, and them, muscular, lying on their backs arms outspread, floating with the sky huge all around them and the ocean deep under them, just these beautiful floating black men talking back and forth to each other in those sweet low voices black men use on each other.

He says, Let me see you swim, and tugs on my ankles, so I slide on in and thrash out a few strokes. Here, he says, let me show you. He holds me floating in the water and moves my arms and legs and straightens my chest, and I love feeling his hands on my skin, how he keeps me horizontal just with his fingertips, and we could be floating in the ocean way past any land, me and Bill and his cousins.

There isn't any point to all this except to touch me underwater, which he does, and I laugh and touch him back. But suddenly we're dead serious, standing there looking at each other, waist deep or so, our hands working on each other for the longest time under the water. He feels huge, and looks it, though the angle of the water distorts the way things look. He's not like the kids I fool around with.

We never have anything much to say, but we swim a bunch of times that summer when the Macleans aren't home, and in August when they go to Colorado for a week, one night when Dad's out of town and Mom's gone to bed early, we swim totally in the buff.

Mom doesn't mind me swimming with Bill.

When Dad isn't home she'll sit and watch morning TV, whatever's on, then go to her bedroom in the afternoon and take a nap. After that she'll stay shut up in there reading or whatever till it's time to go to bed. It's me left to my own devices, which is cool. Of course when Dad's home everything turns regular again, which is cool too.

It's so great being naked and underwater at night. Dark but not completely dark. This glow filters down and we're gliding in shadows, his body dark and mine light, and that's the time he leans me up against the side of the pool saying in my ear, that low sweet voice, Do I want him to? Water halfway up our chests and he whispers, Why don't you grab onto the side there? Rest your elbows there. And I do. I know what's going to happen, and I keep thinking, Please, please let it happen, not just my finger up there or a carrot with some Vaseline once or twice when I was feeling desperate, but to really know what it's like. He keeps saying I won't hurt you, like he expects to hurt me. But he doesn't, even though he's just enormous. Maybe I yelp, but that's just my body being taken by surprise, because it doesn't hurt, really, or it hurts but it also feels terrific and I'm so happy this is happening to me. I say, Bill, you're making me so happy right now and he says, Good, that's what I like. To be making you feel so happy. Bill with his beautiful black skin, not black so much as some kind of cinnamon brown though in the night he's just dark, this hungry spot in the water that's lapping me up.

So why don't your Dad let me cut his lawn? he asks me in my ear. How much he pay you?

Ten bucks, I tell him.

I mow it for eight, he whispers. You keep two bucks.

I can hear the water lapping at the sides of the pool. Bill's keeping up his rhythm, driving me home with it.

Aw, man, he says. He grabs my shoulders and shoves himself way up inside me. I guess I'm feeling a man come inside my ass for the first time in my life.

Shit, Bill's saying between his clenched teeth, his lips pressing against my ear. You don't need the money like I need the money.

———

In the beginning it's mostly *National Geographics* in the garage: boxes and boxes Mom saved, going back to September 1955 when I was born. I'm eleven or twelve when I start going out there and poking around in them, looking for any kind of pictures that'll get me going. Sometimes I'll look all afternoon with no luck, just a half-stiff dick aching for something, it doesn't quite know what. But eventually I find three or four articles that are just great. There's one about a kid whose parents take him to the Amazon to live. They're scientists, and they let him run loose with the Indians in the village they're studying. Lots of pictures in that article, nobody wearing any clothes except the two parents: this blond kid, ten years old or so, standing in a dugout canoe spearfishing, wearing a string tied around his waist and nothing else, or sitting cross-legged with his little dick in full view while some butt-naked Indian shows him how to weave a basket. I practically hypnotize myself staring and staring at his dick, pretending it's me in those pictures, naked as the day I was born.

Then there're the African tribes. I can get dizzy thinking too much about them.

I'll stand there in the narrow space between Dad's Corvette and the wall where the magazine boxes are stacked. Pants down around my ankles, magazine spread open on the hood of the car. If Mom's out shopping and I'm home alone, I'll take off everything. In five years I splatter so much come on that cement floor I'm surprised it doesn't eat right through to China.

There're holy places on this planet. I don't know how I know, but I can tell when I'm in a holy place. Or when I'm making some place holy, because holy places don't just happen, somebody has to make them holy in the first place.

The MacLean's swimming pool is holy. The garage is holy. The book closet back at my old school library is holy.

The sycamores in the MacLean's backyard are holy.

I have so much energy in me sometimes I could fly through the roof. Serious, concentrated energy that I don't know where it comes from, but it's there, I can feel it inside me. Though sometimes I don't have it and I'm totally limp, nothing in the world can wake me up, but when it's there it's this pent-up ball of light waiting to burst out. And I love it. I love that feeling. It's who I think I really am.

So when I get back to Houston from Tennessee, first thing I do is call up Bill. I'm in my bedroom, sitting on my bed, one hand down my pants just thinking about him. Incense burning. I've forgotten what a cool room I used to have here. How much stuff I left behind because I was sure I was coming back.

He doesn't answer; some female comes on the line. I get the impression at least fifteen people live in that house where he lives. Hey, guy, I tell him when he finally gets himself on the phone. I've missed you.

It's been six months.

He's shy, like he's half forgotten me, but I'm not about to let him forget a thing. Some people you just have to keep in line.

I've been saving up for you, I tell him into the phone. You want to see me, man? See what I got saved up for you?

Aw, he says, which means he's not sure.

I don't say anything, so he can have time to think it through. Me, Jonathan, I keep thinking. Remember?

I got other stuff going on, he tells me.

Like what?

Like this chick.

No shit, I tell him. That's insane.

No man, it's real good for me.

That's cool, I say. I have no problem with that.

Though half an hour later we're laying on some tarps in the back of his pickup truck and he's offering me a joint. I tell him I don't do drugs but not to let that stop him, he should go right ahead. He takes a hit while I reach over and open up his pants. What I love about Bill is, he doesn't mind even though he keeps talking nonstop about this chick of his whose name I don't even know.

She's really fine, he's telling me between hits. He keeps inhaling like he can't wait to be stoned. Me, I want to savor all this with a clear head. I don't want to miss a thing.

God's great gift to man, he says. I'm talking about women.

Uh huh, I say, all the time pulling him out of his pants where I can get at him, so ebony it's nearly purple, the color of eggplant I see in

61

the stores that Mom never buys and I never actually tasted eggplant but I've tasted this, though it's been such a long time.

I used to gag but not anymore.

So your old man's going to the moon, Bill mentions while he's running his fingers through my hair. He told me once, You got hair like some little old girl, and my hair wasn't even half as long back then.

I can't answer. Dad *is* going to the moon, but right now I'm thinking, If this keeps up I'll be there first.

I can tell Bill thinks I'm something wonderful. He's got his big hands around my head and holds me there, pressed all the way in against him and I'd breathe if there was room for air in my throat but there's not. With my free hand I'm shucking my jeans, reaching around with a finger to ready myself back there.

When I maneuver to get on all fours, knees and elbows on the hard truck bed, my ass up in the air, Aw man, he says, is that what you want?

You got nobody but yourself to blame, I tell him.

Astronaut's son, he says.

Yeah, I groan. He feels ten times bigger than when he was in my mouth. I relax and relax till I think I'm going to liquefy and he keeps filling me up.

I should of known, he says.

Oh God, I say out loud. It excites me to make noise. He pulls out a ways till I'm gasping to have him back and then he obliges. I love how it practically tears me apart.

I'm for real, now, and I get realer and realer till I can't believe how my body feels being poked to smithereens like this. He bites my shoulder hard and I can feel him spurt inside me. I reach my hands around to pull his hips in against me tight, there must be nearly a foot of him inside me. His sweat's dripping on my back and his rough lips are on my neck, my ear, the side of my face. I can feel his stubble and smell his breath, I think there's whiskey on his breath, and the smoke of a joint. When he pulls out my muscles try to hold him, so that there's a faint popping sound when he leaves me for good that's like a kiss or maybe a sigh.

The pool, I say.

I've gotten him all drunk, which is what I love to do. Now he can't get enough. He can barely drive the truck he's so hot. And I'm so hot too. I don't even remember whether the MacLeans are home, though

62

when we pull up in the drive I can see their cars are gone.

We run across the lawn practically flinging our clothes off, Bill chasing me, catching up with me then falling behind, and in we go with a big double cannonball. He comes up shaking water out of his hair. I love it: those beads of water in his tight rows. I just have to grab him by the waist and he grabs me back. We stand there, waist deep, in our underwear this time like the first time and it's hard to believe that was a whole year ago.

It comes to me how, in a year, I don't know anything about Bill except what sex feels like. Who his people are, what he does with himself. But then I don't know even half that much with most other people.

The way we poke out of our underwear below water level to bump against each other, it's fantastic, like some duel down there but gentle. He's so much bigger than I am.

Yo, he says. Watch out.

And he lets go of me and backs off a couple of steps. I turn around and there's Janine in her black one-piece bathing suit heading right for us across the lawn, but she doesn't notice us till she's to the edge of the pool.

Oh, she says. Then: Hi.

Hey, I say. Bill's behind me, but I know he's about to piss he's so freaked out. And what if he did piss?

This is Bill, I say, and I hear him make some shy noise in Janine's direction.

Hi Bill, Janine says. What would we do without this pool?

Yeah, I say.

Your Dad never had one put in, she says, sitting herself down on one of the lounge chairs. She's got a really great tan, especially her legs, but then she's out by the pool every day.

It just never happened, I tell her. My mom hated pools. Swimming and all that stuff. She hates water, period.

It's freaky saying that to Janine, but it's true.

Funny, she says. I love the water. And your Dad loves to swim.

I must get it from him, I say.

Bill's standing behind me the whole time, and I take a couple steps back in the pool till I knock up against him. He's polite and takes a step back, but I keep moving back till my butt's pressing against him and he gives up and just stays where he is. With both my hands I reach back underwater and cup his thighs to keep him tight against me.

So, how *is* your mom, Janine asks gently. I've been here a week and finally her curiosity's gotten the better of her. I understand that. But I don't really want to talk to her about Mom, even though I'm the dumb ass who brought up the subject.

So I tell her, She's fine. She's happy to be back in Tennessee. Go figure, but it's true.

Now what town is it? Janine asks.

Minerva, I say.

I move my butt against Bill. It's all underwater and Janine can't see a thing, at least I don't think. Anyway it's thrilling and I'm not ashamed. This is where I live, after all. This was my home way before it was hers.

Minerva, she says carefully. I never can remember that.

Yeah, well, there's nothing much to remember.

You hate it there, she says—not a question, only a statement of something she thinks she knows.

Just the town, I say.

She must be a remarkable woman, Janine says. I mean, your mom.

It just comes out of nowhere. I ask her, Why?

Bill's petrified through all this, I can tell, but I have him exactly where I want him. I can feel him swell against me in spite of himself.

To go through what she went through, Janine says. An astronaut's wife.

Well, hold on to your hat, I want to tell her but don't. Instead I say Yeah, well, life's tough all over.

She's pretending Bill isn't there. I can see that. She's frantically pretending, and I have to wonder, will she say something to Dad? Though I have this feeling she won't because she won't know what to say.

And as always, that's what I'm counting on.

Later she knocks on my bedroom door. I'm lying on my bed thinking about Bill, how I spent the spring back in dreaded Tennessee literally aching for him and that I probably shouldn't have called him up like that though I'm glad I did; though I won't see him anymore.

It's just a feeling, but I can tell, so I'm savoring it before I move on.

I feel wrung out, which is probably the sex: sad but not sad, content in some way. Wondering what's next for me and how it could be just about anything.

Knock, knock, Janine says over the sound of her knuckles rapping, like I'm some little kid who needs to be amused.

Because it's off-limits in here, I'm a little annoyed. But since I'm feeling not bad but definitely odd now about the scene at the pool I say, Yeah? and big as life Janine opens the door.

Hope I'm not intruding, she says but I don't say anything.

She takes a couple of steps and just stands there looking around, surveying all my junk. Well, she says all full of cheer, and right at that moment I really hate her. It's . . . different, she says. I always wondered what was in here.

I think how pathetic she looks, dolled up the way she is, and she's going to marry Dad, she's going to be my stepmother. It makes me flinch and I tell her, nonchalantly, Well, now you know.

It's weird. Something in my tone sounds just like Dad.

She must hear it too, because suddenly I see she's actually shy. I've frozen her there with my tone of voice, like Dad must. But she hasn't just come bumbling in: she's made herself do this for some reason, and so then I'm interested.

You know, we sort of seem to avoid each other, she says, or is that my imagination?

Didn't we just have a conversation? I say. I'm wary of these talks with her.

Oh that, she says. She doesn't want to be reminded.

Then what? I say.

Do you mind? she says, and sits on the side of my bed.

I can't figure this one out. I tent my fingers over my chest and study the ceiling.

I bet everything in this room has a story to it, she says. That, for instance, is a very odd picture. She points to this print I bought at the Asian grocery downtown. Ganesh the Elephant God.

I wonder should I tell her anything? So I say, I'm a secret Hindu.

Oh, she says. Reincarnation and all that.

I'm about to think she's the most stupid person in the world till she goes on.

I've been reincarnated, she says. In some other life I died by drowning. I'm convinced of that. Either that or I was a mermaid. I have these strong feelings around water. Like I was saying earlier, but it goes deeper than just swimming. I can't explain it, and maybe everybody has feelings like that. Do you know what your Dad said when I asked him what he was in a previous life?

A falcon? I say off the top of my head.

A wheelbarrow, she says.

That says a lot, I tell her.

Your Dad's so funny, she says. He's always making me laugh.

I almost drowned, I mention. When I was a kid. We'd just moved to Houston and we were down at Galveston at the beach. A jellyfish stung me right across the chest. Man, was I screaming. I forgot how to swim, it hurt so much. Portuguese Man of War—that sounds better than jellyfish. Dad dragged me out of the water. Mom on the beach yelling her head off. I had these huge welts on my chest for hours. But I've never been reincarnated.

No? she says. You don't remember anything at all?

I'm pretty sure this is my first life ever, I tell her.

And it's true. It's why I feel so alive. Everything's brand new. Nothing's run down. I've got millions of lives still to go, more mistakes to make than I can ever imagine, pleasures and heartaches one after another after another for a million years, and only after I've worked through all that am I going to be tired and ready to sleep.

It's a golden journey ahead of me, I tell her.

I notice how she looks vaguely, from this angle, like Mom.

You know, she says, I think maybe I can see that in you.

A DISCOVERY

It's apparent, after a few days, that they actually get along, Janine and Jonathan—at least that's how it seems to Allen's untrained eye. Things have come up at the office, he's not been home as much as he'd like, or at least thought he'd like, and so that unlikely pair has been thrown together. But Jonathan acts as if he's unfazed by Janine's presence about the house. Allen comes home to find the two of them lazing by the pool, or making dinner together. It's odd. As if Joan, that whole other life, never existed, and yet Jonathan's presence signals at the same time so undeniably that it did exist.

One afternoon when he comes home he can hear their voices in the kitchen. He pauses in the hallway to listen. He's always had this inclination to know what people say, how they act, when he's not in the room; it's always struck him as slightly shameful, some kind of deceit, perhaps conceit, he's not comfortable with. Yet the temptation's hard to resist.

"So I told him," Jonathan is saying, with some excitement, "no way am I going to Galveston with you. Let me off right this instant. Now."

There's a pause. Allen's brain spins.

"And did he?" Janine's voice asks.

"Well," Jonathan's voice continues, "he groused about it, but then he did. He was so sure he had a rider to Galveston, even though I told him. So there I am, standing all by my lonesome on the side of the interstate, cars zooming by, and that's when the cops pick me up. They say, You can't hitchhike here, and I say, That's the last thing I want to do."

Fear, cold as nausea, threads its anxious way through Allen. He doesn't know this story. He doesn't want to know it, his son's life which can't be innocent.

He strides boldly into the room.

They're sitting at the kitchen table, coffee cups in front of them.

"You should hear what happened to Jonathan," Janine says excitedly. It's happened only this afternoon. She's been caught up in the telling. He can tell she doesn't know anything about this kid, can't read a single thing he says. Because even his own father can't do that.

I want him out of the house, Allen thinks. Away from here. He can see, in an instant, how Jonathan will wreck everything if he stays. It's just too clear. You need help, he tells his son silently, accusingly, knowing that he's the one who's failed in that help. How publicly disappointed and secretly relieved he was when it was decided Jonathan should go with Joan. And the boy had wanted, impossibly, to stay on in Houston. As if that could have been an option.

He's hesitant to reveal he's heard anything of their conversation. "Jonathan, what's up?" he asks from the door as casually as he can.

Jonathan's answer's a reflex. "Nothing," he says, and Allen wonders if Janine weren't around to lure it out of him, would Jonathan have said a thing? Jonathan's always been one to talk to the women. Allen's come to suspect all sorts of things Joan knew and never told him. And is Jonathan now testing Janine, slyly trying to find her out, win her over? Suddenly Allen's feeling that same insecurity he came to feel in those final fraught weeks with Joan—that she and Jonathan were somehow in cahoots.

"I mean," Jonathan corrects himself, "nothing much. I was trying to hitch a ride, only there was some confusion as to how far I was going."

Allen frowns. "This hitchhiking thing's not good."

"You used to hitch all the time," Jonathan reminds him. "Mom said so. You used to hitch to see her."

"That was 1952. Things were very different."

He must have hitched a hundred rides and never had a problem, but he also didn't invite trouble. Jonathan invites trouble. It's hard to say how. That long hair, his voice, some vague unseemliness in him.

"So do you want me taking the 'vette?" Jonathan asks slyly.

"I was saying he could use my car when I'm not needing it," Janine says.

Stay out of this, Allen wants to tell her—not harshly but very, very gently. For your own good, stay out of it. It's deeper than you are, it goes way back. Instead he says sharply, too sharply, "Why do you have to be running around all the time? Where do you have to go?"

Jonathan doesn't have a ready answer.

Allen punches his point home. "Houston's a big city," he explains. "People are different in big cities. You forget."

Jonathan makes that exasperated face he's been making since he was two years old. "I haven't been away from here *that* long, Dad."

Allen sighs. "I know," he says. Is this a fight worth fighting? As with most such fights, he decides against it—against his better judgment, but in accord with the secret sweat that's popped out under his arms and is crawling down his ribs. It's been a mistake to have Jonathan home. They just don't click, for whatever reason. What law says a father and son have to click?

"If you need to go somewhere," he offers mildly, "I'll take you, or Janine'll take you."

"Buy me a motorcycle," Jonathan says flatly.

"No," Allen says.

"Oh, come on, Dad."

He can feel Janine watching them curiously. It seems vital to be firm. Everything seems to ride on it. "No," he reiterates. "Too dangerous."

"It was just an idea," says Jonathan wistfully.

That the boy's a complete wild card these days is clearly Joan's fault.

Allen pauses, then asks the only askable question that's on his mind. "Are you bored here? I mean, with us."

Jonathan seems surprised, and Allen can register that Janine's surprised as well. It's a question he's glad he's asked.

"I'm having a great time," Jonathan insists. "Terrific time."

"I was just wondering," Allen says. He can feel Janine watching the both of them; her eyes dart back and forth as if to follow the lob of their words.

He realizes he's made his son nervous. Jonathan fidgets, then rises abruptly from his chair. He twists the little leather thing he's got tied around his wrist and says, "Gotta go."

"You're always on the go," Janine tells him, with a puzzling tone of wonderment, and he's out the door.

She shakes her head after him. Allen's grim.

"He doesn't like me," he says, and sits down heavily in the chair Jonathan's just vacated. The seat's warm, and the sensation's mildly uncomfortable. The heat of Jonathan's body.

"Of course he likes you," she tells him. "He idolizes you, in his way. He's just another generation, that's all. But your son's wonderful. He's so much like you. You can't see it, but I wish you could. He has such a zest for things. If he wants to get out of that little town he's stuck in, he should come live with us. I wouldn't have any problem with that, he and I get on so well."

He's never seen her quite so enthusiastic, and he can't find the words to say how Jonathan wears him thin. He himself isn't sure why he constantly feels so irritable around his son, this secret chafing in his presence. The hitchhiking story annoys him. It also worries him, which annoys him even more.

"Have you two been talking along these lines?" he asks suspiciously. "I don't think we should encourage that line of thought for him."

Janine seems genuinely puzzled. She's too good-hearted, and he can see what a beast of a father he's turned out to be.

"Why not?" she goes on. "He really wants to be here. That's plain to see. And his mother, from what he tells me—"

"Let's not talk about his mother," Allen says bitterly. "His mother has him, for better or worse, and let's leave well enough alone."

"She really hurt you," says Janine.

She said that to him before and he was touched—now the words only irritate him. She doesn't understand a thing.

"I'd rather not talk about it," he repeats.

"Allen," she says warningly, "your problem is that you never want to talk about things."

"Let's don't have this discussion," he says. He puts his hands over his ears.

"See, that's exactly what I mean."

It's their first fight ever.

"You have to tell me what you're thinking," she says, reaching out and gently pulling his hands away from his head.

"I've never been much of a talker," he complains. "I'm a doer. I

70

believe in getting things done, not talking about them. That's just the way I am."

He's incapable of marriage, relationships. He should throw himself into what he does best: his work, his rock-steady flying. It's the identity he's always craved, even as a boy devouring aviation journals, memorizing aircraft makes, specs, performances. The Flyer, pure, stoic, silent. Those moments: once they loosed you from the B-52 you'd piggy-backed up, you were self-sufficient and unattached. Like nothing else. Just you and the speed of sound and all the free space in the world. Your life there, the blood and your heart and your lightning-alert mind where everything is clear and cold and perfect.

He sees it the instant he flicks the light switch in the garage, though it takes a couple of seconds to register anything more than that something's out of place. He's gone there with the notion of taking the Corvette out for a spin, something he doesn't do that much anymore—in part because Janine worries, but also because, lately, he simply hasn't felt the need to absent himself from the house. But in the last few days his nerves have begun to fray. Just now, he and Janine have found themselves nearly shouting over some inconsequential wedding detail. She's accused him of being a troglodyte, one of those words she sometimes uses, he suspects, without quite knowing what it means.

Troglodyte. Even he's not entirely sure on that one.

Do whatever you want, he's told her too brusquely, and then is out the door.

What he sees on the Corvette's white hood, over on the passenger side by the wall with its stacked boxes, is a splayed-open magazine. From where he stands it's upside down, and he has to wedge himself between the car and the wall to see. A group of nearly naked African tribesmen stand in a circle. In the middle of the circle are some boys, completely naked, daubed with what looks like whitewash.

National Geographic.

For a moment his mind's a blank. Who's been looking at old *National Geographics*? Then suddenly a faint glimmer, only to be followed by another thought that pushes everything else aside: his pistol. He hasn't thought about it in months, but didn't he leave it out here, stashed away in one of these boxes of defunct *National Geographics* and then never come back for it, in fact fight relentlessly down into oblivion the memory of that October morning?

Frantic, he rips into the box on top, pulling out magazine after magazine, hurling them to the floor, but it's not there. And there are literally dozens of boxes. Suddenly enraged, not so much at the memory as at having made himself forget, he rampages through several more boxes till he gives up in disgust. He's breathing hard, broken out in a sweat. Maybe he did move the gun after all and just forgot. He should remember to check in the dresser in the bedroom.

How can he have forgotten?

But the pistol's not the point. Or it's all tied up with everything else. With the back of his hand Allen sweeps the offending magazines off the hood of his car, suddenly clear in his head, terrifyingly so. He's got to get Jonathan away from here. Out of this house. If he doesn't, his life with Janine will crack up like his marriage with Joan did. It was my son's homosexuality, he's able to say to himself for the first time, that destroyed my marriage.

Joan, Joan, he says aloud. He hardly knows what he's doing till he finds himself standing, breath shallow, stomach roiling, before Jonathan's bedroom door. Quickly, before his nerve fails him, he raps out a brisk tattoo. There's the muffled sound of something interrupted, then Jonathan's voice saying, "Half a second." Allen waits a decent while longer than half a second before turning the knob.

The door's locked.

He rattles the knob and Jonathan's there to open it. Shirtless, barefoot. Allen can see he's been up to something that's left him in a fine sweat. It beads above his lips, along his collarbone.

The room smells sickeningly sweet. Incense in the ashtray. Next to the ashtray there's a little jar of Vaseline, a wad of tissues.

Jesus, Allen thinks.

Assiduously avoiding eye contact, he blurts out the first thing that occurs to him. "I don't like the idea of you burning stuff in your room," he says. It calls attention to precisely that nightstand he'd rather ignore. For an instant he sees why kids have to despise their parents.

But then again, he never abused himself all over his father's secondhand Dodge.

The room's messy as ever, no place to sit, and Allen feels too self-conscious standing there face to face with a son he's just interrupted, presumably, in a bout of self-abuse. He puts his hands in his pockets and takes them out again.

"On-site inspection?" Jonathan says. "Tourism maybe? Borrow some sugar?"

Like one of those Indian scouts who can move through the forest and never snap a twig underfoot, he glides to his bed and sits down. With the back of his hand he wipes sweat from his collarbone.

"Room is kind of a mess, don't you think?" Allen observes as, a little unsteadily, he picks his own clumsy way to the desk chair—it seems the least compromised place to try to sit.

"At least I know where everything is," Jonathan says.

"Yeah, on the floor." Allen delicately removes some wadded-up underwear from the chair. "Do you mind?" he asks.

Jonathan shrugs. "Throw it anywhere," he says.

They both stare at the spot on the floor where the underwear flutters down. Say something, Allen tells himself (why is he so scared?) and then launches into what, standing in front of the door, he'd briefly rehearsed.

"I think," he says, "we need to talk."

It's barely perceptible, but the words make Jonathan flinch. Not much, but just enough, and Allen thinks, Good, at least the kid's not totally oblivious.

He's knows it's a mine field he has to thread his way through, but he charges ahead bravely.

"Look," he says, "I don't know what you do, and I don't want to know, it's none of my business, but it is my business what goes on around my house."

Jonathan's just looking at him.

"I'm talking about some pretty unseemly behavior," Allen goes on. "And if you don't know what I'm talking about, then you need to use some common sense to figure it out."

"You mean Bill?" Jonathan says.

It stops him dead in his tracks. Allen doesn't know any Bill.

The speed with which Jonathan volunteers that name rattles him completely. "You know what I mean," he says in a panic. "Ever since you've been back here this summer, I don't know what's gotten into your head. What on earth was that story about you and the police that I just happened in on? Janine doesn't find that sort of stuff as amusing

73

as you seem to," he adds by way of inspired intuition. "And neither do I."

Unsure where to go next, he pauses, and suddenly Jonathan does the oddest thing. From where he's sitting on his bed, he stretches out on his back.

"Look, old buddy"—Allen tries to modulate his tone of voice—"I know this is hard on you. I know your mother's not the easiest person to get along with, and I wish you didn't have to live in Tennessee. But you've got one more year of school and then you can go do whatever you want. I'm asking you, for your old Dad, to hang in there one more year. Nine months. Things are complicated here, what with—"

"Janine and going to the moon and everything else," Jonathan completes his father's sentence for him.

Put that way, none of it sounds like the excuse he'd like it to be. But then that's overtaken by sudden, furious annoyance—at all of them: Joan, Jonathan. Janine too. My life is a three-ring circus, he thinks bitterly, high-wire acts all precarious and linked, but there's no net. What do you want from me? he wants to shout. They wouldn't understand. It's what he's known all along, his high lonely calling, the courage and the ambition. They've named their lunar module "Raptor," their command ship "Cormorant." Lift-off is scheduled for less than eight months, touchdown at a spot in the lunar highlands known as the Cayley Plains.

"You're throwing me out," Jonathan says simply.

"It's not that," Allen stumbles to say. "It's that, well, I don't think things are working out for you here. This was supposed to be a visit. It's been two and a half weeks. A good visit. But it's time for you to go"—he almost says "home," but fortunately amends that to "back to Tennessee."

Jonathan doesn't say anything. He takes a pillow and hugs it to himself, curls his body around it. He lies on his side, away from Allen; his long hair hides his face. He doesn't say a word.

"Jonathan," Allen says gently. He's so relieved he's brought himself to say what he's said, but it's no relief. "Do you hear me, old buddy?" he asks.

Jonathan gives no sign that he does. He brings his thumb to his mouth, a gesture not so much infantile as simply dire. Silent, he chews his flesh with his teeth. Allen doesn't know whether he should be angered by a kind of insolence in that gesture, or whether, as all at once happens, it should break his heart.

For the longest time they stay like that, Allen in the chair watching his son, curled into himself, Jonathan on his bed, wounded and unknowable. Allen resists the urge to go over and gather the kid in his arms. That would only make everything worse. More confused.

A homosexual.

Allen can't think of another single thing to say. He tries to memorize that compromised figure there. When he's committed as much to memory as he thinks he can bear, he gets up without a word and leaves the room.

He's done it.

He's never felt so deeply ashamed.

RABBIT'S FOOT

When fall came and school started again, the boy from the Travelers turned up in my biology class. I remember seeing him walk into the classroom and thinking, Oh, how odd—almost nonchalant since I'd decided I'd never see him again. But then my heart leapt. At least I would come to know who he was, what he was like. All that sick fascination would gradually be dispelled.

We took seats on opposite sides of the room. The teacher, a burly crew-cut man, reminded us that his name was Dr. Lennox, not Mr. Lennox. "I have a Ph.D.," he told us, though we all knew that. He was famous for being the only teacher at Minerva High who had a Ph.D., and everyone was in awe of him.

His first order of business was to assign lab partners for the year. "I don't want friends pairing up," he told us, "because I've learned that that only leads to discipline problems. So I'm going to choose one from one side of the room and one from the other." I watched as people were paired off. It came my turn.

"You," said Dr. Lennox. "Your name."

I told him "Stayton Voegli" and he wrote it down.

"And you," he said to the other side of the room.

"Jonathan Cloud."

It was the first time I knew his name. We looked across the room at each other and nodded. I couldn't tell whether he remembered ever having seen me before.

Our first lab together, later in the week, featured an African grass-hopper we were supposed to dissect. Dr. Lennox came around to each desk and extracted, with tongs, an immense grasshopper from the large jar where they were tightly packed in evil-smelling juices.

"No pussyfooting around with earthworms," he told us. "Not in my science class. We're just going to hit the ground running." He promised, by the end of the year, to put a fetal pig on each and every lab table.

Mottled yellow and brown, our grasshopper lay obscenely on its back in the metal dissecting tray. We both stood there and looked at it, unsure what to do next, or who would start.

"Actually, I should be good at this kind of thing," Jonathan laughed. "It should be in my blood."

"What kind of thing?" I asked. I felt shy and nervous with him, and I wondered if he could sense the thinking I'd done about him over the last few months—as if some wavelength beyond the audible or visible could convey that sort of thing.

Ignoring me, he circled round the creature, trying to get all the angles. "What if it tries to fight back?" he wondered out loud. He tested the sharpness of the scalpel with his fingertip. "Ouch." He looked at the thin red line that appeared. "Blood poisoning," he told me. "What were you asking about? Oh, the science thing. Do you see any science thing in my blood?" He held up his finger. The little slit of blood looked like a smile. "Nope," he said. "The science thing curdles my blood. But I should have it. I should be shot through with it."

He leaned in close, as if to tell me a secret. His breath smelled like milk. "It runs in my family. It's like a virus. But I don't want to talk about it." He tossed his head, that long fine hair.

I had no idea what he was talking about. It was the first conversation we'd had.

"You're the one who brought it up," I said.

"Touché," he told me, and reached over and touched the tip of his finger to my cheek. I was shocked.

"I can tell," he said, "that you're a very uptight person. You need to relax a little. I'm going to make you relax. That's the one thing I'm going to do this year."

"How can I relax with that thing staring me in the face?" I pointed at the African grasshopper that was still waiting for us to attack.

"Speaking of face," Jonathan said, "You've got blood on your cheek."

I dabbed at where his finger had touched; rubbed the smear of red between two fingers till it was gone.

"Science blood," I said.

"You bet," Jonathan told me. "Blood like that took men to the moon. It'll find the cure for the common cold one day. It's patient blood, but adventurous."

I'd heard Pentecostals profess the Lord in tongues with somewhat more coherence.

But Jonathan had turned grim. He frowned at the grasshopper in the tray. Taking up the tongs, he held the segmented body, then carefully put the tip of the scalpel to its breast. He slit a little ways along and stopped.

An oozy liquid, like licorice, bubbled along the incision. The smell of formaldehyde was pungent.

"I'm going to faint," he said. "This is going to make me faint."

He took a step back from the table. "They'd found the alien's body in the wreckage of its spacecraft," he said in an excited voice, like a rattled radio announcer. "When the team of American scientists cut it open for autopsy, they all noticed a curious vapor, a sweetish smell, elusive yet vaguely enchanting. They thought nothing of it. That, ladies and gentlemen, was their fatal mistake. By week's end, the alien virus had claimed each of them in ways that subtly yet ironically corresponded to their most secret personalities. One man died dressed as the Queen of England. Another barked in his death throes like a poodle. It was humanity's alarming first glimpse into the altogether insidious— though sometimes rather witty—ways of the dreaded Vegan Star Tyranny."

"You talk like a book," I told him.

He brandished the scalpel in my direction. "Don't interrupt me when I'm talking like a book."

"Oh," I said. "Would you get over here and start dissecting this thing before it decides to do something drastic out of sheer boredom?"

He closed his eyelids halfway and looked at me through his lashes. Then he moved in on the grasshopper and very delicately prodded it with the scalpel's tip.

"Anyway," I told him, "I saw the movie. It turned out"—I tried to make myself as unhinged as Jonathan—"that humanity's ultimate revenge was . . . chiffon."

"Oh please," Jonathan said. "I can't cut straight if you're going to be profound. Chiffon. Really."

"I thought we were *trying* to be profound," I said.

"I forgot. Momentary lapse brought on by Vegan fever." He splayed apart the split-open grasshopper. "Chiffon's of course perfect for that occasional profound moment."

I felt giddy, though it wasn't the formaldehyde.

Making his rounds of the lab, Dr. Lennox stopped by our desk. "How's it going?" he asked. "Is that all you've done? There's only fifteen minutes left."

We'd done much more than met the eye.

"We were almost overcome by the vapors," Jonathan explained. "But we recovered. We're back on track. This grasshopper is history, sir."

I could tell Dr. Lennox had decided, then and there, that Jonathan was worthless.

"Keep your mind on your business," he told us both.

"You take over," Jonathan commanded the instant Lennox had moved on. "All this is too exhausting. I think I'll play with the bunsen burner for a while now. I think I'll try to singe my eyebrows. How do you think I'd look with singed eyebrows?"

"Fool talk," I could hear my father say, and I thought, He's right. Still, the sound of Jonathan's voice had lodged in my head like a melody, and I caught myself replaying it at odd moments.

That Friday night when I got to the Travelers, Jonathan was already there. It was the first time I'd seen him there since May. He was dancing when I walked in, near his old spot by the jukebox. We nodded and he beckoned me over. He gestured toward the jukebox: "I like to get my music fresh," he explained, but that was all he said.

For at least an hour we danced nonstop: crazy, concentrated dancing, not interacting in any way, not even looking at each other—just trying to get to whatever place we thought dancing was supposed to get us to.

At least that was what I was doing, and not without a leading edge of panic. Almost overnight I'd come to know this boy who'd made me excited and squeamish when I first saw him. Now I could see, up close, what I'd suspected during the spring but had told myself was impossible: he really was wearing mascara to deepen the effect of his dark brown eyes. Once again my excitement was mixed with a piercing sense of shame.

Out on the sidewalk, hours later, he was still shimmying, tuned to some ultrasonic frequency unavailable to me. "One day," he said, bouncing himself off the side of a building, "they'll design a spaceship that's powered by go-go dancers. You wait."

"I have to go," I told him. "Nobody knows I'm here."

"Nobody knows I'm anywhere," Jonathan said. "It's okay that way."

"Your parents let you stay out?"

"My mom's cool." He grinned. "She's gotta be—they turned off the heat last winter when she didn't pay her bills."

"No," I said.

"That was last winter. We're doing a lot better now." He paused. I was dying to touch him, and that appalled me. "It's what I spent the whole summer negotiating," he said. "For us to do better."

It must've shown on my face that I didn't follow any of what he was saying.

"My Dad." Jonathan snapped his fingers. "The one with the bucks. The man in the moon. Now tell me, are you in really big trouble if you get caught?"

"You better believe it," I told him.

"I love it," he said. "I love living dangerously." He gave me a playful shove. "You scoot on home," he winked.

"I have one question," I told him, "before I go." I looked long and hard at him under the streetlamp, took a deep breath, and then said, "Why are you wearing makeup?"

"Does it make me look gorgeous?" With one hand he piled his hair on top of his head, and smirked.

"Just asking," I said, suddenly unnerved by whatever it was I'd gone and gotten myself into.

Jonathan carried around a rabbit's foot. Whenever he fished his keys from his pocket to open his locker, there it dangled, bright orange, from his key chain. One day, with a quick hand motion, I swiped it from him.

"A rabbit's foot," I taunted him.

"Give it back," he said seriously.

Back in the fourth grade we'd all had our rabbit's foot for good luck. I bought mine from hoarded lunch money and, until the fad passed, carried it in secret because I knew my parents would disapprove. I hadn't seen one in years.

"When're you going to grow up?" I asked Jonathan.

He pounced on me and retrieved his key chain.

"Some hot little number bestowed this on me," he confided, "and I'm not about to give it up to anybody." He let it dangle in front of my nose. "Now, aren't you jealous?"

There was something in the way he said "hot little number," some special emphasis. I had a physical reaction, an instantaneous cold sweat breaking out. I looked around to see if anybody had heard, but we were alone in the hall. Biology class was starting in a minute, and we had another lab scheduled.

I knew he wasn't talking about a girl. I don't know how I knew, but that instant knowledge sparked between us. I turned away.

"Someday when I know you better," I said, bland as I could manage, "you'll have to tell me all about it." Even I could hear how my voice shook.

In lab we went about setting up our table's microscope and daubing the slide with pond water Dr. Lennox had scooped from behind his house.

"Now," Dr. Lennox instructed us, standing on a chair so he could oversee the entire array of lab tables in the room, "partner number one will look into the secret invisible life of a water droplet, and tell partner number two, who will enter it in a log. Then I want you to change places and repeat the exercise. This is an experiment in close scientific observation and reportage. Make sure you report everything you see and vice versa."

"Vice versa?" Jonathan asked as I sat down at the microscope. Fixing my eye to the viewer, I started to focus. Jonathan stood over me with the logbook. Suddenly he bent close and began to whisper into my ear.

What he said was completely pointless.

"I think the idea was to choose one kid from one ninth grade class and one from the other," he said, "because at my old school in Houston there were two ninth grade classes, and so it was me and this kid Lex from the other class, and we were supposed to shelve books during the lunch period when nobody was using the library. The librarian wasn't even there, just us. I think that's how it worked."

"I'm supposed to be the one who's talking," I reminded him. "I see a lot of little transparent things skittering around. Don't you want to write that down?"

Jonathan ignored me.

"We'd do things in there," he said.

A hot flash that started in my stomach spread its way down to the soles of my feet.

"This supply closet behind the checkout desk. Mops and brooms. We'd shut the door. I remember what his sweat tasted like."

I kept my eye firmly glued to the microscope. The pond water was trembling with invisible life. Amoebas, flagellates, ciliates, sporozoans. I could identify all of them. Jonathan's lips were still at my ear. He told me, "We'd just stand there. We'd rub against each other. We'd feel each other with our hands. Like hugging."

I felt sick and excited.

"I used to lick the side of his neck," he said. Then he touched my neck with his hand. "Right there," he said.

It nearly made me jump off the lab stool.

"I used to suck him off," Jonathan confessed into my ear.

He said it so simply.

"Now I've completely freaked you out," he whispered.

"I don't freak out easily," I lied.

"I think you know what I'm saying," he said, then abruptly broke off his whisper. He spoke in a normal voice: "Tell me what else you see." I looked up in a panic to see Dr. Lennox coming over to our table. I was nervous around Dr. Lennox the way I was nervous around police cars.

"How're you lunks making out?" he asked.

I hated that word. It was one of my father's favorite words.

"We're just fine, Professor," Jonathan said. He knew Dr. Lennox had no time for him. As for Dr. Lennox, since he didn't know the whole story, I think he regretted having paired me with a character like Jonathan.

"Let me take a look." He nudged me off my stool.

Jonathan's glance went straight to my crotch. I put my fists down deep in my pockets to hide what I knew he'd already seen. When our eyes met I think he nodded, so subtle I wasn't sure. But I knew, nod or no nod, that he knew. We held there like that, looking each other over while Dr. Lennox fiddled with our microscope.

"This is totally out of focus," he scolded. "What've you been doing here?"

"It won't focus," I told him, not looking at him, still looking at Jonathan. With one hand Jonathan tugged at the crotch in his own pants.

It occurred to me this was probably the most ridiculous situation I'd ever been in.

"I've got it focused for you now," Dr. Lennox told me. He got up from the stool and stood looking at us. "A mind's a terrible thing to waste, boys. Now, you better get at it."

"We've been at it, sir," Jonathan said.

"Well, get at it some more," Dr. Lennox told him.

Jonathan was still looking at me—he never once looked at Dr. Lennox—and as soon as Lennox's back was turned, he arched an eyebrow at me and sort of pouted his mouth.

"At least you have something interesting to think about now," he said, taking out his pen with a little theatrical flourish and readying himself to take some notes. "So, talk to me about pond water."

HIS BEAUTIFUL MOUTH

One day when he's a little child, Krishna's mother finds him sitting in the street in front of their house. He's eating dirt. Picking it up in his fat little fists and putting it in his mouth. She drops what she's doing and rushes over to say, Stop that, that's nasty. But when she pries his mouth open to scoop out the dirt before he swallows it, what she sees isn't the inside of his mouth: what she sees is herself, bent over, opening his mouth, and she sees the street where they are, the houses, the rice fields beyond the village, and the mountains in the distance, and cities on the other side of the mountains, people in marketplaces buying vegetables and nuts, other people inside their houses cooking over fires, talking foreign languages, sleeping, and the dreams they're dreaming while they sleep, and bees inside honeycombs, and birds flying over the desert and the ocean, and the stars, and the indescribable worlds beyond the stars, all the different levels of cosmic beings including the lord Krishna, whose mouth as a baby his mother's just opened to try to find the handful of dirt she saw him eat.

I don't think he's going to let me but he does. I take his face in my hands and kiss him on the mouth, and I can tell nobody's ever kissed him before because he doesn't know what to do, his lips all closed up, and he's completely shocked when my tongue tries to slip its way in. I

84

love that about him. How he's dying to but doesn't know the first thing about how.

When he pulls back a little I'm right there, I hold him, I'm not letting this kid go anywhere till I've got my tongue where I want it. Then if he wants to go anywhere, well, he's free to go, but I figure he'll probably stay. Though I'm thinking he's got to be the most skittish person I ever kissed in my life—probably why I want to kiss him so much. For the challenge of it, to see if I can.

And I do. I get my tongue in there and he just opens up. Delicious. Nobody's been in there before, he's growling in the back of his throat, my tongue lapping and slurping in his mouth, dueling with his tongue and running along his teeth.

There're two kinds of guys: those you have to kiss first and those you have to suck off. I could tell Stayton was going to be a kisser. Not like Mike, that day I don't have any lunch money and say, Spot me a couple and he says, You can suck my dick. To which I tell him I will, you know. Been doing him ever since, though a kiss is something I'll never get out of him.

But that kiss with Stayton, really it starts about three hours earlier when he walks in the door of the Travelers. After lab I don't know if he will, but I'm sitting on a bar stool sipping a Dr Pepper and he slides onto the stool next to me, nervous but at least there. I thought it was going to take a lot longer. It's midnight. I reach in my pocket and haul out the rabbit's foot he started everything off with by teasing me about.

Here, I tell him, I'm giving this to you.

He's hesitating, in fact he's scared stiff of it. But I press it into his hand and stroke it there. Makes him jump.

I send him what I hope's a cool smile and hop off the stool and dance myself into the crowd. Let him come find me or walk out the door.

Then he's beside me, our usual spot by the jukebox. For the first time we're dancing with each other, there's no pretending we're doing anything else. David Bowie's playing "Ziggy Stardust and the Spiders from Mars," and it thrills me, along with the music, to have a boy just where I want him. All that practice in the bars—or when I couldn't get into bars, the parking lots—of Houston.

In my church we're not allowed to dance, Stayton confides to me. The only thing he says for three straight hours.

Welcome to my church, I tell him back.

We both pour sweat—more like running a race than dancing. I make him drunk with dancing, that rabbit's foot agitating in his pants pocket, working its secret luck on him till I take him by the hand and lead him out the door.

On the street everything's deserted, the air's cool. Beginning of fall. I'm so happy right then, the dancing still inside my chest and the night air and this boy I don't know, so shy, so pent up in himself. Such big brown eyes in that lean, sad face nobody, I bet, has ever told him is just beautiful.

This is usually when he'll head on home, and there's some danger he's about to bolt.

I've got all this energy, I tell him. I'll walk you a couple of blocks.

And I start us down the sidewalk. But Stayton shakes his head, squirms out of my grasp. Can't walk, he says.

What do you mean, can't walk? I ask.

Run, he says, and takes off. Just like that, and not just down the street: cuts between two buildings, across an empty parking lot and into some trees. So he's crazy. I take off after him thinking maybe he wants me to catch him, maybe he's taking me somewhere. It's a devious course, well practiced I'd say, skirting backyards, empty lots, down a dead end into some woods along the culvert.

When I catch up with him I say, Stop, and he stops.

We're both panting.

You're crazy, I tell him. Where do you think you're going?

Home, he says.

Like this?

The police are out, he says. They patrol the streets.

The police, I say. I have to laugh.

They keep tabs, he says. They watch me. For a long time. You wouldn't understand.

And I don't. The police, I say, are not a problem. Not at all.

Just let me go on home, he tells me.

Instead I reach out and touch his pants pocket where I know the rabbit's foot is. I can feel the lump there.

You've got good luck, I tell him. You're even invisible. Nobody's going to catch you.

I didn't mean to take it, he says. You should have it back.

It's for keeps, I say.

Kid's stuff, he says dubiously. He has so many defenses.

You never know, I tell him. I put both my hands on his shoulders. His lower lip's trembling, his eyes are big and dark brown. Gorgeous eyes. We're both still breathing hard, but I'm taking my chances it's not just from all the running.

What? he says finally. I can feel his whole body shivering, his heart racing way out ahead of itself. It's starting to rain.

Don't worry, I tell him. I know the feeling too.

What? he says again. That's when I kiss his beautiful mouth.

Mom's still up when I get home. All the lights on, past three in the morning, but she's oblivious. Vacuuming up a storm and singing at the top of her lungs.

Oh, she says when I walk in, you startled me.

She has this bright-eyed look to her. Hectic. Strands of hair in her face.

All the picking up around the house that gets done is my doing, and I don't do a lot of it.

The strangest thing, Mom says, shutting off the machine. You won't believe. This man who came by. Waltzed right into the living room and in fifteen minutes he's sold me this.

She's pointing to a big silver cannister on wheels, its hose with a complicated head.

A prophet right out of the Old Testament, she says.

Hey Mom, I say, what are you talking about?

Ezekiel or Isaiah or some such. Let me tell you: a prophet beard and prophet eyes. Very righteous and totally crazy, spouting Bible up and down and all mixed in with trying to sell me a new vacuum cleaner. Twenty-nine ninety-five a month for six months. With truly innovative attachments. Who can beat it?

I never talk money with Mom, but it's three in the morning, I'm drenched with rain, my lips are rubbed raw from kissing a boy, and

Mom's striking various poses with her new vacuum cleaner. Might as well talk money as anything else.

So where do we get twenty-nine ninety-five a month for six months? I ask.

Funny, she says, I asked him the same thing. I said, Look at me. Do I look like somebody with thirty bucks a month to spend on a machine from outer space like that? And know what he said? He told me, When Elijah was in the wilderness, the ravens fed him. Well what could I say to that?

I hope he accepts payment in bread crumbs, I tell her.

She pouts her mouth, makes sad eyes at me. Very theatrical. She was always a hoot in plays at the community theater.

Oh Jonathan, you worry too much, she says. I used to worry too much too. You get it from me.

I'm not one to worry, I say.

Oh, but you do, she tells me. Deep down. You're worried right now. I'm your mother. I can tell.

And in fact, she can. But I'm not worried; agitated's more like it. Deep, thrilling agitation. When she goes back to running the vacuum over the carpet, I lock myself in the bathroom and stand in front of the mirror to watch myself dance there for a while. No music except what's in my head. I slip off my water-logged clothes and watch the way my hands move, my hips—my bouncing dick and wet swinging hair.

I'm wild there, but only for a minute. The trick is to calm down. So I stand still, count my breaths, watch the mirror while I say words, anything that comes in my head. Semen, I say. Estrus. Lingam.

Watch my lips and teeth, my tongue. My open mouth's a cave, all red and spit-wet and shiny.

Hepatitis and chlamydia and trypanosomiasis.

See how they look in my mouth and sound in my ear.

Telemetry. Circumference. Algorithm.

All we do tonight is kiss and grope, but it's like I'm flying, like the air's wide open and I'm soaring on wings, up in the sky Dad taught me: Nimbus and cumulus and cirrus and stratus.

Words that never bring him back.

Jonathan, I say. And Stayton. And Cloud and Voegli.

I make faces at myself, ugly, haughty, alluring, pissed, crazy, vacant.

All a blur. Which one's mine I can't remember, like shapes in a rubberband. Elastic. I can't recognize myself. I push so far I get scared, then skitter back to my face at rest, tranquil, though that's not it either; my face in the mirror that's never mine, never the way I imagine it to be.

Hardly able to hear myself over the roar of Mom's vacuum, I say more words. I speak very, very slowly.

Libidinous, I say. Catamite. Voluptuary.

Mouthfuls. My face changes and changes. Inside every mouth, I think, must be some kind of universe.

HOME LIFE

The first thing I did when I got home, even before stripping out of my sodden clothes and spreading them in the back of my closet to dry, was to fish Jonathan's rabbit's foot from my pocket and stash it safely beneath a stack of underwear in my dresser. It was too dangerous even to hold in my hand, a token of every illicit thing that had gone on—not just that evening but for the last six months. To have it in the house, even secreted away, made me vulnerable, and I could sense its presence even in the unruly dreams I had when finally I fell asleep.

The next day I was sick and stayed home from school. The rain that had started in the early morning hours was the day's only consolation. As long as it kept falling there was a link, a connection with the night before. But around nightfall the rain stopped, and I felt that everything was over. I'd lived through my whole life in a few hours and this was the end.

Why had I broken that kiss and pushed him away, running through the soaking rain, spitting his kiss out—its germs or sin—again and again, in futility, as I ran?

All day the thought of that rabbit's foot in my drawer gnawed at me. Finally I couldn't stand it. I pulled open the drawer and groped till I found it. I held it in the palm of my hand, an obscene thing, at the same time sad. Some dead little rabbit. I stroked the soft bright-orange fur that was supposed to be good luck. Then I went in the bathroom and threw up.

It was the kind of vomiting you could hear all over the house, and even before I was finished my mother was standing at the top of the stairs.

"Stayton, are you all right in there?" she asked through the closed door.

I wiped my mouth on a washcloth and came out.

"I feel really sick," I told her truthfully. She lay her palm flat against my forehead.

"No fever," she said. "Maybe it was something you ate. Do you feel gassy?"

"No," I told her.

"Diarrhea?"

My mother had a disconcerting way of asking, with an edge of panic in her voice, about every symptom imaginable. I think it was something Africa had taught her. "I'll get you some Coca-cola," she said. "The fizz'll make you feel better."

I drank the Coke, and in fact the fizz did make me feel somewhat better. At least it took my mind off things. I went back to my room chastened but purer.

Crawling into bed, I took my Bible off the night stand. Every morning and evening I still read a couple of chapters—more habit than anything else, since I'd secretly ceased to believe some time before. That night I read the whole of the Book of Zephaniah, which is one of the stranger and scarier books in the Old Testament.

After a while I drifted off to sleep, and when I woke it was just after midnight. The rain had begun again. I debated whether or not to go to the Travelers after all, whether I wanted to see Jonathan ever again, what I was going to do when eventually I had to see him at school— till finally it was too late to go anywhere, and for better or worse I'd lost whatever chance I might have had.

The next Monday Jonathan wasn't in school, nor Tuesday or Wednesday or any of the days that week. Every day I thought he'd be there, but then he wasn't. I had no idea what it meant, but I was terrified that he might simply have vanished in the same way he'd vanished once before from my life.

It seemed not impossible that he was some kind of demonic spirit capable of any number of tricks.

On Thursday night of that week I had a dream in which he and I were sitting on a picnic table in the middle of a field under a gray sky. The field was immense, and so was the sky. Jonathan was holding something in his hand, I couldn't tell what, but then, smiling oddly, he held up his palm to show me. There, inscribed in his flesh, was a living blue eye. Not brown like his real eyes but bright blue, almost like translucent glass except alive and watching me. I knew there was something shameful about seeing that eye, something sickening, but it also filled me with a longing that was related, in its way, to sickness. I reached out to grab his wrist. "Too late," he said, closing his palm into a fist just as I woke up in a panic.

I resolved to go to his house as soon as school was out the next day.

It was a lab day, and in Jonathan's absence I found myself paired with a girl named Ruby whose partner also was absent. Ruby was a country girl who rode the bus in. She had the worst case of acne I'd ever seen, and she wore her greasy hair pulled back in a tight bun. There was something smug and defiant about her that repulsed me. But she carved up the specimen turtle with aplomb, doing all the work herself and licking one side of her mouth as she went.

I longed for chiffon and the Vegan Star Tyranny.

Jonathan had told me once, as we parted in front of the Travelers, how his was the last house on the dead end of Jaffe Road. I approached the low-slung brick house with some doubt. Overgrown bushes almost completely hid it from view, the front lawn was knee-high with weeds. The most disquieting thing: the windows, except for one with an air conditioner in it, were all covered over with aluminum foil from the inside.

Jonathan's mother answered the door. She was wearing a blue housecoat, and fuzzy, light-blue slippers. She held a coffee mug. In her eyes was a kind of grim determination mixed with surprise.

"Jonathan's not here right now," she said. "Do you want to come in?"

Something told me I must have woken her from a deep sleep.

She motioned me inside, and though I didn't really want to, I found myself in the dark living room. Heavy drapes were drawn. Lamps on the end tables on either side of the sofa had been turned on, and it was like stepping from afternoon into late evening. The room smelled of old cigarettes and stale air-conditioning.

"Can I get you a Seven-Up?" Mrs. Cloud offered.

"That's okay," I told her. She'd sat down on the sofa as soon as I was in the door, but I was still standing up. I put my hands in my pockets because I didn't quite know what else to do.

She lit a cigarette. In the ashtray on the end table was a big pile of butts, shocking in their profligacy (no one I knew smoked), and another full ashtray balanced on a stack of *National Geographics*, on the sofa cushion beside her. She saw that I saw the *National Geographics*. "Just catching up on my reading," she explained.

"I'll come back later," I said. There were no pictures on the walls, but stacks of magazines everywhere.

"Jonathan's not sick, is he?" I asked.

"Actually, he's in Texas," she said. "I guess you could call that a kind of sickness."

It made me vaguely nervous in the pit of my stomach.

"Texas?" I said.

She made a clucking noise. In the dim light her face looked puffy, tired.

"His father's getting married," she told me.

The way she said "his father" chilled me.

"For some reason that is utterly unknown to me, and probably unknowable, Jonathan insisted on going," she explained. She looked at me curiously for a long moment—too long, I felt obscurely. There were ice cubes in her mug that clinked together as she stirred with her finger.

"He'll be back on Monday," she went on. "Unless he decides to try and stay. But if I'm so fortunate as to see him again, I'll say you dropped by."

"That's okay," I said. "I'll see him in school."

I noticed that the television set was running afternoon cartoons with the sound turned off.

She drank again from her mug. "How does he do in that school?" she asked me. "Does he like it there? Does he ever say?"

"He's fine," I said, realizing it had never occurred to me whether he was fine or not.

I waited for her to say something else, but she didn't. I stood there trying to think how to leave.

"Are you friends with him?" she asked abruptly.

"I guess," I told her a little dubiously.

"Don't be mean to him," she said.

I didn't have plans to be mean to him, I was about to tell her when she continued, "And maybe you'll come back sometime, right? When he's here? You should, you know."

"You might see me again," I told her cautiously, unable really to believe it myself. She didn't get up from the sofa to usher me out, but I got the sense anyway it was time to go. I stood a second or two longer, just to make sure I'd been dismissed, and moved toward the door.

She didn't say anything. She looked at me, that same curious look as before, as if she were studying me intently, trying to discover something there—I had no idea what.

That night was the first Friday in months that I didn't go to the Travelers. Without Jonathan, there didn't seem any point. At ten o'clock I went to bed like the rest of my family, and then lay there in a kind of rage and grief. I didn't know why I was so angry, and at the same time so sorry.

I slipped my pajamas down and masturbated, a long hard angry masturbation, rubbing myself raw as I lashed away toward some goal I had no clue to. And even coming didn't get me there.

Sleep didn't come either, so I masturbated again, and about forty-five minutes later a third time, taking forever to come this last time, a dry empty come that left me feeling heartsick and disgusted.

When Jonathan came back to school on Monday, he was as scalped as an army recruit. All his beautiful long brown hair was completely gone.

I could hardly look at him.

"Like it?" He ran his hand over the stubble. I followed with my own hand, just grazing the bristle, wild with regret that I hadn't buried my fingers in it the one time I had a chance.

"I don't even recognize you," I told him. "Why'd you go and do a thing like that?"

He smiled a half-playful smile. Then he looked serious. "I hear you went to see my mom," he said. "Why'd you do that?"

"What do you mean, why'd I do that? You disappeared for a week."

"Well, I wish you hadn't," he said, and shut his locker with a bang.

"Is there something wrong?" I asked him.

"No," he said. "Of course not. It's just that now you know."

No sooner had I said Know what? than everything clicked.

"Your secret's safe with me," I added piously.

"You're a fuckhead," Jonathan told me. "And you're coming to my house this afternoon."

The previous family who'd lived there had converted the basement into a dank, forlorn-looking recreation room: plywood paneling, linoleum floor, fluorescent ceiling lights. They'd left behind a brown Naugahyde sofa that was the only piece of furniture down there.

"We could use my room, but that'd be taking chances," Jonathan explained as he led me around to the basement door at the back of the house. "Even though Mom's sure to be what we like to call sound asleep."

"Let's not take chances," I told him.

It turned out that my first visit had caught Mrs. Cloud on one of her rare good days. Usually three-thirty or four was about as far as she could bear to make it through an afternoon. She'd pass out in her bedroom till seven or eight o'clock.

"This is so exciting," Jonathan said once he'd made sure the door leading upstairs was locked from the inside. He was in such a hurry to unbutton my shirt, rub his hands on my chest that I had to laugh through all my throbbing panic.

"What's funny?" he said.

"You," I told him. But I didn't actually, at the moment, think he was so much funny as terrifying.

"I can't stand it," he said. "Feel." Grabbing me by the wrist, he laid my hand on his crotch. "You're so shy. You don't have to just do what I do. Here—touch anyplace you want to. There's nothing to be afraid of."

Though what we were about to undertake with each other was to repeat itself, in various guises, many, many times, I still remember that first afternoon. How, after we'd stripped each other, Jonathan stepped back to let us admire each other's nakedness, exclaiming, "I don't even know where to start. Boy, I could eat you alive."

All those nights when I'd stood before the bathroom mirror: here was exactly what I'd longed to see—another boy like me, slender as a reed, narrow-hipped and virtually hairless except for that dark thicket from which jutted—oh God, I wanted to shout in triumphant blasphemy—an erect, dark-hued, blood-pulsing penis.

Slowly, in a dream—"floating on air," I would have said at the time—we moved together. I could feel his penis bumping against my thigh, every part of me buzzing, his tongue on my neck, my armpit, trailing down my belly as he knelt in front of me, and I held the back of his stubbled head as I came in his hungering mouth.

Then it was my turn. "You're a good learner," he told me. I couldn't get enough of him. The linoleum floor was cold and hard, the clammy surface of the sofa not much better, but for the space of half an hour, an hour—I couldn't have said how long—it didn't matter. It didn't matter that his mom was going to storm down the steps the next instant, or that my parents would be able to tell, immediately, when I got home, exactly what unspeakable sins had covered me in darkness. All that mattered was that those things I never thought would happen to me, kept safe behind the invisible barrier, immaculate, unsullied, were happening to me all at once, filthy and obscene and electrifying in their abandon.

After the third time I came that afternoon, Jonathan kissed me with my semen still in his mouth, passing it back to me with his saliva, warm, salty, slick like snot. In all the hundreds of times I'd masturbated, it had never even occurred to me to taste my own come.

LOWER DEPTHS

Allen, can you hear? Of course not. You were always deaf to the world around you, deaf especially to me. But if you could hear as I can hear, the message would be coming in loud and clear from the basement of my house.

What's in the basement, you ask? Let me tell you. Our son is in the basement of my house, and he's with another boy, and they're fucking, Allen, that's what they're doing, fucking. The sound comes up through the heating ducts and I can hear every noise they make, their grunts and moans, and though I don't want to hear this noise, I can't resist. I sit on the sofa in my living room and eight feet beneath me our son is being fucked. It's like watching an accident happen before your eyes; you don't want to watch, but you can't turn away. And this happens practically every other afternoon, and every other afternoon I put myself through this because I have to. I have no choice. This is life, this is my life, what it's turned into. And when he comes, Allen, our son sounds just like you.

I had to tell you that. I thought it was something you should know.

I don't blame anybody for this; I'm just fascinated by it. Fascinated as I was that day I stood outside his closed bedroom door and heard sounds I couldn't at first identify except as monstrous echoes of familiar pleasures—listened fascinated, thinking how the husk can slough off in seconds to reveal the worm-eaten heart of things.

I'd seen them swim together, black body and white. I'd enjoyed, I

97

admit, the thought of William—was that his name?—fouling the hy-
gienic waters of Frank and Sally's pool. I always hated that pool, at
night it was an open wound, the moon seething there in its unstable
mirror, reflecting that day in '64 when Jonathan nearly drowned and
you made light of it: I could see past the mirage of water suddenly gone
transparent and for my eyes alone, apparently, because life on the beach
unfurled lazily as if nothing had happened except for a shrieking child
held in his father's arms, the red whiplike welts already starting to surface in his flesh. It doesn't particularly bother me now that my son is
a homosexual, though I hope it horrifies you. You contributed, after all,
as much as I.

I want you to feel the weight and the hurt of my accusation. But
you're deaf, Allen, you won't ever hear any of this because you're beyond hurting no matter what I hurl your way. It's always been like that.

My liver aches, Allen. Used to just every now and then, but now it
aches all the time, every day, and sometimes at night I wake up with
it aching. And other pains that migrate through my body. I know it's
because of the drinking, but I'm not going to see a doctor because I
associate doctors with Mission Control and, see, I refuse to buy into
any of that stuff anymore. I know the hurt's because of drinking, but
I'm not going to stop. I have no reason to stop. My drinking has lowered
me down step by step into some fundamental self whom I can live with,
who can name things what they are, who can speak up, if only to herself
sitting in her living room on a winter afternoon listening to her son
get fucked by the son of the local Baptist preacher.

I remember the days when I used to drink simply to get drunk—
dull, gray soviet years, the five-year plan of alcoholism. I was always
afraid to notice the world too much; what I might see, I thought, could
only hurt me. Now I stand and gape, amazed by its unexpected beauty.
The amber light stopped inside a bottle of Jameson at dusk. The fierce
ruby dark of a cheap but ungrafted merlot from some nameless Chilean
vineyard. The sweet awful abandon of fruit brandies: blackberry and
apricot and pear. The rigor of ice cold vodka or, better yet, aquavit.
Gin's juniper piquancy. Bitter Campari a bit of soda water can lighten.
The fierce, heartwarming attack of grappa or marc. Absinthe, the devil's

thirst quencher. Tequila and mescal and ouzo and raki and Pernod. For sheer massive quantities your California jug wines of impeccable murk.

I've become adventurous in the wasteland of my middle age, an explorer. Not one of your narrow-minded alcoholics who finds her poison of choice and sticks with it. No, I'm wildly promiscuous, rooting around like a hog in a forest and bringing up the most marvelous delicacies, pungent with muck and the subterranean distillation of years. I navigate these various liquors like Odysseus, apparently aimless yet epically purposeful. I pursue my course with the passion and fervor of a lover, the cool precision of a scientist.

I even contemplate, in rare fits of disquieting ambition, my magnum opus: The Alcoholic's Survival Cookbook. How to evade hangover (I recommend massive doses of broccoli, strong leafy greens like kale or collards—everything in excess). How to soothe the tender liver, the throbbing pancreas, all the dilated circuitry of the brain. How to ease the diarrheic effusions of the alcoholic body or heighten the bliss of the abyss (the French had it right: certain very ripe cheeses, the moldier the better). How rice vinegar clears the liver, how a cold beer in the morning can set a tone for the whole day. The wonders of megavitamins, of bee pollen and rose hips. How a handful of Bufferin can work. The importance, always, of a strict regimen: stick to clear liquors, or amber, but never mix, and never mix grain and the vine. Red and white in sequence are fine, and beer chasers for the amber liquors but not the clear. Anything that has a worm or a slug in the bottom of the bottle should be reserved for the high holy days of utter madness.

When I'm not drinking, life scares me practically to death.

I try, I honestly try to get a grip on myself. Last night, for example, I decided not to drink. To not touch a drop of the beautiful poison. I thought I'd watch the television instead, and what do I see? These two women friends are getting together. They sit on a sofa, and one of them opens a nice bottle of white wine. Before I know it I'm craving like mad the cool tart sip of white wine, and like a zombie I'm standing at the refrigerator pulling out a chilled bottle, I'm opening it and pouring myself a glass, I'm sitting on the sofa sipping my glass of wine along with those two women as they chat about their lives. I would chat too, only they're so interesting that they engage my attention completely. I'm content to be the silent one, just sit back and sip my wine along with them and listen to their fascinating chatter.

Allen. Here is what finally happened. One day I saw through you to the possibility of my own death. Before, it was always your death I was fixated on, hypnotized by, the dire event that had to come sooner or later, I knew, as every wife of a test pilot knows, and then one day I saw through you to my own death. It took me, I have to admit, by complete surprise. You were standing on the front lawn holding a rake, looking up at the con trail of a passenger jet in the clear sky, and standing there on the other side of you, your body gone transparent, was my own death and it was beckoning to me. It was another, truer version of myself, and after that day I could never be the same.

Oh, I went on with the ordinary things, folded napkins and poured drinks and played hostess when necessary. I carried Jonathan to school when he missed the bus, and cooked his meals and on the weekends, when you were home, I cooked your meals too. All that was easy—I did all that in my sleep. What I kept thinking about, though, was that other self I had glimpsed through your sudden transparency. And I realized why you had suddenly become transparent for me, Allen, why you'd been opaque my whole life and suddenly became transparent. Because I didn't need you anymore. You were blocking my view of my own self wrapped in the terrible legacy of death. And I had never known that. I had always needed you because I never knew I didn't. From that first night we met, McCauley's Restaurant in Armistice, you the friend of a brother of a friend and leaving in a day or so for Korea, the day before Christmas in fact.

We sat across from each other at that festive table, surrounded by so much noise, such a cacophony of urges and needs (we were twenty then), and our eyes met, we kept looking at each other and I remember thinking, He's bearing me up, I'm holding onto him and he's seeing me through all this. Because I was always terribly shy, though I grew out of that in certain ways, I had to, and I was terrified that evening, which was only a slice, wedge-thin but remarkable, of my whole life. As long as I looked in your eyes, I was held steady, I was okay. And I thought, We can hold each other steady, and we did, through that long suspension we called Korea and beyond. I had never met anybody whose eyes offered to hold me steady like that. I was a fool, it was an accident of light or of terror. But at the time it seemed like salvation.

Sweet lure of vodka in the mornings, incisive pleasure of the world split wide open by noon, the black birds that rise from the maw of evening, clear silhouettes in an unimaginable sky. I cherish these experiences like a traveler, I hoard them close in my soul and refer back to them constantly as the constellation or compass points they really are.

I remember one morning, in Houston, not long before the end. I had to go down to the theater to deliver some programs I'd picked up from the printer. Rob was there because he was always there. When he said the theater was his life he meant it.

How you hated him. I don't cotton to men like that, was all you'd say. He made the hair on the back of your neck prickle. He gave you the heebie jeebies. I knew you well enough to recognize the symptoms. You were in a mild panic whenever he talked to you at a party (and mercifully that was seldom).

I adored him, needless to say. That wit that could scald. That lithe body, lithe personality. Scampering about the stage, shouting in mock or real despair at the housewives and retirees he'd conned into the joys of community theater. From that motley lot he chose me for his confidante—he said I had spark. I was his leading lady in "The Thread That Runs True."

That particular morning, ten o'clock at the latest, I was standing there, he was sitting on the stage, dangling his legs down, voluble as ever, and suddenly I realized—a profound shock and comfort—that at ten in the morning Rob was a secret drunk too. He recognized it the same instant, and I remember so clearly: without breaking the brisk stride of our conversation he raised his right hand in front of his face and, with the flick of a wrist, tipped back an invisible shot glass. I nodded, nothing more, a single quick nod. We left the stage crew to their task of hammering together the backdrop for a western town and went around to his cluttered little office in back, paint-smelling and hardly room to sit down, where he rescued from the detritus a bottle of Stalingrad vodka, cheapest of the cheap and foulest of the foul, but we sat there doing breathless shots with one another until before I knew it we were kissing, passionate kisses like I never had, rapturous, though Rob was queer as they come and I was, well, married to an astronaut.

Two parched souls miraculously finding, in the depths of a mid-morning midlife desolation they saw no possibility of ever surviving, the oasis of one another. Half hour of delirious, quenching kisses. But nothing more happened. Got to supervise the ladies, he chirped, smoothing his clothes and running a hand through thinning hair, and it was only a week later that you came home to find me doing, as you so delicately put it at the time, the unconscionable thing to myself.

I should have spoken to him about Jonathan, my worries, I should have gotten his reassurance, but I never did, and instead I spoke those words aloud, Allen, to you.

Can I whisper you a secret? I always knew you would be terrified of your son's homosexuality. That's why I blurted it out the way I did. I could see the terror in you years before I had any words to name it. I could feel it in the dark, as you lay next to me in our bed, wanting to touch me but resisting your desire, propelling yourself away from me with the force of a swimmer and yet revealing in those strokes of dark-ness so much about yourself, your fears. I had no words to encompass the quality of your hands as they ran down my ribs, my thighs, the surprised discovery they made of my breasts, but I knew. I was reading a silent language in everything you did with me, every mute appeal your body made in my direction.

I went along entirely, carried by some welcoming current I had no intention of resisting. It was another way of steadying myself, and I loved, in my way, all those nights when you anchored yourself in me, battened down against storms you never even suspected.

Or did you? What hid inside you during those nights? I could feel it breathing inside your ribcage, a smothered beast lurking in there, never let out, never entirely acknowledged. But you knew—in those moments of hesitation, those gaps between your heart and your groin, I could see there was something you knew. Blindly I tried to ferret it out—by in-stinct, trickery—but it stayed elusive, pent up and panicked, and I caught only glimpses in your eyes, rare flaws in your gaze that surprised me till I grew used to them. Not betrayals but something else entirely: apology, perhaps, or recompense.

DARK STAR

"Extravaganza!" Jonathan said. We were walking down the street and he kept repeating the word, emphasising different syllables, teasing it out, torturing both the word and me. "Extravaganza!" Trying it out for all the heft and life it had.

"Serendipity," he said. "Hootenany."

"Shut up," I said.

"Why?"

"You're driving me crazy."

"Maybe you have a bad attitude," he said. "Maybe you should learn a bigger vocabulary. Maybe you should appreciate the world more. Orgiastic. Promiscuity. Sybaritic."

"Concupiscent," I said.

"There you go," he told me. "I don't even know what that means."

He loved to prowl. At dusk we'd wander the streets to spy on unsuspecting families through uncurtained windows. It was odd to walk around casually chatting, looking into windows, never alluding to what we'd experienced with each other in the basement an hour before.

The voyeuring hour, Jonathan called that fortuitous wedge of time between the turning on of indoor lights and the pulling down of shades, when you were free to peer into windows, catch people going obliviously about their business, entirely unaware they were being observed. Other people's lives fascinated Jonathan—what they did behind closed doors when no one else was watching. He was avid for the least glimpse

103

of such moments. I thought it was peculiar, slightly off-color in some obscure way, but since I was enthralled by even Jonathan's most questionable aspects—perhaps most enthralled by precisely those—I was willing to go along with anything.

Besides, dusk afforded an illusory sense of safety. Walking the streets with Jonathan, I could convince myself that some truce had been declared between myself and the world: for half an hour all rules were suspended, the invisible barrier fell (just as the opaque windows all along the street became suddenly transparent to our prying eyes). Everyone, for that brief space of time, had their backs turned, their eyes on other things, whether preparing dinner or settling down in front of the television. All Minerva was enchanted, and we alone had been vouchsafed to observe that enchantment, to study it, even to classify it.

Over months of prowling the voyeuring hour, Jonathan had devised an elaborate system of classification. "The one thing I've discovered," he confided to me, "is that the Vegan Star Tyranny has made much greater inroads on this planet than anyone has previously suspected. You won't even guess the things I've seen."

Ordinary houses—the continually disappointing ones—he called Nebulas. In those brightly lit rooms, life proceeded apace, clueless and innocent of greater galactic goings-on. A family sitting down to dinner might well mean Nebula, but it might also mean, since the rating system could be tricky, Dark Star. A Dark Star household had its share of brightly lit rooms as well, where children did homework at the dining room table, Mom and Pop played cards with the neighbors, the dog slumbered. But something was different. Nothing you could put your finger on; still, you had misgivings, suspicions. An argument, a fit of crying, a birthday party—these could be interpreted in various ways.

Novas were houses in whose rooms otherworldly activity was definitely afoot. They were beachheads of a sort, rooms where you might observe a cat at play with something invisible, or a person alone in a room talking to themselves. Husbands poring over stamp collections, wives sipping beer in the kitchen. On the Vegan home planet, Jonathan had decided, it was always dusk. Shades were never drawn. It was just possible, here on Earth, that windows left unshuttered signaled some species of nostalgia for that other life.

We had our nightly rounds. The best was a little blue house, comically small, fastidiously kept up though always with a slightly disheveled air about it. Two elderly ladies lived there, Miss Hat and Miss Ryan. They'd been piano teachers, but that was years ago. They must have been in their nineties, still spry and odd and solitary. Inside their cramped house was a marvel. Eight or nine or ten parakeets lived there with them, not in cages, but simply in the rooms of the house, amid potted plants and furniture and two upright pianos set back to back in the living room (that sight in itself a find). We could hear the birds' raucous chatter even in winter when the windows were shut tight— and, since they were both nearly deaf, we could hear the two ladies as well, not the words they said but the singsong chirping as their voices rose above the fray.

"I've thought about this one," Jonathan told me. "It has to do with the dinosaurs."

"What?" I said.

"Listen," he told me. "I've been reading about the dinosaurs. How they didn't go extinct like scientists claim they did. They're still here on the planet with us. Only they changed. Over time they got smaller; but more important, they learned how to fly. And that was so thrilling for them, they were willing to give up everything just to be able to do that. Birds fly for pleasure; scientists know that. It's ecstasy for them. And so the dinosaurs gave up the whole planet just so they could keep flying."

"You should write a book," I told him.

"This is secret knowledge," he said.

"Have you told President Nixon yet?"

He put his finger to his lips. "Only you," he said, "and I want you to keep all this in strictest confidence. It could be very dangerous if it got out. It could have major consequences. Now ask me about Miss Hat and Miss Ryan."

"What about them?"

"Aren't you curious? Those birds are teaching them how to fly. See, they practice at night, in the attic, just the two of them. They sail around up there, they sing to each other in birdcalls. One day we'll all know how to fly. It'll be the end of human life. We'll give up everything, but we'll be able to fly. I think my grandmother turned into a bird before she died. I was just a little kid, but I think I remember that.

Anyway, the Vegans are just a bunch of old women in space suits, but Jesus Fucking Christ can they fly. They twitter themselves silly. Bird-song's the Vegan national anthem."

There was so much profligate talk from him, sometimes it could seem obscene.

Beyond the Nebula houses and the Dark Stars, beyond even the Novas, was that rarest occurrence of all: the Supernova, that happened once or twice in a window-watcher's lifetime.

"They leave you speechless," was all Jonathan would disclose. "But if you ever see a Supernova, you'll definitely know. I guarantee it."

In the house on the corner the father led the family in suppertime prayer. They all sat with bowed heads and tightly shut eyes—except for the little boy, a dark-haired number, as Jonathan would say, seven or eight years old, who looked straight out the window at us, a grave unwavering stare. In the fading light we couldn't possibly be visible to him, and yet he studied us so intently, with such a strange look of recognition.

"Nova," Jonathan said. "Mild nova. We've definitely got the kid. Look at those eyes."

"Whose side are you on?" I asked. "Sometimes I wonder if you're not just another lowly Vegan census taker making his rounds."

"Its rounds. There're seven different sexes in the Vegan Star Tyranny, and they don't make vulgar distinctions between them."

"Oh," I said. "Sort of like David Bowie."

"David Bowie is an angel. Don't compare him to the Vegans. They're like us: shabby arrivistes."

"Shabby arrivistes," I said.

"Well, you know what I mean."

"Sometimes," I told him, "I think your imagination is just too vivid."

"For what?" he asked me.

But I didn't have an answer. I was content strolling beside him, listening to all his fantastic chatter. And I loved Minerva at dusk, the streetlights coming on, some the blue-white of mercury vapor, others the orange of sulphur, the sky to the west crimson, then a cold clear steel-gray fading into black. I felt at home wandering out in that light. Bats flickered, or great rivers of migrating birds—we were in the Mississippi flyway—streamed across the sky for half an hour at a stretch. The police cars still cruised like the silent threats they were—I was as preternaturally alert to their presence as Jonathan was to whatever went on in the houses we prowled. I felt a stab of guilt every time a car would pass us in its own relentless prowling, as if police radar could somehow read the secret crimes in our gait, as if they and we were engaged in some complicated and ongoing negotiation with each other for possession of Minerva's streets at dusk.

One evening we turned down my street. I'd never told Jonathan where I lived, only the general neighborhood. The notion of him dropping by one afternoon and meeting my parents or my brothers terrified me. I was constantly issuing him small warnings in that regard.

I'd hoped we'd pass on by, but Jonathan touched my arm. "Here," he said.

The windows of my parents' house were lit up, the curtains wide open, everything in full view. It was alarming.

"This is where I live," I admitted.

"I know," he said. "I used to see you here. That's your bedroom up there."

It was spooky.

"My job is to know everything," he explained. "I saw you undressing up there one night."

I looked at my darkened window.

"Big thrill," I told him, trying to imagine what secret life he could have caught me in. "When was this?"

"Before I knew it was you. I used to go by your house a lot."

He had to be lying.

"Then what does it rate?" I asked. "Nebula? Supernova?"

Through the living room window my parents looked as strange as any strangers. I'd never seen my house this way, my father in his recliner, feet up, reading the *Minerva Evening Crescent*. For long stretches he remained motionless behind the paper, then he'd give it a shake and crisply turn the page. My mother, meanwhile, marched restlessly in and out of the room, looking for something, apparently, and failing to find it.

Keith and Kevin sat entranced by the television's blue glow.

Jonathan wasn't watching my house but me, his stare cool and appraising. "You tell me," he said, "what they rate. Be objective."

I told him, "I only live there, you know. I'm just passing through."

"That's what you think," he said.

107

"It's what I know," I said. "Anyway, I can't believe you've been spying on my family."

He shrugged. "And now here you're spying on them too. Strange, the things you can get yourself into."

"Let's go." I gave him a little push. "This is too creepy." I thought about how in another half hour I'd be sitting down to the dinner table in that house. How we'd bow our heads, and my father would pray.

I thought about Jonathan's house, the overgrown shrubs, the aluminum foil over the windows so nobody could see in.

"Dark Star," I said as we walked away. "It's definitely a Dark Star house."

"And why's that?" Jonathan asked, putting his arm through mine in a way that alarmed me, even though by now the light had failed and the street was completely deserted.

"Because you've got me," I had to say as I released myself from his grip. "Because I've gone over to your side."

LUCKY STAR OF HIDDEN THINGS

Dad comes and sits on the side of the bed.

It's summer, and I'm little, and I've been afraid because the wicked witch of the west has been standing on the other side of the window looking in. Not doing anything, just standing past the gauze of the curtains. I can see her shape there, and then a breeze blows, but when it stops her shape is there again. It's still light out—in summer I have to go to bed long before it gets dark, though I can never sleep, I just lie and stare at the wicked witch who stands in the window and stares back, and sometimes I hear voices talking inside my pillow before I go to sleep.

Sitting on the side of the bed Dad sings to me. Away, he sings, I'm bound away, across the wide Missouri.

I'm five years old and I feel so sad.

In the winter when it gets dark early I stand in the driveway and wait for him to come home. I look at the stars, and I say to myself, The Wide Missouri, because The Wide Missouri is space, the huge sky at night that he has to cross.

I'm jealous of his family on the other side of The Wide Missouri. I see them standing there on the far side of the sky, thin and silver, and they stare at me with big dark eyes. Their high ghostly singing like cicadas in summer makes me shiver, so I go back inside to work on the map of the moon I'm making.

Or I'm seven, eight, we've just moved into the house in Houston and Dad's off to Florida for a month. Sitting on the side of my bed. Be a big boy, he says, for your mom. Because I don't want him to go. He pulls back the window curtains, whispers, Can you keep a secret? Just between the two of us.

I nod. Cross my heart I tell him. Hope to die.

He says, See those trees there?

Sycamores, I tell him.

Sycamores, he says. Right. Well, here's the secret. A NASA secret just for you and me.

He lets his voice drop low. I can barely hear him.

They're not really trees, he whispers. They're from the future. Another part of the universe. And do you know why they've come here?

I shake my head no.

Leaning close to me, still whispering. They're here to watch over you and your mom. When your old daddy's away. Nothing bad can happen to you when those trees are watching over you.

What are their names? I ask him. He doesn't miss a beat, so I know he's not making it up.

The Owl, he says, pointing to the one on the left, and that other one is . . . the Amateur.

I ask him what's an Amateur.

Somebody who makes mistakes, he tells me. Then says, But don't worry. This one doesn't make any mistakes, because where he comes from Amateurs don't make mistakes.

Where's that?

But already I can tell I'm asking too many questions.

You have to know everything, don't you? he says. Gives my skull a light rap with his knuckles.

Later, after he's gone, I climb out of bed to peer out the window at those trees that aren't really trees. This secret only Dad and I know. They're sort of scary looking, bark all blotched and whitish, pockmarked like the moon and silvery in the dark like the moon too.

Owl, I say to myself. Amateur. Top secret. Classified.

They stand motionless in the winter night, unblinking, not watching me but watching over me. Between them they have more than a million eyes. Nothing bad can ever get past their stare.

Hamal the lamb and Phact the dove, Vega the vulture and Edasich the hyena. Sulaphat the tortoise and Arneb the hare. Algedi, Schedar, Toliman and Altais.

Algorab, raven's wing. Rastaban, head of dragon. Denebola the lion's tail and Zubenelakrab the scorpion's claw.

Algol the demon star.

Dabih, lucky star of the slaughterer.

Cold meat loaf, fried chicken, fish sticks. On Mondays it's always pot roast from Sunday dinner. Stayton's embarrassed by the leftovers his mom packs him off with, but I'm psyched to trade. I haven't seen leftovers in months.

The lunchroom's insanely crowded. "See the cute guy over there?" I say. And I point.

Nearly everything I do makes Stayton jump, if not physically then otherwise. I get a kick out of it. He's got such a long way to go and I'm going to love taking him there.

"Who?" he says, all alarmed at my pointing. "Mike Burns?"

I lean close and whisper, "I've done him." Then I wait a couple of seconds before confiding, "I even convinced him to fuck me. He didn't want to, but I told him it was only fair, if I was going to suck him off, for me to get something in return."

Stayton looks over to where Mike's talking to a couple of females.

"You're a lunatic," he tells me in that earnest way he has when he gets caught off guard.

"Once he started in on me," I say, "he was all eager to do it."

"You have a filthy mind," Stayton mumbles. "And you're such a liar."

"Take it or leave it," I say, and go back to my meat loaf sandwich, which is really delicious. He takes a bite of what used to be my peanut butter and jelly sandwich and chews and chews. I study the way his jaw works. I'm in love with that jaw, its clean lines. He has just the faintest bit of stubble, shaves maybe once a week.

After he swallows he says, pretending hardly to be interested, "So when was this supposed to happen?"

Cat and mouse. But it's fun. I just give him a look and wish we were both naked together in some wide-open outdoors space somewhere, breeze blowing goosebumps over us.

111

He tilts his milk carton to his mouth, and it leaves a trace of white around the corners of his lips I wish I could lick, but I can do that later.

The thought of that makes me so happy. Makes me practically drunk and ready to devour the rest of the afternoon till school's out.

"Mike," I call across the crowded cafeteria—it's a kind of joy, really—and instantly Mike turns around. He comes sauntering our way with that cocky walk of his.

"Jon, my man," he says. I raise my hand and he clasps it in his big palm. "How you been, man?"

He has very greasy, sweet-smelling hair I'd love to bury my nose in, but that's strictly off-limits with guys like him.

"Same old so-so," I tell him. What I like about Mike is, I hardly have to say words to communicate with him. He's more comfortable with looks and shrugs. But some things you have to say. "This is my friend Stayton," I tell him.

They look each other over. Mike's a year older because he failed a grade. He has beautiful sideburns. I can tell they just hate each other.

Mike shrugs. He thrusts out his hips and sticks his hands down in the pockets of his jeans.

"Well, see you later," he tells me, and starts to move on the way he always moves, like there's an invisible rope attached to his dick that's pulling him along. I wait a beat and say, "Hey Mike."

The way I say it stops him dead. That invisible rope goes slack, and his eyes narrow like a cat's.

"We should hang out sometime," I tell him.

He gives me this threatening look. "Sure," he says, all flustered. "That'd be cool." He shrugs again, confused, and starts to move off. "I'll, uh, definitely I'll give you a call sometime," he says.

I can just feel Stayton let go this huge pneumatic sigh of relief.

"See?" I tell him.

"Mike Burns is a beast," he declares fiercely as the lunch bell rings and he takes off from me like a shot.

George and I share what George calls a predilection for what I call dinge. We both like big words and rude words so we get along fine.

Dinge I get from this guy in Houston whose name I can't remember, but he's a scream. From Louisiana and always using words like dinge.

112

But at first, predilection for dinge isn't what I know about George. George doesn't put the moves on. We do banter at the Travelers—evil surmises about the people that wander in and out, an appreciation here or there that lets me know what he sees in things. I'm one of those kids he lets hang around, who could get him in big trouble but won't. Leaning across the bar one night, scouring glasses dry while I sip my Dr Pepper—So, he says, finally taking the bull by the horns, I could show you the ropes if you're interested.

I remember some guy in Houston telling me: You've got sex written all over you.

The ropes, I tell George, and then what comes into my head, more a joke than anything: That sounds like a business proposition.

Money? he frowns. I can do that.

I'm poor, I tell him. You're rich.

Don't I wish, he sighs.

Get paid to learn, I say—thinking, If only Bill could see me now.

Consider it, George tells me, some kind of a scholarship.

I like him. I like his salt-and-pepper mustache and receding hair. His hard Greek body that's been around.

Socrates and all that, huh? I tell him, but he draws a blank.

Back at his house he smokes a joint to get himself ready. He offers me but I pass. He shrugs and takes another puff.

When you're as old as I am, he says, you'll understand.

How old? I ask because I'm curious.

He looks hurt, this sense of hopelessness.

Forty-six, he says.

Don't look a day over forty-five to me, I tell him, and I put my finger on this big ugly asterisk on his left arm, all white scar tissue.

Bullet, he says.

I love how shy he suddenly gets, but I coax him. He tells me the story of his scars. An appendix operation. A slice at the base of his thumb where a glass he was drying broke on him. A brown fissure on his shin, like lips, from when he broke his leg playing soccer and the bone poked through the skin. In Nafplion when he was fifteen, three years before he came to America.

Not a bad way to get acquainted with somebody. Their history. Plus tattoos. I'm crazy about tattoos and George takes me on the tour—his right shoulder, where a compass shows NESW above its points; a butterfly on his hip, right at the fold in his groin; and a skull in a top hat on his left shoulder blade where he can't see.

Why there? I ask.

Unexplored territory, is his answer.

I run my finger around its outline, then I kiss and lick it. George's skin tastes oily and salty.

Now you know that tattoo better than I do, he says, pulling me around so he can kiss me on the mouth.

He proceeds to do some really amazing things to my body.

After, he picks up a book from the nightstand by his bed and reads me a sentence. We come into this world, he reads in his faint accent, with only one possession, the slender word 'I,' and to give it up—in love, in religious fervor—is the ultimate ecstasy.

I tell him, Wow.

Simone Weil, he says, a lunatic but you could say she saw the truth.

Later we talk about wishes, what we wish for most.

Most? he says. I want to touch a Masai before I die.

A Masai, I tell him. I could definitely get into that.

You know the Masai? he asks.

National Geographic, I explain.

Well, for us on this uncivilized continent there's always the Neptune Lounge, he says.

Which is? I say. Tell me about it.

Better, the next weekend he takes me down to Memphis. Chelsea Avenue lined on a Saturday night with tall black dudes in chartreuse pants and outrageous platforms. Afros a zillion miles wide. I'm in heaven. The Neptune Lounge is a low building faced with black tiles and a neon trident above the door. Inside, nothing but wall to wall dinge, as my Louisiana friend would say. George seems to know every one of them. He picks me out a sweet, crazy-seeming brother named Anthony.

The music's not too loud, Marvin Gaye and such, but Anthony leans close. His breath stinks like the cheap wine he's been guzzling.

Because he has such a beautiful body, he confides in my ear, he should be in modeling. Don't I think he has a beautiful body?

And he does. Coal black and beautiful as can be. He also has a gold front tooth, and straightened hair he's slathered with oil that smells like lemons. He puts his big hands on my hips, tells me he can almost reach all the way around—which he can't, but I let myself slide toward him anyway. His body's beautiful but his face is ugly as a sheep's face.

There's a door at the rear of the club, and we're through it, me and Anthony, we're standing in the cool damp night and Anthony is saying, George was telling me about you.

Telling what? I want to know. But Anthony just shrugs. Aw, he says, said you was a wicked dude. You a wicked dude?

He's so ugly, he's driving me crazy looking at him. I love that gold tooth shining in the streetlight.

Show me how wicked, he whispers in my ear. Big hands pawing my butt. All the blood rushes from my extremities right to my head. At the same time I'm spreading my wings to fly. I can feel it. I take three or four deep breaths like a diver, till I'm halfway turned inside out. He's not taking his time. Fingers fumbling at my zipper, exposing me to air. There's nothing to do but bend over, grab my ankles, let him do the rest.

Two, three fingers and then the main event. I practically pass out till I get accustomed, and then I'm riding high on the sweet pain of it, swept right outside myself till I can see stars popping in my eyeballs. Literally. I'm gasping for breath.

When I open my eyes we're not alone. Thinking, Shit—but the brother doesn't make a move. Just stands there half in the shadows looking at us for the longest time. Or not us. It's just me he's studying—and strange how I forget it's Anthony who's working me from the rear. Can't even remember his ugly face. Instead I'm focusing on this dignified fellow in the shadows, his gold wire-rim glasses and calm curious stare, and he's focusing on me too and how can I say it? I feel this love going out—not just me to him, but the whole dark alley caught up in it, sirens out on the avenue and normal traffic as well, a dog barking, the hiss of the streetlight. The city and the river bluffs and the river and delta and all the huge world.

Like a prayer he touches his two palms together, then with a little nod of his head he's gone. Anthony's smacking my buns and shouting, I'm sorry, Jesus, I'm sorry, and that peculiar sensation of having somebody squirt inside your guts. I'm on my knees clambering to clean him off, suck him free of all that blood and shit and come he's gotten himself into with me. This white boy who leaves him reeling with pleasure.

Then I go back inside to find George.

115

A couple of times I wriggle a finger up his butt, but he doesn't really like it. To try to convince him I say, Hey Stayton, you got to come to terms with your asshole if you want to know who you really are.

He doesn't buy it for an instant. Doesn't even like hearing a word like asshole. Or shit or fuck or Jesus Christ. So I whisper in his ear, Fuck, fuck, fuck while he does just that. It upsets him, which turns him on, which upsets him all the more.

I think about that snake from mythology that's always swallowing its own tail. Ourobouros.

Shit and piss, I explain to Stayton, are the stuff I'm interested in. Star stuff, stuff of life. The cosmos and all. I'm fascinated by what goes into me and what comes out. I think the whole process is just amazing.

But Stayton's terrified. When he sees my shit and blood on his dick afterward he nearly passes out. When I clean him off I think he's going to vomit.

It's life, you know. Existence.

Like the time I find a dead cat by the side of the road. First by its smell, then I see it over in the weeds, this mashed little corpse. Really mashed, with the coil of its guts spilled out, and its raggedy fur like the fur of a teddy bear I had when I was a kid, that I used to eat the stuffing out of. Little berry-black eyes, glassy—both the teddy bear and the cat. And this smell, sickly sweet but with a bite to it. Arousing.

Life.

I squat there by the side of the road for the longest time, not able to take my eyes off the thing, daring myself to reach out and touch it. Why not? It won't bite. Won't do anything at all. But I feel squeamish till I make myself and then it's not bad, it's like touching anything else.

Sniffing the tips of my fingers. But can I really still smell it, or is that just my oil and sweat?

Rot. Decay. Decomposition.

Putrefaction.

I know all about it: anaerobic splitting of proteins by bacteria. Which forms incompletely oxidized alkaloids. Which stink.

Poor little cat.

Rigel the foot and Alderamin the shoulder, Caph the hand and Ruchbah the knee. Maaysim the wrist. Alnilam, a string of pearls. Saiph, a sword.

Benetnasch, chief of the mourners. Aldebaran the follower. Suha the overlooked one.

Nashira the fortunate one, Albali the swallower.

Sadalmelik, lucky one of the king. Sadalsud, luckiest of the lucky.

Sadachbia, lucky star of hidden things.

THE DANGER WAKE

All through my senior year, Minerva High was in the grip of a religious revival. A couple of teachers had come up with the idea as a way of encouraging school spirit, and it had caught on beyond their wildest ambitions. There were prayer meetings before classes, Holy Spirit rallies at lunchtime, charity mission projects after school.

In American history we were read aloud to from the Narnia chronicles and *The Late Great Planet Earth*. In math we were lectured on the statistical probability (zillions to one) that the world had happened by accident versus the virtual certainty that God had created it. Before football or basketball games, the whole school would assemble in the gym where Dr. Lennox would lead us in prayer for the team's victory as well as the overthrow of communism. The two were somehow intertwined.

My father, famous for his anticommunism, was a frequent guest speaker at these rallies. A few years before the great Minerva revival, he'd achieved a certain notoriety there, and even beyond, because of the lengths to which he was willing to go in order to demonstrate the dangers of communism. What happened was this:

Halfway through an Easter morning sermon, five armed gunmen entered the church sanctuary. Wearing drab khaki uniforms, their faces covered by black bandanas, they brandished grenades and machine guns. One of them bounded up to the pulpit, thrust my father aside, and announced, in a heavy Russian accent, that the Red Army had taken control of the United States. From now on, he claimed, God and Jesus and the Christian Church were outlawed.

The congregation sat in shocked silence. Two of the Russian soldiers had grabbed my father and were pointing guns at his head. All ministers of the so-called Christian God will be executed, one of them declared.

Just at that moment, a woman in the crowd stood up, cried out, "My Jesus, my Jesus," and fainted.

"She's having a heart attack," her husband yelled. "Please, somebody get a doctor."

There was complete chaos. People screamed and shouted. Above the din my father commanded into the microphone, "One of you deacons go call the fire department," just as the Russian soldiers whipped off their black bandanas to reveal themselves as men—even deacons—of the congregation.

Mrs. Thayer survived her heart attack, but there were some at the church who thought my father had gone too far. In the end, though, it made my father more rather than less respected for his uncompromising views. A television station in Memphis even sent a reporter up to interview him. As Dr. Lennox explained in one of the school assemblies: "Extremism in the defense of religious freedom is, thank God, not yet a crime in these United States."

"Personally speaking, I became a communist in the fourth grade," Jonathan announced to me after one of those rallies. "I organized a cell of the Young Pioneers. During recess we'd hang out down by the woods and try to figure out what it meant to be a Bolshevik. I read all about them in *Junior Scholastic* and thought, Cool idea. We had our five-year plan for taking over the school and turning it into a Stalinist indoctrination camp. And this girl Lisa made red armbands for us to put on at recess. Lisa Lineberry, now there was a budding young terrorist. I wonder whatever happened to her. Probably a lesbian by now. We should've had a revolution, come to think of it, but we were just too young to get it together. I wonder if any of those other kids are still communists. I wonder if I still am. I mean, a good communist, party line and all that."

For several days after he told me that story—who could tell whether it was true or made up on the spot?—he wore a red armband to school. But nobody paid any attention. I don't think they knew what it meant, and so after a while he stopped wearing it.

It was about that time that Dr. Lennox decided to separate us as lab partners. He caught up with me in church one Sunday—he was a deacon there—and apologized for having saddled me with a character like Jonathan. A loser and a deadbeat, as Dr. Lennox said. From now on I was to be paired with Ruby of the virulent acne and insatiable appetite for biology.

In certain ways it made my complicated new life simpler. I would henceforth cease to be seen with Jonathan at school, and only meet him in the afternoons at his house, or for the voyeuring hour's strange interlude, when I absurdly believed I was safe from detection. My parents would ask questions if I spent too much time away from home in the afternoons, since I never had before, so as a cover I threw myself enthusiastically into the school revival. I'd always been, by virtue of my father, involved in church activities, but during that winter and spring I joined every project and activity I could, so conspicuously overextended that I often had to miss one meeting in order to go to another—a flurry of scheduling that allowed me to escape undetected one or two afternoons a week to Jonathan's. There was a particular thrill in steering my way between the twin, conflicting obstacles of a Christian Fellowship meeting and a witnessing trip to the Nursing Home in order to end up moaning my heart out on the Naugahyde sofa in Jonathan's basement.

"Once you get going," Jonathan would whisper in my ear, "you Baptist boys know how to raise hell."

He was right. I was in love with every jolt of agony or bliss I could send through his slim little body.

"Come inside me," he'd urge, his hands on my buttocks pulling me deeper. "I want your come all up in me."

The secret places.

This new self, willing to risk everything, was unfamiliar to me, though I saw clearly enough how it began that first night I sneaked out of my parents' house to the Travelers.

I was not without painful contradictions. I remember one day, as I headed back to class after a particularly egregious assembly in which I had a leading role, I happened to pass the forlorn patch of concrete under the fire escape that served as the school's official smoking area. Students with written permission from their parents could congregate there between classes; otherwise it was strictly off limits. Jonathan didn't smoke, but he was sitting on the fire escape with Mike Burns.

I made to hurry past the smoking area as if I hadn't seen either of them, but Jonathan's reedy drawl called me over.

I glanced around to see if anybody had noticed, and then hurried to them.

What Jonathan thought of my public dissociation from him and my even more public embrace of our ongoing student revival, I had no idea. But in the weeks since Dr. Lennox had reassigned us to different lab partners, he'd allowed me to slip from him, at least during school hours, without a word.

"Just wanted to say hi," he said, though with a slyness in his voice that suddenly put me on my guard. Not for the first time I saw him as the liability he might one day prove to be.

"Yeah," I told him curtly, shifting back and forth, all too clearly eager to get this over with.

"I just wanted to tell you," he said, "I can't wait for this afternoon to be here." As he said it he cupped both his hands over his crotch, a gesture only I could see. Mortified, I fled to the safety of math class. I couldn't wait for that afternoon either.

"You freaked," he accused me. We lay clumsily folded into each other's arms on the clammy sofa.

"No," I said. "What do you mean?"

"You know," was all he said. And I did know.

"It's hard to explain," I told him.

"Sure it is," he said.

And that was it. He never brought it up with me again, but I knew that afternoon, with bolt-lightning sharpness, what nobody else could know: Jonathan Cloud was better than I. Truer, more substantial. Even Mike Burns, that quintessential loser and deadbeat, was truer than I, who received so many brilliant accolades for my hypocrisy. When I thought about it later, after I'd gone home to lie on my bed in a crisis of everything, it brought tears to my eyes as I imagined telling Jonathan the respect I had for him, and how jealous I was. Entirely sentimental, I see now. Silence on both sides was to be part of the bargain struck that afternoon—and by Jonathan so gracefully, I thought, that even to say a word would ruin something I could only name, in my shamed and fumbling way, as holy.

Sometimes Jonathan's mother would be stirring upstairs. I always wanted to slip out the back way, but Jonathan wouldn't hear of it.

"You act like you're ashamed," he said.

"Just naturally cautious," I reminded him.

Mrs. Cloud had fixed herself a cup of coffee. She sat at the kitchen table in her blue bathrobe and chain-smoked Kools. The radio played Minerva's only rock-and-roll station, the one my father had unsuccessfully preached against for years. In our school, I helped lead the drive to get students to pledge not to listen to it, and most did pledge, though I suspect most continued to listen to it just the same. The songs it played were all songs I loved from the Travelers.

Mrs. Cloud smoked her Kools and stared vaguely into the late winter twilight that invaded the room.

"I was thinking," she said.

"That can be dangerous," Jonathan told her. "Sure you're feeling all right?"

She shivered.

"Sometimes," she said, "I honestly don't know how we got through. I mean, got through so well as we did. That's what I was thinking."

Jonathan's attitude toward his mother was ironic, but he could become tender with her in an instant. He slid into the chair beside her and put his hand on her shoulder.

"What's up?" he asked her. It was one of those times when I wanted to vanish. But I also couldn't look away.

"The danger wake," she said. She looked at him steadily. "You don't remember the danger wake, do you? You wouldn't. You were too young, thank God, and we swore we'd never talk about it. Bad luck even to say the words."

Jonathan looked at me over his shoulder, a pleading look that asked me to stay. I stuck my hands in my pockets and leaned against the countertop, trying to become as inconspicuous as possible. There were afternoons when I think Mrs. Cloud took me at best for a ghost, more likely just some trick of light in the dim room.

"Mom," Jonathan said in a calming voice, "you're out of all that now. Light-years away. Tell me what the danger wake was."

She smiled, brushed a strand of thick, gray hair from where it'd fallen in front of her eyes. There was something tight and leathery about her, a squint to her eyes as if she'd lived her life in a desert full of sandstorms. "When your father made his space walk," she said, "and you went upstairs to your room. Remember? You wanted to watch it by yourself. You didn't want to be downstairs with the rest of us."

"If you mean all those people," Jonathan said. He was looking intently at his mother. He was studying her. She took a long drag on her Kool, held it in, then exhaled. All three of us watched the thin blue trail of smoke hang in the air before it disappeared.

"I don't know who called it the danger wake," she mused. "All us wives parked in the living room of whoever was the unlucky one that go-round—smoking up a storm, getting tanked on martinis, counting down lift-offs, space walks, docking maneuvers, the fucking duration. Waiting it all out." She laughed her laugh that always had something disheveled about it. "You know what it was like? A bunch of drunk women waiting around for one of us to give birth to something. And we all knew when it finally popped out, what a monster it was going to be, all bloodied-up, fangs sprouting from it, and we'd have to say something. What in the hell were we going to say? Oh, nice. Well done. It wasn't even born yet and we were already at the funeral. The two-day danger wake, the weeklong danger wake. Till they were back on dry land, or at least the fucking aircraft carrier.

"Oh we had a wonderful life back then," she said, suddenly addressing me as if I'd just appeared out of the woodwork. "Believe you me, we had a goddamn wonderful life. But don't listen to me. Listen to the radio. Do you like this music? Isn't this the kind of music you kids like?" Her voice was all anxiety. Jumping up from her chair she started shimmying in her blue bathrobe there in the middle of the kitchen. "Come on," she invited. "No more danger wake ever."

"No more danger wake," Jonathan said, a little wearily, from his chair.

"Come on," his mother told him. She stood in front of him, both hands out, and he took them, he let her pull him up from his chair. I'll never forget—on the radio Elton John was singing "Honky Chateau." I'd always had a feeling about Elton John.

"It's not good," said Mrs. Cloud, stretching out her hands to me, "if one person holds back. It means the agreement's off, the danger wake's back in force."

"Shake your butt," Jonathan commanded me mildly.

"Life on earth," laughed Mrs. Cloud.

"Here with the stars," Jonathan said.

"Death curled up in a little ball in the center of the universe," his mother shouted with glee.

So I danced, the three of us danced there in the kitchen in the settling dusk and the radio playing song after song I still remember. For about fifteen minutes we danced. Then Mrs. Cloud excused herself to light up another Kool. The dancing fell apart. We all three sat around the table.

"Whew," she said. "That did me some good."

"Mom," Jonathan looked at his mother seriously. He patted her wrist. "It's a real good thing you got out. You know that, don't you?"

"I miss the bastard," she said. "The life. But you're right. You're totally one thousand percent right. Let somebody else do the worrying. My liver couldn't have stood it anyway."

"Are you going to be all right?" Jonathan asked. "I mean, tonight. I could make you some macaroni and cheese or something before I go out."

"I'm fine," she said. "I'll sit here and listen to the radio. You know me, I can listen to the radio all night."

"There's a lot here I don't get," I admitted to Jonathan when we were out on the sidewalk. "It kind of makes me uncomfortable."

"Yeah, well," he said. "You know, Dad's supposed to go to the moon sometime this spring."

I had to stop him in his tracks.

"But that's incredible," I said. "That's fantastic. Don't you think that's fantastic? I can't believe you didn't tell me that before." I had to let out a little whoop even though, of course, I'd never met his father. "If it were my dad," I confessed, "I'd go around telling everybody. It'd be the one thing people knew about me."

"I know," Jonathan said.

"Oh, shut up," I told him, and punched his shoulder. "But seriously, going to the moon."

"Yes, seriously," he said. It was the voyeuring hour. Lights were coming on in all the houses up and down the street, and we made our usual circuit, but it was another window I was interested in peering in that evening. I'd never seen it so wide open before, and the light shining within.

"The first time my dad went up," Jonathan told me as we strolled in the chill air, "I was so scared and furious I wanted to kill him. I'm not kidding you. I was what, eleven? Twelve? My Mom's right. I went up-stairs—we were back home by then. They flew us down to Florida for the lift-off, but we were back in Texas for the walk. I locked myself in my room and watched on the little TV I had up there. There were all these people in the house, but I couldn't stand to be around any of them. You know why? Because I knew what was going to happen. I'd seen it all in my head a hundred times like a movie that just kept playing. He'd be floating there out in space, and the cord just snapped, the one that held him to the capsule. The tether. He'd go drifting off in slow motion, all in full view of the camera, and nothing anybody could do. Calling my name. Calling Mom's name. I had dreams about it. I even had dreams where he sat on the side of my bed in the middle of the night and told me it was going to happen, how he had it all planned, his great escape, and you know what? I never knew whether those dreams were dreams or whether they really happened, and by the time he was up there it was too late to ask. I thought he must hate us a lot, and that was why he wanted to have us watch him float away from us on TV, with everybody watching. Everybody saying, he doesn't want you. There's something out there he wants more than he wants you."

It was more than Jonathan had ever told me. He looked at me. "Sounds crazy, don't it? Don't even answer. I know it was crazy. I knew it was crazy even then. Everybody kept knocking on the door, asking me if I was okay. These people I didn't even know were knocking on the door. That kid Lex's mother, for Christ's sake. If only she'd known. And I wouldn't answer any of them. I just wouldn't."

"You were doing your own space walk," I told him tentatively. It was ridiculous even to pretend to understand.

"I'd fucking cut the cord," he said. "I was already in deep space and nobody had a clue."

MUSIC LESSONS

Amid the balancing act I was always only barely managing, my weekly French horn lessons were an interval of odd repose. I'd been taking lessons for a couple of years, more at my parents' urging than anything else: in Morogoro, one of the Mormon missionaries had played French horn every evening, and the sound wafting over into my parents' walled garden had enchanted my mother.

I'd never thought much about my teacher, Kai Dempsey, a music major from the local Methodist College, except to register that he was black. In those days I was much more racist than either of my parents, though that would never have occurred to me. As I sat before Kai and worked through the week's assigned étude, I'd be thinking all the time, with some strange mix of pride and defiance, He's black, he's a black man, I'm studying French horn with a black man—a litany meant to demonstrate to myself my own enlightened attitudes. That he was scarcely three years older than I didn't quite sink in.

Kai fascinated but also repelled me—his sweatish odor that cologne didn't sweeten; ripe lips and bloodshot eyes, the way his palms were pinkish, not bitter-chocolate like the rest of him. He wore gold wire-rim glasses and a beret, and spoke a full-bodied kind of English. His loafers were more like slippers than shoes, very feminine looking, and he had outrageously colored socks.

He usually took a mocking, ironic tone with me. "You want to know the secret of some great horn playing?" he'd say. "I'll tell you. Tight chops, loose attitude." He looked to see my reaction. "Relax," he told me. "It's just music. It's not like getting married or anything."

There was too much else to concentrate on for me to take his advice. When I was through, he'd pick up his horn to show how it was done. His burnished sound filled the room to the brim, so sweet and liquid we were both swimming in it. It made me dizzy to be so close. My own sound was pinched and stingy.

"Just let it pour like honey," he coaxed, taking off his mouthpiece and shaking out spittle while I tried to negotiate the high register legato he'd made sound easy. "Put the love of Jesus into it," he said. "Rise above all that earthly sorrow."

I had to break off the note I was hitting in order to laugh.

"You say the weirdest things," I told him.

He hit his open palm to his forehead and flung himself back like he'd been wounded. "I'm talking to you about love," he said.

"Sorry." I repositioned my lips on the mouthpiece.

"Just forget it," he said. "The mood's ruined anyway."

He always professed to be shocked by the barbaric way I played. Just as he always shocked me by sounding so serious and soulful about things like the B minor scale.

"I come from a very musical family," he told me once. "One of my sisters sings professionally—oh, she sings beautifully, she has this big rich creamy voice. Pascal leads a church choir in Nashville. And my brother Maxwell plays violin in the orchestra at Radio City Music Hall. Me, I want to be the most famous French horn player in the universe. I want to be invited to give concerts on the moon. Play the Mozart Fourth Horn Concerto on the Sea of Tranquillity."

"At least you're not ambitious," I complimented him, not knowing what else to say to someone like that.

But things changed between us during that winter and spring of 1972. Perhaps I became, despite my best intentions, somehow more transparent to Kai, or perhaps in two years he'd simply grown bored and wanted to know whether there was anything in me worth his time.

"Tell me," he asked one day after I'd made my diligent way through my lesson, "what is the point of playing music?"

"So you can get better," I said.

"Get better at what?"

"Playing the music."

"And what's the point of *that*?"

"You mean," I asked, "what's the point of playing music?"

"Exactly."

I looked for an answer but couldn't find one. I was just blank.

"Can I ask you a question?" he said. "Not about music. About you."

Few things unnerved me more than being asked a direct question about myself.

"What question?" I asked.

"Don't be so nervous," Kai told me. "You act like you're about to get caught."

"There's nothing to catch me at," I said.

There was a silence that seemed to last too long. I knew Kai was looking at me, though I wouldn't look back at him. The room was excruciatingly small.

"Is that true?" he finally said. "That there's nothing to catch you at?"

I just sat there fingering the valves of my horn.

"When I say to you, 'express yourself,'" he went on, "what goes through that head of yours?"

I thought about the way Kai played, how he leaned into the music, breathed it out from his chest. To play like that would embarrass me. It was too dangerous.

"We have different styles," I said.

"What is it you're afraid of giving away?" he asked.

It wasn't something I was going to answer. His shiny spectacles hid his eyes. Underneath my shirt, a single bead of sweat made its way down my side.

"Or let me put it this way," he went on. "Do you have anything there to give away? If that question upsets you, it's meant to." He pulled the mouthpiece off his horn and shook out some spittle, then laid it in the plush of his open horn case. It was as if I were no longer there.

"I'll think about what you've said," I told him politely. He shrugged, and I hated him. I hated his gleaming spectacles and his beret and his large hands. I hated his blackness, his beautiful music. I hated it that he knew who I was.

I couldn't retreat from that room fast enough. I fled to the safety of Dr. Lennox's office and a meeting of the Christian Fellowship.

After that afternoon, I canceled my lessons more and more frequently as other commitments began to encroach on my time. But I had recurrent dreams: we wrestled together, Kai Dempsey and I, hugging, grappling, rolling around on the ground. Finally he pinned me, held me there, then slowly lay down on top of me, the full length of his body spread against mine, the sweet heaviness of him intoxicating like another, deeper kind of sleep.

You've really fallen far, I'd say to myself when I awoke, and in an early morning drowse of excitement I'd relish how far I'd fallen, how deep.

Sooner or later I would have to get caught. I knew that. I was prepared for it, and wondered whether I'd be brave enough to commit suicide when the time came.

One day in early spring I came home from Jonathan's a little later than usual—we'd lost track of time. I can't remember, now, by what subterfuge I had managed to elude all my pressing engagements that afternoon for a couple of stolen hours, but as I walked through the living room my father said simply, without even looking up from the evening paper, "You're slipping, Stayton. Watch that you don't slip."

He said it in such a flat, neutral voice. Somehow he'd managed to discover everything. I stopped dead in my tracks, waiting for whatever came next. But he didn't stir from behind his newspaper. It was as if he hadn't said a word, as if in my deep anxiety I'd hallucinated the whole thing.

After a heartbeat I resumed my stride through the room. Whether the momentary falter in my step was evident to my father, I don't know. But upstairs in my bedroom I practically collapsed.

For weeks the incident haunted me. In my head I heard again and again my father's words, "You're slipping." The matter-of-fact tone, no surprise there, no sorrow, nothing but objective observation: one more heart-sickening piece of evidence that I was rotting from the inside out; that the seamless facade I'd so hectically perpetrated would soon have to crumble in full view of everybody.

The truth was, I couldn't wait to be caught.

Like all the other windows in the Cloud house, the windows of Jonathan's bedroom were covered with aluminum foil. Insulation, he explained. Cool in summer, warm in winter.

We never had sex in his bedroom, just as we never really talked in the basement, only enacted our more or less silent rituals and then ascended to the kitchen and Mrs. Cloud. Each aspect of our relationship seemed to have its place.

His bedroom was full of things. That was what I first noticed about it: the clutter of odd things he'd collected—strangely shaped or colored rocks, polished sea glass, geodes and thunderstones, dried seed pods, driftwood, fossils, shells, a squirrel's tail he'd pinned to his bulletin board. On one wall hung a sign advertising Jack & Jill Soap Bubbles: TO HAVE FUN DIP WAND AND BLOW! (My motto, he explained.) Over his bed were lurid Hindu gods: an elephant, a warrior monkey, a blue-skinned boy with a flute, all vaguely obscene. On another wall hung several posters: Ziggy Stardust and the Spiders From Mars; Pat Paulsen for President; a striking dancer Jonathan identified to me as Rudolf Nureyev.

He always lit a cone of incense when we were in that room, and even today the cloying scent of patchouli takes me back.

I loved all that chaos—unlike my own room, tidy and bright, nothing on the walls except a framed map of the holy land that had been there as long as I could remember, and a calendar of Bible readings by which one could make one's way through both testaments in the course of a year (I had done so three times). The Bible was the only real book in my bedroom. Pamphlets—some from Sunday school, others from after-school activities—made up the remainder of my austere library. Jonathan's bookcase, on the other hand, was crammed with dog-eared paperbacks.

"You must read all the time," I told him, hardly able to imagine when he could find the time in between all his other exploits—unless, of course, as I both hoped and did not hope, most of those exploits were invented.

He lay on his bed; I sat in the bean bag chair on the floor.

"It's like a bad habit, you know?" he said dubiously. "Like I'm wasting my time." He picked up a book from beside his bed, flipped through it impatiently, then tossed it to me.

"*Steppenwolf*," I read off the psychedelic cover. I thought it was the name of a band.

"Hermann Hesse," Jonathan told me. "Cool stuff. But when the message of all his books is how you shouldn't stay in and read books, you should go out and live life, well, then I feel guilty." He shifted his position on the bed and sighed. "Though I guess you have to read those books in the first place, to know that's what they say."

I thought about how I never read any books except for the ones that were assigned me at school. In all my classes I made straight A's, while I gathered Jonathan was often in danger of failing.

"Hey Stayton," he said. "Can I ask you a question? When you read books, do you get a hard-on?"

"What kind of question's that?" I asked.

"I mean literally," he said. "I read *Pride and Prejudice* for English class, you know, and it fucking gave me a hard-on, it was so good. Sometimes I just don't know."

Before I knew it he'd unzipped his jeans and was pulling out his penis. Looking down at it, giving it a good shake. "Hey dick," he said in a gruff voice, "what's going on down there?" Then in a shriller voice he answered, "Just shaddup and mind your own business, will you? Do I tell you what to do?" And back to the other voice. "Well, yes, as a matter of fact, buster, sometimes you do."

To distract myself from his antics, I browsed through his shelves. Allen Ginsburg, William Burroughs, D. H. Lawrence. J. D. Salinger. The Bhagavad Gita. Some I'd vaguely heard of, most not.

"You should borrow some," he offered, but I demurred. I couldn't imagine how any of them could be worth the risk of my parents finding them in my room.

The next thing I knew, he was asking me, out of the blue, "Why do you hate yourself so much?"

The question caught me completely off-guard and I didn't know what to say.

Sometimes we could look one another in the eye for what felt like minutes at a time. A very disconcerting exercise.

Finally I spoke. "There's only one unforgivable sin," I said slowly. "Being born. That's why nobody can ever forgive their parents."

It was a bit of tormented adolescent blasphemy I'd been privately rehearsing for some weeks. Jonathan didn't blink, just continued to look at me. For a moment it felt like we were both traveling along the same line of thought. But then he said, in a grave tone of voice, "Do you know how to tell if your dad's been fucking your sister? His dick tastes funny."

And he threw a pillow at me.

131

"You're one person," I told him, tossing the pillow back, "who's definitely going to burn in hell."

If his stories were any indication, what I said was in fact true.

He told me how he'd borrow his mother's car, a '67 Ford Galaxy, and drive out to Interstate 40. About twenty miles past Minerva, heading toward Memphis, was a rest stop.

"Truckers," he told me. "You wouldn't hardly believe."

His method was this: with his jeans unbuttoned and unzipped, and his penis stroked into an erection, he'd cruise the stretch of interstate near the rest stop. He'd drive up behind a truck and flash his headlights, then pull up alongside, let the driver get a good look, then accelerate and cut in in front of the truck. If the truck blinked his lights, they'd both pull off at the rest stop and Jonathan would clamber up into the cab.

"Truckers," I told him. "Ick."

"Truckers," Jonathan told me, "will do anything to get their rocks off."

His stories could sometimes make me sick with desire.

"I'm up in the cab there," he said, "and it's dark, and this total stranger's banging me silly, but it's like I'm not even there. I'm seeing myself from a million miles away. It's great. It's like getting high must be."

"Getting high," I said. "Is that something you do too?"

But Jonathan vigorously shook his head. "Addictions of various kinds run in my family," he said. "I stay away from that shit. One toke and I'd be a goner. I'd just love it too much. I can tell that about myself. But I have nothing against it theoretically speaking."

I'd thought a lot about his mother.

"It must be hard," I told him.

"It's something you live with," he said. "Like any other kind of disease, really. I've learned some valuable lessons from it. Listen to this: When they were first married, my parents, they lived in this little shack up in the mountains in California. Dad was at Edwards Air Force Base test piloting. It was right after I was born. Mom used to be able to watch his flights from the cabin with binoculars. They were high enough up so she could see everything. There wasn't any running water or electricity. It cost them twenty-five dollars a month. I don't know why they didn't live on base. It was something they wanted to do. I don't remember the house, but I've seen pictures. There were flowers all over. There was something special about that cabin, or maybe it was just that time in their lives. Before everything started taking its toll: the danger wake, stuff like that. It just wore her down. Even when I was a little kid I could feel it: tension all the time. Enough to drive you crazy. Which I guess it did, for both of them."

"Your dad too?" I asked.

"Are you kidding? Dad most of all. But that's the best-kept secret in Houston. All those guys—they're crazy."

I thought about the times I'd seen the astronauts on TV: all-American men with crew cuts and big grins. "They always seemed normal to me," I observed.

"They have to seem that way. Because deep down, some of those guys have completely flipped. If they didn't seem normal on the outside, there'd be no saving it for anybody."

"Oh," I said.

"Now let me tell you," he abruptly changed the subject, "about this fabulous bar I found to go to in Memphis."

The subject of his father seemed to make him nervous. He never dwelt there for any length of time. Everything I got, I got in bits and pieces.

"What fabulous bar?" I asked him.

I knew he'd taken to driving his mother's car down to Memphis on Saturday afternoons, then coming back early Sunday morning. I gathered the Neptune Lounge was in a black neighborhood. That in itself was a little perturbing. The few times I'd been to Memphis, I'd felt outnumbered by the great swarms of black people. To venture into their part of the city seemed perverse and unwise—especially after the 1968 riots, whose pall still hung over the city.

"Watch out for yourself," I told him.

"It's a beautiful place," Jonathan reassured me. "All those hot black bodies. They serve oysters on the half shell in the back room, and champagne. Play Nat King Cole."

"I never know when to believe you," I told him.

"You should come down with me this weekend. We'll find you a nice mulatto boyfriend."

"Stop," I said. An accusation that had long lingered near the surface occurred to me, and I dredged it up fiercely. "Does this mean," I said, making sure each of my words counted, "that you're a nigger lover?"

Jonathan just looked at me, studying me carefully as if somehow seeing me for the first time. "Yeah," he said, "that's what I am, a nigger lover."

He said it so simply and beautifully that I blushed with shame.

"What on earth am I doing with you?" I asked him.

"I could ask you the same thing," he told me.

I couldn't entirely push the phrase "nigger lover" out of my head. I thought about Kai Dempsey, the only black person I actually knew.

I was very perplexed by all this. I didn't want to hear any more about the Neptune Lounge.

"It's a very artistic crowd," Jonathan went on. "Musicians, painters, writers. Drug dealers, drag queens. Pre-Ops. There're black-and-silver banquettes and palm trees, and WPA-style murals on the wall, Martin Luther King and George Washington Carver and Leontyne Price. You'd love it."

"If you think that," I told him with offended dignity, "then you don't really know anything about me."

COMMUNISM

Black man sitting on a bar stool so I edge in beside him. He's drinking a soda and I say, What's up?

The Travelers on a slow night. George is behind the counter serving soft drinks, the occasional beer. He asks if the two of us have met.

Kai Dempsey introduces himself. Offers a big firm hand, peers at me through gold wire-rim glasses.

You look like a prince of ancient Egypt, I tell him.

First thing that comes into my head.

That's so rich, he laughs. I should definitely have that dynastic touch.

He's got a pharaoh's cheekbones for sure. Luscious lips. I've seen statues of his ancestors in *National Geographic*. He cocks his head to one side. His eyes see right through me.

We *don't* know each other, do we? he says in a curious tone of voice.

I try to think. The way he searches me.

George, he announces suddenly, almost with a shiver. I have the most absolutely severe splitting headache. Whatever do you put in the Dr Pepper? I think I'm going to go home. Tomorrow I have to be up with the dawn.

I'm watching him and thinking, I'm what made him shiver. I spooked him.

And you, child, he says, trying to gather himself back together, isn't it past your bedtime? And on a school night when the moon's full . . .

But the moon's not full. I'm always on lunar calendar, so I know. I

135

reach out and touch the palm of my hand to the stubble of his cheek. It absolutely shocks him—he reels back. But he asked for it. And I'm happy to have grazed that magnificent ebony skin.

I'm reprimanded, he says.

Another touch from me, it's clear, and he'll go flying off the bar stool.

George is watching us with a smile. 'Night, Kai, he says, then does what he never does in the Travelers—blows him a kiss.

I'm the only witness. Kai gathers up his leather coat trimmed with fur. At the door he pauses to take one last look at me. Hmm, is all he says.

I told him about you, George explains. He leans close, confidential.

You tell everybody about me, I complain.

I just can't keep a secret, he admits. Especially when it's a secret too good to keep.

He makes me laugh. The feeling comes over me that I want to dance, so I slide down off the stool and head over to the jukebox that's been silent since I got here. Dancing at the Travelers is for weekends—but I don't mind. I slip a dime in and I'm off. I can feel people in the booths watching me. They've never seen anybody dance by himself, but it's the way I dance alone, in my room. It takes me places. Nobody believes that, but I travel. I go all over.

George, at least, appreciates it. He's seen me dance a hundred times, but still he lays down whatever he's doing just to watch. Stands there with his hands on his hips and I can feel his eyes eating me alive— like I'm food, fresh catch from the sea, the most delicious feast he ever tasted in his life. I like his hunger, the way it streams out of him like some kind of light. The way it bathes me.

All the while I'm stalking a memory, about to flush it out, but then it's gone, I've lost the scent. Kai Dempsey, I say to myself as I move, as I travel.

Then the music's over, I'm stranded in silence. People who've been watching look away. Concentrate on their Minerva hot wieners and mugs of beer, check their watches to see when the rest stop is over and the bus for Memphis pulls out.

At the stroke of midnight George turns the place over to Frank and we're out of there. Minerva at this hour's a ghost town. The only other traffic is the cop cars that haunt the streets. What Stayton's so terrified of.

Slowly, deliberately, George meanders us along some circuitous route—side streets, back roads, up dead ends and back, crisscrossing Main in long patient arcs.

Where're we going? I have to ask.

I'm just driving you around, George tells me.

I can tell he's got things on his mind.

He's so terrific, he says after a while. Maybe you didn't see it, but he is.

I like him, I say. Then add, But I think I make him nervous.

He's a deep one, George says, tapping his head. Musician. You never know what's going on up there. I met him in Memphis three weeks ago—total coincidence he was from here. Goes to school at the college.

He bangs on the steering wheel, he's so happy. Tells me, You should hear him sing Casta Diva in the shower in the mornings. Bone-tingling.

He lets me imagine all the rest.

George, I say. Don't feel bad on account of me. We're all in the same dance together, far as I'm concerned.

He puts his hand on my knee, slides a finger in the hole that's worn there in my jeans. I love his touch: I can feel the current of his soul in it.

Kid, what am I going to do with you? he purrs.

We've come to a stop in front of my house. No lights are on. I slide over to him and put my mouth on his.

Cop car slows as it passes. The thing I love about George is—no fear. He keeps his tongue down my throat like he's lapping some sweet honey he's found there.

Oblivious, the cops drive right on past.

A few streets over from where Stayton lives there's a row of new houses. Finished—wall-to-wall carpeting laid down, appliances built in, driveways poured. But nobody's moved in. There they sit empty in a field of weeds and bare dirt.

I get an idea.

I know what you're thinking, Stayton says. And the answer's no.

You have no curiosity, I tell him.

Are you crazy? Get ourselves arrested for trespassing?

There's nobody to know, I say. I just want a look.

I strike out through the weeds. Like I know he will, Stayton follows. With my penknife I jimmy the lock in no time.

You're a lot better at that than you should be, he says—and I tell him, Thanks for the compliment.

Inside it's dim. Smells new, smells of chemicals and plastic and paint. Also stale from being closed up.

I have this sudden urge, I say.

He tells me, You want to be an interior decorator.

I know he doesn't like this. It's why I'm putting him up to it.

I say, Let's get naked.

Of course he's freaking.

No way, he tells me. Are you crazy?

But I'm already doing it. Tug off my sneakers, step out of my pants. I can't get naked without getting a hard-on.

Beast, he says. Put your clothes back on and let's get out of here.

I can tell he thinks they even wear clothes in heaven. I pull on myself a couple times, then step up to him till we're face to face. I tug at his belt.

He says, No, takes a step back, but I'm right there.

Yes, I say.

He pushes my hands away, but I keep coming back so he stops. We stand there a minute, my hands on his belly. I undo his belt buckle and he sighs.

I break into people's houses at night, I whisper in his ear. I sit on their sofas and jerk off. I leave stains.

You do not, he says.

I'm unzipping his pants, reaching in my hand.

Some night soon, I say. Some night soon I'll break into your house. Nothing to it. Jimmy the door. If things want in, they'll get in. Nothing you can do about it.

I've got his fat dick in my hand and I'm making it hard. He's twice as big as I am.

See? I tell him. One day we're gonna live in a house, you and me, no furniture, no books, just wall-to-wall mattresses. Butt naked all the time, Stayton. Sleep naked, fart naked, sit around and talk philosophy

138

naked. Look through the telescope at the moon naked. We'll take showers together and swim in the pool and have cookouts in the backyard.

His knees are getting weak and his big dick is rock hard. I think, Before you know it, Stayton, this thing of yours is going to be inside me.

What about the neighbors? he barely manages. It's hilarious how he keeps trying to have a normal conversation with me.

Butt naked, I say, like us. Everybody. A bunch of guys naked with each other all night and all day.

He's really anxious. He's pretending none of this is happening to him.

And the girls? he says, more a moan than anything else.

They've got their own village, other side of the river. We'll wave to each other. No seriously, Stayton, this is my dream. A bunch of guys who love each other so much they know everything about each other. They can be totally naked together and not have any secrets, not body secrets or head secrets or anything. We want to piss, well, we'll just piss, and we feel like going on a crying jag, we'll just burst into tears. Or take a shit, just squat down and take a shit and not care who sees it. Simple as that. Not be embarrassed by anything. Love everything.

He says I sound like a communist.

I tell him, Face it. Isn't this one of the greatest conversations we ever had?

The light's faded to where we can barely see, but I've got my hand on his dick and he's got his on mine and we're both hard and we're both perfect. I can smell his breath our faces are so close. I'd eat his breath if I could. His lips and tongue.

Not just one guy? he says.

A bunch of guys, I say. The more the better.

But what about jealousy? he asks.

Of what?

He shifts his body even closer against my mine, so our skin's touching.

Each other, he says.

Don't you see? I tell him. They'd have each other. So what's to be jealous of? Every one of them gets to have every other one. You're such a prude.

Well, he tells me, sometimes the choice is clear—a prude or a pervert.

Don't you think it sounds like heaven on earth? I ask him.

It's the warmest night of the spring so far. Our clothes are in a pile on the floor. We go from room to room butt naked. There's a big tile bathroom. All done up, fixtures in place. Apricot color scheme—really hideous. Maybe I *should* become an interior designer. I look at us in the mirror standing there.

Hey, I tell him, taking his hand, putting it on my chest. Did I ever show you this?

What? he asks. Suspicious as always. I make sure he can feel the little nub with his finger.

My third nipple, I tell him. Supernumerary. At night when I'm asleep it turns into an eye I can see through. It's my dreaming eye.

He takes away his hand, tells me, Jonathan, you're just plain crazy.

Still watching us both in the mirror—I have to laugh. Our other silver-star identities staring out at us from the other side.

I know, I tell him. Isn't it just terrible? Crazy and a communist.

Then I step into the bathtub.

Stayton, I say, Let me ask you something.

What?

He always flinches when he says that. Reflex. It's his favorite thing to say to me, and I like to make him jerk that way.

I lie down full length in the tub. Cool—make that chill—against my back.

If I wanted you to piss on me, Stayton, would you do it?

I'm looking right at him, but he won't look at me. All around the room, but not at me.

What kind of stupid question's that? he says.

Reflex.

If you asked me to piss on you, I say, I'd do it in a second.

I wouldn't ask, he says.

I love how his dick stays hard. Majestic, I think. His heartbeat makes it throb. You can't really piss with a hard-on.

But if you did ask me, I say.

You're just strange, he tells me. You're sick.

Somewhere out there, I tell him, there's some gorgeous guy who'd love to piss on me.

You've got a brilliant future ahead of you, he says.

And I can tell he's angry.

When he turns away from me to walk out the door I let out a big roaring fart. To annoy him.

It's some test I think we both fail.

George tells me: the Masai rub each other with mutton fat. All over their bodies. They paint themselves with butter and ochre. The warriors spend hours braiding each other's hair.

They despise farming, possessions except for jewelry. The only thing they love are their cows. They put their dead out for the hyenas to take.

They wear cloaks but nothing else, so when the wind blows you can see their long dicks, and the wind's always blowing in the highlands where they live.

Nyakyusa, George tells me. Kaguru. Kikuyu. Yoruba.

Asante. Nuer. Xhosa. !Kung.

All the brilliant peoples of Africa.

One Saturday afternoon he and Kai pick me up. They've become so thick with each other in the last few weeks, I can hardly tell them apart. We drive out of Minerva into bottom land. April and covered with flood. We ford shallow stretches of water till we come to where they're taking me.

An Indian mound in the woods, a great snake sleeping under earth. Trees disguise its shape. Still, I can hear its heartbeat. I can smell the sheen of its blood.

Nobody knows these people, George says. Mississippi Culture. Before the Chickasaw and the Choctaw.

We hoist ourselves up the muddy bank. From on top you can see the river bottom flooded out for miles. Rich farm land. Fields full of arrow heads, George says. Slender gorgeous things.

I was in Mexico, Kai tells us, with a youth orchestra. We played an open air concert where the Aztecs used to sacrifice. We played Brahms among the pyramids of the sun god.

God, George says, was a feathered serpent down there.

He starts to dance. Starts dancing and chanting. We watch him flail his arms and stomp the hollow ground. Waking echoes all along the spine of our sleeping snake. I have to join in—no choice—and Kai follows, the three of us there dancing and chanting on the back of God the feathered serpent.

We make up words.

Pomo Seri Hokan. Washo Yana Tiwa.

Bemba Ganda Luba. Shona Gola Sango.

We orbit one another, dancing close inside the circle of our breath, arms and legs weaving in and out of the spaces our bodies make in motion. We only stop when we're all winded and sweating. The humid air's cold on us.

Take a smoke, George offers a joint from the pocket of his flannel shirt, but Kai shakes his head.

Messes with my lungs, he explains.

You too, George says. Panting and laughing, he gestures my way. This one here never smokes either. And you know why? Kid's always stoned.

Think so? Kai asks.

Definitely, George says. He takes a couple hits, then snuffs the little stub. Sticks it back in his shirt pocket. Says grandly, Jonathan's got chemicals in his brain like nobody's business. He's got stars up there, regular galaxies. Visions of the white buffalo.

I think I can see that, Kai says.

His look searches me through. But what he finds must keep teasing him. I catch him looking at me all the time, studying me out the corner of his eye. What? I want to say.

Inspired, he takes me by the hand, leads me down the steep slope to where the water laps at the river side of the mound. Squats down, saying, Come here, and I squat down too, facing him. We're all in a trance, I think. Snake-charmed out of ourselves. Kai scoops a handful of cold mud and spreads it on my face. On my cheeks and my chin and forehead.

I don't ask why he's doing it. He looks so serious. He rubs his muddy hands all through my hair.

I don't do it back to him. It's something he's doing to me, not me to him. Some way he has of trying to recognize who I am.

George has followed us down the slope. He stands above us where we squat, hands on his hips, watching us the way he watches me when I dance. He knows how I'm dancing even now.

142

Take off your shirt, he commands. I wad it into a ball and toss it his way. He tells me to take off my shoes and my pants and my underwear. I'm shivering in the raw. He watches while Kai scoops big handfuls from the riverbank and coats me in thick, cold mud. Silently slaps it on thick, rubs it into my skin.

Mud boy, George says.

There's such pleasure in his voice.

A bunch of wise-looking cows are watching us from a dry rise in their field across the river and I wonder what they're thinking.

The mud gets hard when it starts to dry. I can feel it tightening my skin.

I'd keep you two like this, George says. Mud totems. I'd hide you both down here by the river. Come here in the moonlight. Dance. You'd come rising out of the water.

It's his time to talk. Kai doesn't say a word, me either. We both are in George's hands.

Those hands he dips in the water and touches my lips, my eyelids with. He washes the mud out of my hair. He splashes freezing water on my chest, my belly. My dick and balls that have shrunk up to nothing.

Newborn.

I'd circumcise you, he says, if you weren't already circumcised. I'd shave your head and your armpits and your groin. I'd shave your asshole and make you my wife. I'd make you pregnant with my child. My big strong future tense.

George gets me on my hands and knees. Spreading my ass cheeks wide to the cold, licks a finger, touches it to my hole, rubs teasing circles there.

The things I'd do, he says, to get to the galaxies you've got inside.

THE FLIGHT OF THE RAPTOR

Florida in late April, sultry and bedazzled. He's brought Janine here three weeks before lift-off because he's wanted her to see, in person, the rocket he'll roar skyward on. Driving in, they catch sight of the Saturn V from far off, across the Banana River, a great gleaming monolith and its attendant tower rising above the swamps. On Pad 39A's vast apron of concrete they squint in the tropical downpour of light. Janine will watch the launch on TV from Houston.

From swing arm 9, thirty-six stories up, the view is magnificent: down the curve of Merritt Island toward the head of the Cape, where Wernher von Braun and his technicians launched their first V-2 for the Allies after the war was over.

Gerhart Walter, the pad leader, has Allen and Janine suit up at the door to the White Room—smock, gloves, booties, mask—as if they're entering surgery. Allen is familiar with Gerhart's tender ministrations. A little man with thick lenses and an even thicker German accent, he headed the White Room Crew all through Gemini but left when the Apollo program began because of a change in manufacturers. Then immediately after the Apollo I fire he was rehired.

Once inside the white room that encloses the capsule, it's impossible to tell they're so high above the ground. In the capsule's presence, Gerhart speaks in a hushed voice.

"Behold the Cormorant," he says, more like a conjuring magician than a top-flight technician. But then, Allen guesses, he's really a little of both.

"Cormorant" is not the name he'd have chosen, but it's what Walt Hammond, the CM pilot, came up with to complement the Lunar Module's moniker "Raptor." Droll as ever, Walt.

"A big shiny gumdrop," is Janine's normal-voiced response to the immaculate vision before them. "Can the three of you really fit inside there?"

Gerhart looks slightly offended. The capsule's his personal baby, after all, from now till launch.

"That capsule," he tells her, "is large enough to carry the dreams of the human race. This is a holy place where we stand. This is where the future is born."

"My," says Janine, "you really have faith, don't you?"

"With all my heart, Mrs. Cloud," Gerhart tells her. "Your husband's part of a tremendous destiny."

"But does he pick up after himself around the house?" Janine teases.

The future belongs to the brave, Allen remembers, and suddenly feels so sad and empty he could cry. He can't say why it comes over him like that. He looks at Janine and thinks, as he's thought a thousand times, how terrific it is to be married to her, how she settles him, makes him a whole man again. He looks at Gerhart and thinks, Thank God my life is in the hands of somebody like that. Gerhart flew night fighters with the Luftwaffe in the war. Why, Allen wonders, and not for the first time, did we ever fight the Germans in the first place?

Six years ago it was Joan he'd brought to the White Room. Before the Gemini flight. She hadn't wanted to come, but he more or less forced her. Said he wouldn't feel covered going into space without her paying a visit. A ritual, he explained. For good luck.

The week after Chuck was killed, when he told her he'd been moved up to the flight she burst into tears. Only for a moment. Then she said, "That's not fair of me," and was herself again. That's how he got her to the White Room: "It's not fair of you," he said, "not to come."

Joan knew, intuitively, to speak in whispers in the White Room. She understood the clear-eyed passion of a man like Gerhart Walter.

He realizes Janine is talking to him.

"What are you saying?" he asks her.

"You had this faraway look," she says.

"Just thinking," he tells her.

"I was saying, it's a shame Jonathan's not up here with us. He really should be able to see all this. The chance of a lifetime."

You're skirting very close, Allen thinks, but he doesn't say anything because he never does. He hates the way Janine's competitive for Jonathan—but then it's his fault. Or it's the damn vasectomy's fault. Forget Jonathan, he should have told Janine long ago, he's with his mother, he's got his hands full—but he didn't and now it's too late. Nobody, he thinks, would ever do anything if they knew the price they'd eventually have to pay for it.

He doesn't like it when he thinks that way. And even now Janine's blissfully optimistic she'll be able to fix things between father and son. "It's just unnatural," she says. He wants to tell her, If only you knew. But that's her nature, bless her—a fixer-upper. The exact opposite of Joan, all too content to let things go. Attributable, no doubt, to that great falling-down house of her grandmother's where she grew up. Appalling conditions he couldn't wait to rescue her from. Mold and gloom. Air force housing wasn't exactly palatial, but at least it was well-lit and clean. He never could understand her attachment to that house, and he's even surprised she didn't move back to Armistice when she left, but instead went to Minerva.

Minerva, which can only exacerbate morbid memories.

It's been a whole year. She's returned to the Joan she was before she ever met him. That's been her way of rejecting him completely. Well, if she wants to have hurt him, she's done exactly that, he thinks bitterly.

He's glad he's let Janine redecorate the house to suit her sunny disposition. That she's spent hours beautifying the front lawn with bulbs, perennial beds, azaleas. That in eight short months she's transformed it from a place where he happens to be living at the moment to something remarkably like a place to come home to.

He's been asked to make a presentation. Wearing a suit and tie, he stands before an unfamiliar, slightly hostile audience. He shuffles his papers, trying to find his notes, but his handwriting is indecipherable. The audience is restive, they whisper and murmur. It's then he notices viscous brown liquid seeping over the waistband of his trousers. It oozes warmly down his front, chunks of fecal material in a soup of diarrheal acid.

He wakes breathing fiercely. His heart thunders. What worries him most about the ten-day flight are his bowels. Outwardly he's imperturbable, yes, but his body pays its secret price. He's never had an accident. Most of his buddies have been caught at one time or another. It happens—but never, so far, to him.

There's no reason even to worry, but knowing that doesn't ease the irrational anxiety. For the duration of the flight he'll wear a fecal containment garment, a big diaper, really. They'll be on a relentlessly low residue diet. One bowel movement in space, the doctor assures them, maybe two. No problem at all. Allen doesn't volunteer the information that in normal times he's used to at least one a day.

Since 1966, when it was no problem, his secret condition's gotten worse.

One piece of good news handed down to the crew in the weeks before launch: it's been determined that, beginning with this flight, no three-week quarantine of the returning astronauts will be necessary. They're all tremendously relieved. Except for publicity-shy Neil Armstrong—who seemed to like being sequestered away, and might even have preferred to remain there—all the astronauts have complained of the claustrophobia, the sense of letdown and frustration the quarantine induced.

"Ten days with you guys will be quite enough, thank you all," says Charlie Sumner, the LM pilot. "I feel like I'm practically married to you as it is. Especially you, Al baby."

"Look, it's tough on all of us," Allen says. He doesn't like Charlie—never has—but understands how that's neither here nor there. He knows Charlie aspired, at one time, to mission commander.

"The only living organisms brought back from the moon," the Flight Doctor explains to them, "were found inside the camera the Apollo 12 crew retrieved from Surveyor 3. We're quite sure, we're positive in fact, that those organisms date from earth assembly, and they were brought from earth in the Surveyor thirty-one months earlier."

"Thirty-one months," Allen says, "and they managed to survive."

"It's a surprisingly long time," the doctor admits.

Exhausted from fourteen-hour days in the simulators, he's slept soundly in the crew's spartan, windowless quarters on the third floor of the Mission Control Building.

The breakfast is filet mignon, scrambled eggs, fresh asparagus, fruit cups, coffee, biscuits. Except for the asparagus, which he doesn't touch, it's the perfect meal as far as Allen's concerned—though he worries if it's really "low residue" enough.

They eat in studious silence, all except for Charlie. Walt's quiet, dry wit Allen can take—it's something on the order of Frank's martinis. But Charlie's antics can seem a bit much at times. His invented Chinese astronaut, Han Moon Fu, has dogged them all through sixteen months of training.

Today, Han Moon Fu is about to depart, like them, for Earth's nearest neighbor.

"Eawth heavenry sistaw, I coming faw you," Charlie intones. "You bettaw watch out. My wickashaw hawness up to my flock of goose, fry me to moon."

"Fry me to the moon my ass," says Walt. "Anybody want my asparagus?"

But no one does.

Gerhart taps his spoon on a coffee cup and rises. They've known this was coming. He clears his throat. "Gentleman and . . . Gentleman," he says, "it is my great and solemn honor, on behalf of your colleagues at NASA, to present you with"—he pauses dramatically—"the key to the moon. Remember to turn out the lights and lock the door when you leave."

"And flush," says Charlie. The key is plywood, attached to cardboard tubing wrapped in aluminum foil. Passed down from mission to mission since Apollo 12, it's slightly the worse for wear.

"Hey, there're teeth marks on this," exclaims Charlie when the key's passed to him. "Chinee teeth marks. Ah. No. White man."

Gerhart admits, "One of your colleagues, I won't say who, thought there was milk chocolate underneath."

Gerhart never makes jokes. This morning the astronauts' guffaws are loud and relatively unforced.

After breakfast Allen makes a last phone call to Janine.

She's not alone, as he's known she wouldn't be. Sally, Pete Leitner and his wife, other astronaut wives. "Tons of food," Janine says.

She's terrifically excited, he can hear it in her voice, but she's also worried that the TV reporters are destroying the flowerbeds she spent hours planting. She even caught one cameraman standing in the middle of a bed, right under the living room bay window, trying to film through the glass.

"They're just flowers," Allen says. "We'll buy some more when I get home."

"But peeking in the window like that."

"You're right," he says. "That's outrageous."

"Pete went out and told them to cut it out," Janine says. "But they'll be back again, I know it."

"Did Jonathan call?" he asks.

"No," she says disappointedly.

"It's just that he said he might," Allen lies.

She brightens. Her moods are reassuringly easy to read. "Oh, you talked to him then," she says. "Did you tell him I miss his smiling face down here?"

Allen winces to think of the phone call to Tennessee he broke down and made last night.

"I'll give him a call when I hang up here," he says.

If I die, he thinks, what will turn out to be the real story of everything? Not of my death, but my life. The way I've lived it.

"All set?" Gerhart taps him on the shoulder. "We start suit-up in fifteen minutes."

They do last-minute things. Synchronize their wristwatches to Houston time. Make sure their fecal containment garments fit securely, also their urine tubes (leg muscles aren't the only muscles to atrophy in space). Slide into the suits, legs first, ease the head through the neck ring. Don the communications carriers, gloves, helmets. Final checks for leakage, a communications check, oxygen check, hookup to the portable ventilators.

"Hey guys, I have to go pee pee," says Charlie.

"Tough," Allen snaps.

"Sorry," Charlie apologizes.

They're not off, this morning, to a good start. Allen wonders whether he should say something, but decides not to because it's time to go: down the ramp, past TV cameras, a storm of flashbulbs (he waves, wondering, Will Joan see this, will Jonathan?), and into the van that takes them out to the pad. The whole ride he's thinking—irrationally, he knows—Charlie better not jinx this mission. All his talk and antics. Not that Allen's superstitious, and he's not a prude either—he's been around a lot of guys like Charlie—but he does have a certain sense of what's appropriate to the occasion. Some sense of dignity. And he's mission commander, after all—he should set the tone.

He's told Charlie, The moon's not for horsing around. Though he can't imagine Charlie managed to hear.

Allen's sharp words, though, seem to have subdued him. All three are uncommonly silent, watching the dim Florida landscape—it's only five-thirty in the morning—roll past. So green it looks, so lovely. Why would anyone ever want to leave a planet like this?

The ubiquitous Gerhart has somehow beat them to the rocket. When they come up the elevator, he's waiting at the 320-foot level. In good hands, Allen thinks, in good hands. Though his heart is racing. But once he's been fitted snugly into the capsule—he goes first, followed by Walt, who as CM pilot sits in the center, and then Charlie—once his breathing, communication, and biomedical lines are hooked up, calm descends on him. This is his element, this is where he was always meant to be. On the job, and doing what he does better than anybody. Matched only by these two professionals beside him. Whatever their quirks as men, professionals through and through.

Beneath the three of them, like something alive, the great rocket murmurs and groans, its liquid hydrogen and liquid oxygen fuel tanks being constantly topped off. As Allen settles into the countdown, he remembers what someone once told him: that the Saturn V, the moment it lifts off, is eating as much oxygen as half a billion people catching their breath.

He's rehearsed various first words—nobody will remember, of course, what the ninth and tenth men on the moon have to say for themselves, so it takes the pressure off. But he's wanted to do his own modest moment in the history of things some kind of justice.

He stands at the base of the ladder on the bleak, bleak surface and says gravely, "Here you are, mysterious and unknown highlands of the moon. We've come to steal your secrets."

Once out of his mouth, those words, teased and tortured for 240,000 miles from Earth to moon, manage to sound all wrong.

It's been a flight plagued, or so it seems, from the beginning. There's the faulty backup circuit on the steering motor of the Cormorant's engine nozzle that nearly aborts, and in fact postpones for six hours, the Raptor's descent to the surface. Then the steerable camera locks, so there are no photos of Allen's first steps on the moon. Charlie spends twenty minutes trying to get the external equipment bay unstuck, while Allen tinkers with one of the rover's two batteries that's mysteriously gone dead—till it suddenly, for no apparent reason, decides to come back to life.

And the disasters haven't even started.

Charlie loses his grip on the nuclear power plant for the experiments and it slips heavily from his hand. No damage there, they determine after heart-stopping minutes. But as Allen lopes back toward the Raptor, his right foot catches a cable leading to the heat flow experiment. "God almighty," he says, stooping to survey the damage. The cable's come completely unattached from the head of the unit. "I'm sorry, I'm sorry," he says, hoping that will somehow undo the damage, but Houston's already telling him, "Uh-oh, buddy, that looks kind of major."

He knows $1,200,000 is the price tag on that experiment.

"We'll see," Houston says wearily, "what the guys down here can come up with toward getting that fixed. I have to say it doesn't look good. Am I right that it's completely severed?"

"Afraid so," Allen says, holding up the cut cord. "I can't believe I did that. It's clumsier to move around up here than you think."

"And I have another complaint," Charlie pipes in. "Every time I turn my head to read my oxygen gauge, I'm getting an earful of orange juice."

"We copy you on that," Houston says.

Allen's own dispenser ruptured while he was fitting his helmet, and he had to take a ten-minute time-out to clean the headpiece so the juice wouldn't interact with the visor defogging compound.

They take time out, between deploying the Far Ultraviolet Telescope/Camera and unfolding the solar wind collector, to set up the flag. For a moment both of them are silent there, saluting the stars and stripes wire-taut in the airless breeze, drenched, no doubt, by that solar wind whose traces they hope to snare. For the first time since setting foot on the surface, Allen's brain opens up—only for a moment, but a flood of images rushes in. Mostly he thinks, This isn't a simulation, this is the actual thing, and he knows it's the actual thing with a clarity that nearly unbalances him. This is why they train so much, he knows, to avoid just this kind of vertiginous moment. And he's very well trained. He doesn't think another instant about the hereness and now-ness of time—that way lies a nervous breakdown in full view of the whole Earth. What he thinks is what he had planned, ahead of time, to think. About the fallen. The ones who didn't make it: Ted and Elliot and C.C., and Gus and Roger and Ed. Most of all Chuck.

Old buddy, he thinks, you're here with me now. You got here after all. Do you know that?

He'd rehearsed the thought, but he hadn't planned to be so suddenly, horrifyingly choked up about it.

"All right, now let's party," whoops Charlie. And thank God, Allen thinks. You may just have saved my sanity.

Later, after they've taken the rover out for its maiden spin, a couple-mile jaunt to the crater called Spook on the map (though it's hard to find, everything looks different on the surface than it did in the orbital photos), they suit down in the cabin. There's dirt everywhere. Some-how, without realizing it, they've both gotten filthy. And there's the smell, faint but persistent—the other astronauts have reported it as well. A smell vaguely like gunpowder, or wet ashes. The smell of the moon. Of million-year-old dust suddenly released into air—a kind of chemical blooming, one scientist has suggested.

Charlie switches off the cabin mike. "Now houw fow venelable tea celemony," he announces with a small bow. "Han Moon Fu honoled to be of selvice."

"Have some more orange juice," Allen suggests.

"Smokee opium now. Rerax and enjoy."

"Give it a break," Allen says sharply just as Houston comes on: "We've got a couple of lovely ladies here would like to say a few words to you cowboys."

"Hi hon." Janine's voice drifts in from 240,000 miles away. "It's me, Janine. Everything okay up there? It sounds like you guys are making out like bandits."

"Really terrific," Allen says, just as Janine says something further that manages to get lost in the time elapse. They speak again, but once again their voices tangle.

"Two second delay," he reminds her.

"It feels so odd," she says. And pauses. "Who's paying for this call?" she wonders.

"Your tax dollars," Charlie says.

"Hello up there, Charlie," greets Sandy.

They talk for a while, and then Janine is back on.

"You're in my thoughts," she says.

"I love you," Allen tells her. It's all he can think of to say.

"Okay," Houston interrupts. "We should wrap this up. It's bedtime for you lunks up there."

He wakes, several minutes before wake-up call's due, to an uncomfortable sensation and then realizes: he's ejaculated.

A wet dream on the moon.

He feels vaguely embarrassed, but also amused. Not the first man to get to the moon, but maybe the first to come there. He has to grin, sheepishly, though there's no one to see. Charlie slumbers uneasily in the sleeping sling.

What his medical telemetry's just told Houston is anyone's guess. A sudden telltale flurry on the monitors down there, some knowing grin on the face of the medical staffers on duty—*they* can read what that quickened heartbeat is all about. Well, well, Commander Cloud, they chuckle among themselves.

Sleeping at one-sixth G scrambles the brain even worse than weightlessness. The old moon's definitely got them in its grip.

Then without warning he remembers his dream. He remembers it so clearly that he has the momentary sensation it wasn't a dream at all. It actually happened. He and Charlie really did unstrap themselves, sometime in the bright lunar night, from their sleep harnesses. They really did open the hatch and descend, once again, the ladder to the dazzling surface.

It's nothing they've planned, an unscheduled EVA, but they move as if having mutually agreed beforehand. Climbing into the rover, powering it up, they set off.

Their journey retraces their route earlier in the day, that dreamy bouncing motion as the wire mesh tires engage the powdery surface. The moonscape's gentle, draped in a fine dust that softens the edges of everything, though here and there rough boulders, easily avoided, stick through the surface. But this time, when they get to the crater dubbed Spook, they don't turn back. They head around, negotiating the lower slopes—not much of a grade there—go up over a rise. That's when they see them.

Rover tracks heading off into the distance, where no rover tracks could possibly be.

Something settles in his spine, not so much a chill as a spooking. It flows out into his limbs, a tingling, mildly electric sensation. The hairs on the back of his neck prickle, an itch creeps along his scalp.

Etched precisely in the dust, clear as if they'd been made just moments before, the tracks lead down into a broad valley. And far in the distance, a brighter spot of light amid the brightness, they see the other rover.

It's stopped at the edge of a crater, slightly at an angle. No sign of motion. They approach it slowly.

Its two astronauts, seated, do not move. Their gold visors make it impossible, of course, to see their faces. On the arms of their bulky white spacesuits, a million, ten million years old, is the American flag.

On the moon I've dreamed about being on the moon, Allen tells himself, just as the wake-up call—the Symphonie Fantastique—blares from the intercom.

But why he should have ejaculated . . . he won't allow himself to think about that dream for another instant. He consigns it to oblivion as Charlie groans, sniffles, then farts.

"Out of the sack, partner," Allen tells him, "there's chores here to be done. And please, don't stink up the living room."

"I always fart after being sodomized," Charlie says.

"Hey guys, can you tone it down?" Mission Control breaks in. "That's a hot mike you've got there."

"Oops," Allen says. "Shouldn't it be shut off?"

"I thought it was," Charlie tells him.

"Well it's on now," says Mission Control, "so you guys clean up your act up there."

The third and final EVA is scheduled to take them, via the rover, seven miles to North Ray Crater. It's as far as their safety margin will allow them to venture from the ship, especially with an on-again-off-again rover battery.

"Another gorgeous day on the moon," Charlie announces for the benefit of planet Earth as he climbs down the ladder. "A hundred and thirty fahrenheit in the sun, minus a hundred fifty in the shade."

"Bracing," seconds Allen, though he's not feeling too well this gorgeous morning. Five and a half hours of uneasy sleep, and now his breakfast—peaches, beefsteak, bacon squares, spiced fruit cereal, a cherry food bar, all indistinguishable from one another—is sloshing around in his stomach. Plus what feels like gallons of the potassium-laced orange juice they've been consuming as an experiment to counteract muscle loss. He's actually thankful his damn helmet dispenser is broken, though he thinks he's getting some residual seepage. It feels like he's got orange juice in his hair, his helmet misted, despite his labors, with a fine fog of orange juice. "I haven't had so much citrus in twenty years," he groans as the rover starts up, and begins its jostling ride across the surface. "I think that's what's giving us the you know what's."

"You guys are just going to insist on keeping the conversation in the gutter," sighs Houston. "Now what are you seeing up there? You have to help us out." The rover's high-gain antenna is malfunctioning, so the quality of the TV reception back on earth, Houston tells them, is disappointing.

As they've found on their first two EVAs, it's difficult to tell where they are. The features don't match the maps.

"I'm just continually surprised at how beat-up things are around here," Allen reports. "There're some really big, old subdued craters on the right that we don't even have mapped on our photo map."

"We copy," says Houston.

"I think that's Buster crater over there," Charlie says. Today's his turn to drive.

"Buster's only forty meters, this one's got a diameter of at least seventy-five," Allen tells him. "There're some boulders on the bottom, you can see them, they must be five meters across."

"Still no outcrops or bedrock," Charlie says. "Should we stop along here? I want to get a soil sample. Get some of this regolith layer."

"I'm reading 313 gammas on the magnetic field," Allen reports.

"I think that's a record," says Houston.

"The big surprise is that it's practically nothing but breccias, everywhere," Charlie says. "There's no volcanic here I can see anywhere. Zilch."

"We got a bunch of guys down here trying to rethink all this," Houston tells him. "You've made their life a lot more complicated."

"Anything I can do to be of help. This should be good for a dozen or so NSF grants."

Charlie's on his knees, cracking open a fist-sized rock. "I'm getting black clasts in a white matrix here," he says. "All this rock shows signs of having been metamorphosed by shock. I don't know what this is staring up at me, Houston, but I'm going to pick it up."

"Anything that stares at you, you better pick it up," Houston admonishes.

"It's crystal," Charlie says. "Feldspar probably."

"Well, bring it on back," Houston tells him.

Allen's known all along: when Charlie's good, he's really good. Nobody better for the job. Any unseemly antics come with the territory.

North Ray crater, when they reach it, is dominated by an enormous rock.

"We discovered it," Charlie says. "I think we get to name it. Go ahead, Al, you name it."

"House Rock," Allen says off the top of his head.

"House Rock it is," Charlie agrees. "You copy, Houston?"

"Roger. We've got a suggestion down here: maybe you could do a shadowed sample around there. See if we can get any volatiles that haven't been boiled off."

"I'll get that," Allen says. He kneels in the shadow of the rock—it really is as big as a house, though he wishes he'd managed to think up, on the spur of the moment, a better name. Well, House Rock it'll have to be, his deathless little contribution to selenography.

A moment of faintness comes over him. Stab of urgent pain, followed at once by a loose flow of diarrhea. He grimaces at the sudden onslaught. He'd known it would have to happen. Now he'll be wearing it all the way home.

"We've got a bio-med spike here," Houston reports. "Everything okay up there, Allen?"

"Whew," Allen says. "That orange juice has just about done me in. I feel better now."

Or worse. He's popped out in cold sweat, would love to wipe his brow but of course, in the confines of the suit, can't. Would love to wipe his burning butt as well.

"Fascinating, just fascinating," Charlie is saying. "This one is white clasts in a black matrix. I'd say we came to the right place for all the wrong reasons."

"That's what we're in it for," Houston comments.

On the ride back, they cut loose. The worst is behind them. All the way back to the Raptor, they're kids on recess. Whoo-ha, Charlie shouts. He's got the rover up to speed, eleven miles per hour.

"Slow down there, sailor," Houston reminds him.

"I read you," Charlie says. "I just wanted to see what she'd do. Tell the guys at Boeing they've done one fantastic job on this vehicle."

"Ditto," says Allen as he hangs on for dear life.

Leaving the moon is leaving some kind of home, as craters and ridges, alien three days ago and now familiar landmarks, recede into the larger, less familiar landscape of the moon seen from ten, twenty, sixty miles.

He's left behind a small cache of personal objects, mementoes for the million-year anniversary. Some stamps, trinkets for friends, a statuette given him by a Dutch sculptor: "The Fallen Astronaut. In Memory."

A photo of himself and Joan and Jonathan, circa 1967, shortly after Gemini. They'd driven to Ohio to visit his parents whom he hadn't seen, for various reasons, in years. In the photo the Cloud family stands, husband and wife and child, on the front steps of the old frame house where he grew up. The huge sycamores of the front lawn dapple them with shadow. Joan has her hair pulled back. She wears a simple blue shift that becomes her. Allen's got one arm proudly around her shoulder. In front of them, eleven-year-old Jonathan looks skeptically at the camera, as if he doesn't trust it. He's got his hands pushed down in the pockets of his jeans, the way Allen's always scolded him for doing. Shoulders back, he says, chest out: you'll ruin your posture.

"Manure's what ruins a pasture," Jonathan retorts. Then: "Please don't hit me, sir, please don't." As if Allen would ever do such a thing.

Putting his hands up to shield himself, grinning the whole time.

It was a joke.

Allen's not sure why this is his favorite picture of the three of them, there in the shade of the sycamores with his parents' house behind them.

Walt's smiling face in the hatchway greets their return to the Cormorant.

"Hey, you guys," he warns, "don't track up my clean carpet." They've radioed in to say they're filthy, the moon dust they can't seem to clear the cabin of. It bothers their breathing at night, makes them sneeze.

When they turn on the Cormorant's vacuum, it runs for two minutes and then quits on them.

Figures.

Nervous over the Cormorant's balky engine nozzle guidance control, Houston's decided to break them out of lunar orbit a day early. It means their final tasks on board the Raptor—transfer the two hundred or so earth pounds of lunar materials, the film canisters; prepare the ascent stage for jettisoning—have to move along more speedily than Allen would like.

The last to leave, he takes a quick, farewell look around. Old ship, he thinks, you served us well. We owe you one.

Then he closes and secures the hatch on the greatest chapter of his life. He feels it as a lump in his throat, a heavy door swinging shut. The uncoupling is undetectable, but there it floats, several hundred yards from them in more or less synchronous orbit, a golden, forlorn thing.

"Let her rip," says Houston, and Walt relays the signal that should fire the Raptor's small thrusters to send the empty spacecraft plunging into the moon. Seismic packages from four missions are waiting to register the shock waves of its impact.

But nothing happens.

"Onboard computer can't comply," Walt reports. For several minutes messages fly between the Cormorant and Houston as Allen keeps watch, out the small window, on the recalcitrant voyager. What the problem is gradually becomes clear. Allen reaches it a moment before either Houston or Walt. He groans aloud.

A circuit breaker he forgot to close when leaving for that last time.

"Well, boys," Houston says. The disappointment in that voice is palapable. "We shouldn't've broke you out of there so soon. Our fault entirely."

There's no specific information immediately available on how long the Raptor might stay in useless orbit around the moon. But with no atmospheric drag, Allen calculates, it could well be millennia.

When he gets back to earth, he thinks, he'd like to sleep as long.

A VIRUS

1969, that overcast Sunday afternoon in July when the Apollo 11 astronauts landed on the moon: I was seized by anxiety so intense it kept me rushing back and forth from the television set to the bathroom. I'd sit on the toilet and expel a jet of fiery liquid, wipe myself gingerly, then return, shaken, to the living room where the rest of my family kept vigil.

"Honey, you're so fidgety," my mother said. "Can't you keep still?"

"Upset stomach," I told her. "I must've eaten something that didn't agree with me."

"The canteloupe," she diagnosed. "It tasted off."

"Quiet," my father commanded. Hunched over, chin propped on fist, he watched the screen with grim attention.

I perched on the edge of the rocking chair, my heart pounding so fiercely I thought everyone in the room could hear. I wasn't sure exactly why. I'd been made to follow the space program for years; at school the science teachers dutifully wheeled out the television set for every launch, every splashdown. I'd felt nothing but the dull throb of headache from watching television in the daytime. But that afternoon was different. I was certain I was about to witness something terrible. What, exactly, I didn't know. But something terrible. I was sure of it.

Tension made my head spin: the room itself, in fact, was plummeting, free fall, toward the lunar surface. I hung on for dear life, counting silently down from twenty to touchdown, but every time I reached zero the lunar module was still descending, and so I'd begin again.

"Stayton, you're making all of us very nervous," my mother said, and touched the back of my rocking chair that I had unconsciously propelled into furious motion.

My bowels were about to explode again.

Three times I completed my silent countdown, till on the fourth try Neil Armstrong announced, not a quaver in his voice, "Tranquillity Base here. The Eagle has landed."

As if our house itself had come gently to rest on some alien surface, the Sea of Tranquillity itself, there was a moment of complete silence from all of us. Then a cheer went up from my brothers. My father stood, abruptly, and inexplicably stalked out of the room. As I rushed to the bathroom, fumbling to undo my trousers as I went, I could hear him slam the front door behind him.

When I came back, much relieved though painfully scalded, the moment had dissipated, but my father still hadn't returned. He paced the front yard—a trapped creature, it seemed, hemmed in by his own version of the invisible barrier. I watched from the window, agitated by such mysterious conduct. Later, at supper, he was moody and subdued. I sensed some great inner disappointment, though in whom, exactly, or what I couldn't say. But it was as if we had all, in some way, failed.

Since it was Sunday, we went down to the church for evening services.

My father spoke that night on the subject of Adam and Eve. Quietly he conjured the two of them in the garden, how terrific they were feeling, what a party they had going. Getting thoughtless, forgetting the rules that had been clearly and explicitly laid down by their stern but loving Father. More enthusiastically he told how, drunk on the wine sap of apples, they cavorted and frolicked, so proud, so pleased with themselves, and then right in the middle of that little party of theirs— suddenly my father burst into a deep, blustery voice, the voice of the Lord:"All right, you lunks. Lights on, everybody out. Adam, Eve: party's over." And with a jerk of his thumb he showed them the exit.

The congregation loved it. Because they hadn't witnessed my father stalking the yard that afternoon, they didn't understand. But I did. I understood exactly his troubling message, and felt vaguely ashamed of whatever illicit exhilaration had taken hold of me earlier. Like when the music suddenly is turned off, but for a few moments longer the couples go on dancing to silence.

That had been in 1969. By the spring of 1972, flying to the moon had become, if not routine, then at least no longer disruptive of ordinary life on earth. Time didn't stop when men made the descent to that almost mundane surface, and I probably wouldn't have bothered to watch had it not been for the chance, finally, to catch Jonathan's father.

For weeks I looked forward to the opportunity to glimpse this man about whom Jonathan practically never talked. It wasn't because he disliked his father, or was indifferent to him. Rather, I sensed some silence that had to be. That's how I put it to myself. There's something Jonathan, talkative to a fault, has to be silent about.

The newspaper talked of the "lunar window," that three- or four-day advantage when the Earth and the moon were in favorable alignment with one another for lift-off. But in my head I conflated it with those other windows of our voyeuring hour, as if this mission were a ten-day window of opportunity in which I would be able to spy out some truth about Jonathan by way of his father the astronaut.

I think, in those days, Jonathan held me in such a terror of myself that I simply had to look for clues that would explain the hold he had come to have over me. Only then could I break free—or surrender in good conscience, as the case might be.

I also think, though only in retrospect, that in some terribly complicated way I had conceived a crush on Jonathan's father—not the fact of his father so much as the idea of him—and that this crush had something, in some equally complicated way, to do with my feelings toward my own father.

At the time I wouldn't have comprehended any of that.

In the weeks before lift-off, Dr. Lennox embarked on a curious campaign to convince his students that men had never actually walked on the moon. He pointed out that the whole event of a moon landing could easily be staged by what he called the secular media. Was there any one of us, he asked, who could really say for certain that those pictures were coming back from the moon rather than a studio in Hollywood? He mentioned, darkly and impressively, that in the German language the word "Hollywood" meant "Hölle-Wut," the rage of hell.

"Think about it," he said. "It's all pretty clichéd when you start to consider the space program from an analytical point of view. Let's face it, these so-called rocket scientists aren't all that smart a bunch."

I looked over at Jonathan, but he sat composed and unreadable. He didn't even roll his eyes, as Dr. Lennox tended on occasion to make him do. It seemed impossible to me that no one in the school knew that Jonathan's father was about to walk on the moon. But apparently I was the only one who knew, and I wasn't always sure even I'd got Jonathan's story entirely straight. When I brought up the subject of the approaching lift-off, he'd shrug and say, "Yeah, there's always a clock running somewhere in the world." I consoled myself by admitting I couldn't imagine what he might be feeling.

The weekend before the flight, Jonathan confided to me, "I'm going to lie low for a few days, okay? I'm going to cool everything."

That was all he said, but I knew it meant he didn't want to see me.

I told myself not to feel rebuffed, but of course I did.

I kept up my own danger wake.

The three-man crew conducted banal interviews as they hurtled moonward. The only moment that caught me was Commander Cloud observing, "You look at Earth down there and you think, everybody I've ever known in my life, everybody I'm ever going to meet, they're all of them right there on something that looks the size of a half-dollar. And I can blot it out with my thumb." Two days later, ghostly-looking due to troubles with the high-gain antenna that was sending their TV signals back to Earth, Commander Cloud and mission specialist Charlie Sumner loped about on the lunar surface, knocked golf balls into the distance, took clumsy joyrides in the rover. They seemed at once wonderstruck and vaguely bored.

I couldn't get enough, though there was something tedious about the whole process. Tedium enlivened by the ever-present possibility of catastrophe. But catastrophe didn't strike. The astronauts folded up their experiments and, in a lift-off televised by the camera they left behind, headed back to the command module circling above. Afterward the camera showed the deserted site crisscrossed by footprints that would last a million years. Tossed by the thrust of takeoff, the flag leaned precariously, its stars and stripes frozen in a windless wind.

With splashdown I breathed a sigh of relief. Helicopters plucked the men from their floating capsule. They walked shakily across the deck of the U.S.S. *Ticonderoga* to the cheers and waiting microphones. Cameras focused closeup on a smiling, ill-shaven, leathery-faced man who made my heart stop.

It was the first clear sight of him I'd got, and I hadn't seen the blood connection clearly till that moment. Jonathan's delicate and loose-jointed beauty fleshed out into the full, military stature of a man. And yet what struck me was how fragile, how vulnerable all three of the astronauts appeared after their flight, completely at odds with the heroic task they'd just accomplished. It seemed impossible that these men who were being handled with such care—almost as if their ordeal had made them eerily unfit for human contact—could have stormed the heavens and gotten away with it.

Windswept at the microphone, bouyant and yet oddly regretful—was that possible?—Commander Cloud tersely thanked the carrier crew, the helicopter pilots, Mission Control back in Houston. "Terrific" seemed to be his favorite word. The flight, the lunar rover they'd tested, the view from the moon, the sense of homecoming he felt just now aboard the U.S.S. *Ticonderoga*. "Terrific to be back on terra firma," he said, "even if it's not quite firm under us yet."

So tight-lipped and correct. And I thought about Jonathan loping along the streets of Minerva at the voyeuring hour, testing the air with profligate and polysyllabic concoctions he'd gleaned who knew where.

This man who'd seen mysteries, who seemed both compromised and utterly untouched by them—I leaned close to watch him on the screen, thinking, I've seen mysteries too. I've known your son, I've been inside him. The thought made me flush with regret and desire and wonder, so that I shivered, icy lightning down my spine even as my brothers continued to parrot, from their perch on the sofa next to me, Dr. Lennox's assertion that the whole event had been faked.

What indeed was real? My whole life that year had been a complete sham, a deception I'd given myself over to so fully that I was no longer in any way distinguishable from it. Commander Cloud's repeated "terrific" was equally, it seemed, a sham. Like mine, a sham meant to cover the truth of some experience he couldn't begin to convey.

At school the day after the splashdown, Dr. Lennox was incensed that a quarantine of the astronauts had been deemed unnecessary. The other quarantines had turned up no evidence of alien virus, but Dr. Lennox fumed. "What if this alien virus is so alien they can't recognize it for a virus? What if it isn't detectable for months, or even years? Those astronauts could carry it around inside their bodies and infect half the planet before anybody caught on. And by then it'd be too late."

I remember that afternoon so clearly. I hadn't seen Jonathan all week, but with splashdown he was back in the classroom like clockwork, hearing out Dr. Lennox's inanities with cool indifference. When school was out I made my way to his house. Without a word he let me into the basement through the back door, and I remember I lay on the sofa in the basement while he sucked me off, and told him, as I ran my fingers through his hair now grown long and fine, all the other theories Dr. Lennox had propounded to us in the week of classes the boy with science in his blood had seen fit to miss.

How, if Dr. Lennox was right about the media, then we had nothing to fear from space diseases unless we were afraid of deadly alien viruses emanating from Hollywood.

THIS CHILD BORN OF WRECKAGE
AND FLAME

Today I've been accusing you of some kind of murder. This cold after-noon in late spring—dogwood and redbud light up the dark woods behind the house while clouds scud passionately across a slate-blue sky. I have peered out the back door to register astounding weather, this terrible sky that sends me scurrying back to the safety of indoors. Yet I have brought in with me the faintest whiff of spring, anarchic and bold, almost more than I can bear, and I'm accusing you of murder.

Do you remember Nora? Of course you do. *Oh yes, Nora,* you'd say. Nora with such a good head on her shoulders. Nora with those terrific legs. A fine woman. You actually said those things to me. Our closest friends, Nora and Chuck, those first years after we moved to Houston.

Was it Christmas 1965? Their living room with the silver artificial tree decorating the corner. All evening that tree held aloof from our enforced cheer, a disguised presence in our midst, and I drew comfort from it, however cold. I couldn't stop staring at that tree: it drew me out of the room and into some frigid place of far horizons where I could breathe. You seemed to think I was in one of my moods, which I sup-pose I was, because when Chuck hauled out the big band albums, tunes from our youth, and set them spinning on the hi-fi (you took both my hands and pulled me up from the sofa saying, Hon, let's dance) those melodies plunged me even deeper into melancholy. But we danced till breathless, laughing and giddy like the teenagers we'd been years before, living through the war years, the four of us now adults, wildly successful in ways we'd never have guessed, whooping it up the day after Christmas 1965 in that large, newly redecorated living room with the sectional sofa, the home entertainment center, the sliding glass door whose heavy pleated drapes banished the wintry night. You were flushed, excited—you always got that way toward the end of our social evenings, you loved them so much and were in a kind of panic that they were ending, and Chuck the same way, the two of you comically dancing together, frenetic, while Nora and I waited that one out, Nora refreshing everyone's drinks—Wild Turkey always the drink of choice at the Brittains'. You both knew what you would never tell us, how despite your unrelenting optimism into which, like everything else, you'd been assiduously trained, you knew how possible it was that each bit of carousal might well be your last, though you were denying it, you had to deny it. You were living it up because death in the form of that silver tree was watching, was watching. Was I wrong, then, to sit and stare? Because I knew it too; I also, in my way, lived with it. And Nora.

You proposed, I remember, a toast. Why could you never resist a toast? What odd emotion did that stir in you: some urge to commemorate what you already knew (but never would admit) was doomed? To our friendship, you said. Forever.

To our friendship forever, we all echoed. Beautifully liquor flushed, we had all moved into that golden parenthesis of euphoria that made life possible from terror to casual terror, and it was then that Nora burst into tears. I remember that so clearly. I had seen them coming, blind and inopportune, welling from some dark shaft sunk deep in her misery—only I'd thought they were to be my tears, that in the next instant I would be the one to break, but at the last moment those tears, deflected from me, found their surprised outlet in Nora. And I'd secretly thought I was the fragile one. Nora had never shown herself like that, and I realized why. It was simply too shocking. We were all shocked. You and Chuck cleared out, I remember—scared little boys, suddenly, and Chuck wanted you to look at a faulty dimmer switch in the dining room chandelier. I sat by Nora on the sofa, put my arm around her, said, Here sweetheart, what's wrong with you?—so deft and responsible, though I knew through the platitudes of our common script exactly what was wrong with her, I could peer over her shoulder at that silver artificial Christmas tree in the corner, convenient and modern—*I'm so tired of messing with live trees*, she'd said several weeks earlier, in that brittle, slightly nervous way of hers, when she picked it up at Sears. *Especially just the two of us*, she said, *and Chuck's never here*. . . .

Chuck's the sensible kind, I assured her, though in fact he'd been grousing to me on the very subject of that tree earlier in the evening as we two stood in the kitchen and listened to you and Nora laughing it up in the living room: good-natured as usual, but beneath all that ease the coals of resentment smouldered dully.

And I could feel as I held Nora, quieted her sobs, that tree casting its cold lunar light over the room, its death glitter, so pure and implacable it held us all, in our various ways, under its spell that evening, and I knew what a terrible mistake it had been, one of those little moves (only a purchase, after all) you think is unimportant but that alters everything, tips some invisible balance. None of us knew, at the time, exactly what balance had in fact been tipped—but we would find out.

Then you and Chuck ambled back into the living room, ready for a final refill on the Wild Turkey—*Honey, we should probably call it a night* because you were off to Seattle tomorrow—Nora's sobs banished as if they'd never been, and as far as you and Chuck were concerned they never *had* been. Like a good astronaut wife, I'd rendered them invisible by offering up only a small part of my soul.

Allen, we never talked about any of this.

You liked Nora. I even confess, at this far remove, to a pang or two of jealousy, though of course there was never the remotest likelihood. But they were never really your friends, Nora and Chuck, because I suspect no one has ever really been your friend. Only acquaintances, buddies, colleagues. But you never really had a friend, Allen, in all the years I've known you. You simply moved from one set of people to the next, and it served you well, no doubt, because you moved among people exactly like yourself, whose expectations were never any different. How could you have friends, when you knew all this—even life itself—was always so temporary? And yet every day you pretended it wasn't. You greeted whoever was currently on the scene with great heartiness, you drank all those toasts to eternal friendships (how many of them I've witnessed on sodden evenings), but how many of those people do you still know, Allen? Or did you ever know?

After the accident there was no place for her. Simple and irrevocable as that. We all knew it. She knew it clearest of all. I saw it in her face that afternoon she heard the news. Would I have managed so lucidly? After she moved to California, we never heard from her again except that she married an auto insurance agent in Bakersfield. As far removed from her former life as possible. *It all seems like some bad dream, and so faraway*, she wrote me. *Like something that never happened.*

Like none of us ever happened. That's what she meant, and her words haunted me. I never wrote back because I knew she was right. Like all of us she'd been entirely expendable, her place guaranteed only by the role she happened to be playing at the time and now there was no reason for Nora Brittain any longer.

She was not unproblematic. In other circumstances I might not even have liked her very much—though life, I've found, is never about other circumstances. Still, she was a friend. She should have remained, past grief and forgiveness, a friend. We had made a pact. We were secret allies in the face of the courageous future: she would watch through the night with me, I would watch through the night with her.

I don't forgive you, Allen, for Nora. Not you, or any of your cronies at NASA, the whole murdering crew of you. I say that and raise my glass in a toast years overdue. Here you are, dear Nora. Take this. You're finally getting back your own.

Some days I have the world inside my head. It rings in me like the clapper of an elephantine bronze bell. I sit awash in life on the living room sofa with my stack of *National Geographics* that I continue to receive through some whimsical dispensation since my subscription must certainly have lapsed years ago.

I doze off and dream, only it's far too vivid for any ordinary dreaming. I'm on a barge at twilight, sailing slowly along a broad canal of black water, and both shores of the canal are lined with ancient buildings, their sandstone stained gold by a last outburst of raging sun from the west. Basilicas with great domes, some collapsed, split open like pumpkins, some still intact. Broken arches, fluted columns flowering into ornate capitals, the long splendid line of an aqueduct linking two hills. Burnished mosaics visible on the facades of grandiose public buildings flaunt saints and sinners caught out in a rain of golden fire. Our barge has moved into a deep still pool, and in the center of this basin are

169

leaping sculpted bronze dolphins, whose mouths issue powerful jets of water. There are plazas along the shore, great paved areas utterly deserted of people. In fact there is no one in this city, it is a ghost capital of a vanished empire. With stately languor the barge moves past unbreached massive walls.

I have journeyed to Constantinople. It is all so clear in my head. So solemn and grand and still.

Other days I travel elsewhere, to the ruins of Angkor Wat; fortress cities high in the Himalayas; secret capitals where no westerner has ever ventured. I have watched festivals, cumbersome processional carts hauled through narrow streets, clangor of temple bells and the screech of monkeys. I have seen shaved saffron-robed monks, girls with tambourines and drums, a raving hairy yeti brought down from the high ranges in a wooden cage.

By day I read *National Geographic* and its merely colorful world is small and tawdry, no match for my vistas. Why should I ever leave this sofa, this bed, this house that sometimes, in the middle of the afternoon, leaves its moorings and begins its own astral or oceanic journey?

It is, I know, the fine madness of alcohol, its delirium and blue devils, its not inconsiderable raptures of the deep.

At night, still seated on the sofa or awake in my bed, I dream myself free of this house, wander the empty streets of this miserable, murdering town, drift down to the bus station, the bar there, TRAVELERS etched in neon, where I make myself available night after night—men take me home, abuse me for a few drinks, drive me in their cars to the banks of rivers and beat me senseless; I can feel the sharp points of their cowboy boots as they kick and kick, listless with a despair that is more than sexual and less than religious, till I lie bruised and battered, sand in my mouth.

I take another fine swallow of sweet, sweet bourbon, Tennessee sour mash.

I listen to my boys fucking in the basement, and do you know what, Allen? I join them down there. Never moving from my sofa or bed, I am there with them, Allen, some terrible afternoons I am that sweet skinny Baptist boy fucking our son. Conned into these monstrosities, I am in that room, willed there precisely in order to locate myself in Jonathan's joyful sobs, to register exactly the source of those ecstatic moans I have made myself come to know so hideously well.

To mortify myself.

I have even, Allen, been to the moon. You didn't see me there but I was there, standing in shadows, your silver moonwife watching over you the whole time. I arrived the instant you arrived, left the instant you left. Only a single thing surprised me. I realized, standing on that nearly featureless plain, that I had always been coming here.

Outside my bedroom window the limbs of a large sycamore beckon me nightly. In order to resist their call I have covered the windows with foil, but I find myself out in the night anyway, scaling that motley tree trunk past waist-thick boles and generous branchings, smaller and smaller capillaries of twig bleeding into thinner and thinner air. It's not as distant as it looks, the moon: as near, really, as a balloon caught against the ceiling. From my perch I can see the house, the neighborhood, the fields and woods beyond. I can see the streets leading to the business district, the court house and bus station, Highway 45 that leads out of town, where my parents met their fiery end so many years ago, that summer night of 1934 that is my earliest memory. They lifted me out untouched by the carnage, child born of wreckage and flame, though my parents were burned, like Gus and Ed and Roger in their capsule, beyond recognition.

Drunk driver, they said. Reeking of corn liquor, survived without a scratch. Speeding on the wrong side of the road. For years, I'm told, there was a commemorative white cross, though no more. And though I no longer drive, I've become that drunk driver.

But I'm tired of looking. I hoist myself up onto the moon's pale surface, a continuation, really, of the shedding bark of the sycamore. There are pebbles everywhere, each inscribed with a human face. I hold them in my palm like coins, their lips move incessantly as if they are speaking urgently to me, but on the moon there is no sound. I stuff my pockets full. In the morning when I wake my hands are skinned and bruised, my hair littered with leaves, twigs, moon dust. Somewhere in a drawer I must have secreted a trove of moon pebbles, each minted with a human likeness, that I add to each night.

Prodigious, battering thoughts.

She, on the other hand, got a crater on the moon named after her. Two weeks after you're back, and that's what I read in the newspapers. Crater Janine on the back side of the moon. It's nice to see what my reward would have been if I'd just hung on.

Well, Allen, I don't want a crater on the fucking back side of the moon named after me, thank you very much. I don't want my name commemorating some minor lunar catastrophe a million years old. I have my own life, after all, and it fits that bill quite nicely.

THE POLICE PAY A VISIT

With graduation came an enormous sense of relief. I've never hated myself more than during the final praise-laden weeks of my high school career. I won Best All-Around Student award, and Civic Leader. I went to the senior prom with Alice Todd, a sturdy, studious girl who, at graduation ceremony, was to play salutatorian to my valedictorian. My speech at that ceremony was, characteristically, all sham and sanctimonious lies, which didn't stop Dr. Lennox from loudly proclaiming it the best graduation speech ever given by a graduating senior at Minerva High. My father, clearly impressed, told me I had the makings of a man of God if I could put a little more fire under the kettle. I smiled in the afterglow, and shook hands, and felt like a desperado, never more so than when Jonathan, looking incredibly beautiful in his black graduation robe, came up to me with his mother in tow. It was the first time I'd ever seen her outside the spaceship-like confines of her house. Dull-eyed, shallow-skinned, the makeup she'd put on was, more than anything else, an act of desperation. She looked a mess.

Jonathan touched a finger to my cheek.

"What?" I said. It made me jump.

"Eyelash," he told me. "Got it."

I knew there was no eyelash.

"You have a very nice speaking voice," Mrs. Cloud complimented me. "Very firm and decisive."

173

"You should come with us," Jonathan said. "We're going to go have breakfast at the International House of Pancakes."

"It's eight o'clock in the evening," I observed.

"We decided," Mrs. Cloud explained, "that we wanted Belgian waffles to celebrate. What we really want to do is immigrate to some other country. Say Bulgaria, or Turkey. Pack a backpack, hop a plane, wander. We could go overland to India, take at least a year, maybe ten. Follow Alexander the Great. Maybe die out there."

"Hey Mom, you never mentioned any of this to me," Jonathan said.

"We'll talk, you and I," she told him. "But Stayton, you should come join us."

"I'm having dinner with my folks," I demurred, conscious that my family had been waiting patiently on the sidelines during our conversation.

"Come to a party with me later," Jonathan said insistently.

"I can't," I told him. Dinner with my folks was really a Praise Banquet at the church. Those of us who had graduated were being anointed for our commencement of the world.

"Midnight," he said. "Sidewalk in front of your house. I'll be waiting."

Then he and his mother, arm in arm, the strangest pair, were gone.

"Who was *that?*" my mother asked with distaste.

"He was my lab partner for a while," I explained, "in Dr. Lennox's class."

With that half-truth, the summer began. It opened up inside me like a well, and I could hear my words falling into it.

In September I'd be going off to college at the other end of the state: full scholarship at Billy Hightower Memorial Baptist College in the mountains of east Tennessee. With a pang I realized something was over, something that had seemed vast and endless and that I hadn't properly taken account of.

That night I escaped my house the old way. It was like going through the motions of an old crime, the way ghosts must. I'd felt so much safer having relinquished the Travelers months before; relieved that, whatever might happen to me, getting caught at that place was a fate I'd managed to evade.

Jonathan was waiting for me on the sidewalk, his mother's unmuffered Galaxy parked around the corner.

"If I have to wake up the street," he said, "at least it won't be your street."

"I shudder to think," I told him, "what dreams they're dreaming in my house right now."

What I couldn't know was that it was the last time I'd see Jonathan for thirteen years. He was wearing a blousy apricot-colored shirt, tight white jeans, black motorcycle boots. In the last several months his hair had grown long again, nearly as long as when I first glimpsed him. Silky and dark, it fell nearly past his shoulders. The mascara and lipstick he'd touched himself up with heightened his terrific girl/boy beauty in all the ways that could upset and excite me.

George's house as we approached was a bright roaring furnace of activity. Music blared; loud conversation. Squeals of delight stalked the night air. In back there was a pool into which large resistant bodies were apparently being thrown.

George at the door was florid with what I knew must be alcohol. I staggered back from his unexpected bear hug. He smelled overwhelmingly of cologne.

"Of course I remember you," he told me. "How would I ever forget dark eyes like that?" He turned to Jonathan and put his arm around him. "And how's my crazy little genie? Now you boys help yourself to anything that comes your way, flora or fauna or combination thereof. I have to go turn down that music. Aren't your eardrums splitting? I have neighbors, after all."

All the time a great space was opening up in my chest, a hollowness. There was nothing but men here, I noticed. It was a terrible mistake.

"Isn't it a trip?" Jonathan enthused. His face was lit with excitement, and I realized that, in some way, I'd never really seen him before, at least not in what I could grasp at once was really his element. He seemed to know everybody. Men put their arms around him, he bumped hips with them playfully, teasingly; with his finger he touched their cheeks.

"This is Stayton," he introduced me all around. "My best friend. We go back forever."

He kissed me on the cheek.

"Not forever," I said cautiously. Everyone regarded me with admiration, and all I could do was bask rather uneasily in their glow.

If Jonathan had turned to me at that moment, and confided in a low voice to play it cool, that this house he'd brought me to wasn't, in reality, George's at all but a secret beachhead of the Vegan Star Tyranny, a clandestine supernova house, I'd have absolutely believed him. About thirty men were there—mostly middle-aged, but also three or four of those mysterious kids from the Travelers whom I knew, in a sense, but had never spoken to.

I saw, with a feeling of profound unsurprise, of something like calm acceptance, that Kai Dempsey was also there. As if holding some kind of informal court, he sat on the arm of an armchair and conducted an elaborate monologue for the benefit of three listeners at his feet.

"So I turned to her and said, 'High heels and some foofy dress do not a drag queen make, my dear.' Well, she just looked at me, poor thing, and *bawled*. Right there in the middle of the Neptune Lounge. Imagine coming all that way just for that."

Seeing me, Kai shrieked. That's what it was—it came out, "Oww!" and he jumped up and ran to where I stood. I felt embarrassed but resolute. He hooked an arm around my waist and drew me to him. I tensed up at his touch but resisted the urge to flee. I willed myself to relax.

"I suspected," he said. "I just suspected. But it's always lovely to know." He looked from Jonathan to me, and back again, his mouth open in mock surprise. Then he laughed his odd laugh I knew from the few times in the practice room when I managed to say something he liked or, more frequently, when he himself said something he liked. "I can't believe she was keeping us a secret from each other," he told me.

"I didn't know," said Jonathan, one arm around me and the other around Kai. "Honestly I didn't. But I think it's perfect."

"What's going on?" George asked.

"It's the recognition scene," somebody explained.

All the time I was intoning silently to myself, in my head, in measured tones verging nonetheless on hysteria, This room is full of homosexuals. George is a homosexual. That man he's talking to is a homosexual. Kai Dempsey is a homosexual. Jonathan Cloud is a homosexual.

I'm a homosexual, I said to myself for the first time in my life.

"I thought you weren't coming," Jonathan was ribbing Kai.

"I keep changing my plans all the time," Kai explained. "One thing comes up, and then something else, and before you know it I have a million things on my calendar. And then something else comes along and I'm back to square one. So there. Life always presents me with so many options."

I marveled at how, in a room so full of white men, Kai looked completely at ease. He stood there in his red polo shirt and khaki trousers, one hand in his pocket, the other holding a drink. Freed to watch him in a way I'd never before dared, I said to myself, He has an expressive face. His arms, where they vanished into the short-sleeves of his shirt, were dark and lightly muscled. His forehead was high and gleaming, his hair in tight coils against his skull.

Then, in the confusing flux of the party, I lost him. I found myself with other men who were talking to me, asking me questions I tried to answer, then with still other men as if the party were a kaleidoscope shifting every few minutes into different relations, conversations, men standing in one room or another. Everyone was very friendly and kept offering me beers. I kept telling them I didn't drink. Never had alcohol seemed such a dangerous thing as now, in this room already rife with so much terrifying temptation.

In every conversation I could feel undercurrents, hints that I resolutely ignored.

"You're so serious," a balding man told me.

"Oh, that's him all right," said Kai, who in the latest kaleidoscopic shift had reappeared at my side. "You should see him with a horn to his lips."

"I'd like that," said the balding man, touching me just for an instant on my elbow. "Will I see you with a horn to your lips one day?"

I didn't know what to do. I was self-conscious in a way I'd never been before: conscious of being not only myself but something else, a thing. A homosexual. My mouth was full of that dire word as I wandered from room to room of George's house, alert to every wayward leer or wisp of conversation that filtered through the overlay of loud, loud music pummeling my brain—as if suddenly I'd been transported to the very insides of the Travelers' lighted jukebox.

In the kitchen the phone was ringing. A man dressed all in white picked it up. "I can't hear what you're saying," he said in a reedy voice. "I can't hear what you're saying," he repeated to whoever was on the other end, and he hung up. The phone rang again. He picked up the receiver and laid it on the kitchen counter and resumed his shouted

177

conversation with one of the Travelers kids, a slightly surly-looking type.

In the next room, suddenly quiet, the stereo turned abruptly down to normal volume, I found George again. "Doing okay?" he asked me. "Why?"

"I couldn't tell," he said. "You seem very shy." He wiped sweat off his forehead, even though the room was cool with air-conditioning. "I just can't drink when the weather's warm," he told me.

I'd never been in the presence of an adult homosexual before, and it both thrilled and unsettled me to think that, those weeks Jonathan and I had danced at the Travelers, the man behind the counter who served us up our Dr Peppers and watched us dance had been a homosexual.

I found I still liked him. Despite his mustache and fierce eyes there was something sweet, almost mothering about him. He had a hideous scar on his arm; it kept peeking out of his short-sleeved shirt.

"There goes that music again," he said. "I think that stereo has a mind of its own." And he was off to turn it down again.

In the next room, a bedroom, I could see with some alarm that several men sitting or sprawled on the bed were passing around a joint. I'd never seen a joint, but I knew that was what it was. I could smell its ropey scent. "Excuse me," I said, backing out of the room. One man held it out to me, but I shook my head and continued to retreat. I'd read that even being in a room with marijuana smoke could get you high.

I wondered, in fact, whether I was somehow high anyway.

I hadn't seen Jonathan, it seemed, for ages. I went looking for him, but there was no trace, and I started to worry that, for some reason, he'd gone home. I contemplated leaving myself, beginning the long—too long, I realized with a sinking heart—jog back from this house that was miles, it seemed, from anywhere.

Having exhausted the indoors, I wandered out onto the back deck. The music was still so loud I could hear it throb against my rib cage, tunes I'd first learned to dance to at the Travelers. Then abruptly the music disappeared again. "Aww," said a voice somewhere out in the dark backyard.

"You could hear that music on the fucking moon," said another voice, and there was laughter.

What replaced the music was a rise and fall of cicadas, slow undu-
lating waves of sound. I felt wonderfully free out in that night and
sudden silence. Breathing deep gulps of air, I strode down the length of
lawn that stretched from the house to a far line of trees.

Coming out of the dark, Jonathan's voice surprised me. "Who's that?"
he asked.

"It's me," I said.

"Latent Stayton," said Kai's voice. "Come on down here and join
us."

I'd almost stepped on them. They were lying, side by side, on their
backs in the grass.

I sat down next to them. The grass was wet from dew. "What're you
guys doing?"

"Jonathan has been telling me the most fabulous lies," Kai said. "Did
you know he's an encyclopedia of untruths?"

"Tell me about it," I said. The fact was, no one knew useless facts
the way Jonathan did. He had a kind of genius, I'd decided, for knowing
all the wrong things.

"What's he been on about this time?" I asked.

"He's been telling me," Kai went on, "and correct me, Jon doll, if
I'm wrong, that at this very moment we are all of us lying here exposed
beneath a gigantic meteor shower. A spring storm from outer space.
Isn't that glamorous?"

"The Eta Aquarids," Jonathan said. "A May swarm the Earth passes
through."

"Meteors," I said.

"Soon to be meteorites. Now lie down on your back. Get comfortable."

"Jonathan says you have to be very very quiet," Kai explained.

"Speculative," Jonathan admitted. "But I think it helps."

"You know all these things," I said.

"Science in the blood," he explained. "Now lie back and look."

The sky was enormous. We lay underneath it, overwhelmed. No one
could speak. Finally Jonathan said something.

"When I was a kid," he said, "I thought the sound of the cicadas
was the sound the stars made when they twinkled. I told my dad and
he laughed, he thought it was the funniest thing. I only told him after
I knew better."

And Jonathan himself laughed, a low private chuckle in his throat.

I watched the stars twinkle and listened to the cicadas, their alien sheen of sound. It occurred to me that I'd never in my life lain on my back and watched the stars. Simply stared with no end to my staring.

It occurred to me that I'd always been afraid to pay too close attention to anything.

The night swallowed me. All my staring fell and fell into its great gulping throat. I felt dizzy with the abyss of infinite dark above and below us.

"I feel," I said aloud, to steady myself, "like I'm falling straight up into the sky."

"Grab onto the grass like I'm doing," Kai suggested. "It's the only thing holding me back."

"Help," I said, "I'm starting to go. My grip's loosening."

Our voices were beacons in the dark to show one another we were still there.

"Shh!" Jonathan whispered. "You have to be quiet to look for meteors. There one went. Did you see it?"

A spit of light, gone almost before I'd caught it was there.

"Now we have to be completely quiet," Jonathan said. "Concentrate on one spot and wish for a meteor."

Almost instantly, in my quadrant of sky, another meteor flashed. As if in answer, music from the house blared once again—but only for an instant. Then the cicadas or twinkling stars. Still, something had made me shiver—the rising dew, the night air, the three of us lying there. The word *homosexual* was still in my mouth, huge and dark. I felt its strong black hands on me.

I thought about my parents, my brothers slumbering unaware of the whole secret life of us, the rest of us of whom I was now a part. The way we flared and subsided, like music that couldn't be bridled. An ecstasy akin to nausea rose inside me, a trembling.

Abruptly Kai sat up. "This damp," he announced, "is going to give me rheumatism. And I, for one, have to stay limber for a few more years at least."

"It's the tail end of the storm," Jonathan admitted. "Earlier in the month was better. Anyway, we should go back to the party. George'll think we started some vast sodomitical orgy without him, and will he be pissed."

"George," I said fiercely, "is a silly old queer." Kai helped me to my feet. I'd never clasped his big dry hand before.

"George," he corrected me, as you'd correct a child, "is an ancient galactic queen of the supreme order. So there."

Shouldering his way between us as we walked back up the lawn, Jonathan linked his arms through both of ours and pulled us tight, just for a few steps, as though we were a single striding creature glimpsed dimly by meteor light.

We'd just stepped inside the back door when, from the front of the house, there was something of a commotion. Someone was at the door, a couple of people, then I heard ring out through the house the single word, chilling and electric, "Cops!" and it was like a glass shattering: the room broke apart, people scurried out every available window and door while, in the distance but approaching quickly, I could hear sirens as all the dreaded police cars of my childhood converged on George's house.

CALENDAR OF STORMS

Spring ushered in by the lyrids.

May's Eta Aquarids and the Delta Aquarids of midsummer. August's Perseid storm and October's Orionids.

South Taurids with the Leonids close on their heels.

The Geminids and Ursids and Quadrantids of deepest winter.

When I'm nine or ten I make a calendar of meteors and have the crazy idea we'll live by it, Dad and Mom and me. Mom thinks it's a good idea—why not? she says—and I'm so excited to show it to Dad, I can't wait till he gets home. Time's ruined till then. I walk around the house clapping my hands. In my bedroom I play with myself for an hour at a time, lying on my bed with my hand down my pants squeezing and pulling and bothering. I'm too young for anything to happen; it's just something to *do* to ease the time.

The year divides into ten storms, some longer and some shorter. The big months are Quadrantids and Perseids and Geminids. Holiday months, when people can take off from work or school and lie out on their front lawns and watch for shooting stars the whole night long. There won't be any wars or crime then. People will live longer.

Sure as shooting, people say.

Sure as shooting stars.

I'm a genius and the Meteor Storm Calendar is my masterpiece.

I wait up for him late but I fall asleep before he gets home, and the next day I have to go to school before he's up. That afternoon when I get home—school's out early because of the snow—is the afternoon our neighbor next door gets killed in a plane crash, but I don't know that yet. When I get home there's nobody there. I walk all over the empty house feeling odd, like something's not right, and it's an hour or so before Mom comes over, looking all upset and teary, telling me what's wrong, and will I be all right by myself for a while because she needs to go back over next door. And after hours of television, when they do get home, I show Dad the calendar. His breath smells like whiskey. He takes the calendar and looks at it, and I can see that he can hardly hold it steady because his hands are shaking so much.

Or I'm twelve and for a couple of weeks I've had a hard knot in my right nipple. Sensitive and it won't go away, so I show it to Dad. When he presses lightly with his fingertips: Ow, I tell him. The next night the two of us take a walk around the neighborhood. A clear night in spring, all the stars out.

I talked to the doctor today, he tells me, and the doctor says it's not a thing to worry about. But it's probably a good time for us to have a little father and son talk.

I'm so happy to be walking around the block with Dad. Lights on in all the houses, curtains drawn, blinds closed, a feeling that we're making the rounds, the two of us, making sure everything's safe and sound, putting the neighborhood to bed.

It's that time in life, he says. Your body's starting to go through some changes. Hormones, things like that. It's called puberty. Have you studied any of this in school?

A little, I tell him. I'm becoming a man.

Exactly, he says. And that's why you have that little knot there. It's your glands changing. Like growing pains. The doctor says give it a month or two and it'll go away. There'll be other changes too. You'll start to grow body hair. Your voice'll get deeper.

He punches me lightly in the shoulder.

You'll go and get interested in girls, he says.

I feel, tonight, like I can talk to him about anything. It's great. It's what being an adult is going to be like. A man.

My penis, I say, using the correct word I've learned in health class. Sometimes it sticks up. And it stays that way.

Well, he says with sort of a laugh. I wouldn't worry too much about that. It's normal for boys your age. Just don't go playing with yourself. That's a nasty habit to get into.

We walk for a few minutes while I try to absorb what he's just told me.

Hey Dad, I say, because tonight we can say anything to each other. Why didn't you and Mom have more kids after me?

It's because of me, something I did. That's been my worry. Adults, I know, don't have worries like this. They ask each other questions and get answers.

Dad sighs. He pops his knuckles. Well, old buddy, he tells me, it's complicated. We did try.

I'm all scientific curiosity.

How *do* you try to have kids? I ask. I mean, two people. What do they do to have kids, exactly?

I can't see it, but I feel it. Dad goes tense. Some kind of drawing back.

All in good time, he tells me, all in good time. And he sighs again—I know that kind of sigh from Dad. It's when he thinks I'm being impossible.

I don't go down for the launch. I don't watch it on TV. I don't do anything for that whole week except stay inside with Mom while she smokes cigarettes and drinks up a storm. The old danger wake, this time with hurricane force winds. She holds together really well, considering. We hardly ever mention it. Once she says, day two of the mission. Well, I guess if something goes wrong, we'll be the last people on the planet to know.

But that's about it. We fix TV dinners and play Scrabble a lot. I spell words that she keeps calling me on, but I usually turn out to be right.

Occultation, I spell out. Sidereal. Halcyon. Gibbous.

Random words that occur to me.

There's a chance at Sagittarius, but proper nouns don't count.

I think about the constellations. Who first saw them, who named them. And one day will there be new ones? In a million years the sky will have rearranged itself, the old constellations won't make sense any more. I make new ones in my head. The Astronaut. The Drunk. The Boy.

The Lawnmower. The Masai.

For days that week I don't know what the weather's like outdoors. It feels too unsafe even to open the front door. Only if we huddle here very quietly will the danger wake pass us by.

For that whole week I don't see Stayton. He's so polite he stays away, which is the signal I sent and he's good that way. And I don't have sex or jerk off or do anything for that whole week. Hands off myself. It's my secret arrangement to bring him back to Earth safely.

Back to Earth. I say that and it sounds so odd to mean it literally like I do. Sometimes I think I could go outside and watch him climb the sky like a ladder, using all my favorite stars as handholds in the huge vertical cliff that goes to the moon. I imagine him in the arms of his silver star family. I imagine them singing together and swimming in the sea of serenity. I imagine him thinking about us, across the wide Missouri, and barely remembering who we are. Not even remembering our names.

I think about Janine and she's the one I feel sorry for. I talk to her on the phone when she calls but not this week. The phone rings and rings but this house isn't answering. We're underwater, out of range. There's our own dangerous passage down here we have to attend to.

It's strange how Janine confides in me, since I never confide anything back. But for months she doesn't notice. Too busy planning how to get me back to Houston. Back into the fold, as she says. And I come to realize the amazing thing, how she's got it in her head that I walked out on her and Dad. Left for some selfish reason Dad's been sparing her the details of.

So she keeps calling.

I don't tell her Dad threw me out. I don't remind her he never calls, not a single time, and this thing about me coming down to live with them in Houston, one big happy family, is Disneyland and nothing but.

If you have to have a family, I want to tell her, then go and have babies of your own.

Instead I don't say a word and when Dad calls the night before lift-off, first time in nine months, to say, Wish me well, old buddy—I won't talk to him. I hang up.

I can't believe he lets her think I stormed off and now she's the one who's got to coax me back. I just can't believe he does that.

It hurts.

It hurts a lot.

Lying out on the lawn in the tall grass that needs to be mowed: Hydra, I can see. Libra and Gemini to the south, Ursa Major and Minor to the north. Draco and Cepheus and Corona Borealis.

Boötes with Arcturus hanging bright, and Virgo with Spica and Leo anchored by Regulus. Perseus and Cassiopeia barely visible above the trees of the neighbor's yard.

Sky of early May.

Blue-skinned kid Krishna playing on his flute to draw the beautiful boy Radhu out by moonlight. And when Radhu comes into the forest clearing, all on fire with that melody, his thirty-three friends come with him, and with each of them thousands more boys from the village, all carrying flower garlands and musk and saffron, all singing and shouting. Krishna doesn't know what he's gone and gotten himself into. Drops his flute and his lotus flower in awe. Yellow robe slips right off his shoulders.

Shy Radhu offers him betel leaf to chew, and Krishna chews. Then Krishna takes the betel leaf out of his mouth and gives it back to Radhu to chew, all delicious and soggy with Krishna spit. Then witty Krishna does the eight kinds of intercourse with shy beautiful Radhu, kisses him the eight mysterious ways, and what he's doing to Radhu he's also doing with the different parts of his body to all the different parts of all the other boys' bodies, entering into every orifice and being entered. With nine hundred thousand boys he's nine hundred thousand blue-skinned Krishnas, on backs and bellies, messing their hair, ripping off their clothes, in their mouths and up their asses, every blessed combination and permutation, this cosmic storm of sound so loud it makes time lurch to a stop. The gods watching in heaven, elephant gods and monkey gods, shower down lotus blossoms, go faint with desire, and the saints shower down musk and the goddesses saffron and I love it that Krishna gives so much and gets it too. Nine hundred thousand times nine hundred thousand blurs in the moonlight and they're all happy, they're all laughing because each one of them gets Krishna and thinks he's the lucky one.

Makes me laugh.

Makes me laugh, too, when the cops swoop down on George's house like they're raiding a serious bomb factory when it's just a bunch of sissies with the music cranked up too loud. What else except laugh? It's completely bogus, noise or no noise. I know all that. I also know how for them it's serious stuff, but I don't know why that has to be. And it drives me crazy. It makes me really furious.

Of course Stayton freaks. Turns white as a corpse. It's the worse thing that could ever happen to him, and I don't see till right then how it's the worst thing. But watching them bundle him off to the squad car, I remember how scared he always is about everything but especially about cops.

It takes a while to get things sorted out.

Kai shrugs and says, Nice knowing you, girls. George's handsome face is so pent up and red it looks like he's going to explode, scars, tattoos and all.

Cop tells me to drive the Galaxy home and he'll follow. He wants to have a little talk with my mom. Remand me to her custody, as he puts it.

Cop car with no siren but its lights flashing behind me and poor Stayton in its backseat. I never think I'm going to get to be so crazy about him but one day I just am. No questions asked, I'm just there. That's what I'm thinking: how when I first meet him he's somebody I like to tease and mess with, so serious, but underneath he's just sparkling. It's there in his eyes, the kissable corners of his mouth. No dancing allowed in his church, but what a dancer he turns out to be.

Mom does herself proud keeping sober all day for graduation, which seems such a long time ago. She sits up there for me in the bleachers all by herself, stone cold sober. Cries her heart out.

She comes to the front door in her blue bathrobe, listens while the cop explains about the party, the noise. Routine noise ordinance violation, he calls it. How he's remanding me to her custody because I'm a minor—two months to go, so what difference does it make?—and that party was what he calls a doosie. Does she want to hear about it?

She looks at me the whole time he's talking. Sad, serious. When he's finished she says, Since when is it anybody's business what people do inside their own houses?

He mentions alcohol and drugs.

Not me, I say truthfully.

He has to admit I'm not stoned and I'm not drunk.

So what, then? Mom says.

She's watching me with, I swear, a twinkle in her eye. I'm awestruck. I think the cop can tell she has total contempt for him. What he stands for. But he's in a pretty good mood. Thinking the whole thing's sort of funny, and not taking either of us too seriously one way or the other.

You know this fellow George? he asks her, but she shakes her head.

He's certainly getting some reputation, he explains.

Mom says, Aren't we all?

I don't know you, lady, the cop says, but I can just imagine.

He's exasperated.

He says, Let me give both of you a little piece of advice. From an old hand at this, okay? George Mitropoulis is bad news. All those fellows. It's fun while the party lasts, but the party don't last forever, you know what I mean? If you have a minister, a family doctor—somebody professional you can do some serious talking with. You and your son both.

Please, let's get this over with, Mom says. Aren't there murderers or something you should be chasing out there?

The cop's a good sport. Slow night, he admits. Just think about what I'm telling you.

Goodnight, Mom says. Grabs me by the arm and hauls me inside. Then when she closes the door behind her, practically in his face: Well, she says to me, do you have something you need to talk to me about?

Well, I say, looking right back at her, not unless you have something you need to talk to *me* about.

That gets her. She just laughs out loud.

I hate those people, she says. I hate them, I hate them. They remind me of your father. Men in fucking uniforms.

I can see her point. We're both hilarious there for a minute or two.

What a pair, she says. What a fucking pair of birds we are. I don't know how we got ourselves into this mess.

Practice, I tell her. We work hard at it.

Like your father always said, I mean says: Practice makes perfect. Well how about this for perfect? Once upon a time, in a land that God forsook, there was this mother who was a lush and her son who was, well . . .

Well, whatever, I say.

And together they lived in a shoe . . .

Yes, I say, exactly, ruby pumps with retro rockets strapped to the sides . . .

And at night that shoe would *fly* through the universe . . .

Kicking ass, I shout.

Why not? she says. Then, looking more serious: What about Stayton?

His name from her mouth startles me.

He's going to catch hell with a capital H, I tell her.

That just makes me too crazy, she says.

Before I know it she flings open the door and is practically down the front steps. Blue housecoat sailing out behind her.

Mom, I say.

What? She stops, turns around.

What're you doing?

What does it look like?

I'm not sure, I tell her.

Well, come on, she says. He's *your* boyfriend, not mine.

She could punch me in the jaw for all the difference it makes. I'm so dizzy I just reel after her down to the car. Drives us down dark streets, exactly the route I took about three hours earlier when I went to pick up, as she puts it, my boyfriend.

You don't have to worry, Mom tells me. She lights a cigarette and talks to it so she won't have to look at me. I worked through all this. I've come to terms with it. I used to think it was something I did. I guess that's how I was trained to think about it. But then the more I thought about it, I decided that was just insulting to both you and to me. So there.

So there, I say.

Then, after about half a minute while I take things in, I say, Hey Mom, can I tell you something? Since we're talking here?

Anything, she says. Why not? The one day of the year I decide not to drink.

When I was little, I tell her—because right now I can tell her anything—I used to think the reason you didn't have any more kids was something I did. And when you went away to that hospital to try to hide.

She puts her hand on my neck and rubs. Oh honey, she tells me. That wasn't it at all. Not at all.

That's when we pull into Stayton's drive. The cop car's gone, but the instant I get out I can hear a roar coming through the open windows of the house. Roar as big as an elephant in frenzy, *National Geographic* style.

The front door's unlocked, Mom pushes her way right in. For once I'm just following along, no idea what's gotten into her, but it pleases me.

Don't take a step into this house, Mr. Voegli yells the instant we barge in. Standing in the middle of the living room and he fixes us in a really fierce stare. I can feel Mom falter. I'd falter too except she's the one taking the brunt of it.

You people go back where you came from right now, he orders us.

He's got a ridiculous-looking beard. Bloodshot eyes. His teeth are yellow.

Stayton stands cowering. Tears streaming down his face. I've never seen him cry. His dad's been holding him by the shoulders and shaking the living daylights out of him.

What are you doing to this boy? Mom says, but her voice goes all shaky.

I realize we two really must look the pair, especially Mom in her blue housecoat and hair like a banshee.

Mr. V. turns to face us full on. He's really raging. I don't know you, he says, from Adam.

Take a good look, Mom says, because as a matter of fact you do.

I look from him to her. She's flustered but has decided to stand her ground. There's a blaze in her eyes.

Please, Stayton tells us. Just go. You can't help. I got myself into this. I have to pay for it.

This *boy* here—Mr. V. flings his pointed finger my direction—*he* got you into it, and I'm going to pull you out of it, for the love of God, if it's the last thing I do.

The way he spits out *boy* is like nothing I've heard.

You're the one, Mom reminds him fiercely, who sold me that damn vacuum cleaner. Do you remember that? The body ash siphon, of all the shameless frauds.

I can see he does remember, vaguely, but he doesn't look ashamed in the least.

And I've used that vacuum cleaner, she continues, a royal piece of shit if ever there was one.

The filth in that house, he says, nothing could scour clean. But I can see you probably feel mightily at home there. It probably fits you both to a T. In fact, why don't you both scuttle on back to your dirt and filth and leave this Christian family alone.

This Christian family that's all there: Stayton's creepy brothers gloating and gawking at the top of the stairs; beaten-down Mrs. Voegli with prayerful hands and mumbling words over and over to herself.

That man should be against the law. But then I think, well, people like him *are* the law.

Now get out, he says, or I'm calling the police.

I can tell he's used this tactic before.

Mom doesn't budge. But she doesn't say anything either.

Stayton, I pipe up, come spend the night.

His brothers standing at the top of the stairs are eating all this up. I never knew all the stuff he was running from. And I think he's actually going to do it, come running to me, but Mr. V. accosts him. Grabs his arm and literally twists.

Let go, Stayton says—his voice a sharp, surprising command. I said let go, he repeats, though less firm. And Mr. V. literally flings him across the room. Stayton stumbles into a recliner and then sits down, all in a loose heap, on the floor.

You can't do that to somebody. It shocks us all. For a second there's not a sound. Nobody moves. Then one of his brothers giggles while Mrs. Voegli rushes over to Stayton to help him. But he's not letting her touch him. She's wringing her hands like I've never seen anybody actually do.

Please, you people, she pleads with us, just go away from here.

Suddenly I know—Mr. V.'s hit her too. At least he's threatened. He can't open his mouth without bullying somebody.

This is private property, he's saying. I am the master of this house, legally and spiritually and financially. Nobody can tell me how to run my own family.

Stayton, Mom says, you don't have to stay here one more instant. You know that, don't you?

He certainly does have to stay here, Mr. V. roars. You'll be cursed, he tells Stayton, turning his finger on him. If you make one move to walk out that door I'll see to it you're cursed with the curse of Ham.

Stayton looks stricken at that one. The man's clearly a psychopath. But I have to burst out laughing. I can't help it.

Mr. V. turns his laser beam on me. Vegan Star Tyranny all the way.

Look at him, he shouts (meaning me) to everybody in the room, but Mom in particular. Look at your son. Look at his hair, look at his clothes, woman. He's wearing . . . makeup. This *boy* is wearing makeup. And you think you deserve to be called a mother? You're a disgrace. You're an abomination of a mother, and he should be taken out of your hands like a loaded pistol. I intend to see to it, in fact. I intend to make telephone calls.

You're ridiculous, she tells him simply.

That may be, he comes back at her, but I'll say one thing to you. I'd rather be ridiculous in God's powerful order of things than lost like you are outside it. Now get out. Don't ever let me see you two flaunting yourselves around here again.

I see now's my chance.

Stayton, I call out. Get your pretty face over here.

What I wish I could tell him is—*Super Nova.*

Get out, Mr. V. roars. And you, he collars Stayton, lifts him up to his feet off the floor. Say it. Say what you have to say.

Stayton hesitates. I can tell his dad's hurting him, and not just physically. He's wincing like some abused orphan cat. I can see Mr. V.'s got a lot of secret ammunition, stuff that goes way back and deep, and that I can't know anything about.

I want to say, Go ahead and get it over with, Stayton. Whatever it is, go ahead and say it. It can't be that terrible.

Say it so there's no mistaking it, Mr. V. orders him.

Stayton looks at me with this look of pure agony. Jonathan, Jonathan, he says.

I don't know what he's going to say till he actually says it, the words out of his mouth.

Jonathan, he says very slowly, very clearly, though his voice is trembling something wild.

I renounce you forever, he says.

PART TWO

HOUSTON, 1990

There's the day Allen runs into Frank in line at the 7-Eleven. A Saturday morning in June. Frank's filled his Mustang with gas, Allen's buying eggs, bacon, orange juice because he's gotten it into his head to surprise Janine with breakfast on her birthday.

He hasn't noticed Frank in line, though he noticed the red Mustang. If he'd put two and two together, he might have headed off to another convenience store down the street. For the last several months he and Frank have been assiduously avoiding each other—as much as that's possible for two men who've been named co-defendants in a civil suit.

"I should tell you," Frank says, "I'm going to have those sycamores taken down. Damn nuisances. I should've done something twenty years ago when they were still halfway manageable. I got some fellows coming over. There might be some limbs falling on your property, but don't fret. I just wanted to warn you."

You might've warned me about the things that really mattered, Allen thinks. But his wounded honor won't let him say anything. He's been as correct with Frank as he can manage.

"When's this going to happen?" he asks casually. This isn't, he thinks, a necessary conversation. They could have nodded hello and been on their separate ways. They could have ignored each other.

"I think this weekend. You know that colored fellow Bill. On a different schedule from you or me. Always has been. Why I put up with him like I do, I have no idea."

"You've been saying that forever," Allen remarks, annoyed by mention of that name, though Frank can never have known anything. Whatever there might have been to know.

"Yeah," Frank says, "I guess I have."

He genuinely liked Frank once, he remembers. Now he feels nothing but a dull anger, a wincing shame. Irrationally, he hates even to be seen standing in line at the 7-Eleven with the guy, as if everyone will know their crime.

It was Frank's idea, though Allen can see now how all too willing he was, in the heady greed of the early eighties, to be talked into anything. Laid off in the August massacre of 1976, Frank didn't waste time. Within eight months he launched two separate companies and negotiated, through Grumman, a guidance-mechanisms deal with the Iranian Air Force so sweet even revolution couldn't erode it. After the Shah's overthrow, he continued to make trips to Teheran on behalf of Grumman—"not secret," he explained, "just very low-profile."

What he proposed to Allen in the summer of 1981 sounded simple enough: Allen would lend his name and credibility as an astronaut—an astronaut who walked on the moon, no less—to Frank's new company, InterTech. To all appearances, the venture was entirely aboveboard: develop the technology to monitor the devices used to prevent mechanical breakdowns aboard aircraft. A redundant safety feature, but they'd both learned from NASA that, when you're talking safety, redundancy is the only name of the game.

Frank had rounded up some forty investors, nearly two million dollars in all. For his modest share in the profits, Allen flew to various luncheons in Tucson, Denver, San Diego to talk up the project. He'd done the same countless times for NASA. There was nothing to think twice about, and once he'd done his bit he put the whole thing out of his head.

Ten years later came the lawsuit: seven investors from Arizona filing a civil suit charging fraud, intentional misrepresentation, breach of fiduciary duty. InterTech's promised technology somehow never got developed and Frank had funneled the money into other partnerships he controlled. And Allen, according to the lawsuit, had knowingly abetted him in the fraud.

Frank's explanation was straightforward. "I was trying to juggle too

196

many balls at once, and I dropped one. I'm sorry, guy, it had to land on you. Jesus I'm sorry."

Janine was furious. "You trusted him," she said. "And he broke that trust."

"Well," Allen told her. But he knew she was probably right.

"That's no friend," she went on. "And I hate to think how all those years you considered him one."

It unleashed something in her the likes of which he'd never seen. He hadn't thought her capable of such a sense of betrayal, and if he'd been inclined to forgive and forget, insofar as that was possible with a million dollar lawsuit hanging over his head, it was clear she wasn't going to let him. Frank and Sally had been her friends as well—it was, after all, by the side of their pool that Allen and Janine first met. It was in the depths of that blue water that they first made some kind of contact. She's swum, through the years, in that pool. It's why he never had one put in for her in their own backyard. But now she's given it up. Now she swims, when she swims, at a health club.

Deep down, he thinks: who hasn't been guilty, from time to time, of juggling too many balls? Who hasn't been unlucky? But surprised at the level of Janine's hurt, disappointed he can't find in himself a commensurate portion of rage, he's learned to emulate her response as best he can. He knows it's because he feels guilty—not about Frank's so-called betrayal, but other matters of his own he's kept secret all these years, his own little betrayals whose consequences, should they ever come to light, he greatly fears.

"I always liked those sycamore trees," Allen says absently. "Magnificent trees." What Frank has told him begins to sink in only now, as Frank hands bills to the cashier. "Ten on pump four," he sings out heartily, then, "See you around, Al."

"Wait," Allen tells him. He reaches out and grabs Frank's arm.

Frank looks surprised, even alarmed.

"Al," he says sharply.

It's Allen's turn to pay. There's a line behind him.

"Oh, never mind." He releases Frank from his grip.

"You're all right, aren't you? I mean, you look like you've seen a ghost."

Allen blushes, confused. "Maybe I did," he says. "Maybe I just did."

The eggs, the bacon, the carton of orange juice wait for him on the counter. He fumbles in his wallet for cash and watches uneasily as Frank climbs into his red Mustang and roars off in an early morning sunlight tinged, as so often these days, with the acrid hint of smog.

Who am I to judge? he's thought time and again. There are days when the episode of Fiona Root, now years in the past, still worries him like a loose tooth.

After the moon he spent five weeks in bed, an exhaustion both mental and physical. He could barely, in those weeks, lift a hand. Janine was wonderful, bringing soup and sandwiches to his bedside, pitchers of iced tea. Thinking he might enjoy the distraction, she wheeled the television set into the bedroom. But he wanted none of it. Drawn blinds, peace and quiet. His mind, he remembers, was only a blank.

NASA doctors could find nothing wrong. A touch of flu, they had diagnosed at first. Weightlessness makes the body susceptible; it does strange things to the immune system. Other astronauts had suffered, though it had hit Allen, all the doctors agreed, particularly hard. Post Lunar Depression, they half-jokingly named this species of pyschosomatics.

But it wasn't a joke. Allen's bowels, never in great shape, tormented him relentlessly: severe constipation lasting a week or longer, followed by bouts of lava-fierce diarrhea. These things tend to strike, the doctors told him, where you're most vulnerable. Interested, they poked his private parts, fed tubing into his orifices, pumped him full of noxious compounds.

If there was a bright side to his incapacitation, it lay in his forced abdication of his role as primary spokesman to the minor flurry of journalists who harried his hapless colleagues in the weeks after the flight.

"I can see who's the smart one here," Charlie told him over the phone. "Bailing out on us. What's this I hear about a hysterical pregnancy? Remember, the kid's half mine even if it looks like Satan."

"I don't feel up to kidding around," Allen told him with more listlessness than he perhaps actually felt.

He was relieved to be avoiding those endless, senseless interviews. Why couldn't reporters pool their questions—they always asked the same ones—and let them get it over with once and for all? What did it feel like to be standing on the moon? they asked. Did you have any special thoughts at the time? Did you sense eternity, the infinite? What is your opinion now of man's place in the cosmos?

It would disappoint you, he once told a reporter, if I could convey just how ordinary the whole thing was. You'd regret spending all that money on something so ordinary.

Most of the reporters, he'd discovered, regretted it already. They were a jaded, dismissive lot.

Which made him all the more surprised to find himself, one mild day in autumn after he was more or less fully recovered, giving permission over the telephone to an Irish reporter to come to his house and interview him. She was in America visiting relatives, and happened to be coming to Houston the next weekend.

Some dark lilt in her voice attracted him: he imagined a moody, vulnerable young woman with pretty features and long brown hair.

When he met her a week later at the front door—Janine had left for lunch with a friend—he was struck by how utterly mistaken he'd been. Fiona Root was intensely, even shockingly redheaded, an air of dishevelment made more so by her habit of heaping her hair up on the top of her head—idly, with one hand—as she talked. She wore unbecoming heavy-rimmed glasses. Her skin was peculiarly translucent.

The first thing she asked, after limply shaking his hand, was whether she could use his toilet. Why, he wondered—as he heard, quite distinctly, the sounds of vomiting—had he consented to this? But she reappeared, looking unperturbed by whatever had transpired in the bathroom, and seated herself on the sofa across from him.

"Do you mind," she asked, gesturing to the small machine she extracted from her large black handbag, "if I record this? Testing, one, two, three." She cleared her throat. "September 25, 1972. Interview with Allen Cloud, 1604 Culvert Lane, Houston, Texas. Here goes."

Again she cleared her throat. He remembered that she had vomited in his bathroom.

"One prominent newspaper," she said, "passed this judgment on your mission: quote, A scientific triumph, a mechanical boondoggle, unquote. And that seems to have become the standard line on the flight of the Raptor. Would you care to comment?"

It was everything he hated about the press—and in his own living room too.

"I would just like people to be aware," he said carefully, "of how monumentally difficult every single step in a project like this is. The number of things that can go wrong—I mean, mission-threatening details—is truly staggering. People don't appreciate that. All this carping about minor malfunctions, countdowns on hold. Your real miracle is that the countdown ever proceeds at all. Just to get the rocket off the ground—that's the miracle, and it's only the beginning. I don't think your ordinary person quite grasps that. And you could almost say it's our fault for making the job look so easy. When I say 'our,' I mean all the technicians and work crews and safety inspectors. We astronauts are just along for the ride. We're the ones who have the easy job, though we're also the ones who get all the credit."

"The human factor," Fiona said. "You don't give yourself enough credit. And yet"—her tone, for a moment reassuring, turned vaguely ominous—"many of the mistakes in this mission were directly attributable to human error. I could list them—"

"I'm well aware," he said.

"Well," she went on, "some critics are maintaining that unmanned missions could accomplish everything manned missions do, even more—and at a fraction of the cost and none of the risk."

NASA had coached him well. "I can't begin to stress," he said mildly, "the terrific importance of having human beings on the spot. Hands-on experience. Somebody once said, some famous philosopher or other, that if Time's the fourth dimension, then the fifth dimension is Consciousness. I really believe that, and that's why there's just no substitute, never will be, for men to actually and physically walk on the surface of the moon."

"And women too, I presume."

"Women too, God bless them. Kick up dust and pick up rocks, and if they go tripping over some power cable, well so be it. Consciousness, perception. The fifth dimension."

He'd risen, he felt, to the occasion.

"Come fly away," she laughed, "in my beautiful balloon."

He didn't get it.

"You're certainly very passionate about all this," she observed.

"Well, in fact, I am. And people who try to call this into question—it's my whole life they're trying to call into question. My buddies' lives. Guys who died so we could do what we do."

What he said next surprised him.

"Astronauts don't go around calling reporters' lives into question, I might add. Though what they do for a living is certainly questionable."

Perhaps it was the enforced inaction of his long recuperation that fired him up. He stood back from himself and took a good look as he sparred, head on, with this feisty Irish woman. He was being testy, out of line, and yet he found himself enjoying this give and take. There was intelligent life here.

For her part, Fiona remained unfazed; she met him feint for feint—rare in the women he'd known. But he liked it. And her Irishness added to the charm. He'd never been to Ireland, but had always had an idea of the place—solitary vales and desolate bogs, mournful music in touch with something far back, something lurking and primeval. Some far distant time lying close to the surface.

It was almost a vision, so intensely did it come to him as he watched her there on the sofa, heard the mysterious cadences of her speech, the hard questions she drove home. Because now she was asking, shifting gears and catching him off guard, "Is it true that around NASA you and your crew were known as the Partynauts?"

She'd been talking, he could tell, to Charlie. Partynauts. One of Charlie's unflattering sobriquets for the three of them back in the early days of training for the mission—and all because of some raucous nights on the Cape when Allen had found himself caught in the hell between marriages. Thankfully it was a phrase that fell out of use early on, superceded by Charlie's Venerable Chinese Astronaut schtick. Had Charlie, Allen wondered, told Fiona about that as well?

He found himself saying, defensively, "I've been known to have a good time. We astronauts in general are known for living with gusto. It comes with the job."

She looked at him wryly.

"I understand there's a powerful lot of drinking goes on."

There *was* a lot of drinking, to be honest, though NASA had always warned them to play it down if anybody should ask.

"No more than's healthy," he ventured cautiously. "But then"—he turned sly—"I expect you people should know about that. Your readers, I mean."

He thought she might take it up—tit for tat—but she didn't. Instead she shifted ground once more to ask, "So, Allen Cloud, what do you worry about the most? From your mission. What still bothers you, wakes you up at night?"

Yet again she'd surprised him. Before he realized it, he was answering more frankly than he'd intended. He told her, "It's not something that happened on the moon per se. Something before. When they told us . . . When the flight doctor . . . See, all the moon missions up to that point, when they got back to Earth, they had to undergo a three-week quarantine."

"I know about the quarantines," she said briskly. "And for your mission they ended them."

"Yes," he said. "And what the flight doctor told us when they decided to forgo the quarantine was that on the previous flights they hadn't found any evidence of any life forms."

He wasn't sure whether he should go on. Surely the information wasn't classified or anything like that. The doctor mentioned it so casually, and that very offhandedness was part of what he remembered.

"Well." Unconsciously he rubbed his thumb with his forefinger. "Actually there *were* life forms brought back. Nothing, really. Just the camera the Apollo 12 team retrieved from the Surveyor. But they found microorganisms inside. Nothing alien, just Earth contamination that survived inside that camera on the moon for quite some time. That's all."

"And you're saying . . ." she probed.

"I just think about it, is all. I don't know why. I'm not sure 'worry' is the right word."

He hadn't told anyone this—not Janine, not any other reporter. But Fiona didn't seem particularly interested.

"Anything while you were actually on the moon?" she asked. "Some thought or emotion you had?"

He knew that, in some indefinable way, he'd bested her. He'd lobbed his bombshell and it exploded without her noticing. But he'd done his duty—the thing got said, off his chest. The press, namely Fiona Root, could make of it what they will.

He was tempted to go on and tell his lunar dream, but decided not to. A new emotion had invaded him—pungent and inexplicable, and yet, he realized, present in some shadow form in their colloquy all along. He resented Fiona's questions, her smugly businesslike air. He didn't like her at all, and now he found himself ferociously attracted.

His postlunar depression had extended to things sexual. That strange dream by Earthlight, his secret ejaculation: it drained him of something. His one or two abortive couplings with Janine since had left him too pent up and baffled to want to repeat them.

He could count on the fingers of one hand his infidelities down through the years, all pointless and minor, all within his marriage to Joan and having, he was quite sure, no identifiable consequences whatsoever. She never knew, never had any reason to suspect. Don't start now, he thought, with Janine. But this curious desire overwhelmed him. How, he wondered, did you go about seducing a reporter who was skeptical, as far as he could tell, of every single thing about him?

He decided to try to turn the tables.

"Can I ask you," he said, adopting her tactic of abruptness, "just why you wanted to do this interview in the first place?"

He'd surprised her, so he went on.

"To be frank, you don't seem to care about any of this stuff whatsoever, unless you can tear it down. I think you wanted to show me up for some kind of fool," he concluded fiercely. He'd never tried anything like this, and he was suddenly pleased with himself.

But she had her own store of surprises. "At least we're getting somewhere now," she told him point-blank.

All at once the room was sheer awkwardness. He'd already made the quick, forlorn calculation: Janine wouldn't be back for a couple of hours. It was his mission, as he saw it, to subdue this agent of the skeptical press. Win her over.

From here on out was all uncharted territory. He cast about wildly. "You know," he told her, "I think you're a very impressive young woman. I think you're better than coming here to make a fool of me. I think you're fascinated, quite frankly, by these things you don't understand."

She asked simply, "Are you coming on to me?" looking at him with that clear, unafraid stare he remarked from the first.

He felt sick, giddy, awful. In answer, he glided from his seat to the spot on the sofa beside her. This is power, he told himself. Pure and available and brutal.

She didn't resist. The force of their kiss dislodged her glasses from her nose.

"Oops," he said, then, "Oh my God."

"What?" she asked.

"Hot mike," he said, reaching over to the coffee table to shut off the tape recorder.

"Don't worry," she assured him, her hands everywhere. "I'll erase it all later. None of this will ever have happened."

Later. But now was now. He took her by the hand and led her upstairs. He didn't know why, but it was to Jonathan's bedroom he found himself taking her. That room he never went in.

It was no longer the mess it used to be. Jonathan had carted away most of his more egregious paraphernalia when he left last summer. But the room remained some kind of hazard anyway. Michelangelo's *David* with its obscene crotch continued to leer from the wall. Black sheets still covered the bed.

Fiona hardly gave him time to think, however, before she was on him, wild and loud and hell-bent, he thought in a panic, on consuming him utterly.

Before he fully knew what he'd gotten himself into, though, it was mercifully over.

"Wham bam," she said in that odd, slightly mocking tone of hers, "thank you ma'am."

He lay supine on the bed, stunned, while she padded naked and shameless down the hall to the bathroom, returned briskly to dress, collect her things. "I've exhausted you," she told him matter-of-factly. There was a note of satisfaction in her voice that chilled him. "Don't get up," she commanded, and he didn't. He lay there, hands behind his head, staring at the lips and tongue of David's crotch. He willed her to vanish. Which, in fact, she did. The front door slamming shook the whole house. Then the sound of her rented car in the drive.

He realized he'd utterly forgotten to confiscate that tape of hers before she left.

When he pulls his Towncar into the driveway, he realizes with annoyance that he can't remember a single thing about the drive he's just made from the 7-Eleven. He's gotten like this recently. Careful, he warns himself, you'll end up like Charlie, who wrapped his TransAm around a tree and didn't walk away.

He scares himself sometimes.

Janine's not up: she loves to sleep late on the weekends. She loves, in fact, to sleep period. Her favorite thing about life, she told him once. He thinks it odd, but what can you do? His own sleep has been fitful these past few years. Often he'll spend half the night sitting up in his recliner in the den, or at the kitchen table looking out the window at the slow, slow progress of the night. His doctor's diagnosed a spastic colon, but even when his insides are calm, he still can't sleep.

He fries bacon in the big iron skillet, scrambles eggs with a bit of tarragon and some Swiss cheese. Janine's fifty-two today—hard to believe they'll have been married, come October, nineteen years. Hard to believe the things they've survived. Or, more precisely, hard to believe the threatening things that never, miraculously, came to pass. Fiona Root's incriminating tape that disappeared without a trace. He's expected it to surface, but each year that passes he worries less. Only today, for some reason, he's thought of Fiona.

Couplings and uncouplings. It's seeing Frank that's unsettled him. Or it's not Frank. It's something else—elusive, vaporous—that worries him as he raps lightly on Janine's door, walks in bearing breakfast on a tray and singing "Happy Birthday."

"Oh," she says, sitting up and rubbing her eyes, gazing upon the eggs, the bacon, the butter-drenched toast. "You've made me heart-attack food for my birthday."

"Well," he considers.

"But I love it. Did you make yourself some? It's nice outside, isn't it? Can't we sit on the terrace?"

"The terrace it is," he tells her. "At your service."

"I'll be out," she says, "in a minute. Just let me throw something on."

He wonders whether, instead of breakfast, he should have slipped into bed beside her. Made gentle love like they never do anymore. But it's not something he's thought of till now, ambling outdoors onto the terrace, setting around plates, glasses, napkins. Sex, he's decided, just makes things tense. They're better off without it. He's nearing sixty, after all. The system's beginning to slow down.

"This is terrific," Janine tells him. It's a word she never used to use when he first knew her. She's tied her hair up, put on a magenta bathrobe and fuzzy blue slippers. "I can't believe you actually remembered."

He has, after all, forgotten more times than not.

205

"I'm getting better in my old age," he teases. And he's almost forgotten—"Wait," he tells her, and shuffles indoors to get her present. *Some guys get the wife lingerie, for Christ's sake*, he can hear Charlie's ghost exclaim. Well, people get peculiar as they last with each other. Various compromises, accommodations. This marriage hasn't been a bad thing, after all.

"How'd you know?" she says when he hands it over.

"You told me, remember? A couple months ago. I didn't wrap it."

She hefts the thing—he loves the way pleasure shows in her eyes. She can't hide it.

A long-bladed poacher's spade from Smith & Hawkin. Inveterate gardener these days, Janine's transformed the soothing lawn into a confusion of shrubs and flowerbeds. The less they connect in bed, the more time she spends with her hands in the dirt. Poor Joan, Allen thinks, wouldn't recognize the place anymore. Nor would Jonathan, his room long ago remodeled into a cheery, perfectly harmonious guest bedroom. It laid to rest, and for good, the fantasy that he might one day be coaxed to join them in some ersatz family.

Other memories, of course, it laid to uneasy rest as well.

Janine's testing her new tool. "I can take up those hostas now," she says. "Divide them like they should be."

"Have breakfast first," Allen tells her, picking up the orange juice carton to pour into glasses. But midway through the motion he stops.

He's looking right at them. Immense, majestic, they cast dappled morning shade all across the lawn. He has to crane his head to see their tops against the hazy sky.

Companions of lo these many nights and years. Whispering confidantes. Fellow voyagers.

"Allen?" Janine says. She steps in front of him, waves a hand across his field of vision. "Earth to Allen."

Those sycamores.

TEMPUS FUGIT

The day before I was to leave Minerva for east Tennessee and college, I'd walked by Jonathan's house. It was the first time I'd dared. The grass had been newly mowed, the unkempt bushes hacked from around the foundation, aluminum foil removed from the windows. A FOR SALE sign had sprouted in the front lawn. Jonathan and his mother had simply vanished—and just as well, I thought. The austere purity that had commenced in my soul that summer was deeply satisfying to me, and now that two months had passed I could even convince myself that the various humiliations I'd undergone in the weeks after George's party had been entirely worthwhile if they had indeed cleared my head of all that miasma I had been wandering lost in for the previous nine months.

There was the trip to the family doctor, who examined me, especially my genitals, poking and prodding with what seemed excessive zeal. My father stood, arms crossed, and watched the whole procedure. Dr. Percy bent me over the metal table, put on a plastic glove and pushed his finger up inside me. "Oof," I said as he probed. He'd managed to hit a spot that made my penis go erect despite everything I could do to control it.

My father just stared at me—furious, I suppose, with my body for betraying me the way it did.

While I got dressed, Dr. Perry washed his hands thoroughly, for what seemed like minutes. Then he dried them just as thoroughly. Turning around to face us, he said to me, "Son, did you know you've gone and gotten yourself a dose of gonorrhea? You must've noticed *something*."

If I had had any lingering doubts about my renunciation of Jonathan, those chilling words finished them off. I'd steadfastly ignored the deep sting I'd felt the past few weeks whenever I urinated.

"Can you cure him?" asked my father.

"No problem. Though it'll smart a bit. You'll be a lot more careful in the future, I can guarantee that."

"Your mother," my father told me sternly, "doesn't ever need to know."

As if I were about to tell her. She'd taken to her bedroom and refused to come out. "I just wish," she'd called out that terrible night, "that I'd never been born. That I'd never gone and brought you into the world. How could I have done such a thing?"

I saw something about my mother just then—how she had turned the guilt from me to herself. "Cunning" was the only word I had to describe it, and in retrospect I realize that it was in that instant that I turned against my mother forever.

And then there was George, whom I read about in the papers with the moral equivalent of averted eyes. I felt no pity for him, only a kind of awe at what had happened, what the headlines reported, and a terror that, if I looked too closely, I'd be able to detect my own terrible complicity somewhere in all this.

How I survived that summer I'm still not sure—I suppose by putting my head down against the storm and, like any dumb beast, simply outlasting it. But I knew I could never be the same; my relations both with my family and myself had changed irrevocably. I'd fallen, in full view of everyone, and the stain would always be there. The only solution was to put as much distance between myself and the scene of my fall as possible.

About my four years at Hightower Memorial Baptist College I have little to say, except that I excelled there in all the odious ways I'd excelled in high school, minus the compromising subterfuges. I gloried in my chastity, my scrupulous devotion to my studies. I kept myself apart from everything, and secretly despised my teachers and fellow students alike for continually failing to live up to the stratospheric standards to which I held myself. They rewarded me with their unstinting admiration. For what little it was worth, I was Hightower's star scholar, and in the spring of my senior year I was sent to represent the school at a collegiate evangelical conference in Virginia Beach.

To keep down expenses, delegates were expected to share hotel rooms. My roommate introduced himself as Larry from Bob Jones University. He sat on one of the room's two double beds and chatted with me while I unpacked my suitcase, some story about his bus trip up from South Carolina. Meaningless chatter, in the midst of which, without missing a beat, he said, "Maybe we should just hop in the sack together right now." I couldn't believe what I'd heard, but the look he gave me made it clear I wasn't hallucinating. I felt such a surge of sick terror that I could hardly even speak.

"You've got a strange sense of humor," I managed to tell him. He only smiled, got up, and went out onto the balcony to watch the ocean. There has to be some misunderstanding here, I told myself furiously, there has to be.

For his part Larry pretended nothing had happened, and perhaps nothing *had* happened. We went off to that evening's dinner and keynote address and fellowship hour, and when we got back to the room nothing at all was amiss. While he was in the bathroom I slipped under the covers of my bed and made as if to be sound asleep. But of course I couldn't sleep. I lay wide awake, vigilant lest he should try something, hoping that he would, praying that he wouldn't, and the whole time thinking, thinking, thinking. It had been nearly four years since I'd last seen Jonathan, and except for the occasional dream in which he figured prominently, and from which I would wake feeling sticky and devastated, I made myself never consciously think either of him or the abyss he represented, whose awful pleasures I had tasted with such avidity.

All day at the conference I found myself watching Larry. I hated him, the way he smiled, his musical voice, the flutter of his hands. All the ways in which he served to remind me of that figure I thought I'd banished for good.

I remember the dessert that evening was red Jell-O, and I watched him spoon shivering cubes of it into his mouth. Repulsed and sick with desire, I couldn't stop watching him.

That night I again got myself protectively to bed while he was washing up in the bathroom. When he came out, he was naked. He simply walked over to my bed, lifted up the covers, and slipped in beside me.

"You need a bunch of good loving," he whispered in my ear. There was nothing to it. His warm body pressed up against me while, under the covers, I ran my hands all over him.

I'd told myself earlier, ominously, as I watched him eat his Jell-O, I could have you for nothing but the price of my soul. At the time I'd shivered with nausea, only to find myself, a scant two hours later, paying the price gladly, with such fantastic relief. Paying it again and again through that long night. I returned to Hightower devastated, to spend what remained of my final semester in prayer, loathing, and various forms of futile expiation.

I suppose it's never any surprise that a sham, when it falls apart, falls apart so quickly and thoroughly. Shortly before graduating I announced, to the consternation of my parents and teachers alike, that I had decided to postpone the calling as a missionary to darkest Africa that had seemed so evident for the last couple of years, and instead to move to Washington, D.C.

Why Washington? everyone asked. I had no reason. Larry had grown up there, though that was no reason, since I couldn't imagine the circumstances in which I'd ever try to get in touch. And sometime during that delirious night of ours, he'd mentioned D.C. had a "scene," but that was hardly a reason either.

"Eventually," I lied reassuringly to myself and everyone else I knew, "I'll accept Christ's mission for my life. I'm as sure of that as the day is long. But right now I need to do battle with the secular world. I need to test my strength and confirm my faith."

Put that way, they could hardly refuse. Armed with cautions of every kind, I threw myself headlong into that city of secular temptation.

It was nearly two years before I ventured into my first gay bar. Such was the depth of my terror. To my utter astonishment, within an hour I had let myself be picked up by a long-haired boy from Pittsburgh who took me back to his dormitory at George Washington University for a night of unforgettable initiations. The next morning, as I made my way home, I felt not terror, as I'd expected, but delight and relief. I examined myself, all the next week, for signs of panic, but there were none at all. The only regret I felt was in recognizing, once and for all, how susceptible I'd always been to self-deception, how I'd wasted so many years fastidiously constructing a self only to have it crumble out from under me—if not at the slightest provocation, then at least with a minimum of promptings.

It was a lesson, I told myself, I'd make sure never to forget. Whatever happened.

I saw that boy several more times, and then we both moved on, easily, without recrimination. He introduced me to his friends, who introduced me to their friends, and before I knew it I was deep in the world I'd always wanted to be a part of.

Then one sultry summer night in 1981 I was sitting with friends in a cramped, crowded Ethiopian restaurant in Adams-Morgan. We were admiring the high, aristocratic cheekbones and clean lines of our waiter when I heard, from a nearby table and clearly aimed at us, the exclamation "Yeow!"

It was a sound that made my heart stop.

I looked up. A figure was rising, moving toward us.

"I don't believe my eyes!" he said. "Tell me I'm dreaming. Tell me they put hallucinogens in the chicken ethiope."

For an instant I considered denial, or even flight, but then as I stood up to meet him I said, with surprising calm, "Kai Dempsey."

That I remembered him so easily shows how little, despite everything, I'd really forgotten.

"Latent Stayton," he said. He'd moved on impulse but now seemed unsure quite what to do next. All the complications of the past surged into view.

"Not so latent anymore," I confessed with a smile.

He eyed my companions appreciatively—a Georgetown law student named Robert with whom I'd been carrying on a bit in recent weeks, and Denzel, co-worker at Lambda Rising and frequent companion in exploring the city's sordid and opulent nightlife.

"Join us," I invited Kai.

"First, a hug," he said. "A kiss."

I'd never hugged or kissed him, except in dreams. We embraced long and hard, I breathed in his rich scent of sweat and cologne, as he kissed me first on one cheek, then on the other, and finally full on the lips. I'd never been held like that, and I think I must have sighed audibly with the pleasure, the surrender of it.

"Such a long time," Kai said, "and no see. No nothing. What on earth are you doing with yourself these days? And don't tell me you live in this swamp town too? We can't begin to catch up like this. Besides, I have to return to my retinue. Professional obligations." He gestured in the direction of three somewhat staid-looking white people. "Wind jocks," he whispered, "talking trade. Mouthpieces and valve oil. But we should really see each other, you and me: we have hours of chatting to do. I have antique postcards of Minerva I can show you."

"I'd like that," I told him as we exchanged phone numbers.

"Stayton Voegli," he shook his head in parting. "It just does my heart good to see."

"Well," said Robert once Kai had returned to his table. "Impressive. You never cease to surprise."

"A long story," I told them. "My fetid Tennessee past."

"Which you never divulge one iota to hungry gossips. We should get that big beautiful girl over here and do a little interrogating."

"He was my French horn teacher," I said, "when I was in high school."

"That, certainly, must have been fun. He's welcome to play *my* horn any day."

"Oh you," I said, tapping Robert's shoulder.

"Stayton in high school," Denzel sighed. He was five years younger than either me or Robert. "That was back before they invented gay, wasn't it?"

What I had liked about Washington, from the beginning, was the clean break it afforded. Minerva, Hightower: I'd laid both those ghosts to rest. Still, I wasn't alarmed by this intrusion of the past. Better Minerva than Hightower I thought later, when I excused myself from Robert and Denzel's foray to a drag show at Tracks in order to take a long solitary walk along the Potomac before heading home. I remember that stroll so well: how thrilled I was, an inexplicable buoyancy that promised to float me right over the rooftops. I hadn't thought of Kai since that party at George's; along with everything else that was too painful, I'd put him completely out of my mind. Now I remembered the surprise I'd felt when I saw him in George's living room, that moment when it clicked in my head—oh, so Kai Dempsey's gay too. My French horn teacher. Of course, of course. And now to meet him again was nothing less than redemption. Kai of the chocolate skin and sweet high horn notes. Kai who had made me squirm all those afternoons with the terrible suspicion that he was somehow able to see right through me. Kai whom I'd dreamed of, who'd made me come in my dreams, and whose image when I woke had stirred such a sense of taboo and shame.

I felt, that beautiful summer night as I walked on and on, powered by such erotic excitement, that this was nothing less than my chance to come full circle, to look my panicked younger self calmly in the face, to forgive that terror-stricken kid I had been.

That white kid secretly set on fire by the sight of a black man's beauty.

Kai would get to know me, I resolved triumphantly, and he'd be amazed at this gay man I'd finally managed, against all odds, to become.

Because I had *become* gay. Almost through an act of will, I had made myself embrace this new identity of mine and never look back. I had gay friends, I ate at gay restaurants, I went to gay bars. I had my apartment near DuPont Circle. After two years at a Walden bookstore, I'd begun working recently in the mail order department at Lambda Rising. My parents had gone from concerned to alarmed to panicked to silent. I spoke to them rarely now. All their worst fears had been confirmed: the rising tide they'd thought Hightower might succeed in damming had turned into the dark flood after all, and their firstborn had been swept away.

A week after our chance encounter, and feeling inexplicably nervous, I plucked Kai's number from my wallet and called him up.

"Stayton, honey," he said. "I was just thinking about you. About how delicious it was to see you the other night, and I was saying to myself, I should invite that boy around sometime soon, and then the phone rings like magic. So: can you come to dinner? Are there things you can't eat? I'll roast a chicken. It's the only meat I touch, but I do love chicken."

"Sounds fabulous," I told him.

"And fabulous," he promised, "it will most definitely be."

Kai's apartment was in a grand old building. He met me at the front door, wearing a flowing white robe, and embraced me and ceremoniously kissed me, as he'd done in the restaurant, on both cheeks and then full on the lips. "Welcome," he said with somewhat theatrical solemnity.

"I feel overdressed," I laughed, "or maybe it's underdressed."

"Oh this," he said. "I asked myself, should I be formal, or should I

213

just be myself. For you, I decided to just be myself. Isn't it a hoot? A friend got it for me in Morocco. He had one, and I wore it around the house all the time—he never got to put it on—and so he got me my own. It was the end of our relationship, too."

"You never can tell," I told him, "about relationships."

"That is one thing that is simply too true," he laughed as he led me through his spacious set of rooms—"The obligatory tour," he apologized, "but face it, everybody wants to see how you live."

"I love house tours," I allowed.

"There could be more furniture," Kai judged, as if noticing for the first time the spareness of the rooms. "But I'm doing it one piece at a time, and I want to get it right."

"Plus," I told him, "you have expensive tastes." The few pieces he had, mostly French, were clearly extraordinary.

"The bane of my existence," he said airily, "believe you me."

It was all rather a lot to take in, so I handed him the bottle of wine I'd been carrying.

"Ah," he said, "merci. Shall I pour us some?"

I followed him into a kitchen resplendent with all the latest gadgets. "Well," I said as he filled our glasses, "you certainly seem to be doing well for yourself."

"Black faggot makes good," he said, raising his glass in a toast. In the years since Minerva, he'd cropped his hair very short, grown a neat goatee. A big hoop earring of gold dangled from his left ear. I hoped I had changed as much.

"To faggots in general making good," I told him.

"Amen," he said, looking right at me, his eyes glittering, teasing—the fascinated way he'd used to study me back in Minerva. For a moment, everything in the room was perfectly still—between us as well. It was all so strange to be here, especially now that our initial banter, that had carried us along so successfully for the first few minutes, had slowed a bit.

"I want you to tell me," I said—not in desperation but just as insurance against any silence that might break out—"everything that's happened to you."

"What you want," he said, "is my resumé."

"It's the eighties," I joked.

So I sat at the kitchen table watching his white-sheathed back as he made a salad and treated me to the obviously well-rehearsed story: how he transferred from that small college in Minerva to Oberlin for three bone-cold years, then more cold years at the Boston Conservatory followed by a stint with the New Jersey Symphony, a felicitous audition with Mstislav Rostropovich, and—happy ending—his present position as second French horn with the National Symphony. "That," he said, turning to me with a final flourish of the salad spinner, "is when my jet-setting life may properly be said to have begun. Meaning I have played the capitals of Europe, the outback of Australia, the unspeakable provinces of the People's Republic of China. Not that I saw so much of any one place. Hotels and concert halls and waiting rooms. I can tell you where the public conveniences are located in most of the major airports of the world. If you ever need to know."

"I'll keep that in mind," I said. And we both laughed, and looked at each other, and then Kai, taking a peek in the oven, said we should move out to the dining room table because the fabulous chicken, voilá, was done.

"More wine?" he offered, but I shook my head. I hardly ever drank, and the single glass had me floating quite pleasantly. I knew well enough where a second glass would send me.

"Me either," he said. "I just can't drink. Dries out my mouth all the next day, and if there's one thing a horn player needs, it's his spit."

"I think I must have Baptist genes," I told him. "Grape juice for communion and all. My mother used to tell me, if you were meant to be an alcoholic, one drop of the stuff would do it."

"Baptists," Kai said. "All that religion stuff makes me shiver. Let's don't talk about Baptists. Let's talk about love and life and happiness."

"Then talk on," I urged him. "You gave me the resumé, but you left out the love and life and happiness."

"You mean the sexy parts," Kai said. "Admit it: you want the sexy parts."

I loved this: how easy it felt to be here, eating fabulous roast chicken and parsleyed potatoes and admitting, "Sure, the sexy parts. Tell me the sexiest affair you ever had." Maybe it was the glass of wine that made me bold that evening. Or the exhilarating sense that I had fully, and finally, come into my own in the difficult world.

Kai tilted back his head and touched his finger to his chin. "Let's see," he mused. "I should first of all tell you that I am just getting over

215

six months with a ballet dancer, which was definitely not the sexiest affair I ever had. In fact it exhausted me, and I have since joined a health club. The sexiest affair I ever had wasn't even an affair by most people's standards. It took just three minutes, and we never touched. And it happened to me such a long time ago. But you'll appreciate it. I never told anybody else, because who else would appreciate it like you will? This Memphis club I used to flee to from time to time when Minerva was feeling just too small to endure another minute. Not a sex club or even a dance club, just a club where queens who were brothers could hang and not get hassled. And there were all kinds there, too—a real mellow joint. A dive, really, but I loved that place. And out back was this alley, dark except for the light hanging over the back door, and you could step out there if you had some business or wanted a break or whatever. I'd never done shit like that, but that one night, I don't know why, I slipped myself on out there."

Smiling, he paused to remember.

"Funny how I still think about that night," he said.

I asked him, "So what happened?"

"Oh, I'm doing all the talking here," he said. "You should talk some now."

"Kai," I complained. "I want to hear your story. It was starting to turn me on."

He laughed that rich laugh of his.

"No, really," I insisted, and there we were looking at each other again over the remains of the roast chicken. We're going to sleep together, I thought. I'm going to make it happen. I have to.

"What I saw out in the alley," Kai said bluntly, "was this white boy getting fucked by one of the brothers. I just stood there and watched— I'd never seen anything like it. Never seen black on white. You know, salt and pepper. It was this big rowdy brother I happened to know, but I don't think he saw me. Had his mind on other business. But that white boy—he was just a kid, seventeen years old I later found out— he sure saw me. Looked right at me while he was taking that brother's tool. And such a look on his face. I could see it in the light of the streetlight—just him and me looking at each other, and I swear we were the only two people in the universe just then. Soulful. It like to killed me, it was so soulful between us."

Instinctively I knew. A shiver went through me.

"You're talking about Jonathan Cloud," I said.

"Yeah." Kai sort of laughed quietly. "First time I ever met him, too. Back of the old Club Neptune. Turned out he was down there on a visit with George. First time I met either one of them."

The world had quietly dropped out from under me. Terror and wonder were what I felt, ice-cold and burning. To have him present with us like this—I realized, with something of a shock, he'd been here all along, powerful, unacknowledged, ever since I walked in the front door.

"I thought I should tell you that," Kai said, "before we move on to anything else."

I decided, with some desperation, it was my turn to talk. "Jonathan and I used to fool around down in his basement," I confessed. "We did that for almost a whole year. It totally freaked me out. Then that night after George's party—I denied him. Did it right to his face. Looked him in the eye and completely renounced him. Like I was pronouncing him dead. And to me he really was dead. It was the last thing I ever said to him."

This was all so painful. For years I had commanded myself, every day, not to think of any of this.

"I wondered," Kai said, "if we were going to end up here. Jonathan Cloud. George Mitropoulis. We have so much past together, you and I."

"I never knew George," I told him. "Jonathan was the one who knew George. I was just at that party because Jonathan took me there."

"Well, I was good friends with George," Kai said. "Knew him even better than I knew Jonathan. See, I never made it with Jonathan, unless you call what happened behind the Neptune making it with him. But George . . . he was a saint of a man, if you ask me. If folks had any self-respect they'd tear down that bus station brick by brick and put up a shrine to his memory. They used to do that in Greece, you know—shrines for beautiful lovers. Plant groves of trees. Set up stones. Nafplion, the town where George was from—it was on a bay, and he told me how there'd be storms up in the mountains, and the light coming down across the water was out of this world. His grandmother used to say, The gods are walking. You know, when the light was like that. He told me about it. He was crazy out of this world about Jonathan, you know."

I didn't know.

"Lord," Kai burst out. "I hate those people. I hate them, I hate them."

He didn't have to say anything more. All these things I'd buried, as if hiding them from myself could make them go away. The police had taken George to the county jail for making a nuisance of himself when they came to his party. He was drunk, he was irrational, so they booked him on charges of disturbing the peace, serving alcohol to minors, possession of marijuana. They entertained him, apparently, with other possibilities, including an investigation of the Travelers. But for all that, it was standard lockup, nothing that didn't happen to dozens of people every month at the hands of the Minerva police.

When the guard came to George's cell in the morning he saw him— not hanging, just crouched, slumped over, his feet touching the floor where the shoestring he'd tied to the light socket had stretched itself out with his weight.

He didn't die instantly, said the coroner's report. He thrashed about for ten minutes before he suffocated.

Seeing the headlines on the front page of the Minerva *Evening Crescent* I'd averted my eyes in terror. My parents didn't mention it, though surely they knew the connection. For days I waited for the police to come ask questions—but they never did, and that was almost worse: the waiting, day after day.

What unnerved me the most was this: for a single instant, before I'd even heard about George, I had also considered suicide. A vengeful, insinuating whisper in my head. No matter how I tried, I couldn't shake the uncanny feeling that George had somehow committed my suicide for me. And then, on top of that, Jonathan's empty house, the FOR SALE sign on the front lawn.

These were not things I could say, even nine years later, to a living soul.

"Jonathan took it very very hard," Kai told me quietly. "It broke his heart. I was worried sick for him."

"He just vanished," I said, "off the face of the planet."

"As far as anybody knows," Kai confirmed. "As far as anybody knows."

In the lengthening silence between us I studied my plate, the chicken bones, the congealing grease. I felt an odd relief come over me: we'd put Jonathan to some kind of rest.

Strange, I thought. After all these years.

Self-consciously, Kai cleared his throat. "I'm thinking," he announced, "we could use some salad about now. Clear the palate, as it were."

Or break the spell.

"Salad," I said, "sounds great," and I followed him toward the kitchen. In the doorway he turned around, arms open, and I walked right into his embrace.

I'd known, that first instant I saw him in the Red Sea Café, that sooner or later we'd have to become lovers. The only thing that surprised me was that it happened so quickly. Afterward I could only marvel: how we moved fluidly from that embrace into a long kiss, from which I drew back to say "This makes sense, doesn't it? Tell me it makes sense."

"Yes," Kai told me, "it makes perfect sense."

During my time in Washington I'd skirted relationships, preferring the magic and romance of one-night stands, breathing a sigh of inward relief (no matter how outwardly disappointed I might profess myself to be) when the rare two- or three-week affair finally ran out of inspiration. I was conscious, on waking beside Kai the morning after, that this was going to be different. That this had been in the making for years. I remember I raised myself up on my elbow in that huge four-poster bed and watched him. He was still asleep, facing away from me, his bare back lustrous in the early morning sunlight that filled a bedroom redolent with the odor of our bodies: our sweat, our come, the exhalations of our lungs. I breathed in that aroma hungrily. I watched the rise and fall of his shoulders. No panic: nothing but a sense of completion.

What I remembered as I lay there, propped on my elbow, was a book that sat on the shelf in our living room in Minerva: *The History of the Voegli Family in America*. Some distant relative had compiled it in the late 1950s, and by chance, though as if marking the end of something, my birth was the final entry in the text. One item fascinated me as a boy: a bill of sale from an 1828 auction, in which the heirs of my great-great-great-grandfather Tyler Voegli had cashed in his estate. He'd been a farmer of some substance, and alongside his cattle, horses and tools, a number of his slaves had also been sold off. With their curious names like Juba and Linen, they'd fetched several hundred dollars apiece.

I could only laugh quietly, with sweet satisfaction, as I thought about our coupling, the fantastic intimacies, Kai's penis touching tender places inside me no one had ever touched. I nuzzled against him, my erection pressing itself along his warm backside, and he murmured drowsily, reaching his hands back to hold me against him. I pressed my face into his satiny shoulder, tasted his salty skin with my lips and tongue.

From my childhood I remembered only this: God sees everything.

IN THE ATTIC

What a strange day it's been, Allen thinks to himself.

Janine's downstairs in bed asleep—what better birthday gift than a full night's peaceful, luxurious, uninterrupted slumber? Allen can hardly imagine such a thing anymore.

Sitting at his desk in his study, he thinks about what Janine asked him earlier tonight in the Mexican restaurant. They seldom talk these days, as if they ran out of things to say years ago and subsist on a mutual fondness that needn't speak to be heard. Joan, on the other hand, was always asking him things. Even when she didn't ask, when he signaled to her he wasn't in a talkative mood, still there was the pressure of questions in her that she'd have liked to ask. A quality their son inherited. At the time he'd felt it something of a trial, all that stray chatter. Janine, though, asks so very little of life, which is comfortable but—he admits to himself—he misses the pressure. The sense of being scrutinized. Fiona Root pressed him—that afternoon he's never forgotten, only shunted to the hidden space where he thinks perhaps he really lives his life. The space strange things occupy. Where the Owl lives, and the Amateur. From way back.

So much has surfaced today.

And tonight, perhaps because it's her birthday, because he's made her the gift of a spade (she spent all afternoon rooting up things, digging and planting and carrying shrubs to and fro in the wheelbarrow) Janine has asked, "If you could wish for just one thing, what would it be?" Her tone was dreamy. The second margarita had, predictably enough, gone to her head.

"The one thing I wish for." He felt stumped. He wondered, even, if it was a dangerous question to go asking. She had told him, long ago, she was a mermaid in a previous life.

"Actually, I'd have to say I'm a pretty contented guy," he was beginning to tell her when he stopped. What he found himself saying instead was, "I wish I hadn't lost so many people. I mean, all down the line. I wish none of us had."

It shocked him to hear himself say that, but he couldn't take it back. And what he did next shocked him even more. The catch in his voice that those sentences provoked turned into a full-fledged sob. There was no missing it.

"Honey, I didn't mean . . ." Janine said.

"No," he told her, observing with half a laugh still verging on tears, wiping in fact a tear from his eye, "Those chilis are really something else. Man alive." Discipline. Calm. Control. Everything would be okay.

And for the moment it was. The waitress happened by—nothing could have seemed more fortuitous. Janine ordered a third margarita, he ordered himself another Dos Equis and—for good measure, calling the waitress back as an afterthought—a shot of tequila. Clearing his throat, wiping his eyes again. What plants, he asked Janine, was she thinking of transplanting? And plant by plant, in great and saving detail, she told him.

Later, at home, standing in the doorway to the bedroom she said, "You don't want a good night's sleep for once?" Though most nights she took herself off to bed with only a brisk goodnight, sometimes she lingered like that. She wore a pink nightgown—all hope, all expectation—that could break his heart. He understood, of course, but it had been such a long time since he'd taken her up on her offer. The empty feeling afterward wasn't worth it. In any event, there was way too much thinking he had to do tonight to even dream of sleep.

I know I'm losing you too, he thinks. Or already gone and lost you. That look of quiet defeat, not only in her face but her body as well. But tonight's not the night.

"I'll come to bed in a bit," he lies, and trudges upstairs to his study in the attic. Here he'll often spend hours alone, reading newspapers, magazines, clipping articles for his files or sorting the folders he's already stashed away. There was a time when he thought about writing some kind of memoir, but astronauts, he realizes, are a dime a dozen these days, good only for selling used cars or fronting bogus corporations. He's done his time on that one.

For him there's only withdrawal. Silence. What gets to him is the sheer solitude, some space that's opened up around him, an invisible circumference of indefinable radius. No matter how he tries, he can't get close to anybody. Always thinking of himself as something of a loner, he's never really been a loner at all. His life's been lived, all along, shoulder to shoulder with other people—which is why this space seems so lonely and so wide.

He draws from his files one of the magazine articles he clipped several months ago. Recently he's started to brood on certain items in his collection, returning to them night after night—in search of what, he can't say.

Inside the tomb of the exploded nuclear reactor, he reads, *there is only lethal darkness and the spewed and hardened magma of 171 tons of radioactive fuel which huddles like some horrific pestilence in solitary confinement. Unbelievably, a half dozen Soviet workers, as dedicated as they are doomed, venture inside the 20-story sarcophagus daily and probe the dangerous mass with pikes and radiometers.*

"The guys are great," says Victoria Ivleva, a Soviet photographer who has gone inside the reactor twice to take these photographs. .

From inside the sarcophagus. He adjusts his little halogen desk lamp to better study the photograph he's already studied countless nights before. Amidst the tangled debris, the sandbags and lead dropped by doomed, dedicated helicopter pilots, two tiny human figures dressed in white antiradiation suits pose for the camera in a single ray of sun that penetrates the tombal gloom.

"The guys are kamikazes, working for 1,200 rubles a month, and they're absorbing 200 rems and more," she says. The salary is four times the national average and the radiation dose hundreds of times the safe maximum for nuclear-plant workers.

Short and kinetic, red-haired and articulate, Ivleva is now a favorite of the six men of Chernobyl's interior "expedition," as their project is formally known. She laughs at the scientific conceit of the flimsy plastic antiradiation clothing, which does nothing to block the deadly gamma rays. "You take your last breath and last glance at the trees," she says. "You climb the small,

223

absolutely vertical staircase and rush as quickly as you can through the high-rem field into the deadly dark. You've no time inside, every thought is a rem," she says. *"When you get a dose in there you feel sleepy at first, and later you have this feeling of . . . I told the guys: 'You know what I'd like to do now? Go back inside.' And they said. 'Now you understand us.' "*

These frail figures in Victoria Ivleva's photos—dead by now, or soon to be dead, mirror-astronauts in a world stranger and braver than any he's trod the surface of. Bio-robots, they've been called. Human where no machine will do. Some rapture of the deep pulls them back. He thinks, in some odd way, he understands. Just as he finds himself drawn back to these men, night after night. To Victoria Ivleva with whom—is it possible?—he thinks he is in love.

Uneasy—as ever, these days—he slides the article back in its folder. When his colon's acting up, there's just no getting comfortable. It spasms. He shifts this way and that in his desk chair. Best is to remain as still as possible.

Outwardly motionless, his gut spasming away, he stares out the attic window at the sycamores in Frank's backyard. How the moon rises in their arms, sparkles in the mirroring water of the swimming pool below. For close on a quarter century he's seen that simple phenomenon—and in the meantime been there and back. Never, never, never to return. Dreaming always that somehow he might—as if he left something there, some part of himself, he can't go on without retrieving.

Tomorrow, or next week or next month—depending on the ever unreliable Bill—those trees will be down, sawn up, carted away. There'll be left only the vast space of sky, an emptiness whose prospect, all at once palpable, sends him into a tailspin of terror. Sitting motionless in his chair, he feels a hole open up, a gap right beneath him he could fall through and no one would ever be the wiser. He wants to reach out, grab hold of something—but there's nothing, just that gaping sink-hole in his heart.

The next instant he's better, he's fine, that bit of turbulence is safely behind him. He hardly knows what came over him.

Jeez, I hate Mexican food, he thinks. The heavy way it lingers in his stomach. There was something a little forlorn about that dinner at La Casita. Other years there might've been Frank and Sally, or if not them then other old cronies from NASA. Funny how he's caught somebody else's guilt. How he's marked with it now, contagious himself. He suspects the lawsuit's giving him an ulcer, and that's what he can feel dinner working on inside him. That burning in his gut.

All these things. The moon looks exhausted, wizened up there in the sky, its face pockmarked by craters, blemished by seas. The Chinese see a rabbit there, the Laplanders see a reindeer's horns. He can't help it; even though he's walked its surface he's always, since his father pointed it out to him as a kid, seen an old man's queer face leering down.

It's cleared the branches of the sycamores, that face, and sails free into the hazy night sky. Moonlight used to be brighter, he thinks, back when he first moved to Houston. Brighter still when he was a kid. Now there's rarely a smogless day or one of those bracingly transparent nights of old. His gaze keeps returning to the sycamores, their pale stout trunks so earth-rooted, gnarled hectic branches poking skyward. Gesticulating, he thinks. Or better, yearning. Trees like those you could climb halfway to the moon—and suddenly he's thinking of his father, he's thinking of that telephone call from his mother early one morning in December of 1982.

He'd been negligent, hadn't stayed in touch—perhaps always a failing of the Cloud family, some self-sufficiency, lack of sentimentality. Perhaps only a coldness around the heart. You could construe it any number of ways. But once out of the nest, the Clouds have always struck out on their own. Never looked back. His own father did it, he's done it, and look at Jonathan.

(I'll never have grandchildren, Allen thinks with a pang. This is it for me, the end of the line.)

He remembers how his father expressed surprise, even annoyance, when Allen once took the chance to call him on the Watts line from Bitberg. Something stern in his voice: "In my day, you know, when you left home you left home." Perhaps he hadn't meant it unkindly, merely as an observation. But Allen felt the sting nonetheless. And he'd gotten the message.

One of the only times he went home was the occasion of the hero's parade Armistice threw for him some months after the moon landing. A tedious processional took him down Main Street, perched between the Mayor and the district congressmen in the back of a Cadillac convertible, itself sandwiched between the Fighting Panthers marching band and the Ladies' Auxiliary. All the great spreading shade elms of his childhood had died, and unaccustomed sunlight beat down fiercely on the heads of the crowd.

A decade passed before he returned. They'd brought his father back from surgery in Toledo, installed him in the downstairs bedroom because he could no longer negotiate stairs. We can make him comfortable, the doctor said, but that's about all. Cancer of the liver, cancer of the pancreas.

Allen's mother was stoic. She'd aged tremendously. Her flesh looked gray, unhealthy. She looked, in certain ways, worse than his father. He was never that close to her. She hadn't wanted him to take flying lessons. She'd wanted to keep him close, a Mama's boy, and instinctively he'd fled her at an early age.

They shared meals at the big dining room table, and tried to make conversation.

"Tell me if I'm wrong," he said. "And maybe I am wrong. I must be wrong. But I seem to remember, when I was little, there were always these men sitting around the table at dinner. I never knew who they were. Strangers. They never said anything. Did I dream that up?"

"I'm surprised," his mother said, "you remember so far back."

"I must've been very young," he told her.

"I'd imagine four or five," she said. "We took in boarders for a while. Railroad men, mostly, who'd spend the night between shifts. I had no idea you could recall that. It was the middle of the Depression."

What he didn't tell his mother was how, as a child, he used to watch them—how they ate in silence, paying attention only to the food on their plates. He scrutinized their short hair and dull eyes, the drab clothes they wore.

They were the dead men.

If ever they spoke, it was only in secretive murmurs. He wondered if they communicated by the dull sound of their forks against their plates. Cautiously he tapped out a code on the side of his own plate. No one noticed except his mother who told him, "Eat your carrots." She was in collusion, he'd seen her accept money from these dead men. She leaned over his plate and cut his carrots into slices, urging "Go on, they'll help you see in the dark."

After dinner the dead men retreated into the front parlor where it was always dark. Their eyes lit by carrots, they read newspapers in the dark, played checkers in the dark, listened to President Roosevelt talk on the radio in the dark.

He was afraid to go in there for fear of being contaminated by them. He feared their musty smell, the stubble on their chins, the stubborn dirt that was always under their fingernails.

He'd stand at the door filled with fascination and anxiety. One of the men coughed persistently. Several were smoking cigarettes.

His mother called him to her, back along the dark hallway to the kitchen where she was washing up. Huge stacks of plates tottered beside the sink. She plunged her hands into the soapy water as if wrestling some big fish.

"Don't bother the men out there."

"Why?"

"They're tired. They don't want to have to go messing with some little boy."

In his sleep he could hear them murmur deep into the night. Sometimes he crept downstairs to find them still sitting, motionless, just as he'd left them when his mother took him up to bed. Only they'd shrunk since then, they'd hardened into their true forms—large mummified grasshoppers with twisted limbs and enormous liquid eyes. Their talk was the parched noise of cicadas rasping summer nights away.

In bed he'd wrap himself tightly in his covers, a mummy himself, protected against the dead men's claims. But when he was asleep they'd lift him out of bed. Gently they held him suspended, carried him slowly through the house, down the hallway to where the stairs led up to the attic, and up those stairs through the door into the attic with its stacks of boxes and old bedsteads, the blemished mirror. Then out the open window, floating above the backyard, lifted up over the roofs of the houses of his street, and the train tracks and the water tower, faster now, out over the corn fields, out past where the train wreck spilled a load of grapefruit down the embankment and all the kids in town scrambled to fill bushel baskets, past the Toledo highway, the river winding black like a snake through bottomlands.

For a whole week Allen and his mother kept their vigil. Every day Allen's father moved perceptibly closer to death. He lay unspeaking in the dark, the rasp of his breathing becoming inhuman, unearthly. Every day in that house Allen seemed to remember more. To escape he took

227

long walks only to find other memories thronging close. He wandered the streets of town, replanted with saplings he'd never live long enough to see grow into the splendid shade he remembered from his childhood. Then farther afield, he'd head out along the train tracks, past the coal bins, the water tower, to the river, hugging its shore then cutting over to the old Brewery Road that led past the grass runway where an old Bavarian named Bruno Knappertsbusch had given flying lessons during the war years.

All this he had erased clear away. How at age fifteen he and Kite Baxter would bicycle out to take turns at the controls of Mr. Knappertsbusch's Aeronca Champion as it carried them high over familiar landscapes, allowed them inside the secret life of clouds. Kite Baxter, with whom he'd built rubber-band–powered models, devoured aviation journals, filled notebooks with scraps of information about makes of aircraft, specifications, performances.

In the attic, away from adults, they'd play the flying game. In the corner by the chimney had been stored the skeleton of a magisterial iron bedstead and coiled boxsprings. Stripped to their underwear, they'd take turns clinging to the bottom of the boxsprings with fingers and toes, moving around down there like spiders, rubbing chest and stomach and thighs and groin against the bedspring while one boy, perched on top of the boxsprings, tried to break the other's grip with tickles and well-aimed jabs. Hours flew by that way, they'd work themselves into that great aching excitement they called flying, always promising themselves afterward not to fly again—it was growth-stunting, health-destroying—but nevertheless they always did.

In the lonely wasteland before girls, Kite Baxter had taught him a thing or two. But the flying game was soon forgotten, mere child's play superceded by the real, the exhilarating thing. It wasn't often they could go out to the Brewery Road, but whatever chance they got they took. The war was being won—though slowly, at great cost. Friends of the family were returning dead. Black wreaths hung on front doors. Mr. Knappertsbusch refused lessons on credit, and nine dollars a lesson was like grasping for the moon, especially when Allen made forty cents an hour working at the pharmacy. Kite was luckier, his Dad ran the bank: for every minute Allen spent in the air Kite spent five, till one day Allen and his father, driving along the Brewery Road, passed a field and in the middle of the field an Aeronca Champion in flames. They hadn't seen it crash, had heard no drone of a plane's engine, no explosion, and yet the plane must have crashed only minutes before. Other cars had stopped, people milled about, unable to do a thing. Black smoke rose from the flames. The tail section was still visible, as yet untouched. Then a dull blast as the gas tanks went.

No one needed to tell Allen who had died there.

He didn't say a word. At home he bolted up the stairs to the attic and shut himself in. Wouldn't come down for supper or the gentle pleas of his father, who knew enough about grief and boyhood to leave him alone after a few minutes. All night he sat on the floor in the attic and watched by faint moonlight that iron skeleton of a bedstead, Kite's underwear-clad ghost shuttling back and forth on the underside, the strange way he had of cocking his head when he smiled.

Sometime in that dreaming night the dead men came to him. He hadn't seen them in years, hardly even remembered them, but lovingly, with the great reverence of the dead for human destruction, they brought Kite's charred and featureless head to the attic. They had gathered it from the wreckage. It smelled bitter, like gunpowder or wet ashes.

Rapture of the deep.

Three weeks later Allen began flying lessons with another aviator, also a German, who lived in Toledo.

And he had thought Armistice could hold no memories. He could no longer recognize the field where the Aeronca Champion took off and landed, where Kite and Bruno Knappertsbusch met their end. Somewhere along the old Brewery Road, it was, but how many times had those fields been plowed and planted or lain fallow since then? And how strange that he'd so thoroughly forgotten all that—had he remembered, he might have privately commemorated Kite and Mr. Knappertsbusch on the moon, the first of all his losses to the devouring goblins of the air. One more thing not done on the moon he'll never return to.

He returned to the house that evening to find that his father had quietly passed away. He went to sleep after lunch and didn't wake up. It was that easy, his mother said. Dry-eyed, composed. How long ago, Allen wondered, had she become resigned to this? In her voice there was no other note so strong as the note of pure relief. He had to admire how capably she performed the tasks at hand—talking to the police, the coroner, the man from the funeral home.

For his part, he called Janine. Not even on the moon had he been so relieved to hear her voice. The voice of safety, of home. It was perhaps the first time he'd fully realized: home was Houston, his house there, his wife.

"I'll catch the next plane up," she said.

"I don't really see the point," he told her. "It's not like you knew him. It's strange. I feel like *I* hardly knew him. Either of them."

"I wouldn't be coming for them," she said. "I'd be coming for you."

"No," he resisted. "Just let me get through this. I can't wait to get home."

Not so much to escape the expected pall of his father's death as all these other ghosts who should long since have been laid to rest.

And he did get home. He escaped. Only tonight, years later, up in his attic retreat, they are all with him again, these ghosts, his head so full, so haunted. And the strangest bit—so strange there's no accounting for it, but around which everything revolves in slow somber orbit—has come at noon, a rare letter from Joan, no return address but postmarked Alanya, Turkey. Türkiye Cumhuriyet. He's grown used to strange stamps, outlandish postmarks. He shivers to think how he never, in all those years they were married, knew a thing about her.

He draws the flimsy piece of airmail stationery from his shirt pocket, unfolds it and lays it in his lap. He doesn't need to read those words. He's been reading them all day, dipping into them the way a secret alcoholic will take nips from the stashed-away bottle through the fraught, solitary hours of an afternoon.

He knows, by now, this letter by heart. Henceforth he'll always know it by heart. Never forget it as long as he lives.

At the same time he will always be averting his gaze.

What he feels, oddly, is a sense of enormous obligation, as if some forbidden knowledge has been vouchsafed him: a burden he must carry, unholy and at the same time holiness itself.

He will not, he thinks, say a word about any of this to Janine. Would he even be able to say it? She hasn't, so far as he knows, been in any kind of touch with Jonathan for years. Certainly she hasn't mentioned his name in ages. He's as dead to her, apparently, as he is to his father.

It quickens him to anguish. He stands up, restless, fraying inside, frustrated with pent-up grief. He wants to shout, to storm down the stairs and out into that moonlight, the fierce spell of those sycamores.

Trample on Janine's carefully tended flowers, dance himself to drunken collapse on the lawn, dive into the mirroring depths of Frank's swimming pool and never come back.

He paces back and forth in the confines of his attic study, rubbing his thumb with his forefinger. It's carried him through before. He's floated in space above the world. He's walked on the moon. He's breathed its dust in his nostrils, felt its chemical bloom in his lungs. None of it matters one bit.

Dear Allen, Joan has written. *I'm sorry to have some bad news. Jonathan writes me:*

". . . So, Mom, this is it. What my system's been warning me about for the past several months. This thing in my blood that's a point of departure for the most horrible occurrences all through my body. I never wanted to look it squarely in the face, and now I'm having to learn to adjust myself. Learning with difficulty, Mom, and such sad amazement. I wanted you to know. Tell Dad as much as you want to or think you should. . . ."

As you can see, Allen, I think you should know everything.

BOUND AWAY

When I first told Allen I thought I was pregnant, winter of 1955: "Impossible," he told me flat out, his first panicked response. But it wasn't impossible, though that's how we referred to the sickness in my belly for the next eight months—"Impossible." And even after the child was born, six weeks premature, that was still his name.

How's our Impossible? Allen would ask when he'd come home from a week or month of training fighter pilots at Cazaux or Freiburg or Fürstenfeldbrück.

Impossible, I'd say. Just impossible.

As if reluctant to pin down this strange little creature in our midst, it was a full year before we finally settled on a name.

It was nothing I'd consciously intended—more a mother's hapless, spur-of-the-moment tribute to the beautiful child who'd seen her through so many shameful months—but the day Jonathan graduated from high school was the day I stopped drinking. And as that day wore on, as my racing, irregular heart seemed gradually to calm and I went through the kitchen cabinets pouring bottle after bottle of the perilous stuff down the drain, it was with a sense of amazement that I found myself growing not more desperate, as I'd imagined, but less. So I just kept going, through the unfolding events of that night and on into the terrible next week when it became clear what I had to do.

I have always been resourceful when it was necessary, it's just that for years my life hadn't in any sense *been* necessary. But that all changed. Jonathan sat on the sofa clipping his toenails while I tried to make light of the previous night's episode. The embarrassed policeman who escorted him home—"such a gentleman," Jonathan observed with a wry grin; all-knowing Mr. Voegli standing dumbfounded and apoplectic in the middle of his living room; his wife wringing her hands and those ghoulish boys cringing at the top of the stairs. I conjured the whole pathetic cast, invoked poor Stayton's name with a freedom and familiarity I wouldn't have dared only a day before. And Jonathan answered my banter in kind, rose to it effortlessly, and I thought, What we're forging here is so remarkable—when suddenly a black man stood knocking at the door.

I had never laid eyes on Kai Dempsey till that moment, never even heard his name spoken, but I knew instinctively from his way of holding himself, the lilt in his voice, that he would be a friend of Jonathan's. With a single look he dismissed me as he strode into the room, Jonathan glancing up from the sofa in surprise as in a single swift motion Kai went down on his knees in front of him.

I might as well, at that moment, have been invisible. Kai lay his hands on my son's forearms, caressed him urgently while saying, barely a murmur but full of such grief, how there'd been an accident, or not an accident at all, but something too terrible to do anything but blurt it out:

George was dead.

This name I'd only heard for the first time the night before, and now with meteoric force this George assumed a body, a life, a terrible mortality before my eyes. In the darkness I saw him flare and suddenly go out.

What happened next I can never forget. With such a lunge he sent him staggering, Jonathan pushed Kai off. He sprang up from the sofa and plunged headlong toward me, throwing himself into my body with all the shock of his grief, burrowing his head into my breast and howling as if a name alone could call George back. I held him in my arms, hardly aware what was happening, aware only that I had never held a human being together—literally, the force of my arms wrapped around him keeping him from exploding. I had never done that before, I have never done that since, but you could say it was the one truly irrevocable act of my life.

One does not hold a human being together only to abandon him later on.

To this day it seems barely conceivable that a week later we found ourselves bound away from all that. Minerva, Houston, the whole country we'd despoiled and made our home. Memphis to Atlanta to Frankfurt in gleaming Germany to that farflung Constantinople I had visited so often in my delirium and now chose in lucid desperation. Because I saw so clearly that for Jonathan to stay another instant in this place would be nothing less than the death of all that beautiful crazy energy I held and couldn't hold and that was my impossible son.

When in doubt, Allen used to say, do anything—the one piece of useful advice he ever gave me. It seems somehow right that the sky, for so many years my deadly adversary, should have become the avenue of our escape. Thunderstorms dogged us the whole way. I knew I was in some sense throwing everything to the winds. But having done that, I was free to enjoy the buffetting, the surges, the bottom dropping out from underneath our fragile craft as it made its way across the Atlantic, the whole of troubled Europe, to the beckoning edges of Asia. Jonathan was in no shape to do anything but acquiesce. I felt like shouting, or singing. I felt like clapping my hands and laughing deep down in the heart of me. Instead I held Jonathan's hand through all that mighty turbulence. Held on for dear life, his and mine alike.

The Turk in the seat beside us was returning to his homeland after years of political banishment. He spoke to us in broken English, broken German, long episodes of staccato Turkish. As we circled in for landing, he became more and more agitated, straining for a glimpse out the window. And then he saw it—the great city, its domes and minarets and glittering garland of waters. City of the world's desire. "*Herrlich!*" he exclaimed. *Magnificent.* A cry so heartfelt, I had never heard a cry so heartfelt. He was home.

I became, in that instant, an exile forever.

Constantinople, Byzantium, Istanbul. It was not the city down whose broad and nonexistent canals of black water I had so often made my way in waking dreams. Why should it have been? And yet it matters

234

intensely to me, even now, that these two superimposed visions should co-exist—the one monumental, defunct but splendid in ruin, the other humming, sooty, traffic-snarled, alive.

Those first hours are etched in me. Our scant baggage stowed at a seedy hotel, nothing but adrenaline buoying us up, we roamed the chaotic streets overwhelmed, turning to each other in disbelief to shout, It's only a dream. It could only be a dream, vast and intricately worked but finally incomprehensible. After some time we found ourselves in the vast square outside the university. Vendors hawked radios, tools, bootleg liquor, tawdry gadgets of every description. Someone had set a small windup toy in motion on the pavement, some kind of top that played, as it spun, a tinny and haunting melody. It took me a moment before I recognized that waltz, so long forgotten but still sad and lost, the ineffable still lurking somewhere within it. Ridiculous in this guise, utterly improbable—but still achingly familiar. Both the music and, I suppose, myself. Always to re-encounter. Always to be haunted. Never to find. The city had offered up its provocative early warning and I had heard. With a shiver of recognition, I had taken note.

Then the crowd pressed us and we moved on out of earshot—safely, I thought, out of reach.

Some time later we found momentary refuge from the city's rampant energy in a patch of tumble-down tombstones by the side of a mosque. Odd, turban-shaped affairs, amid which hollyhocks bloomed in profusion and scrawny cats lazed. We sat on a low stone wall and Jonathan began idly to whistle, a few unrecognizable notes and then . . .

I touched his arm. He looked at me and I thought, my heart sinking, Why have I done this to you? What madness ever made me think I might save you?

Why, I asked him, *are you whistling that?*

Whistling what?

What you were whistling. Beethoven. Für Elise.

But I could tell, even as I said those words, that he had simply no idea what he'd been whistling, had picked up that splinter of song unconsciously amid all the cacophony of sights and sounds, carried it around lodged somewhere inside him for that quarter of an hour while gradually it worked its way back to the surface. Now that I'd called his attention to it, the tune slipped completely away from him.

You've got me, he said, laughing a little at the strangeness of it. Whistling again to try to find the thread, but of course it had vanished. And he was wrong: I didn't have him. I had, in that moment, nothing at all. Only the endless looking for.

And what does one do? How does one live? A little man by the name of Cenk, a schoolteacher who heard our English in a tea shop and began a conversation, took us in hand, found us rooms in an apartment building inhabited, it seemed, entirely by his cousins once and twice and three times removed, immigrants from the distant Anatolian provinces, as new to the city and stunned—in their way—as we. The idea of Americans living next door delighted Cenk, especially the prospect that he could practice his eccentric brand of English on us at will.

Two narrow iron bedsteads, a sagging sofa, a quirky electric burner. An incongruous oil painting of mountains and what looked like a Bavarian farmhouse.

Home.

Five times a day, from just across the street, the minarets of the Fatih Mosque blared the call to prayer into our window.

Jonathan slept fourteen, sixteen hours at a stretch, a slumber so moody and deep that he'd emerge from it blurred, incoherent—hardly remembering, so it would seem, who or where he was. That small apartment reeked of his sleeping, the sweat and turmoil of it. He is recovering, I told myself, from a death wound. He is awaking on the far side of his life. There is nothing I can do but wait and watch.

Whenever I left the apartment the women of the building were shy with me, the men formal. I felt in equal measure their caution and their curiosity. I could see the speculation in their eyes. This oddly mismatched pair—what did we want here, lingering long after the other tourists had gone? What kind of criminals or refugees or lost souls had we become?

What Cenk told them, I have no idea, but his young wife Aslihan knocked on our door, took me by the hand, led me around the neighborhood. From a cart of vegetables she'd pick an eggplant, hold it up saying, Yes? and I'd nod, say yes. *Patlican*, she'd say, and I'd dutifully repeat as the vendor looked on in bemusement. Thinking hard, she would produce the occasional word in English. Otherwise our colloquy took place entirely in her strange language, whose nouns and adjectives

I learned with time to recognize, but among whose daunting compound constructions I had no luck at all in finding my way.

In the evenings Cenk would stop by to check on us and to have English conversation. Clearly he considered us something of a catch. Discreetly ignoring me, he addressed himself to Jonathan—but Jonathan, groggy from just having been dragged back into the world of consciousness, was unresponsive at best. He sat looking drugged and miserable. Cenk was perturbed. Your son is very sick? he would ask me with concern, wary of my repeated assurances to the contrary. The death of an American in his apartment building would not be so fine.

Lacking Jonathan, he resigned himself to conversation with a woman. At least I was American. He and Aslihan brought Jonathan sage tea—bitter but healing. They brought blue glass amulets to ward off the evil eye. Aslihan sat in silence throughout our laborious dialogue. She herself, Cenk told me one day, had been marked by the evil eye when she was a girl in her village. A stranger with blue eyes had looked at her, called her by name though she had never seen him before. He confessed to me that they could not have children for that reason. Her village was in the south, he said, on the coast of the White Sea. It was beautiful there, all along the coast. Antalya was the most beautiful city on earth. The glorious Atatürk visited Antalya seven times in his lifetime, it was so beautiful. And Alanya too, where the mountains ring the bay and beneath the castle are healing caves known only to women, and further east still other cities, also beautiful, that must be seen to be believed.

About the evil eye, Cenk said. Aslihan had wanted me to know. She had wanted him to tell me.

Aslihan smiled. She leaned close, held my hand, stroked it.

I was no longer a stranger.

Days passing into weeks and then months as the golden autumn became sullen, winter rains set in, the city steeped under a daze of smoke and soot. I haunted the American Express office, coaxing funds from the country I'd fled: seldom touched monies held in my name for so many years, insurance settlement from my parents' fiery appointment with a drunken destiny speeding toward them on the wrong side of the road.

And Jonathan began to stir from his slumber. Slowly he began to come around. In the afternoons he'd go out on his own, stay away for hours. He'd come back with his mouth full of strange words, whole sentences, a tongue he was learning with the same unconscious ease he'd taken *Für Elise* into himself and then offered it back to the world.

When he began to disappear for three or four days at a stretch I always felt a curious lightness not unlike the lightness I used to feel in the California hills as I watched Allen's X-100 drop from its B-52 piggyback into the treacherous abyss of air.

No danger wake, I reminded myself. Never again the danger wake. In my heart the all-clear sirens sang and sang. Barely believing, I emerged from my underground bunker into the brilliant light of day. No bombs fell. No astronauts. I could walk for hours in my raincoat, scarf wrapped tightly about my head. Constantly I was being surprised, astonished, flooded with odd shards of clarity. Emotions I had entirely forgotten in the dull stupor of the danger wake. I stood on the site of the ancient hippodrome and gazed up at the fine domes of the Blue Mosque mounting one on the other in perfect accord. I wandered steep narrow alleys whose unpainted wooden houses leaned out crazily, where women poured slop buckets in gutters and children chased madly after a rubber ball as it bounced along the sloping sidewalk. I blocked its escape, tossed it back to them as they cheered this strange foreign woman, and the boldest little boy introduced himself—My name is Ali—then pointed to each of his companions in turn, saying, My name is Mehmet, my name is Hakkan, my name is Abdul.

My name, I told them, is No One.

No One, they repeated. *Bayan* No-One. No-One *hanım*. They thronged about me, laughing, asking for coins, but I had no coins to give and they were off, distracted by a cat, a shout, an old man trundling a cart of potatoes.

I wandered deep below the city, the ancient cisterns with their rows of columns rising out of black water. Carved peacock eyes stared back at me. A precarious boardwalk took me far back into the gloom, to where two great Medusa heads rested, half submerged, inexplicable stone women whose secrets I nevertheless could guess—their abandonment, the serenity of their grief—and to whom I made pilgrimage often, to drop offerings in the still water, to read their lips and their silences. To wonder.

I would allow the city to swallow me up. Only by surrendering in that way would I ensure Jonathan's safety and my own. That was my bargain.

And always he reappeared, safe, untouched and seemingly untouchable, grinning and full of stories. I made myself listen; I made myself learn from him. What he had to teach was a single thing: trust. Immense, joyous trust in whatever would happen. We became conspirators together in this mad act of trust called life.

The promise of fresh cherries lured me into his shop. An American woman alone presented such an irresistible opportunity. I sat with Osman, sipped tea, ate fruit from a bowl as he chatted me up with furious enthusiasm. His English was limited, but his hunger for conversation knew no bounds. I kept concentrating on his mustache, the way it moved as he talked. The process was oddly exhausting, though by no means unpleasant. I felt peacefully surrendered over to the circumstances of the moment—whatever would happen would happen and besides, the cherries were dark and delicious—but as our talk began to circle back on itself for the third or fourth time I made firmly but politely to leave.

Please wait, he said with such insistence that I sat back down in the chair I'd risen from. There was a question he wanted to ask me.

I braced myself for the proposition I felt coming. He looked around quickly, as if afraid he might be overhead, and then said, in hushed, urgent tones, Had we in America been told the truth about Neil Armstrong? The truth about what had happened to him?

My first response was laughter. Then I shivered. Someone, my grandmother used to say, is walking over your grave. To say I felt frightened would be untrue, but I felt the shadow of unease enter the room. Nothing, I thought, can be sloughed off. Nothing.

I decided to keep to myself the compromising information that Neil Armstrong was a former acquaintance of mine back in that other world. No, I told Osman, I did not in fact know what had happened to Neil Armstrong.

He shook his head with wonder. He spoke with gravity: we Americans had not been told the truth by our government. We alone did not know what the rest of the world knew. We alone did not know that Neil Armstrong, on his return to Earth from the moon, converted to

Islam. On the moon he had seen the truth and understood.

He did not resign from NASA: he was forced to retire. And did I know where he was now?

I did not.

Somewhere in the east of Turkey. Osman gestured vaguely. He is living in a small village as an imam, a muezzin. As a holy man.

This was God's truth.

You must promise me, Osman said, to tell America the truth. And in fact I promised. He was, as it turned out, only the first of many to whom I made this promise. In restaurants, in taxicabs, on the decks of ferry boats, in Istanbul and Antalya and Alanya, wherever my travels have taken me—I have invariably been asked this burning question. I have been handed ragged, much-folded xeroxes of affidavits concerning the truth of this rumor. I have been shown blurry photos from magazines. And invariably I have promised to tell the truth. And why not?

Sorry to disappoint you, I told Osman that first time, but I happen to know that Neil Armstrong is retired and living in Ohio.

Ah no, he said sadly, shaking his head at my naivete, the depravity of my government that would go so far to conceal God's truth from its citizenry. That man is not Neil Armstrong. That is a double paid to live as Neil Armstrong.

Day after day I would see her: slumped in a doorway behind the Shehzade mosque, more a bundle of rags than a human figure, an old woman but difficult, through the lines on her face, to tell how old. I thought she must be dead, the first time I saw her—no living body could look so defeated—but as I passed she looked up at me and held out her hand to beg. Thickly covering her open palm were intricate red tattoos. Then I looked in her eyes, unearthly green and piercing. I was so startled I fell back a couple of steps. She uttered something in an incomprehensible tongue as I groped for a coin to drop in her outspread hand. With the other hand she kept touching her forehead, tapping two fingers to her skull and bowing slightly with each tap.

Day after day she was there, and I came to depend on her being there, to depend on giving over my insignificant change into her red-tattooed hand. As much to sustain myself as her, I realized; realizing also where I had seen her face before, mysterious, even uncanny: the stone Medusas in the ancient cistern under the city, to whom I also made offerings.

A tribe from far in the east, beyond Gaziantep, beyond Urfa, speculated Cenk when I described the woman to him. Nomads. Mountain Turks. A barbaric people.

But how had she come here, so far from everything?

Cenk answered so simply it chilled me to the bone. Something terrible, he said, has happened to her.

There was the day in 1979 a man lay dead on the sidewalk near the university. A nervous crowd had gathered.

He was sprawled face down, his thick glasses wrenched from his face, briefcase spilled open. In the warm breeze densely handwritten pages blew down the avenue. Bright blood pooled around his body—he'd been shot many times. He must have stepped out of his shoes in the surprise of it all, or perhaps the impact of the bullets had knocked him out of those elegant loafers with tassels, newly shined; perhaps he had even had them shined that morning by one of the shoeshine boys who flocked the streets. I couldn't take my eyes off them. And his feet in their brown argyle socks. It was somehow unseemly to be all dressed up like that and not wearing any shoes. Blood was darkening his natty suit. How carefully he had clothed himself that morning.

A university professor, someone explained. Having failed to catch the fleeing gunmen, several of his students who'd been with him when he was shot returned to the scene. Police were trying to calm the students, but the students would have none of it. Some of them tried to gather up his papers, but the police forced them away from the body, the scene of the crime. The students shouted at the police, pushed them; the police pushed back. One of them pointed a machine gun in the direction of the students and motioned them to back off. Another policeman with a megaphone told us all to disperse.

I walked for several minutes, quickly, till I was well away from there, then had to sit down as panic overtook the curious numbness I'd felt at first. I sat on the curb in the hot sun and considered. Rumors I'd been hearing, disappearances and assassinations. The car bombs and the strikes. How the military lurked like some sad reminder in the democratic melody as the country lurched its way toward anarchy. The city,

Cenk had told me darkly, is like a melon that is sweet today but already begins to taste of rot. One morning soon we will wake up to the army. They will go house to house. They will clean the city up.

He looked at me with an expression I could read all too well. This vast cosmopolis was really only an overgrown village, and everyone who lived here, who worshipped in the mosques and chatted in the tea houses and played backgammon in the cafés, was related to everyone else in ways I never would fathom, a labyrinth into which Jonathan and I, increasingly out of our element, in over our heads, continued blithely on.

Perhaps, Cenk hinted, the time had come for us to return to our home.

I have no home but this, I told him bravely, though I too knew that the golden nimbus of safety, of untouchability that surrounded us, was growing more fragile with every passing day. I knew that Cenk had come to know about Jonathan, his frenetic hungers, his endless searching by night for loves or abasements or cessations I dared not imagine. I could tell that the mood in the apartment building had subtly shifted against us. If I blamed Jonathan, I also remained loyal to him. If I watched with dreadful fascination, I also watched because if I didn't, then he would simply disappear off the face of the Earth. How little could he know that it was only by dint of those sleepless stone Medusas half sunk in the black water of the cisterns, only by dint of a green-eyed beggar woman at the gate of the Shehzade mosque that he stood safely out of harm's way? I paid the secret price for his charmed life. And yet I had made my vow.

I considered the possibility that, in my madness, the thing that was not possible had nonetheless occurred. That I had fallen in love with my son.

Not with Jonathan but with the abundant energy that lived in him. The electrical charge that was passing momentarily through him. That fed off him the way a blue tongue of fire feeds off fuel. I held that burning in reverence and awe. I never pressed him on the details of his nocturnal rampages, perhaps because I was mortally afraid if I asked he would tell me—forthrightly, without shame, in a blaze of truth I would not endure. More than I would ever want to know, and yet so craved to devour. Breathtaking possibilities I absolutely forbade myself.

So we lingered dangerously on. I waited and watched. Jonathan came home with a black eye and split lip. He came home with a strange rash on the left side of his face that didn't fade for weeks. He came home with a chipped tooth. He came home bearing flowers and baklava. One day he came home to say, Hey Mom, you'll never believe this, but you're famous.

When I asked what he meant, he told me how friends—those mysterious friends I so seldom met—had told him about a crazy American lady who was seen everywhere, on the morning boat to Heybeliada, amid the graves in the old cemetery out in Usküdar, haunting the shrine at Eyüp where nervous young boys are brought to celebrate their circumcisions. One man claimed to have seen her eating fish in Anadolu Kavagi, where the Bosphorous meets the Black Sea.

I knew, Mom, it could only be you.

He seemed enormously pleased, enthusiasm for the crazy American lady I had become radiating so abundantly from him it almost cast shadows. I told him grimly, Then we're both famous.

We would be travelers once again.

A HAUNTED HOUSE

We moved in together. Or rather, I moved in with Kai. I left my bright, shabby rooms for his grander, tastefully underdecorated space. I developed an interest in furniture of the Second Empire, an appreciation for old china picked up in antique shops, a resigned acceptance of the armloads of flowers he insisted on bringing me home—so many unaccustomed flowers that I finally had to tell him, "The worst thing I can say about you is, you buy too many flowers."

"And how many, pray tell, is too many flowers?"

He had a point. I found it difficult to allow myself a life in which someone brought me flowers. It took a discipline and grace I lacked the training for.

Once a Baptist, always a Baptist, Kai teased. He'd been raised less severely as an AME, and seemed to have left all that constricted life light-years behind him. The world, he insisted, was a delightful place— if only you knew how and where to look. He dragged me to the zoo to see the pandas, to Washington's myriad museums (the more obscure the better), to foreign films of similar obscurity or cafés whose brunches he had read reviews of in the *Post* or the *Blade*. I began attending orchestra concerts—at first merely to hear him play, then out of genuine enthusiasm. He took it on himself to tutor me in the classics, and to this day I can never hear the rousing fanfares of Janacek's *Sinfonietta* without recalling the rainy afternoon we came home drenched from the record store with a new CD of that work. As brass answered brass, we dragged towels from the bathroom, stripped each other bare and, throbbing with the restless pulse of the music, made exultant love in the rain-darkened room. As the music surged to an end, so did we.

Those were days of delirium, lasting through winter and on into the next spring. Never had I felt happier or freer, as if, for some brief space, the whole weight and shadow of my past had lifted. I remembered the days when I used to sneak out my bedroom window in Minerva, in quest of something so undefined I could barely even imagine it. Life, I was able to tell myself now. I was after life, only it had taken me so long to get there.

One morning that spring, the phone rang sometime before dawn. I answered, still tangled in the confused dream I'd been having, to find a voice asking for Kai.

"No, this is the right number," I said. "Hold on a second."

Kai groped in the dim light for the receiver I was handing his way. "Oh," he said groggily, "Pascal. How's it going? Uh huh . . . I see . . . that's too bad . . . when? . . . okay . . . okay . . . fine. I'll see you then."

He let out a long weary sigh. Early morning phone calls are never good news.

"That was my brother," he said. "My grandmother passed away last night."

I'd never heard him mention his grandmother. He lay there, cradling the receiver on his chest, and stared at the ceiling. Gingerly I retrieved the receiver from him. "Were you close to her?" I asked.

"That old witch," he said, and then he laughed. "Really," he went on, "she *was* a witch."

"No way," I said, elbowing him gently.

"No two ways about it," he went on. "Spent half her time trying to scare me to death when I was a little kid. She'd sit in this old wicker rocking chair chewing tobacco and spitting into a coffee can. I'd have to go up, give her a kiss. She'd grab me by my shoulders. Pull me in close. Smack her lips so the spit drooled down, then whisper in my ear so nobody else could hear a word: You're no 'count, you're no 'count, you're no 'count. I was all of five or six and I used to tell her, Yes I can count. One, two, three, four, five."

I had to laugh too.

"Evil old woman," he said. Then, more seriously: "Pascal says I have to come down for the funeral. Says he knows something I don't."

"What's that supposed to mean?" I asked.

"Pascal lòves to fool with me. Always been like that."

Pascal was musical like his brother—in more ways than one.

"We'll drive down, drive back. I've got a concert that night."

"We," I said.

"You'll have a ball. Meet my relatives and everything."

"Ha," I said. "I'm staying away from relatives. Mine or anybody else's."

He rolled over and lay on top of me. "I'm asking you to go," he said. There was a certain tone he could get. He held me pinned to the bed.

"You win," I told him. "But you owe me one. Remember that."

"I owe you one," Kai promised. "And don't be afraid. My relatives don't bite."

"No teeth," I giggled, and he tousled my hair.

Though he himself had grown up in Richmond, Kai's family had originally come from the Virginia tidewater, and the funeral was at a country church in whose graveyard many of his relatives lay buried. It was a dreamy, backwater landscape the highway took us through. Spring was just beginning to green the fields. Kai had timed our arrival exactly right. When we arrived at the little whitewashed church, the service had already begun. Cars filled the dirt lot; the sanctuary was full to overflowing. We stood in the vestibule, at the back of the crowd, though our arrival did not go unnoticed: people craned their heads around to nod to Kai, to register my presence at his side. Nothing hostile—only curiosity. I felt, in spite of myself, how strangely powerful it was to be in a church again.

The preacher had begun to eulogize the lady he called Meemaw Jewel. He was a little mummy of a man with oversized black-rimmed glasses. Oddly listless at first, by degrees he came to life as he spoke. His voice rose and fell in sonorous cadences, anchoring everything to the refrain "She was a *fine* woman, very *blessed* of God with *abundance* overflowing," to which the congregation chorused, "Yes she was" as the preacher's voice, buoyed by their approbation, rose higher and higher.

It was so unlike the strict proprieties of the services I used to attend, and I thought how my father might have envied this preacher his lively congregation. My father who had loved to preach bush meetings in Africa from the back of a flatbed truck.

Then the music started in, the choir began to sway, imperceptibly at first, then picking up the rhythm from the upright piano and gently twanging electric guitar. At my side, unconsciously touched, Kai too began to move with this joyful noise unto the Lord. I found myself at once spoken to and repelled. The dead woman lay in the open casket, nearly obscured by mounds of white flowers. It was a funeral, but such a sweet funeral. A pang of remorse shivered through me as, resolutely, I made myself stand apart from all that ecstatic grieving. I hated all this, hated it.

Never had my own family felt more inaccessible, my own childhood more dead and unmourned. What would my father think if he could see me now? It was a mental exercise I often caught myself in, whether wandering down P Street amid men holding hands, or in a loud bar teeming with handsome guys, or quiet evenings at home with my black lover as he lounged in an armchair perusing the newspaper while the stereo played Mozart.

I had come to the conclusion, over the years, that my father was neither evil nor a fool. And far from having abandoned the code by which he lived, I had merely eked out my own stance toward it, in relation to it, firmly within its purviews no matter what thrashing about I might do. The most I could ever manage was to catch myself in the act of being the person I had no choice but to be. I could lard my behavior with all sorts of correctives to that identity, but I could never succeed in shuffling it off. I could be a recovering racist. A recovering fundamentalist. A recovering homophobe. More than those things I never could be, and to pretend so would be insidious.

The music had risen to full pitch. No one in that cramped space was immune. There was something so determined, so joyful, so alien in its cadences.

I told Kai, touching him lightly on the shoulder, "I'm going to wait outside. I can't breathe in here."

He nodded, and I stepped out into the sunlight. I felt so strangely disembodied, as if I'd somehow forfeited all my substance. Outside the house of worship, the sound of the singing became more tolerable, just another part of the peaceful landscape around me. I walked down a stretch of lawn toward the road and the music grew fainter, less insistent. On the other side of the road lay a stretch of newly plowed fields, and beyond that, some woods. Blue sky and scattered clouds. Two turkey buzzards circled languidly in the warmish air.

247

The run of the narrow county road into the distance looked so inviting, I surprised myself by starting to jog along it. It felt good to shed the numbness that had come over me back there. I ran quite a ways, feeling incredibly light on my feet, barely touching the earth in between strides. My wind seemed to last forever. Only when a sharp pain stung my side did I stop. I'd put the church quite a ways behind me; it lay hidden past a curve in the road. There wasn't a soul in sight, and I thought: I could just keep going. The county road led out to a state highway. I could hitch a ride. I could disappear, the way I used to see Greyhound buses pull away into the beckoning night outside the Travelers in Minerva. Kai would never have any idea where I'd vanished to.

I'm not running away, I told myself. But I was. It had happened the moment I sensed Kai move beside me to that gospel music from his past. In all our days and nights in Washington, I might pretend to know him—but really I knew nothing about him. Nor he about me. For an instant I glimpsed something like the truth: how my whole life with him was based on a yearning for something I still couldn't see. Something still ahead of me in the mists—looming, enticing, terrifying. But it wasn't Kai. Kai was just an excuse.

A surge of nausea overcame me, rising without warning in my throat, and I bent over the ditch at the side of the road and vomited long and hard. Surprisingly, it made me feel better. I spit several times to clear the acid taste in my mouth, wiped my lips with my handkerchief, and straightened back up. My head was clear; the act of vomiting had returned me to myself. And I was standing on an empty road with absolutely no excuse in the world.

I found, as I started to walk back toward the church, that I'd run much farther than I thought, as if my body, in blind panic, had taken me over for several minutes my brain had no conscious memory of. As I walked on and still no church, still only myself and the two buzzards, now far off in the clear sky overhead, I felt another kind of panic. I didn't do this kind of thing. I didn't leave people in the lurch.

The panic gave way to a sense of doom, and the sense of doom to a sense of calm. When I finally reached the church, I felt completely at peace.

A great crowd was milling about in front; cars were beginning to pull away. I'd missed the whole thing—the closing of the casket, the procession down the front steps and twenty-five yards out to the grave-site, the final prayer and lowering of the coffin into the earth.

I saw Kai talking to a short, stout woman and a handsome man who could only be Pascal. He broke away from them as soon as he saw me coming.

There was an edge of alarm in his voice. "I was looking all over for you, man." He grabbed my arm. "Where'd you take yourself off to?"

"I just went down the road a bit," I apologized. "I lost track of my-self."

With a forced cheerfulness he ushered me ahead of him. "Mama, Pascal: this is my roommate Stayton."

His mother scrutinized me warily. I held out my hand, and after a moment's hesitation she took it limply. Pascal, though, clasped my palm firmly and held there, squeezing tight before he let go. A look passed between us, an acknowledgment.

"Come back to Aunt Lila's," his mother said. "She's got a ham. She's got your favorite casserole." I could tell she wished I might vanish.

"Got to get back to D.C. Concert tonight," Kai told her with a briskness I could only admire. He hugged her for a long time, smoth-ering her in his embrace and rocking her slowly back and forth.

Over her son's shoulder, she looked straight at me and her eyes were cold and fierce.

"Hang loose," Kai told Pascal. A river of energy flowed between them, so palpable I could almost put out my hands and wash them in it.

Pascal nodded affably to me, and Kai was already dragging me off to the car.

"Whew," he said when we were safely ensconced. "I shouldn't have put you through that."

I'd been prepared for his anger—or, at the very least, disappoint-ment. Instead, he was the one asking, his hand caressing my cheek, "You doing all right?"

"I'm fine," I told him truthfully. "I just have this thing about churches. I'd forgotten how allergic I am."

I was surprised—even, to tell the truth, disappointed—how easily he seemed to accept my explanation. He's not hearing me, I thought with a tinge of bitterness. Though what it was I expected him to hear, exactly, I couldn't have said.

We drove down the road I'd run along. A mile or so past where I'd stopped, Kai turned the car onto a dirt track and stopped the motor. High tension wires on big metal pylons stretched along the edge of a field. On a low rise in the middle of the field sat an abandoned house. Two stories, tin roof, a sagging front porch. It needed paint and repair something desperate.

"Let's get out," Kai suggested. "Walk on up there. I've got something to show you."

I was still feeling bad about having abandoned him. "You're going to rape me and then kill me," I joked. But he didn't seem to hear me.

As if carrying on some other conversation entirely he said, "It's so odd."

"What?"

I followed him along the muddy track.

"She left me this place," he said. "In her will. That's what Pascal had to tell me. Meemaw left him the fifty acres across the road, and me the house and some thirty acres this side."

"You're kidding," I said.

"That's what I told Pascal," Kai said. "But it's all written down."

We'd come up to the place. No one had lived there for a while. Wisteria vines ran rampant along the front porch, and up close the chimney looked precarious. All the windows were broken out, and we peered in on empty rooms. Kai kicked at a loose floorboard that came up under his shoe. Then he hopped down to sit on the edge of the porch. I leaned against a rickety railing and watched him. He sat there taking deep breaths, as if taking it all in.

"She didn't live here," I said to make conversation.

"Not for years. She moved to Richmond to be near my mother. Had a nice brick house in the suburbs. But we used to come out here when I was kid. Man, I hated it, so far out in the country. I never could sleep. Kept hearing so many strange noises. And there was this whipporwill that kept up all night long. Used to drive me crazy. Plus, Meemaw told this story about the palm wine man. Terrifying story. I was afraid to go to the outhouse to pee once it got dark, afraid the palm wine man was hiding down there in the pit, just waiting to grab me and pull me down. I'd wrap myself up in a blanket when I went to bed even though it was a hundred degrees and all the windows were open. And I'd shut my window tight so the palm wine man couldn't climb in. Lie there sweating, but I thought if I was all wrapped up in a blanket, then the palm wine man wouldn't see me."

"You're still afraid of the dark," I mentioned.

"It was Meemaw who put that fear there," he said. "She just loved scaring the living wits out of me. And what do you know? She went and took a shining to me."

"Maybe there's a curse on the place. Maybe it's haunted."

Kai slapped at me playfully. "Now don't get me going," he said. "Don't you even start."

"So what'll you do with it? Sell, I should think."

"Pascal warned me it's pretty worthless. A little field and a lot of swamp. Those power lines cut it right down the middle, plus Pascal says they're going to build a jail through the woods over there. He thinks minimum security. Still . . ."

"So you should sell while there's still a chance."

"Yeow," Kai suddenly shouted. "I own property!" He jumped up and did a little dance in the weeds that had grown up around three or four beleaguered old apple trees. "What do you know? I guess Meemaw knew a no 'count punk when she saw one. Guess she liked what she saw." He hooted. "Me and Pascal."

"Then it's sort of a scandal," I said.

"Except I don't think anybody knows about Pascal. He's been wary. Saw what could happen."

"Your mother doesn't much approve of you."

"Scared of what she doesn't know," he said. "Maxwell—he's the oldest—skipped on the family completely to make his own in the Big Apple, and I was second, and now Pascal. Mama has to suspect. It's hard for her. She did everything for us she could."

I came down the steps to where he stood surveying his bit of swamp and field. "Kai," I said, putting my hand on his shoulder. "I ran away from you back there. I wasn't there for you."

My seriousness took him off guard. "Hey," he said, turning and putting his arms around me.

Perhaps I should have kept on running, but I didn't. Instead I settled for something. This was where I was. This was where I made my stand. Knee-deep in weeds outside that abandoned house, I held onto Kai more tightly than I'd ever held anyone. "Hey," he said again—surprised, I think, at the strength of my need. And he didn't know the half of it.

It was some months later that Kai inadvertently renewed my acquaintance with my own estranged family. From time to time he'd watch the Christian channel on TV: ferocious ranting and spurious healing, incessant shameless pleas for money.

"I thought all that religion stuff made you shiver," I told him the first time I caught him at it.

"It does," he said, "but I'm fascinated by it. I can't turn it off."

After what I'd seen of his grandmother's funeral, I knew to let well enough alone.

One evening I came home from work to find him watching with rapt attention. A stern, slightly wild-eyed man with a prophet beard and accusatory finger waxed fiery.

"There is a plague," he raged, "that is striking the homosexual dead even as we speak. And why the homosexual? Because he has sinned against the law of nature. He has flaunted his unnaturalness in the face of almighty God. He has lowered himself amongst the animals to commit filth in the name of love. He has defiled the temple of the holy spirit. You cannot flaunt the law of the almighty God without paying a terrible price. You cannot, you cannot, you cannot."

"Man," Kai said, "do you hear the kind of things this guy is saying? Before you came in it was quarantines and tattoos and shit like that. It's insane."

"That guy," I told him, feeling more numbed than surprised, "is my father."

"No way," Kai whooped. "That's your old man? From Minerva? Did I ever meet him? You have got to be working me."

"How many Voeglis do you think there are in this country?" I asked him.

"Yeow," he said. He looked like he'd touched a live wire. "I don't want to know that about you, Stayton. You got that bad blood running in your veins."

"I've got lots of bad blood running in my veins. You should know that by now. But can we turn this shit off?" My father's presence in our apartment was just too unnerving.

I reached for the remote to flick off the set, but just at that moment my father pointed directly at the television camera and shouted, "Don't touch that dial. I'm talking to *you*, sinner!"

I practically dropped the remote in the instant before I started to laugh. It was an old trick, and I recognized it across the passage of years. Of course I was slipping. I had always, every instant of my life, been slipping and waiting for someone to catch me at it. Only now I'd had enough.

I sat down next to Kai and pulled him close to me, kissed him firm on the mouth, a deep kiss, my tongue slathering in his mouth. I think he was startled but not displeased. It was a majestic kiss, even as my father went on to thunder, "God has made a natural law. And He made it for a purpose. But man insists on testing the limits—when will he learn? God offers us infinite protection. He has granted a prayer shield over the faithful. But let yourself outside His hands, and God can only look on in great sadness at the things that shall come to pass. Because man will not listen. He will go his own way and not repent. I am the way, said the Lord, and the truth and the light, and no man cometh to the Father but through Me. Can it be any clearer than that? I ask you in all honesty and humility: can it be any clearer?"

Getting fucked wasn't something I'd ever liked—a pain in the butt, I used to joke with a grimace—but with Kai it was an exquisite agony I never could seem to get enough of. In his arms I felt not so much safe as mastered. Slipping from him, I padded into the bedroom and returned with a condom, and there on the carpet in front of the sofa I had Kai fuck me, deep soul-satisfying thrusts while my father preached his heart out on the TV screen, and the choir sang, and the demons of my childhood were for the moment either engaged head-on or kept more or less firmly at bay.

IN THE CITY OF GOD'S SHADOW ON EARTH

I play the cave game. Cover myself completely with blankets pretending I'm trapped, the cave mouth blocked off by a rockfall. I see a glimmer of light, crawl toward it. The tunnel narrows and narrows, I can just barely fit, and I can peer out the hole where the light is, but no way will I ever fit.

Trapped.

That's when it starts. This panic. Squirmy and delicious, but real panic. I lie there trying to resist but it's unbearable. I'm suffocating, I'm going to explode if I can't move my arms and legs.

I have to throw the covers off.

I'm four years old, I'm five.

I'm thirty-five, waking up at night broken out in itchy sweats, shivering, trying to catch my breath, but I can't get enough air in my lungs. My body I'm suffocating inside of. My skin I need to burst out of. Otherwise I'm going to die.

I'm going to die anyway.

Do the astronauts carry cyanide pills? I ask Dad once. Because, twelve years old, I'm fascinated, also worried—what happens if they get stuck in orbit, oxygen running out, no hope of rescue?

Contingencies, Dad says. A new word for me. No cyanide capsules, he laughs. You're always afraid if you prepare for something like that, it might actually happen. So you just make sure it doesn't.

Contingencies. Call everything by a different name. I understand it even back then.

Which is to say I don't believe in AIDS.

Still, I feel it for months, almost three years in fact. Some shadow I can't pinpoint, but there's one night I jerk awake ridiculous with cold sweat. Towel myself down, climb shivering back in bed and try to drift off. But every time I'm almost asleep, this explosion in my ears and I jump. Some part of me touching a live wire that sparks. A charged fence I keep stumbling into.

Spooky.

I can feel myself collapsing inside.

Or there're the shits. A year and a half of nonstop firewater hissing out my tender rear end. Three trips to the toilet, four trips, five.

I'm always fascinated by the stuff that comes out of me, since I was a kid. Hard shit and soft shit and runny shit and some with amazingly varied, intricate textures. Piss and come and snot and phlegm and spit and tears and sweat and pus and blood. My fingernails and toenails. My hair.

My whole interesting bag of insides I keep from the world.

Viscera.

Alanya was Alaja was Kalonoros was Coracesium was Korakesion. Pompey defeating pirates here. Anthony presenting the city to Cleopatra. Alaeddin Keykubad who calls himself God's Shadow on Earth ruling from his winter palace on the promontory. Time all piled up like old carpets on the floor of a mosque.

We're five years in the Yayla Palas, what Mom dubs the Heroin Hotel and it sticks. Tall narrow building hanging off the steep hill of the old town, scary balconies with fabulous views. We have the whole fifth floor to ourselves. Big rooms, Arab-style toilets. Wash basin in the hall.

It's not the best place or the worst, just where we stop for some weeks that turn into years. But after Istanbul I'm glad to be away from all that craziness. Those dusks in Gülhane Park below Topkapi, all the men walking in pairs, arm in arm, or alone, the ones I'm after. Snatches of love in the weeds that've overgrown some collapsed building with columns. Some itch and craving I can't get over, for semen and shit and mucus and blood.

Liminal things.

There's a saying in this place: The earth that feeds you one day will eat you.

My eyes are closed, but I can see clearly. George is sitting on the side of my bed. He sings in a low voice. Across the wide Missouri, he sings. Then: Masai. He mouths the word and grins. He's a blur, a bit of fog. I can see through him. I'm not scared at all.

Asante, I murmur, not sure whether I'm asleep or awake. Nyakyusa. Kikuyu. Kaguru.

Hey, George, I tell him, look at me. I'm halfway to Africa.

He puts his lips to my ear. His breath is cold. Whispering: here's what the Kaguru say. Those newly born and those just out of it, there's no difference between them. Squawling babies and corpses growing cold. They're both provisional. Undecided which side of the spirit barrier they want to be on. A lot of back and forth in those first months.

Why'd you do it?

He looks wily.

Decided, he says, to give them the slip.

Me too?

Everybody, he says. It was slip-away time. Travel time.

George, I say.

George in his coffin in the heavy clay soil of Tennessee. Anaerobic splitting of proteins by bacteria. Forming incompletely oxidized alkaloids.

Rot. Decay. Decomposition.

Though they probably shot him full of enough embalming fluid to last a lifetime.

Maybe they took him back to Greece. Cremated his corpse and scattered the ashes in the beautiful bay of Nafplion where he grew up. Where the Gods go walking in the sky over the mountains.

Maybe the Masai spirited him away by night. Maybe the hyenas of the high plain made sweet feast of his bones.

Every day of my life I miss you so much. Your filthy mouth and generous brilliant mind. When you told me about the astral flights you took beyond the grip of the solar system, you made me feel so powerful and so free.

On the floor below us in the Yayla Palas some Germans just a few years older than me are camped out, about as permanent as we are. Three or four girls—all blond and I can't keep track, one thin, sick-looking guy and another guy who takes my breath away. The smell from their hash pipes drifts up all hours. I'm crazy about the smell.

I see them selling handmade jewelry to Scandinavian tourists in Alaeddin's castle courtyard, but when tourist season's over they don't do much of anything. Neither do we. We wait for the odd check from America.

Funny I'm not better friends for living so long near them, but finally I do know them.

Let me fix you up my friend, Uwe says.

I'm looking at his hollow cheek, the stubble I want to kiss. He's so sweet and really into one of the German girls and there's no chance anything'll happen unless some reality changes. I take a long draw on his pipe.

It's dreamy. You could give up your whole life. A door and it opens just a crack, but enough for me to see. I'll always know. I'll remember.

His low laugh, that grin he gets and his blond hair falling in his ice-blue eyes. Legs spread wide where he's sitting on a cushion on the floor in boxer shorts, and I can't take my eyes off one of his nuts I see hanging heavy in its sac. My mouth dry and my head fuzzy. He keeps laughing, scratches himself there and I'm up and moving over to the cushion where he is, I'm slipping my hand up the leg of his shorts. Slow to react. He holds my wrist but not hard while my hand explores. *Herrlich*, I whisper, *nefis*, and there's that low laugh again, his eyes closed, his hands not pushing me away while I ease him out of his shorts.

My head's spinning. I feel like vomiting. I go down on him.

Hey, hey, my friend, watch that, he says, pushing me away—but gentle. He taps me on the head, laughs that low laugh. Crazy, he says.

I don't like the way I feel afterward. Itchy and dry from smoking.

I lie in bed at night listening to him fuck his girl and jerk off in time to all the noise. So why am I into him like I am, and for so long? Months, in fact. A major source of itch.

Once in a blue moon we get high, I grope him and a few times I actually make him come. Lick the magic off his belly. His creepy friend with the cough's the one who's got his eye on me, though. Two or three times before my head gets straightened out I find myself on the receiving end of what he calls his fat sausage. His hands are cold on my rib cage and that shallow cough racks him the whole time he's doing me.

Schatz, he always says when he pulls out. *Mein schöner Schatz.*

We range up and down that coast, Mom and I. My *arkadaş*, she starts calling me, slang for road buddy, because for a while it seems the only time we see each other is when we're going somewhere. She hears about things and wants to go, and we end up in amazing places.

There's the chimera at Olympus, a fire burning in midair up on the mountaintop and if you douse it, it starts to burn again immediately. A pale blue flame. In ancient times they could see it far out at sea. Nobody has any explanation.

There's the entrance to hell, the Corycian Caves, another idea of hers, though she tells me she doesn't know why she's so keen to see it. Sure she'll recognize it immediately as somewhere she's already been half a dozen times at least. A guide takes us down endless narrow steps past bushes tied up with wishing cloths and then we're at the mouth. *Dikkat*, he says. Caution. Not to kneel or crouch or fall down on the ground. He gestures with his hands. Deadly gas rises up to the height of three feet. Priests used to carry birds into the cave with them, and when they came out the birds were mysteriously dead and the priests unharmed.

How they maintained their authority over the people.

Nothing changes, says Mom.

The air's thick, cool, muggy. An old abandoned church that was a temple before it was a church guards the entrance. Roof gone. Frescoes all graffitied up. Looking back from the belly of the cave, we can see it silhouetted against the sky.

We half slide down a mud slope till we can hear the roar of the underground river. Where it comes from, nobody's discovered, but it enters the sea a couple of miles away with such force it pushes the salt water back, and animals wade out into the ocean to drink from that tongue of sweet water.

The river Achilles' mother dipped him in when he was a baby, Mom tells me. Except the heel she held him by.

Mom's so taken with the past, all these myths and legends.

You should go back to school, I tell her. Become an archaeologist.

Don't tempt me, she says.

I tell her that's exactly what I'm trying to do.

The river roars like some great monster trapped down there trying to break free. The countryside's lousy with the haunts and lairs of defunct monsters. One chasm goes three hundred feet down, no way in or out. Trees growing down there don't reach even a third of the way up the sheer cliffsides. Where a hundred-headed serpent was kept that roared like a bull, barked like a dog, spoke the language of the gods. The devil, say Muslims, in only one of his many memorable disguises.

Or there's the ancient ruined city the Turks call Kanlidivane. Crazy Place of Blood. Nobody knows a thing about it—not its ancient name, or its history, or why its people chose to perch their city on the very edge of another one of those gaping holes in the earth. Middle of nowhere. The locals say the inhabitants kept wild animals down in the chasm—there were lions here then—and threw criminals and foreigners there to be devoured.

At sunset the walls of the great sinkhole turn blood red. We sit on the edge, dangle our feet down, foreigners, criminal too, probably. The angle of light picks out a relief carved way down on the cliffside. Ancient figures of men. The sight makes me shiver.

Truth is, I'm taken with all this stuff too.

Walking down the street and a man sitting in a chair outside his shop greets me.

Merhaba, I tell him. Nasılsınız.

Turkish, he says with surprise.

Çok küçük, I tell him.

You walk this street often, he says. Come inside.

There's something in his smile I have to trust.

CARPET REPARATOR says the sign above the door. The dark room he leads me into—the ceiling's a huge dome. Everywhere's hung with carpets and the air smells like tobacco and the barnyard reek of old wool. Beyond the wall I can hear girls laughing, splashes of water.

Very old hamam, he explains. This part is my shop, but back there is still hamam. Perhaps we will go there one afternoon. But now you would like tea, yes?

He assumes he knows about me and maybe he's right.

Sit, he says, gesturing to a stack of folded carpets. Be still and listen. There is much you can learn here.

Just like that. I'm willing to be captive for a while.

His name's Demir, and in this dim light he could almost be the spitting image of George, who hated the Turks so much—it was the one thing that lit him up.

Something in my heart goes out.

Teach me, I tell Demir. I want to learn.

We sip strong tea.

In Istanbul, he says, I was many years a banker. Life is too short. A filthy city. The crowds, the traffic. Three, four times a day I changed my white shirt to keep clean. No, I say, to ugly life. I choose to live in a surround of beauty.

Before I know it he's unfurling magic: carpets he lets loose with a flick and shimmy of the wrist. They settle on top of each other, their voices speak to me, I can hear them as Demir delights in naming their names: Doşemealti, Tashpinar, Ushak, Adana.

Scorpions, he says, pointing out details. Ram's horns, sheep's eyes. Flowers and mountains and those are stars.

Tells me about the yayla, the high pasture where the nomads take their flocks in summer. Every Turk, he says, has nostalgia for the yayla. Deep in the blood, like those fish who are swimming upstream.

Salmon, I say.

I tell him the hotel where we're living is the Yayla Palas.

See? he says. Then spits. What a dump, he tells me. From now on you live here.

Hours of my life go by, whole lifetimes. I learn my way around. Ensis and kapunuks to cover the tent door, chuvals to store supplies, torbas for the household goods, asmalyks to hang from the camel, yolami to tie up the tent. Mafrashes to cradle the infant, namazlyks to pray on, turbehlyks to spread on the grave. Weaving their way from birth to death.

The tribes Tekke and Salor and Yomut and Arabatshi. The color red from madder roots or insect bodies, brown from nutshells and oak bark.

Saffron crocus yellow and indigo blue. Mordants of alum and iron.

When that summer comes I strike up conversations with tourists, bring them back to the shop, melt into the shadows to watch desire light up their eyes as Demir shakes out a golden carpet from Milas, soumak weaves, a dark Herki kilim with a constellation of stars.

Their breath goes and so does mine. Demir plys the pile, folds an edge over to show the knot count. Snaps his fingers to order me out to fetch apple tea. After each sale he stuffs my shirt pocket full of lira.

He lives in three rooms with a wide balcony behind the shop. The view's not as grand as from the Yayla Palas, but it's still grand—the bay all blue and shining, the pink-gray mountains rising past the banana plantations.

He'll have Mom over, Attila and Tolga, the other runner boys in the shop, his nephew Shahin, who's just come in from the country. Cooks feasts for us there, grill kidneys and lamb chops, tomatoes and peppers. Bowls of cool yogurt and cucumber, fresh bread from the bakery down the street. Sweet round watermelons cracked open to finish us off.

He recites to us from the love songs of Hafiz and Jalal ud-Din Rumi. Sitting cross-legged on a cushion, sings us ghazals in a clear high voice. Persian, the most beautiful language. Like the music of the dove in the rafters.

A little wine, Demir says, a song of love. Friendship. What could be better?

You wonder, he says, am I married? I will tell you that I have two sons, a wife. They live elsewhere. I see them once a month. It is better that way.

He drinks too much raki, gets sentimental with Mom, putting his arm around me and her both, teary-eyed, telling her how I must be Turkish in the blood. Telling her, You are his mother but I am his father, no? No one but my own son could be like this to me.

Which Attila and Tolga, who've had a couple of glasses of raki, think is a hoot, and Shahin sits there smiling politely, deliciously, never saying a word.

Shahin which means Falcon, raptor, bird of prey. I know him by his laugh too—not low but full in the throat, some pure delight at the world that sweeps me off my feet. He laughs at a taste of ice cream, the look of old rugs, bats in a storehouse, cool water he washes in. Laughs at sunlight like it tickles him. I've been waiting for this boy my whole life. Crooked teeth and dark, close-cropped hair. Obsidian eyes all the way from the Mongolian steppes. He's young, barely seventeen, and it's hard to believe I'm going on twenty-six already, but boy am I smitten.

I never look Uwe's direction again.

We go to the hamam behind Demir's shop and I eat him up with my eyes. He sees me, splashes water my way, we chase each other around the pool. It's late afternoon, no one else around. Two birds have gotten inside the dome. Our cavorting startles them, they fly up noisily, circle around the patchy tiles of the ceiling. Then settle on the ledge up there. White doves, and their dusky cooing covers us when suddenly we stop our frolicking. Both breathing hard, looking at each other across the pool.

Please, please, I'm thinking.

I don't know what he's thinking.

We walk through the water toward each other, waist deep. Walk right up to each other, face to face. My heart setting off depth charges inside me. No sound except the lap of water and those doves purring and trilling low. I work up the courage and then I reach out and put my hands on his waist. He flinches at my touch, then laughs, a soundless laugh in the back of his throat. I could drown in all this. I hold my breath and move my hands down. He pushes them gently away. Laughs again. I touch him there again, and again he brushes me off, but so gently, and when I touch him again he closes his eyes, tilts back his head. His hands find me and touch me back the same way I'm touching him.

At dusk Demir takes us round to the Kuyularönü mosque for prayers. I wonder if he can tell.

If our bodies are glowing. Our eyes on fire.

I'm in love with how there's nothing but empty space in a mosque.

Islam. Total submission to the will of God.

Muslim. One who submits totally.

Demir teaches me to wash at the fountain in the inner courtyard: first my hands and wrists, then rinse my mouth, my nose. Wash every part of my face three times: ear lobes, forehead, under the chin. The right arm to the elbow and then the left, the hair on my head, the holes of my ears. My feet and ankles and in between my toes.

Five times a day, he teaches, we are asked to pray. But once is enough. When I cook the other night, you notice I leave for five minutes? I am in my room praying. I say to God, My friends are here, there is food. Already God knows that. And what I do not say also. Because we say: God alone knows the secret things.

On the floor of the Kuyularönü mosque, carpets lie a foot thick. A hundred, two hundred years of carpets, Demir says. The dust rises thick as he peels back layer after layer. Gift carpets, offerings. Births, marriages, death.

There is a strange fever, he says. Perhaps it is in the dust. Yayla fever. It is like nostalgia, but it is a madness. A beautiful madness for carpets. For some a way of life. Perhaps I am not wrong to say you have caught this fever. Your temperature is a few degrees elevated, or you have chills.

I have to laugh.

It's possible, I tell him. It's very possible.

At night when I'm asleep someone comes in my room. A feeling I have when I wake up.

Hey Mom, I announce. Guess what? My room's haunted.

She's eating figs on the balcony.

I dream of blood on the walls, she says. Bloody handprints. When I was in Istanbul I dreamed there was a tidal wave of blood that knocked down the city walls.

She outdoes me on that score, I think.

I go back to my room and turn the place upside down while she goes off to the Radiation Cave, which she says makes her feel better. A room of red rock under the castle promontory.

Early the next morning I understand everything. A kitten's asleep at my feet, though I startle it and it leaps to the windowsill. Pure black, little body quivering. Look of terror in its eyes.

But it doesn't leave. We watch each other.

I'm always dropping scraps of food under the table and they show up out of nowhere. Drives Mom crazy. A plague of cats, she says. And word seems to have gotten around about what a pushover you are.

I reach out slowly, slowly, toward the windowsill. Stroke it lightly with my fingertips. No bigger than my palm I scoop it up in. It's got some kind of eye infection. Poor little cat, female I see, and I can feel its heart beating.

So you've heard about me, I tell her.

We take a motorboat around to the phosophorus cave. Bright sun on the water, salt spray, suck of waves on the red rocks at the base of the cliff. The cave's a mouth and it swallows us, we're inside, its walls all glimmering blue. Turning our skin blue, our hands and arms and faces. Our lips and tongues.

I kiss this ticklish boy all over and he laughs with delight. Doesn't say a word. Doesn't have to.

Or we lie on Cleopatra's Beach and we're all talk. Is there bread in America? he asks me seriously. Are there any trees left? Did I live in a skyscraper there?

Is it against the law for black people to live in certain states? Is their language outlawed, like the Kurdish language is in Turkey?

Is it true that everyone in America has AIDS?

Where does he get these things? I laugh. He's infinitely curious.

Turkey is very beautiful, he tells me with eager pride. It is good to live here.

It is good, I agree.

Better than America, he says tentatively.

It's so strange to hear that word.

Back in his village, he says, his family has chosen him a bride. He will have strong sons.

When, he asks, laying his head on my bare chest, will I get married?

When God wills, I tell him.

A girl from my village? he asks. Have my parents chosen?

I stroke his scalp, run my fingers through his black hair. Falcon, bird of prey. Raptor which always sounds to me like rapture. He has just the barest beginnings of a mustache.

This single moment, here and now, I'm so in love I could die.

Arjuna and Krishna in the war chariot. First day of the great battle. The white horses snorting, stamping the dust with their hooves. A hundred thousand men suited up to die. On both sides: fathers and grandfathers, teachers, uncles, brothers, sons, grandsons, friends, companions, lovers.

Arjuna's mouth goes dry, his body shakes, his skin burns.

He's overcome with compassion.

Why are they about to go through all this?

Teach me, he turns to Krishna.

Krishna turns himself into a billion billion worlds. The entire universe with everything moving and not moving standing together in his body. It's magnificent and scary and shot through with fabulous joy.

Everything there is. Action and inaction. Purpose and accident. The transitory and eternal.

Then Krishna turns terrible. Fire burns in his bright eyes. He becomes Time itself.

Even if you don't do a thing, he tells Arjuna, all these soldiers will cease to exist. The families they left and the villages they grew up in. The forests and mountains, the stars and the empty space between the stars.

Time, he says. Cause of world destruction. Cosmic annihilator. Without lifting a hand.

Time will wipe out everything.

JONATHAN'S ARK

"Hey Stayton," said the voice over the phone that day in 1985. Musical, drawn out in a gentle drawl. At first I couldn't place it—but only for an instant, because then with a thrill of terror I knew.

"You tracked me down," I said to him, the first thing that came into my head.

His voice was blurry through a storm of static. "I've come back to haunt you," he said. "Your worst nightmare come true. Were you trying to hide from me?"

Yes, I thought. Go away and leave me alone. Leave us both alone. But I didn't say that. I had felt this moment once before, back in high school when Dr. Lennox had assigned us lab partners, and I'd looked across the classroom to meet Jonathan's eye for the first time and thought, Oh, of course. It has to be this way.

Part of me had never doubted I'd have to come across him again.

"This is a really terrible connection," I said. "Where on earth are you? Did you die or something?"

All at once the noise vanished and it was as if he were right there in the room with me.

"Yes, as a matter of fact," he said.

There was a pause, then a resurgence of static.

"Well," I said—shouted rather, as if that might help—"which way did you go? Up or down?"

"Sideways. I'm in a phone booth at the post office and these little

266

flashing numbers say I've got a minute and a half left on this call. So what do you want to chat about? Let me tell you about this gorgeous shoeshine boy who hangs out on Atatürk Boulevard."

His voice weaved in and out of audibility, and maybe he wasn't saying what I thought he was saying.

"So where are you really?" I asked him.

"Turkey," he said. "The country, that is."

"This call must be costing you a fortune."

"That's all you can say?"

"I don't know what else to say," I said. "I'm speechless."

"Well, I'm coming to see you, so get prepared. Now write this down."

And he gave me the date and time and airline of his arrival.

"I don't want to have to come looking for you," he said. "I really, really want to see you. I can hardly wait."

Then the line went dead.

I wasn't without misgivings. "It's just been such a long time," I told Kai when he got home, "and I was incredibly mean to him. I was a coward."

"I'm sure if he called you, he forgives you," Kai said.

"But I don't forgive myself. You don't know what a coward I was."

"I'd say you've paid for it by now. I'd say your account's in order. If that's the way you want to think of it."

"He's going to change things," I said. "He changed my life once. If he comes here, no way will he not change things."

"You're still in love with him," Kai diagnosed.

"No," I lied, "it's not that."

"Don't worry," Kai assured me. "If it's any consolation, I'm still in love with him too."

Which of course only increased my vague sense of dread. Despite all the ways I knew I'd changed for the better, the prospect of having to know Jonathan again—of having, at the very least, to renegotiate all the old terms—took the form of a depressingly obvious recurrent dream in which I tried to bar the door against somebody, then flung it open and started chasing, with murderous fury, whoever it was who'd been trying to get in. But then I could never find him, and I'd wake up itchy with sweat, my heart still racing after that invader I'd turned the tables on.

When I first caught a glimpse of him several weeks later at the arrivals gate at Dulles I recognized him instantly, which was more than I'd been afraid might happen, but I still didn't know what to do next. He came toward us, smiling radiantly, arms outstretched, and my first impulse was to flee. "You go first," I told Kai, though in the end it turned into an awkward three-way hug that was, I think, just fine.

"I would ask which of you is which," were Jonathan's first words, "but I'm pretty sure I remember."

I remember thinking when I saw him come through the gate, He's not as beautiful as he used to be. His head was practically shaved bare; he wore a beard that was more stubble than beard.

He'd stepped off the plane carrying nothing but a small, impractical-looking wicker basket. It turned out to be all the luggage he had.

"And you wouldn't believe how much trouble I had getting this through customs," he said.

Inside the basket was a little black cat.

"Say hello," Jonathan said, "to Scheherazade. And Scheherazade, say hello to . . . well . . . you know, guys, this is scary. I don't even know you anymore. Do you feel incredibly scared too?"

He held the cat up for us to see—a scrawny, not very attractive thing. It hissed defiantly, or in terror.

"She barely speaks English," Jonathan apologized, "and she's jet-lagged and suffering a bit of culture shock. Like me. So I'll be up front about things. Can I stay with you guys for a while? I mean, like a few weeks. Till I see what's up? I don't take up much space in the world these days. You'll hardly notice me."

"What an odd thing to say," Kai told him. "I'm counting on you to be very loud and sassy and rude. To keep me company. Stayton's always so quiet."

"I am not," I protested.

"Well," Kai said, "getting better, I have to say. Becoming something of a political activist," he told Jonathan.

"You?" Jonathan asked.

"We've all got to become political," I said, "if we're going to survive."

"I *have* been away a long time," Jonathan said. "It'll be good to be home, I think."

Home, as we showed him around, mostly amounted to all the evidence of our life together. The big double bed. The guest room where he'd staying.

"You own so many things," he said, not so much a challenge as simply an observation.

For her part, Scheherazade took imperious possession at once, gamboling about, exploring under the furniture and inside all the closets. She stalked us cautiously. Satisfied, for the time being, with her new space, she climbed into his lap, burrowing her head fiercely into his chest and kneading urgently with her claws. "Looking for the nipple," Jonathan said. "Desperate for that nipple. Ow," he laughed. "It's my third nipple she really likes. The magic one."

I'd forgotten all about Jonathan's third nipple. On his right side just below his regular nipple, hardly distinguishable from an ordinary mole, it nonetheless used to make me vaguely squeamish, as if all my doubts about his body were somehow confirmed in that nub of uncanniness. Now the mention of it brought him all back to me in a way he hadn't been brought back by the oddly subdued drive home from Dulles. I'd been disconcerted by how shy I felt with him, how tentative. By how quiet he was with us.

Having found whatever fugitive contentment she was after, Scheherazade commenced a deep purr. "Malnourished as a kitten," Jonathan said. "Probably a bit of brain damage. But she makes up for it by sheer force of personality. Sort of like me."

He had an easy, loose sort of laugh that I didn't quite remember. An odd tone of self-deprecation. His eyes were bright, slightly hectic. Years in the Mediterranean sun had left him very dark.

Because Kai had a concert in a couple of hours, he excused himself to the bedroom to dress.

"There's so much I wish I could tell you," Jonathan apologized, "but I don't know what to say. Where to begin or where to end. Let's just say lots of stuff happened to me, most of which you wouldn't believe even if I told you. Let's just say I'm here. But I do have some plans, you'll be thrilled to hear. I'm not here as a bum or anything. I'm going to be very responsible and start a small business. I'm going to open a carpet store."

He didn't say it as a joke, though I certainly thought it might be.

"How bourgeois," was all I could think of to say.

Jonathan beamed. "That's right," he said, playing a bit of drum riff on his knee, all at once the antic Jonathan I remembered. "Pay taxes and everything. Hey, I'm looking for investors."

I'm not sure what I'd expected, though in the last several weeks I'd done my share of romantic imaginings.

"Well, you always were full of surprises."

"The drag is, I can never surprise myself. Same old stuff, over and over. That's why I came home."

"Ta da," Kai said, appearing in his tuxedo.

"I love men in suits," Jonathan said. "Can I come? I never heard you play. What exactly do you play again?"

"No," Kai told him gently. "Not tonight. You're jet-lagged and culture-shocked, remember. You'll fall asleep and snore. Plus you barely speak English, or was that only the cat? Come next week. I have a nice violist who would love to meet you, I'm sure. There's plenty of time for everything. *Plenty* of time."

To me Kai said, a few minutes later and privately, "Don't keep him up, you hear? That child needs rest. He looks exhausted."

They were our first words together about him.

"Go sleep," I commanded Jonathan after he'd made much of the tuxedoed Kai, who did look extremely elegant all dressed up, and then Kai was finally out the door.

But Jonathan couldn't sleep. After half an hour he wandered back into the living room in his boxer shorts and socks.

There was something both stirring and sad in seeing that body I'd made love to all those years ago.

He watched me looking at him.

"Still so skinny," I said, since I had to say something.

"I must have a tape worm or something," he laughed. "You've done a bit of filling out."

I patted my little pot belly that wasn't, I hoped, too noticeable.

"You and Kai both," he said.

"Domesticity, you know."

"I just can't get over it," he exclaimed as he settled himself next to me on the sofa, so close his bare leg rubbed up against my clothed one. "Stayton Voegli and Kai Dempsey. Just blows my mind."

"Five years," I told him. "It's kind of amazing, really. We might just be together for life. What do you think about that?"

"You want my approval," Jonathan said.

"I just want to know what you think," I told him, though of course he was right.

He laid his head against my shoulder. Put his arm around me.

"When I went away," he said, "I told myself I wasn't ever coming back. And to tell you the truth, once I was over there I never missed a thing about this place. Not a single thing. Like it never existed." He turned to face me. "Are you disappointed?"

"You really loved George," I told him.

"And you," he said. "I loved you too."

"Ouch," I told him.

"Why ouch?"

The weight of his body against mine was thrilling. "Oh," I sighed, feeling desperate inside. I'd made my choices, and I'd stick with them. "I shouldn't ever have lost you," I told him. "I shouldn't have, but I did."

With that, he sort of butted his head affectionately into my shoulder, and I rubbed the back of his neck. I could see he was poking out of his boxers. I wanted to cry tears, but I just held him like that for a full minute or two, his head butting my shoulder and my hand on the back of his skull till he murmured groggily that he guessed he really was very, very tired after all.

Jonathan's arrival sent us into a strange sort of flurry. It wasn't just Kai, in whose behavior I recognized some traces of his manic ministrations toward me when I first appeared on his horizon: I noticed it in both of us—how we seemed afraid to be still with Jonathan around. We were constantly arranging things to do, places to go, friends to meet. We gave dinner parties for people we otherwise hardly ever saw, danced at clubs we never went to, attended twice our quota of chamber music and ballet. Jonathan was game, though he remained detached from it all—as if he were watching from a great distance, deciding whether he should venture among us or not.

One cool day in autumn when we were starting to run out of ideas to keep ourselves busy with this friend so recently returned from the dead, we packed a picnic basket from the gourmet deli around the corner and drove down to Virginia to visit Kai's property. It was the first time we'd been there since his grandmother's funeral some three years earlier. The house was much the worse for wear—still salvageable, but just barely. The tin roof had rusted through in places, the front porch was pulling away from the main structure. Another year would tip it irreversibly toward ruin.

We feasted in a little falling-down arbor of climbing rose, long since bloomed. Late season yellow jackets buzzed over our spread, and Kai would yelp whenever one came too near.

"They're trying to sting me on my lips," he said. "Ruin my brilliant career."

Jonathan kept trying to coax one to land on his finger, to no avail.

The woods beyond the house failed to hide the buildings of the recently constructed New Kent County Correctional Facility.

"It truly does ruin the view," Kai lamented. "Pascal was the smart one. At least he got a few dollars out of his acres. All I get is to pay taxes on property that's unsellable."

Jonathan had said little all day, but now he perked up. "Not property," he corrected. "Real estate. In fact, very real estate."

I remember he said it with such strange insistence. He walked around the weedy yard, touching the trunks of the old apple trees, that same apartness about him that hadn't faded the way I'd thought it might. The ground beneath the trees was littered with windfall.

"Here," he said, scooping up a couple of the stunted fruit and tossing one to each of us. "Eat and be happy."

Kai bit into his and then spit it out. "Well," he said, though only to me, "it certainly is tart enough."

Since Jonathan's attention had wandered on to something else, I discreetly laid mine aside.

"That boy," Kai shook his head as we both watched that slight, lost-looking figure negotiate the brambles down by the field. Odd to think, after all these years, how we two were the couple and Jonathan was so alone. Was this what they meant when they said a life had come to nothing? I winced even to think it, but I knew that probably it was true. He gave the impression of someone who'd been knocked violently off course, and had struggled for some time, unsuccessfully, to find his way back.

"Hey," he called out to no one in particular, then came bounding back over to where the two of us sat. He dropped down abruptly between us. "I have an idea," he said.

"It's too nice an afternoon for ideas," Kai told him lazily.

"I'm serious." Again, there was that intensity about him. He looked from Kai to me and back again. "We should build an ark here," he said simply.

I laughed.

As for Kai, there was a wry tone he could sometimes adopt, the verbal equivalent of a raised eyebrow. "You mean like Noah's ark, that kind of ark?"

Jonathan was looking at us with unrelenting seriousness. As if he'd seen a ghost and we didn't believe him.

"Apres moi," he said darkly, "le deluge."

"Yeow. Where'd you learn to talk like that?" Kai told him. In an instant things had turned strange, like a cloud passing across the face of the sun. We all felt it.

But then it was gone. "Oh," Jonathan said offhandedly, "long ago, in a distant galaxy far, far away. You haven't lived till you've seen *Star Wars* dubbed into Turkish. Believe me."

I was a little annoyed with him. "What about the carpet store?" I asked. "I thought your big idea was to open a carpet store."

"That too," Jonathan said. "I have lots of big ideas."

I'd forgotten just how spacey he could be.

He jumped to his feet and started pacing in narrow circles on the grass. "What you two have been needing," he diagnosed, "is some kind of fabulous adventure in your lives. I can read the danger signs. That apartment you've got, for example, has got to go. Washington—got to go. All that scene. It's going to suffocate you if you don't watch out."

After all we'd done for him in the last few weeks, this seemed a little unwarranted.

"You need," he went on, "to be living in some kind of real place. Real life."

"Real estate," Kai said.

"That's *exactly* what I have in mind," Jonathan shouted. He put his arms out and started to twirl. "This is making me dizzy," he said.

Then you should stop, I thought.

"What's this got to do with building an ark?" I asked him, and he abruptly came to a halt.

"An ark," he said, almost as if he'd forgotten. He paused. "Well, we have to build it in order to find out. That's why we *should* build it. So we'll know. Maybe it'll go to other galaxies. Maybe it'll be orchestra powered. Maybe we'll get Beethoven to be the pilot and Captain Nemo on drums. Maybe Esther Williams can come along. And a library of Persian love poems. Plus many, many shoeshine boys—I know most of their names—off the streets of Constantinople."

By the end he was practically singing.

"See?" Jonathan said. "I told you I was serious. You let me live here, do whatever I need to do. In other words, trust me. And you'll be so surprised at what happens. You'll love me for it."

"Don't you think this needs to be, well, thought through?" I suggested.

Jonathan flashed with impatience. "No," he said furiously. "Enough thinking. Please, Kai. All you have to do is say yes."

I made a skeptical face at Kai, though he didn't respond the way I'd expected. He frowned at me in what I took to be reprimand.

"I thought you were still interested in trying to sell this place," I reminded him.

"I'm thinking," he said brusquely. "Don't distract me when I'm thinking."

I'd never seen him quite like this. It was Jonathan. Why was he here with us at all? I didn't dare look his way, afraid I'd betray myself.

Jonathan whistled a stray bit of tune, then broke it off.

"Okay, Jonathan," Kai said—a little impatiently, I noted with satisfaction. "You build us an ark."

"Yes!" Jonathan whooped.

"Oh brother," I said without quite meaning to. Jonathan dropped to his knees in front of where I sat and grabbed my shoulders. His breath was sour in my face. "You may think this is part of the Vegan Star Tyranny's master plan," he said feverishly, "but I assure you it's not. It's a guaranteed countermeasure, in fact."

"The Vegan Star Tyranny?" asked Kai.

"I'll tell you about it sometime," I told him grimly. Meanwhile, I could only wrest myself from Jonathan's grip. Getting to my feet, I headed for the car. Just beyond the camouflage of woods, the afternoon sun glinted off the barbed wire of the prison.

Our trip back was marked by complete silence. Exhausted by his appeal, Jonathan slept in the backseat. Between Kai and me there was some odd constraint, as if we were both vaguely embarrassed by what had happened, what we had let each other see of ourselves. But more than that there were the things in Kai I didn't know about. What he really thought or felt about Jonathan, for example. What he really thought or felt about me.

I only hoped that by the time we were safely back in our Washington apartment, the one Jonathan had so airily disdained, all this would be mercifully forgotten.

But Jonathan didn't forget. I remember that time so well. For the next couple of weeks he practically disappeared into the library. Then one night he was ready: he spread his plans out on the coffee table and took us through them. He'd worked hard, there was something almost touching in the way he'd drawn everything up, and I remembered him telling me how he used to make moon maps as a kid, a calendar based on meteor storms. How it used to drive his dad crazy.

What he proposed was this: bring the house back into shape, cover the roof with solar panels, then add on a greenhouse in back, the two wings intersecting in an L. Inside we'd grow herbs and greens and vegetables. One hundred percent self-sustaining. He'd done the research. We could live in the house and off the greenhouse, so to speak. We'd sell the herbs and greens to local restaurants. The vegetables we'd keep to feed ourselves.

He foresaw a fish pond, some chickens.

"I trust you completely," Kai said. I said nothing. It wasn't my property, after all, though I sensed that more than just property was going to be affected by all this.

In the interval between his phone call from Turkey and the moment he stepped off that plane, I'd wondered how he was going to change us. Vague, looming anxieties—but you never worry about the one thing that's actually going to get you.

I confided to Kai later, as we lay together in bed, "This will never become a reality. You know that, don't you?"

"Probably not," he told me. "But personally I think Jonathan's a genius. I always have. So there."

"You really are in love," I said, not without a tinge of jealousy, or alarm, or admiration, some tricky admixture whose complexity, I knew, Kai would definitely be able to hear. All he did, though, was shrug his shoulders.

Suddenly I found myself angry. "Who is this person," I asked, "to just walk into our lives like this?"

"What are you so afraid of? Because there's something you're terrified of, I can tell."

"Him," I said. "I'm afraid of him."

Kai was silent for a minute. "No you're not," he told me. "It's yourself you're still scared of. Unfinished business you've still got."

I'd decided the best course of action was to stand aside. Not to hamper in any way, but also not to give one bit of encouragement to Jonathan's madness. In spite of that, he ended up talking me into it with all the ease in the world. "I need to go up north," he said. "There're some places I have to see. Prototypes. New Alchemy Institute. Solviva. There's this lesbian collective in Vermont. Hey Stayton, can you drive me?" He hadn't, of course, had a driver's license in years. Before I knew it, I'd taken some of my vacation time from the bookstore and, while Kai was deep in the winter concert season, we headed north.

We arrived at the lesbian collective on a snowy day in early December, the first blizzard of the season, and were greeted by a woman dressed in bib overalls, a flannel shirt, and carrying a pitchfork.

"Perfect," Jonathan said as we got out of the car.

Meg was our self-appointed guide and guardian. She led us into the long greenhouse filled with plants of unimaginable lushness. The very air glowed green with them. Outside the double windows a foot of snow covered the ground.

Ten women lived here at the collective, she explained, though not all at the same time. One was a lawyer in Burlington, another ran a candle shop in Rutland. But this was their spiritual base. They all came back from time to time for soul nourishment.

There was profit here as well: they'd grossed $70,000 the previous year in sales to local restaurants. The secret of their success, she told us—pausing for full effect—was chicken breath.

She pulled open a door on the side of the greenhouse and we were confronted with a long, narrow coop of chickens.

"Just think about it," she said. "Each individual chicken generates eight B.T.U.'s per pound per hour. That's two and a half gallons of fuel oil per chicken per year. We've got seventy chickens and two roosters, which times two and half is—well, whatever the hell seventy-two times two and a half works out to be."

276

"One hundred eighty," Jonathan said.

"I'll take your word. But a lot. And on top of that there's the chicken breath."

Jonathan thought for a moment, then he said, "Carbon dioxide. Of course."

"The CO_2 content in here's four times normal. The plants go wild. They're growing faster in the dead of winter than they would in the peak of summer outdoors."

"Smart," Jonathan told her.

"And something else. Stick to chickens. We got the bright idea of using rabbits, but forget it. Before you know it, five hundred mean, vicious little bunnies. The male ones try to kill each other. You have to keep them apart."

"Leave it to the males of the species," Jonathan said. "Fortunately they'll soon be extinct and the planet will be ruled by peaceful lesbian communes."

"I hope you're not joking," Meg told him.

I think the lesbians liked Jonathan because that day he was wearing, over his jeans, a bright tie-dyed skirt and orange plastic beads around his neck. With all his hair cut off, he looked beautiful and strange and not at all like any man you'd ever seen.

We ate at a big communal table—thick stew of root vegetables, chewy black bread. Homemade candles cast their wavering light. Afterward we were led to the guest room. The greenhouse flowed seamlessly into the living quarters—it was hard to tell where one stopped and the other began. Even in the cubbyhole bedrooms there was room for a plant or two. So-called beneficial insects from the greenhouse drifted about, a little disconcertingly, in the air.

On the double futon that nearly filled the room, we lay together, drowsy from helping chop firewood, gathering greens, a long intense discussion about lesbian separatism—of which Jonathan heartily approved. "Men are just loaded weapons waiting to go off," he had told them. "Women shouldn't have them around the house. Not if they want to get on with their real lives. It's too dangerous."

That had seemed a little extravagant, but I wasn't going to say anything. It occurred to me that the one thing I knew absolutely nothing about was how men and women related to one another. My life had never been about that. The lesbians referred to me as Jonathan's "shy

277

friend," and that was fine. To tell the truth, I was intimidated. Something in those women reminded me of Jonathan's mother, her power and unpredictability. Her volatility.

"This is the first time," Jonathan observed as we lay side by side under homemade quilts blazoned with Amazon ax handles, "that you and I have ever slept in the same bed together. Isn't that extraordinary?"

"No," I said. "That can't be true."

He snuggled in close, his body radiant with warmth. "Then when? That old sofa in the basement doesn't count."

"I'd almost forgotten," I laughed. I was glad to be alone with him like this.

"Naugahyde," he said. "How could you forget? We were pretty great together, remember?"

"I meant I'd almost forgotten the sofa," I said. "Not anything else. Speaking of which," I went on, emboldened by our reminiscence to reach out and rub his bare stomach, "do you think the inside of this place has ever seen one drop of semen?"

"My belly?"

"No, silly. This place. Lesbian Collective."

"Feeling subversive after all that power talk at dinner?" he wondered. "Or just plain horny?"

"A species soon to be extinct," I quoted disapprovingly. Taking him by the wrist I directed his hand under the covers.

"Nice," he said. Then he shivered violently. "Oh, I am so excited!" he exclaimed. I thought he might mean by me, but he went on: "I have so many great plans for us. Our little ark in the countryside. I'm just on fire."

"They've been so friendly here," I said, a little disappointed by the direction of his ardor, though he kept stroking me languidly. "So helpful."

"You sound surprised."

"I didn't know what to expect," I conceded.

"The sisters in the village across the river. Remember? They're our friends."

I hadn't thought in a long time about that empty house where we'd trespassed once, the crazy talking he'd done there.

"You really meant all that."

"I always mean everything I say," he told me. "You just never believe that."

"Well, given what you say, sometimes it's kind of difficult."

"I found lots of guys who were willing to piss on me, by the way."

"You're disgusting."

"See? No faith."

"Yeah, right," I said sourly, "I lost all that some time ago."

It felt good to have my hands on his skinny body once again, though after Kai's solidity, Jonathan felt so insubstantial. I thought of Kai only to will him, for this briefest of interludes, out of my thoughts. Just fifteen minutes, I told myself. For old times.

There was something desperate in our grappling with each other, some ravening hunger that had been pent up for way too long.

I tried to kiss him but he shifted slightly, only to hug at me harder, his hands clutching at my buttocks, roughly massaging my ribs. I took his head in my hands and guided him lovingly down my body.

"Go on," I murmured.

But his lips didn't open.

I ran my fingers through the stubble of his hair and realized with a slight shock that I'd been fantasizing exactly this moment, in various guises, for weeks.

"Suck me off," I whispered in his ear, that phrase with which he'd once so tormented my boyish imagination. I gave him a nudge and then felt his warm, welcoming mouth.

Almost immediately I was over the edge.

He sat up, wiped his mouth, then turned away from me.

"That was a crazy, stupid-fuck thing for us to do," he said flatly.

I reached out and touched his shoulder. "I'm not feeling guilty," I assured him, "so you shouldn't either. It wasn't a betrayal of anybody. It was a reaffirmation."

"I didn't mean that." He turned and looked at me. "It's got nothing to do with that. It's just that you have to never, never let me do anything like that again."

I laughed. Visions of me and Kai and Jonathan all entangled in our big bed together made me unaccountably happy. Suddenly I could see the future. The utopia he'd talked about all those many years ago, when I was young and prudish and afraid. Now I understood.

"Oh," I told him, "we'll have lots more times like this. Believe you me. We're just getting started."

"Stayton," he said, and the tone of his voice stopped me cold. "I was going to talk to you about this. I was going to talk to both of you, but I got scared. I still am scared."

My mouth went dry. I could feel my heart empty itself out.

"Nobody can touch me anymore," Jonathan said in a strained voice. "I'm poison."

"I don't understand," I said dully, though in that instant understanding shot all through me.

"Tears," he said. "Saliva. Snot. Semen. Everything. It's in my blood. You have to stay away, Stayton. Everybody has to stay away."

Why, of all things I'd expected I hadn't expected this, I don't know. I held him by both his thin arms.

"Have you seen a doctor?"

He shook his head. "I don't have to. It's something I already know."

"Are you sick? Do you have symptoms?"

Without a word he reached over and flicked on the lamp that was beside the futon. Pulling back the covers, he pointed to his ankle. There, under the ankle bone on the inside of his foot where it was hard to see . . .

I'd seen spots like that. Lesions.

I remembered having thought so clearly, with such relief for all of us: Jonathan's been away, he's missed all this.

Hardly conscious of anything, I got up and furiously started putting on my clothes.

"What're you doing?" he asked.

"Going for a walk," I told him. "This is some pretty major news you're dumping on me. I have to give my head a chance to clear."

"It's the middle of the night, Stayton."

"So?"

"It's Vermont," he said. "There're wolves out there."

"There's wolves in here," I told him, pointing to my heart.

He turned out to possess a surprisingly practical bent. With indefatigable energy, he enlisted the volunteer labor of all sorts of people—the woman who ran the local post office, a marine biologist, a Williamsburg antique dealer who specialized in, as he rather grandly put it, "colonial pewter, Chinese lacquerware, and undergraduates of the male persuasion," one or two of whom he always seemed to have in tow. Weekends and holidays became an excuse for work parties followed by potluck suppers that lasted late into the night.

As for myself, I quit my job in Washington and moved down to Virginia full time. Kai and I had talked about it, and we'd decided I should be with Jonathan as much as possible. After that night in Vermont, I wouldn't have forsaken him for anything. And Kai joined us whenever his impossible schedule permitted.

Even in Kai's absence, though, music filled that house, overflowed doors and windows flung open to receive the mild springs and falls of the tidewater. Not the jukebox tunes we used to dance to at the Travelers, but under Kai's influence cello sonatas by Bach, Stravinsky ballets, the songs of Schubert. The strains of *Rosenkavalier* and *Arabella* accompanied our sawing and hammering. Elizabeth Schwarzkopf sang the *Four Last Songs* ten thousand times.

I was never happier. "The Opera Gang," people took to calling us when they'd come out for a work weekend. And Jonathan would advertise: he'd phone friends up and say, "It's *Götterdämmerung* this Saturday. Feel like laying down some brick?" Or sheet-rocking to Rossini, painting to Benjamin Britten.

He had a cache of tapes he'd brought back from Turkey—keening women, whirling dervishes—but those drove everyone crazy, so he never played them except when he was alone. There were times I'd turn up the long dirt drive and hear, a quarter mile away, some furious lonesome song wailing out over the treetops and know I'd find Jonathan perched on the top of a ladder, doing some dangerous task he should really have waited for us to help him with but happy by himself, moving with that sinuous music.

That kid who'd danced so frenetically by the jukebox at the Travelers all those years ago: now I watched him, shirtless and brave, hammer in hand and dying. Something welled up in me that threatened—or promised—to carry me out of myself, some buoyant upsurge, not lightheadedness but lightness, a feeling of having gone completely transparent in the full glare of day. It's hard to explain, except to say that I loved Jonathan very much.

For about eight months his health held steady, and then there began

281

a slow but perceptible decline. His throat started bothering him, he had a cough that wouldn't go away. Sweats woke him three or four times a night. And another spot appeared behind his knee. I told him I thought he might be pushing himself too hard, but he only looked at me and said, "I'm already being pushed. This is just me pushing back."

He was in a race to finish.

The house as viewed from the dirt road that led up to it hadn't changed much since that first day we saw it two years earlier, except for an array of solar panels flush against the roof. It was on entering that Jonathan's hand became apparent. He'd opened the downstairs up into a single room. Off to the right, three steps led down to a brick-floored, sky-lit kitchen. To the left, a stone hearth took up most of the wall. From the front door you could look right through the house to the lush riot of the greenhouse beyond.

At the far end of the greenhouse, taking a cue from the Vermont collective, a coop held three roosters and forty chickens. By the time we finally got the greenhouse up to speed, six months and a number of glitches later, not only was it producing all the vegetables we could eat, but also eggs and greens—leaf lettuces, herbs, nasturtiums, borage blossoms—that we sold to local restaurants like the Trellis in Williamsburg.

Where the greenhouse connected with the house there was what we called the airlock, a double-storied room busy with banana plants and avocado trees and flowering jasmine. Its ostensible function—Jonathan's nod to Kai's and my squeamishness—was to keep the ladybugs and wasps that teemed in the greenhouse from drifting into the rest of the house, though that met with only mixed success. In the middle of the airlock, on a bright green carpet of baby's tears, sat a huge, old, claw-footed bathtub Jonathan had salvaged. Especially on winter days he'd lie in that steamy, verdant room for hours—reading, or singing to himself, or just gazing through the glass at the inhospitable world outside. As often as not Scheherazade perched high and dry on his chest, kneading with her claws, looking for the third nipple. Once or twice I came in to find him masturbating there—languorously, unashamedly.

Upstairs, a rustic bathroom filled with more plants and a couple of stone gargoyles from a demolished church in Norfolk connected two large bedrooms, one for me and Kai, the other for Jonathan. A tattered, water-spotted poster of blue-skinned Krishna—sole relic from his cluttered bedroom in Minerva—hung above an austere futon. Turkish carpets and cushions covered the floor, more carpets hung from the four walls.

By the door, Scheherazade had her favorite carpet she was in the slow process of clawing to death. "Of course it's one of the nicer ones," Jonathan lamented. "But she's only interested in that one, crazy thing, so I suppose it's my offering to the little princess."

He scooped her up. "You're a terror," he told her as she squirmed, then went limp in his arms. "Yes, you are," he said.

She was always pissing somewhere, or vomiting on the stairs where you'd find it underfoot. But Jonathan's devotion knew no bounds. They'd go for long walks in the woods together—she'd trail along at his heels like a dog. Every night she slept on his chest. The only food she'd touch was food he set out for her.

"She's afraid you might try to poison her," Jonathan said. "See, she's a harem cat. She's learned to be very cautious if she wants to live to be a hundred years old."

Beyond the various rooms of the house, Jonathan liked to claim, lay an invisible room, the orgy room, which was nothing but wall-to-wall mattresses and oiled, naked bodies sucking and kissing and licking and fucking.

"Alas," he said sadly. "Not meant to be. Another time, another place. But I can see it so clearly. We would all have had so much fun there. Do you ever think about that? All the fun we might have had?"

To furnish the visible house we scoured the Tidewater for second-hand furniture and antiques. "No faggy stuff," he announced, twirling the plastic beads of his electric blue necklace. "Nothing prissy."

A sprawling, riotous party in July of 1989 inaugurated the house. A D.J. friend of Kai's came down from Washington; music blasted into the night. At someone's insistence, "It's Raining Men"—an old favorite from the early years of that difficult decade—played about sixty times. What the guards and inmates a quarter mile away at the New Kent County Correctional Facility made of it all I can only imagine, but once or twice they trained their spotlights our way. I didn't care. We were here to stay, and there was nothing anybody could do about it. I remember at one point in the party walking out to the field so I could see the prison lights flickering through the woods. A warm breeze stirred the leaves, fractured those lights so they looked insignificant as fireflies. Seventeen years ago, when I was seventeen years old—another summer, another party. Halfway between my birth and this moment now. George had been dead seventeen years. I remembered we watched for shooting stars at that party, and I thought perhaps we should watch for them now, only when I looked up I saw that a haze of clouds, maybe an approaching front, obscured the sky. It had been the end of something, that night seventeen years ago, and also, I saw now, the beginning.

For Kai and Jonathan to wander down just at that moment would have been perfect—some healing symmetry. I lingered for a while, but neither came, though in a pause in the music I could distinctly hear Kai scream "Yeow!" in response to something or other that was happening back at the house. It would be my private commemoration, then, a silent offering of thanks—but to what? The random things that happen, I said to myself. The complicated design.

The music had started up again. Once again it was raining men. With a calm, resigned heart I walked back up to the lights and splendid noise of our party.

We'd lit an immense bonfire of wood scraps, rotten floor boards we'd replaced from the front porch, the detritus of our construction work. Someone had dragged an old sofa outside, and a floor lamp connected back to the house by an extension cord. Jonathan held a kind of court on the sofa. He sat with his arm around someone I'd never seen before.

"Hey Stayton," he said. "Meet Marco from the Philippines." Marco was dark-eyed, pretty—a slip of a boy, but Jonathan was keen on pretty slips of boys these days. There was something almost forlorn in his attachment to them—met mostly through the offices of our friend Julian, the Williamsburg antique dealer. As for myself, I preferred to keep the company of men my own age.

Given half a chance, Marco would've slept with Jonathan that night—he made that perfectly clear—but Jonathan wouldn't allow himself any more of that. "I've put myself under strictest quarantine," he told Marco. Though the Filipino boy remained undaunted. "Nope," I can still hear Jonathan saying when Marco tried to kiss him. He placed the palm of his hand gently but firmly on Marco's chest. "I'm off limits these days. Sorry."

POSITIVE OUTLOOK

Our haunted house, Stayton calls it. Never believes in that old house for one instant, skeptical the whole way, and I think, Here I go again, dragging him into one thing and another.

What I don't tell him is, every morning at three-thirty exactly something in the walls wakes Scheherazade. Oddest thing. She'll be asleep on my chest, then flex her claws, a strange low meow, a prowl around one spot near that wall. So intense, seeing or hearing or smelling something I can't. Something that surfaces there for about fifteen minutes, then fades back to wherever it comes from. A secret eye that opens and closes in the middle of the night in my bedroom. Or a window, maybe a door.

I lie awake for hours and listen to the whipporwill, its clear, liquid call testing all the hours of the night. Sounds right up under the eaves, though I know it's down in the field. The sicker I get, the better my hearing. Crazy.

One night I'm going to hear what's behind that wall.

The *Washington Post* quotes an astrophysicist as saying, If dark matter does exist, and most of it turns out to be unlike the ordinary atoms of stars and people, it will be the ultimate Copernican revolution. Not only are we not at the center of the universe as we know it, but we aren't even made up of the same stuff as most of the universe. We are just this small excess, an insignificant phenomenon, and the universe is something completely different.

A feast for sore eyes.

Don't you love the sound of that? I say. A feast for sore eyes.

It's what I call Kai to his face since I hardly ever see him. Never any time between rehearsals and lessons and concerts. The fabulous life he's made for himself.

He's down for the weekend, though. We walk in the woods while Stayton, bless his heart, runs errands for AIDS shut-ins in Williamsburg—what he does every Saturday morning. Scheherazade tags along behind or races yards ahead, then waits for us to catch up before racing on again. So much crazy energy in a late winter thaw, the ground all soggy, pungent with pine needles, air full of cold mist. Things starting to wake up inside rotten logs, tree stumps, lairs, under rocks.

Kai likes to make a circuit of the property, touching the iron rods and fluttering orange flags that mark the corners. We head out to the power lines, follow their clear-cut up to a little ridge where you can look back to see the house and greenhouse settled among the stunted old apple trees and the relics of last summer's garden. The whole outfit ramshackle and hayseed but alive as anything here in these woods. Flotsam ark tossed up on shore by the storm.

Something's been spotting the leaves of the lettuce brown, and I think it's excess ammonia from the chicken shit, and I think I can fix it by venting the ammonia into the soil. I hope.

The old homestead, Kai says of our vista. Who'd have ever thought?

Wood smoke curls from the chimney.

Here I'm nearly forty years old, he goes on. My career continues on a definite upswing. I am in thrall to two beautiful white boys. I live in a country haunted by AIDS, racism, poverty. And I am, despite all that, unaccountably happy to be here on this planet. Today I'm not even going to complain about sweet Stayton. Or about you.

But go ahead and say it, I challenge. You're jealous and that's a problem.

I'm just in Washington, he says, and all this is down here.

You don't have to be in Washington, I tell him.

No, he agrees, but the National Symphony Orchestra does.

Fuck the National Symphony Orchestra, I tell him.

Oh, honey—he looks at me—you just don't understand, do you?

I understand completely, I admit. I'm just being peevish. This disease makes me peevish. I come out here in the woods sometimes and just let loose this string of words. Evil words. Things I'd never say except alone in the woods. One day God'll strike me dead out here. I'll go up in my own private forest fire.

I grip his arm, lean into him as we walk.

Promise me one thing, I ask. I want to be cremated. I want half my ashes scattered here, and half in Turkey where Mom is. Can you do that for me?

Kai shakes his head.

Listen to her talk, he says.

I'm serious, I tell him. I don't think you're listening to me.

I would listen to you more if you went and saw a doctor on some regular basis.

I put my fingers in my ears to signal it's my turn not to listen.

So he pouts. Draws away from me, and we walk apart. He looks so good these days. The white turtleneck he's wearing. Green trousers. He's got fine muscles from a Washington gym. They're not happy together, Kai and Stayton, though they don't know it. Or if they do it doesn't change anything between them. It's the way they've decided to be, and I admire so much what they've done with themselves. Though it breaks my heart, all the things they can't know about each other.

All I have to say is thanks, I confide in Kai. For lending me Stayton like you did. Throwing him my way.

Choosing my words a little carefully.

You mean like the Christian to the lions, Kai says. You two had unfinished business. I could tell.

I feel like I've barged in and wrecked something sweet, I tell him. What you two were trying to put together. All because I panicked.

I hate talking this way, but I can see he's hurting some.

Besides, I finish, we all have unfinished business.

We both stop walking. Stand there by the little pond that marks the north edge of the property. More just a depression where water collects than a pond. In summer it nearly dries up.

You and I have unfinished business, I say. Reach out and tap him lightly on the chin. You and I never made it like we should have.

That makes him nervous. He laughs.

I tell him, You fucked George, but you never fucked me.

287

True, he says. True. You know, George was very proud of that asshole of his. You might even say vain.

It's my turn to laugh.

I can just imagine, I say, though I never fucked George. He was always the one on top. He said, Teachers should be the ones on top. It's the bottom who learns everything.

Wily George, Kai says.

Now where the fuck did he get off slipping out on us like that? I have to shout, I'm suddenly so furious. All the waking woods can hear me.

I never thought he did, Kai says in a matter-of-fact voice. A voice that says he's done a lot of thinking on this one.

I grab Kai's arm and hold him for a minute. I say, What are you telling me, man?

The breath goes all out of me. I remember George's cold hands layering me with river mud. I can feel his touch on my shivering body.

Just what I said, Kai tells me. I never thought George did that to himself and I still don't.

No, I say.

I always thought they were teaching us a lesson. You know, on top. You and me and Stayton. Who knows who else? That's why we have to be together like this. We can't ever let one another down.

Suddenly I'm shaking and it's not just the chilly air that's inside and out. My stinging lungs. I'm shaking and sweating and my heart's pounding in my chest.

Those fuckers, I say.

Yeah, man, Kai says, so quiet and calm I could die. Those fuckers, he says.

I head down to the pond, scoop up some mud in my hand. Smear a handful across my face. It's bitter mud. Freezing.

What're you doing? Kai says.

I tell him I don't know.

Don't go crazy on me, Kai says. I cup another dollop of mud in both my hands, but then I let it slide back to the ground. Our commotion's spooked Scheherazade up the hulk of a dead tree, where she watches suspiciously. I'll get a chill, pneumonia probably, though now's as good a time as any to let the other shoe drop.

My head seems very clear. Come here, I tell Kai. He doesn't move, so I bound over to him, grab him around the waist and tell him, Man, you should fuck the living daylights out of me. Throw me down in the dirt and do it. Because I'm fucked, Kai, and there ain't no tomorrow for me, none at all.

I turn myself around and push my butt into his crotch. I can feel the lump in his pants rub against my crack. Reach my arms back to hold him pressed there against me, my muddy hands spoiling the flanks of his white turtleneck, his handsome green trousers. He runs his hands up under my sweater. Pinches my nipples hard and kisses the back of my neck.

Such a skinny body, he says. Like a damned skeleton under there.

His hot breath on my freezing neck.

Oh baby, he moans. I love you and Stayton too much.

I say, I know. I know.

Holding me tight across my chest with one arm, reaches around and undoes the front of my jeans with his free hand. Nestles me in close against him, the covering warmth of his body, his hand finding me in there, pulling me out, hand warm and rough on my sensitive skin. I grab his wrist, pull his palm up to my mouth, drool some spit. He works me smooth and steady, hand slurping up and down on me coaxing me hard and harder till I groan, thinking even as I'm coming. What's the point of coming? and my sweet poison spurts out on the damp ground.

This is the time, I think, I'll probably catch pneumonia for good.

When it starts to happen I don't tell anybody. How Scheherazade practices alone in the big living room downstairs when no one's around.

I stand just beyond the doorway and watch as she stands on her hind legs, holds the edge of the sofa, then launches herself and staggers precariously on two legs. Tipsy like a drunk. A kind of tiptoe across the Persian carpet.

Learning to walk upright.

She sees me standing there watching her, and she just smiles.

April and the cherry blossoms are out. We're in Washington for the weekend to hear Kai play the Mozart fourth horn concerto. High point of his brilliant career. What we always say: his brilliant career. And what's been my brilliant career?

Stayton and Kai make the rounds, visiting various friends of theirs, but I'm not crazy about their friends so I go it alone. Dusk in the city and I decide to prowl. The voyeuring hour from way back when. Living so far out in the country, there's nobody's windows to look in except our own house lit up and transparent for all the world to see. The correctional facility down the road's got no windows. And in Turkey all the houses are turned inward—private, discreet. You never knew what went on in them. Even after fifteen years I never really knew what went on inside them.

Or in America either, for that matter. I'm always having to make it up for myself.

That, in a nutshell, Jonathan, is the story of your life.

In the lighted windows all I see are families of men. Men alone, men together: men just home from work loosening their ties and drinking white wine and roughhousing with their Samoyeds or Chow Chows, men getting ready to go out, men settling down for the evening in front of the television.

The neighborhood's Dupont Circle, so what else is new?

A black man lifts weights on a complicated machine he's installed like a piece of furniture in his living room.

Two Asian men are feeding one another rice with chopsticks while a calico cat looks on.

In one almost empty room, a sterilized chamber, a gaunt man sits alone, IV pole beside him, glucose bag and the tube leading to the catheter in his arm that leads, I know, into his heart.

I still feel the same things I always felt when I hungered for glimpses, except now I can see myself too. I'm exhausted. I have more spots. When I cough it hurts. One day soon I'm going to have to check into a hospital and never check back out. Well, I won't do that.

I'm being impossible, I know.

Most of Kai's concert I spend trying not to cough. The seat hurts my thin rump but he's magnificent. In the slow movement I think I'm going to have to cry, but I haven't cried since George, and so I don't now. Stayton holds my hand in the dark the whole time, and I'm pretty sure I can see tears when I look his way. Oh, I think, he's still that same scared kid I knew. All the things I lured him into and him wanting to let go so badly but afraid to let go. Never let himself get fucked. I can see that even now, fifteen years later, Stayton never lets himself get fucked.

He's always holding my hand these days, like he's afraid he'll lose me in the crowd if he lets go.

After the concert Stayton has a bottle of champagne waiting back at the apartment. Since none of us ever drink, it goes straight to our heads. *Their* heads, since Stayton won't allow me more than a sip. Then giddily up to bed for the two of them. I try to sleep, but I can't, so around one I go out. Feels somehow like sneaking out, though there's no climbing out the window and across the roof. Just pocket the keys and I'm off.

Sometimes when I think about Stayton, the way he was when I first met him, I'm just amazed. Those nights dancing at the Travelers.

I walk six blocks down P Street to a club I've heard about. Positive Outlook, where everyone's in the same boat. Two in the morning and it's packed. No different than any other bar, except for the secret in all these guys' blood. I order a juice, but like most things these days it tastes terrible. Next to me at the bar's a guy who's drop dead gorgeous, as they say. He's sipping a beer, eyeing me across the pool table. Funny how I never learned to play pool, or to drink for that matter. I feel totally out of place. You will die far from home, a man I made a connection with in the Luna Park in Antalya told me once. And it's true. He didn't know how true it was.

I remember I sucked him off in a little alley between some animal cages—a mangy zoo tucked away in a neglected corner of the park. A baboon watched us from its cage. Sad, intelligent eyes. Reproachful look I'll never forget. Face pressed against the bars.

What Stayton and Kai don't know is, every day I'm here I'm on the verge of running away. Escaping their gorgeous, smothering love. When thin blue envelopes come for me in the mail, nobody has any idea how my hands are trembling or my heart beating when I open them up. Just to see Demir's scrawl, the words I can't always make out, or Shahin's beautiful clumsy sentences telling me nothing at all except that he's still Shahin. That I am like a brother to him. That his two sons are healthy and big. That he worries that God is no longer much obeyed in the world.

He shouldn't worry so much.

It's why I came back here. Submission. One who submits. After Shahin's wedding in the village, the bottomless well of relatives, the gifts of goats and rugs and pots and pans, the feasts and the dancing late into the night, it was the only gift I had to give.

In the palm of my hand he places a blue glass eye. Nothing evil, he tells me, can happen to you if you keep this. Kisses me on both cheeks, then full on the mouth one last time. Looks in my eyes. One day soon, he says with a smile, I will come to your village in America. I will see you married there.

Demir stands beside us. He knows. He nods to me gravely, and I release Shahin from my hold. I let him go.

You will go home now, Demir says gently. I will send you carpets there. We will both become rich men. And Shahin and his sons.

The dazzle of free enterprise glints in his eyes. Demir, who spent five years of his life in prison but never speaks of it. Who has terrible white scars on his back.

Oh, I want to die in Demir's carpet shop. I want Shahin and his two big, healthy sons to take my body by motorboat out into the bay and bundle me off. No, I want them to shroud me and bury me in some shady, peaceful old cemetery with a marker of wood above my head that time will weather to dust. I want to be cremated, have my ashes scattered in the ruins of ancient cities up and down the coast. Anamurium. Elaousa/Sebaste. Olba. Dio-Caesarea.

Coming back to America was such a terrible mistake, or the best thing I ever did.

Everything gets baffled.

Deflected. Checked. Perplexed. Turned aside from its course.

I want to get fucked, somebody really to fuck me, no condom, nothing, I want guys to come in my mouth and in my ass. I want to lose myself. My life, my heart, my soul.

Same as I've always wanted.

Say to myself, Jonathan, Jonathan. Your head's spinning. You can't put yourself together anymore. Can't add yourself up.

Who said a person had to add up?

I ditch the crowd at Positive Outlook, the drop dead gorgeous guy I could have with the nod of my head if I wanted him, but these days everything tastes terrible. Don't want to be in a room full of dead men. Don't want to be a dead man myself.

So I go to the Circle, where in the dark between streetlights men as dangerous as I am are prowling for one another. Catching glimpses, little bared moments of body or soul. But I don't want that either, so I let myself back in the apartment.

Baffled.

Next day I wake around noon to find that Stayton's gotten the strangest notion in his head: we have to see the AIDS quilt that's spread on the ellipse in front of the White House. Why he thinks I'd want to see that, I have no idea. My head's still groggy from last night. I'll be there all too soon, I tell him. Now if they buried the bodies there, a grave mound on the ellipse, a tumulus. Stranger, go tell the world we lie here, having obeyed the call of love. Of cocks and throats and assholes.

I know I'm raving.

Okay, okay, he says, putting up both his hands to slow me down.

But later I relent. He's in the kitchen making the healthy food he insists I eat. Salad of blanched cauliflower, broccoli, cabbage, bean sprouts. I can hardly wait.

Sneak up behind him and put my arms around his waist. Nuzzle his neck.

Let's go, I tell him.

What are you on about now? he says. I'm trying to make us some lunch.

He gets so irritable these days.

But then I also know I have long conversations in my head and forget time's gone by and I'm the only one having the conversation.

The quilt, I say. We should go see it.

No, he says. You're right. The quilt's a stupid idea. There's an ACT UP demonstration at the White House tonight. I'm going to go to that. I'm going to get myself arrested, I decided.

You'd rather die than be arrested, I say.

Just you wait, he tells me severely. Then shouts, shaking his fist in the air. Die, shock troops of the Babylon war machine.

He turns to me and grins.

All right, I tell him.

And I think, I've missed out on so much of him.

In front of the White House I hold his hand. He's made contact with his affinity group, he's got his instructions. There's a lawyer who'll bail them out when they get down to the jail. He's all ready.

I'm the one afraid of losing *him*, I think.

You don't have to do this for me, I say.

Oh, you, he tells me. I've given up on you. You're not even going to see a doctor until you go and collapse on us.

No doctors, I tell him for the hundredth time. No drugs. No poison. I have to do it my way.

Well, he says, and I have to do it mine. With a last squeeze he lets go my hand. Walks toward his affinity group where they're clustered at the floodlit gate. Lots of cops in white latex gloves, and some of the ACT UP boys are taunting, Your gloves don't match your shoes. The cops are stony-faced, even bored-looking.

I don't know why I do what I do. Reach in my pocket and take out the blue glass eye Shahin gave me. Toss it over the White House fence where it falls with a loud splintering crack on the pavement. Like a rifle shot. That does it. The police go crazy. They move into the crowd, the affinity groups who aren't sure what they're supposed to do now. So they all sit down. The cops want a fight but nobody's giving it to them. And in the gather of shadows where I'm standing nobody's seen me throwing my charm.

Hands in my pockets, I whistle a tune, some melody that comes into my head from who knows where.

Two cops move in on Stayton. Take him by the shoulders and lift him to his feet. He goes limp, lets them drag him off to their van. Stayton who used to jump every time he saw a cop car. I'm standing there looking at him and he's looking at me as they drag him away and there's the most peaceful look on his face.

I go to whistle that tune again, but it's gone. I've forgotten how it goes.

HAVOC

An infernal racket wakes him. It takes a minute before he can identify the sound as a chain saw.

Midmorning. He must have fallen asleep around five on the futon he's put in one corner of his attic study. His joints feel stiff, his head's in a fog, but for a blissful instant he can't remember a thing.

Then it all comes back to him. He groans aloud and lets himself fall back on the futon. Not to face any of this. Put it out of his head. Not to think.

Insistent, relentless, the snarl of the chain saw up in the branches of the sycamore won't let him stop thinking. And he can hear Janine downstairs rattling around oblivious. She's got the radio on for easy listening. It's what she spends most of her time doing—aimless little errands that have come to infuriate him if he thinks about them too much. "Just keeping busy," she apologized once when he lost his temper and shouted, "Stop piddling, will you?" He must drive her crazy as well. His irregular hours and nocturnal prowlings. She doesn't complain, though—only winces in sympathy for the travails of his spastic colon. Whenever he's stayed up all night he feels an odd sense of guilt, as if that wakefulness constituted some infidelity to Janine. And not without reason. He's realized a terrible, irrefutable thing: every night he watches through, he loves her a little less.

"So they're finally cutting down those trees," she'll say when he descends from the temporary haven of the attic. Already he can hear her tone, cheerful and conciliatory. She won't even say *sycamores*. To her they're only trees. And it's Frank's property, after all. Even while not speaking to their neighbor, she'll still respect his property. It's how she was brought up. How they were all brought up.

And somehow it's failed all of them—though he's the only one, it seems, to see it clearly. How could he have put up with her all these years? Let her live his life with him while Joan traipsed herself silly halfway around the planet and Jonathan managed to go and catch AIDS. What's been wrong with all of them all these years?

The letter lies unfolded on the desk where he left it, and as he refolds it and puts it back in his shirt pocket he wonders what to do. He can't carry it around forever, and yet he's afraid to let it out of his sight— afraid that, on its own, it'll mutate into something worse. But what could be worse?

Peering out the window, he can see Bill's dark figure perched high and precarious. The chain saw surges through a thick branch, sends it crashing earthward with a thud that shakes the house.

He'd better have insurance, up there like that. But then Allen thinks, Go ahead and fall out of that tree. Fall, fall. He's shocked, but the fervent words are there in his head. He turns from the window and for a full minute just stands, staring at nothing, as Bill and his chain saw proceed with their terrible work.

His life must have been very precarious to fall apart so easily. As he contemplates the wreckage—all laid out there before him in his mind's eye—he's simply amazed. But it's not the first time. All his life he's moved from stability to stability, and each one has proved, if anything, more unstable than the last. Joan with that pistol and the empty bottle. Her words to him, simple and—once said—irrevocable: *You should know that our son is a homosexual.*

You should know.

Joan's been waiting twenty years to be able to deliver him this latest blow. And what a mess, what a nightmarish mess Jonathan's gone and gotten himself into. Couplings and uncouplings. And in between, pure and simple, the abyss.

He rages at both of them, but behind the rage, threatening even to overwhelm it, is something else—some monstrous mutation born of shame, fury, impotence. It can't be tenderness.

He doesn't remember when he first heard mention of AIDS: it was just there one day, not yet fully formed, incipient rather. Did they even have a name to call it back then? The strangest thing is, he thinks he remembers thinking about AIDS before it existed, or before they said it existed—but how, in what manner, eludes him. And yet he knew. One of those mysterious fevers out of Africa: Ebola, Marburg, Lhassa. Green Monkey Fever. Whole villages afflicted, hospitals filled, hundreds dead. Photos he's seen: health-care workers evacuated from the field in special containment garments, rushed to research hospitals in London or Bonn, and this was in the sixties, the early seventies.

But he averted his gaze because he never believed he could know these things in advance. How could he have known, when no one knew?

And it continues. Only last year there was an article—he rummages in his file to find it:

Lagos, Nigeria, April 20 (AP)—An unidentified disease that is fatal in six days has killed about 600 people in southeastern Nigeria and prompted thousands to flee, doctors and community leaders say.

The disease is "characterized by fever, general body pain, jaundice, vomiting of blood, restlessness, inability to pass urine and coma, followed by death," Dr. Samuel Idiagbe told reporters on Friday.

That was it, a tiny item tucked away at the bottom of page ten. Yet another mysterious disease out of Africa. He waited for some kind of follow-up but there never was any, just as there never was any follow-up for all those other warnings down through the years; and he's remembering now, funny how he never put it all together, the flight doctor in Houston, Dr. Hal Roberts from Kansas City, tall and square-jawed, exuding the kind of confidence and competence NASA just loved—Dr. Roberts giving them the good news that quarantine procedures were being rescinded for their flight because there'd been no evidence of microorganisms.

Only the ones brought back by Apollo 12 inside the camera part retrieved from Surveyor 3 and not to worry: that was terrestrial contamination that had somehow survived eighteen months on the moon. But he knew. Even then he knew.

He remembers the gunpowder smell inside the lunar module after the EVAs, all that moondust they tracked in. Its chemical blooming, as some NASA know-it-all called it. How he took to bed that following summer, swollen glands, swimming head, some fatigue he just couldn't seem to shake. And they've all gone funny, haven't they? All of them who were there. Buzz and Gene and Jim and Pete. Neil.

It's too much even to contemplate, this sudden putting together of odd, disconnected things. But, he thinks, what if right now, this morning in June, the year of our Lord 1990, he simply refuses to go on with it? Abdicates something he's not wanted for a long time. Some complicity in life, some terrible shaming share in the spoils. What if he simply locks the door, if worse comes to worst barricades himself up here with the notes he's been collecting, his suspicions, convictions, graphic evidence of something no one else seems willing to face. The end of a certain kind of living. But it's been coming for some time, hasn't it? Those sleepless hours, those nocturnal musings no one should pursue except with some express purpose in mind and he's had, up till now, no purpose, express or otherwise. But now . . .

His mind has never worked this fast in his life. It covers light-years, and with such rampant lucidity. He's exhilarated, skittering along the trajectory of these thoughts, recalling how he read, somewhere, about the thirty-six just men of Jewish legend, how it's only by their secret presence in the world that the world continues at all. The thirty-six who watch through the night. He too has watched through the night, but he's not one of the just—no, he's guilty, he knows that, but the thirty-six just men imply their own balance, don't they? The thirty-six guilty of which he, Allen Cloud, is surely one. Oh, clearly he's one, called not only to watch but to confess and testify and sit in judgment of the crimes in which he himself has taken, he knows now, all too enthusiastic a part.

The crimes of the species, its blood madness and high rapacity, brood of infinite hungering desires. Some people might think he's crazy, off the deep end, but he's definitely not that. Off the deep end, maybe, like a diver into an abyss. Rapture of the deep. He thinks of Victoria Ivleva as she lowers herself down into the sarcophagus. Because surely she's one as well, the tribunal of the guilty.

Oh boy, is he ever going now. Faster and faster, like the dead men used to propel him out the window at night, over fields, the river, by moonlight—but where is he going?

His mind spews a pyrotechnics show of facts, figures, speculations—all devastating, all pertinent. He's sat himself down, poured his files out on the desktop. The clamor of the chain saw buoys him up even as it wreaks its savage work on the world. Before it's done an arm will have to be cut off, a leg; perhaps a head will have been severed. He skims over the burning world, rainforests of Brazil, scoured old growth stands of the Pacific Northwest, Mexico City Lagos Bangkok suffocating in sewage and smog, thinning protection over the Antarctic and Arctic, spent and seeping nuclear reactors dumped on the overfished ocean floor that the mind reels from, can't register so broken out in a sweat as he slows, holds a single article in hand. All these atrocities ruminated over one at a time, night after night these last several months but now amassed in a single drowning upsurge—gasping for air, steady, steady he tries to catch his breath by reading single sentences. One at a time. At a time.

Usti, lying black in its own sticky soot, spews carbon monoxide, nitrogen oxide, sulfur and heavy metals from chemical, glass and cooking-oil plants. Sulfur in the air here has been reported at 20 times the permissible level. Forestry experts meeting in Prague last week cited a stretch of some 250 miles where more than 300,000 acres of forest had disappeared and surviving trees were so sick their lifespan would be short. East Germany reported the loss of more than 125,000 acres of woodlands as well as some damage in 35 percent of its forests and severe damage in 20 percent. Acid rain has killed as much forest in Poland as in East Germany, and almost 60 percent of the pine forests are affected. The Czech Academy of Science says the famous forests of North Bohemia are more than 80 percent damaged.

It helps a little. He feels calmer. A deadly calm. Eye of the storm where there's no longer the vanity of hope. For the first time since reading Joan's letter nearly twenty-four hours ago—is it possible he's lived with it so long?—he bursts into tears. Not a welling in the eyes, a sob choked back, but full-blown tears like he hasn't cried since—well, since Joan left him twenty-two years ago. Great unmanning tears the whole neighborhood surely can hear.

At least Janine hears them. She comes tentatively up the stairs, hesitant as always to interrupt his work space, as she calls it. Sacrosanct, one of her favorite words. If only she knew what terrible work has been done here.

She raps lightly on the door.

"Al, honey, is everything all right?"

Everything is definitely not all right. "Go away," he says, conscious how futile such a thing is to say. "And leave me alone."

He's said such things before. Funny that he was thinking about that other attic only recently. The one back in Armistice. And the dead men—when they come to him this time, whose charred and featureless head will they bear on a platter?

Janine tries the door, but he's had the foresight to lock it. She rattles the handle.

"Allen," she says, the pitch of her voice rising in concern. "Allen, what's going on in there?"

Rattling the locked door handle to Jonathan's room one afternoon, unthinking—the kid fourteen, fifteen, the throes of puberty: *Jonathan, what's going on in there?* Suddenly realizing, going hot with shame. Backing off.

"Go away," he shrieks, not so much to Janine as to the others here: because he's not alone here in this room. Hasn't been alone for days, months. Hasn't been alone for years.

Very quietly, even delicately—as they've done from time to time in his life—the Owl and the Amateur surface within him.

Episodes he's always kept under wraps, even to himself. Impossible to say when they first showed up. Sometimes it seems they've always been waiting in the shadows, occasionally stepping forward into view, then for months or years receding into a kind of slumber inside him.

Now they are wide awake. Beneath the sound of the chain saw, beneath Janine's heavy knocking on the door, the shrill upset edging its way into her voice—if he concentrates, Allen can quite distinctly follow the strange, quiet monotone of their voices.

He can't repeat their individual words, though he can understand perfectly well the drift of their speech. And he can see—somewhere within the space where the wall should be—their eyes, glassy and huge.

The Owl and the Amateur. He's been waiting for them, he realizes, for a long time now.

This hastily arranged tribunal. War crimes court. He only wishes Victoria Ivleva were here to stand by his side, to hold his hand in this darkness. Her calm courageous presence, her knowledge of the sarcophagus's secret life. He feels borne down on relentlessly by these two familiars—no longer the shabby figures of old, whiskey-breathed and sallow from riding the rails, redolent of hobo songs and odd sleights-of-hand, but fully resplendent in their true forms and he can address them as they are: bitter archangels of the thirty thousandth or millionth century.

His mouth is too dry for words. With a flurry of metallic plumage, a rustle of exoskeletons, a vast clearing of the air as after a storm, they indicate the tribunal is about to begin.

Before his eyes—are they open or closed?—an old movie rolls. Something excavated from the ruins, time capsule or coin hoard, meticulously examined and re-examined by the future's great dark eyes. It begins with streaks of light, slippages across the screen, then the shantytown outskirts of a vast city whose distant skyscrapers are dimly visible through a sepia smog. Garbage piled high as a mountain, and on that mountain, scurrying like ants, hundreds of human beings. Knee deep in filth, they scavenge. Many are children.

Close-up of a dark-eyed, dark-haired girl barefoot and in rags. Ten or eleven. Transparent as a mote, an ornately lettered placard floats before his eyes: THE DISCOVERY. In the child's palm lie a dozen exquisitely glowing blue stones. Like glass or diamonds. Like beautiful staring eyes. Excitedly, the child calls out her discovery to the other kids. Laughing, they slide the blue stars into their pockets, put them under their tongues. Sound of singing. Sound of flutes and drums. An improvised dance. *Magic!* A father comes into his sleeping daughter's room to find the blue pellets shining brightly in the dark. Scenes of people wearing the stones as charms, putting them in a baby's crib. Crushing them into sparkling powder and sprinkling them on the dirt floor of their hovels, constellations that shimmer in the night.

Then the scene shifts: a squalid urban hospital where the children have been confined. QUARANTINE! reads the caption. Long-range shot from a safe distance. Children peer out a second-floor window, their expressions sad, puzzled, frightened. Four have died, twelve, twenty-eight, their inner organs burned by radiation. Close-up of the doctor who himself feels nauseous, faint. White-suited hazardous-waste teams combing the garbage heaps discover illegally dumped Cesium-135. Industrial waste.

A last shot of the empty hospital window. A black flag flying.

The lights go up, the jerky picture fades to reveal the Owl and the Amateur in dinner jacket, tails. Rail-thin, the Amateur plays violin in an exaggerated gypsy style. The Owl tap dances, a melancholy entertainment. Somewhere a great bronze bell is tolling and it goes on, lush violin and somber bell and the Owl dancing, dancing till Allen allows himself to be taken by the hand, led down flights of steps. Before a rusty metal door they pause. The Owl puts a finger to his beaked lips as an out-of-tune piano stumbles through a score that is long on hysteria, though not without ominous quieter interludes. Inside the laboratory the Amateur—wig askew, garishly rouged cheeks and lipsticked mouth—is diligently at work. His strapless dress reveals shoulders starred with dark lesions. THE EXPERIMENT announces one floral bit of handwriting, bordered with vines and grinning skulls, as it drifts down. With a broad gesture the Amateur indicates a great cast-iron cylinder lying on its side in the middle of the room. The Owl removes his homburg and sails it slow motion through the air where it stops, hovers, remains. In dumb show, the Amateur—looking oddly like Fiona Root, or perhaps it is Victoria Ivleva, her features dramatically altered by the radiation—readies herself for immersion in the sarcophagus. Gallantly, the Owl helps her up three rickety steps. She stands on the threshold, curtseying coquettishly. Then she disappears. The great door clangs shut. The Owl stands at the controls, feverishly twisting levers and thumping at stuck dials. A sudden jet of steam hisses from a vent. The Owl leans his ear against the side of the cast-iron cylinder. He raps there with his knuckles, listens again.

Inside the sarcophagus, Victoria Ivleva's puppetlike body floats suspended, levitating. Suddenly it shudders, some great force hurls it against the sides of the chamber with terrific violence. In her eyes there is terror, her mouth opens in a soundless scream. Then just as suddenly, all is completely still. Outside, the Owl, his head cocked to one side, is still listening. A title announces THE VOICE. Victoria Ivleva, her voice small and frightened as a child's, begins: "Today I approached the third door. . . ." Immediately a sudden stillness comes over the laboratory, the music drops sotto voce and creeps close to the floor. Dread surrounds the third door. Everyone in the movie theater can feel it. "There is a force," she says, "that I can neither resist nor control. . . ." An icy spasm grips the room as the reel catches, the projector light sputters and now Allen himself prepares to enter. Clothed in the flimsiest of protective gear, he lowers himself down the narrow ladder. Roentgens speed along his body like iron filings, worm under his skin into bone and brain. Four-winged birds fly in and out of fissures that have opened up in the sarcophagus's outer skin. Allen can hear their rough-throated caw, a note of terrible longing and pain. He can hear the lumbering beat of wings in the cavernous space around him.

The bottom of the ladder eases him out onto a clean tiled floor. It's not what he expected. Stories told of a mammoth debris-littered cavern. Instead he is standing in a small, brightly lit room. The walls are white, the ceiling, the tiles on the floor. There is a sofa along one wall. He is wearing the biological isolation garment he wore only in rehearsal, years and years ago.

He does not need to guess that he has just come back from the moon.

The Owl and the Amateur are, as always, nearby. He can't see them, but they're here. They've been with him on the lunar surface. They've been there to prepare the way. Now perhaps they are resting on bunks in other rooms, having blood drawn in the lab, inner organs monitored. Their exotic excrement is being avidly studied by a team of specialists.

The quarantine facility is larger than it looks, a warren of small rooms he's soon lost himself in. Lab after lab ready for work, instruments gleaming, needles and protective masks and gloves.

But then he comes to a flight of stairs that lead down into what appears to be a basement room. ERECTED BY DREAM ORDER reads a plaque on the wall. He doesn't remember these stairs. In contrast to everything else, they're ancient, filthy, in need of repair.

The door at the bottom hangs open on its hinges. Inside, the floor is pooled with water. In the middle of the room, a great cast-iron cylinder lies on its side. On the wall are control panels, cranks, dials. He opens the lid and climbs in. He lies down inside. Invisible hands sustain him. It's like a coffin, and suddenly he remembers: a dread surrounds the third door. "There is a force," he hears a voice say, "that I can neither resist nor control. . . ."

And there he is.

The third door is not a door, it is not a place at all. At the bottom of the mind there is no other door. A fine cold sweat has broken out all over him. There is a force he can neither control nor resist. With a shout of misery he thrusts open the door.

"Hi Dad," says Jonathan. He is sitting on the sofa. Purplish-brown lesions, like eyes, cover his face, his neck, the backs of his hands.

A BIRTHDAY PARTY

Every few weeks a shipment of carpets arrived at the Richmond airport from Alanya, and soon thereafter Jonathan would always throw a Turk-ish dinner party. He spent the day rolling minted rice in grape leaves, marinating chicken and lamb for the grill, roasting peppers and eggplant tender till they slipped from their charred skins. He'd invite friends, the clients he'd gotten to know, and after the feast he'd unfurl his latest offerings.

It was a particular Jonathan I'd never seen: the flash in his dark eyes, the thrill in his voice as he fingered the pile, admired a mellow bit of color, traced a certain design of interest.

He waxed most enthusiastic about details that could seem flaws to an untutored eye—some blatant irregularity in the pattern, a sudden disregard for symmetry that almost bordered on the inept. But those disconcerting accidents were exactly what he loved. He told us, urging us into his vision of the faded beauties of an old nomadic piece, "The women who weave the rugs—because it's only women—if they make a mistake, they don't go back and correct it. They just incorporate it into the pattern and keep moving on, making adjustments as they go. This mistake over there means something new needs to happen over here, see. So the mistake you don't stop to unweave stops being a mistake anymore. It becomes the thing itself."

He stood there looking down at the carpet he'd spread before us. It was at moments like this that he seemed most unknowable, all the

305

strange or riotous life he'd lived in that country forever inaccessible. What spoke through those carpets was the gap of years.

"Sometimes," he said, more to himself than to us, "I think these carpets are so very wise. But then other times I think, carpets are the madness of those women. And probably both of those things are true."

I don't think Jonathan would've parted with a single rug if he hadn't needed to raise money. The best ones would stay at the house for months before finally, reluctantly, he'd move them to the shop for sale.

The "shop" was actually space in a corner of Julian's crowded antique store, a pile of rugs situated somewhat incongruously between the colonial pewter, the Chinese lacquerware and Julian's lounging entourage of undergraduates of the male persuasion.

Julian wasn't particularly to my taste—his effusive high style put me off. He pulled back his sandy hair in a pony tail, wore a little diamond stud in his left ear and could have afforded to lose thirty pounds. He had a distracting way of calling everyone he met "Darling." Years of pot smoking had left him habitually unfocussed. But he inexplicably endeared himself to Jonathan the night he announced to everyone that he'd bought a new car. When Jonathan asked what kind, Julian answered regally, with a vague but capacious gesture, "Oh, Darling, it's midnight blue."

It was through Julian that Jonathan first met, the night of our grand housewarming party, the last love of his life. Looking hardly more than fourteen though he was actually twenty, Marco was utterly devoted to Jonathan. Willing, compliant, docile, he was also oddly oblique, even opaque. I have to confess that I didn't see a whole lot there, but then Jonathan had other eyes. It was a curious relationship. As far as I could tell, they never had sex of the old-fashioned kind—the kind we were all nostalgic for—nor even sex of the new, careful variety. The most they ever seemed to do was bathe one another in the old claw-footed tub so publicly situated—what *were* we thinking?—in the airlock room. But who was I to say? I wasn't the most objective person about Marco. Shadowing every moment and detail of the life we all led together, there was some haunting other life, the life where only we two were together, Stayton and Jonathan forever. And yet, disturbingly, when I tried to make any of the specifics of that vague dream come clear to myself, I couldn't do it. There was only this life, its complicated texture, its palpable pleasures and frustrations. Including Marco. Including Kai. Our one big happy family, as Jonathan was fond of proclaiming.

I was by that time working for an advertising agency in Richmond. Marco and Jonathan divided the carpet duties between them, and the three of us together maintained the greenhouse.

When he was down for weekends from Washington, Kai and I would often play duets. I'd taken up the French horn again after many years, and though I wasn't very good, Kai insisted I'd improved beyond recognition. It's because you're a better person now, he sweetly claimed. He was, as always, a demanding teacher.

Jonathan liked to hear us two play. "Don't stop," he'd call from upstairs where he was taking a nap.

"Aren't we bothering you?" I asked.

"It's soothing."

"You just like knowing where we are," Kai told him. "And that we've got our paws off each other."

Jonathan stood at the top of the stairs in the bright red flannel pajamas he'd taken to wearing because he got cold so easily. "Actually," he said, "I don't think you two make passionate love quite often enough. But that's none of my business. What I was going to say was, I was lying up here and I thought, it's like they're wrapping me in a winding sheet. The music, I mean."

"That's morbid talk," Kai told him. "No morbid talk, remember?"

But Jonathan said, "You've got it wrong. I felt safe. Peaceful. I was being taken good care of."

When he'd gone back into his bedroom Kai started to cry. It wasn't something I thought would happen, because in general Kai and I were very stoic with each other. He sobbed quietly so Jonathan wouldn't hear, and I held him. I could feel his silent shudders go all through me. He's sick too, I thought with sudden alarm. He knows it, and he's not telling anyone. But then I calmed myself. We'd always, from the very first, been safe with each other. As safe as anyone can be under the circumstances.

"He'll wonder what happened to us," Kai whispered after a minute. Releasing me, he resolutely took up his horn and sounded a long, pure note, caressed from pianissimo to mezzo forte. I joined in a major third lower and we held that sweet concordance, welling and subsiding. Then he changed his note, a whole step up, and I changed too, a half step down, the sound of our two horns mingling, calm and sustained. Sustaining.

Like angels, I thought, hovering near to Earth. Like the angels of death.

We both loved Jonathan very much, though he went his own way. It was curious. I hadn't been sure what to expect when he first showed up—anything can happen, I'd thought, any new configuration is possible. But there was, finally, something oddly tactful and reserved about this new Jonathan, as if, for whatever reasons, he were particularly mindful of the two of us, the fragile balance of our relationship. He stood gracefully aside.

The irrevocable fact was, I'd renounced him, cast him off, and he'd gone on alone, or with others; in any event, without me. I couldn't ever make that up to him, that moment when I threw him away. We could go on, we were in fact going on, and sometimes this all seemed like some miraculous second chance, but the fact still remained that when it counted, I'd denied him.

At the time I hadn't understood what now I know so well. That you can't take anything back. That you can atone, you can be forgiven, but you can't take anything back.

It was the mild late June night of his thirty-fourth birthday. Fireflies were out, and the fields beyond the windows glimmered with their apparently random but purposeful lights.

"No fuss," he'd said when I asked him what he wanted to do. "A simple nun's meal. Just the two of us. Quiet prayers of thanksgiving. Early bedtime."

"I thought," I told him, "I'd at least invite Marco."

"No," he said. "I see that boy all the time. Tonight, just the two of us."

All day long the phone had been ringing with birthday greetings from friends. From would-be lovers he'd stopped, here and there down the line, with a gentle hand placed on the chest.

Unable to come down because of a concert, Kai had sent regrets and a new CD of David Diamond symphonies. I'd made a roast chicken with potatoes and brussels sprouts—favorites of Jonathan's, though his appetite wasn't particularly good these days. He picked dutifully at his plate.

"Why would anybody want to touch his tongue to somebody else's asshole?" he asked between bites. "Because," he answered himself, "it's there."

He was oddly exuberant, chattering away in the midst of what I suspected was probably a siege of nausea or some other discomfort.

Much of the time I managed not so much to forget Jonathan's condition as to underestimate its ravages. Still, I had to admit to myself how spookily he'd come to resemble one of those concentration camp inmates who peer out at us from old—and not so old—photographs. That drawn face, the eyes unnaturally large and bright. He kept his head closely shaven, wore an invariable uniform of tie-dyed skirts over faded jeans and black T-shirts enlivened, on special occasions like his birthday dinner, by a necklace of bright plastic beads.

"You know," he said, "I never can think of birthdays nowadays without thinking about the way, in Turkey, boys get circumcised when they turn nine or ten. The parents make a big to-do about it. Dress them up in caps and silver crowns, parade them around. Throw a party for them. Then the next day, it's the knife."

"Sounds totally barbaric."

"Well, I'm not sure it is barbaric. How you behave at your circumcision is very important. It's what you're remembered for for the rest of your life. I knew this boy there, and the thing he was proudest of was how he didn't flinch when they cut him. Showed character."

"Or lack of nerve endings," I said.

"Oh, it was definitely character. If you'd known Shahin. He had plenty of nerve endings." He laughed. "So now I'm always a little suspicious when people throw me a party or make me dinner. Wonder when the knife's going to be."

"Sorry," I said. "No knife. Not even a cake since you're not eating sugar."

"Well, while we're on that subject, did I tell you I bought myself a present?"

He hopped up from the table, went off to his room and came back brandishing what looked like a shoe box.

"A rare and antique dildo," he explained as he opened the box, "purchased from a very exclusive mail-order concern. See, this masturbation thing is starting to ruin my eyesight. I can tell. Doesn't it look huge? I have only one request: you have to volunteer to use this fabulous instrument on me. Hey Stayton, will you do that?"

He laid the dildo on the table beside my plate. I was too surprised to say anything.

"You know," he said, "it's hard to fathom that this could be my last birthday."

Something in me broke. I blurted out what had been on my mind for a long time. "I keep having this dream," I told him. "I'm in some strange city, like an Arab city, all white-washed, bright sun, and it's like a labyrinth. You're chasing me, and I'm running away from you. I don't see you, but I know you're there in that city somewhere. There's no one else. It's deserted except for you and me. The reason I'm running from you is because you want to fuck me and give me AIDS too. I'm really ashamed I have that dream, but I do. Sometimes I wake up and I think, I should let Jonathan fuck me and then we'll be in the same boat. I really do think that sometimes."

"It's because you never liked to get fucked," Jonathan said. "It made you feel like you were losing control."

Tears were running down my cheeks, and I knew he could see. What he could never see was the life Kai and I had when we were alone.

"I don't want you to do this without me," I told him.

"I can't help you," Jonathan said. "I wish I could, but I can't. Life's fucking you and you're still afraid of losing control."

"That's a stupid thing to say," I told him sharply. For a moment I gave way to a surge of bitterness. "Do you ever wish all this never happened? That we'd just never been born? So we wouldn't have to get sick and die as a way of getting it all over with? That the real problem is that we ever existed in the first place?"

Jonathan looked at me with such gravity I've never forgotten. "The only thing that counts," he said quietly, "is that I fell in love with you way back when. That first lab day in Dr. Lennox's class. Do you remember? What a freak he was. And that awful African grasshopper." He laughed, then said seriously, "I guess you could say it was the Vegan Star Tyranny that brought us together."

I said I thought it was chiffon.

"The secret weapon," he declared.

"It's still the secret weapon," I said.

"Fuck AZT," Jonathan shouted. "Where's chiffon when you need it? The Vegan Star Tyranny invented AZT."

We were both laughing in spite of ourselves.

"Come here," he told me. With his fingertips he wiped the tears off my cheeks. He tasted them. He could still do that. Sometimes I thought he had all the freedom in the world.

Taking me by the hand, he led me into the room we called the airlock. Some time before, he'd started setting out candles all around the room: he liked to take long baths by candlelight. Now he went around lighting them till it glowed in there like a shrine, warm and flickering, and the fireflies past the windows. From his bedroom he brought in a shabby, much faded prayer rug he professed to adore. I undressed him slowly. He'd lost a lot of weight. His ribs stuck out, his arms were thin. In that light he looked younger, he looked like a boy again. He knelt on the rug, touched his forehead to it, raised his hips in the air.

It wasn't an act I'd ever imagined. Or not in these circumstances, and certainly not with such utter tenderness. Inserting the dildo in him slowly, gently. Pausing to let him accommodate it. Pushing past his sphincter muscle, into the forbidden cave of his insides. I felt him stir under my motions, his body answering back. This was the saddest thing I'd ever done, I thought.

The most full of love.

I rubbed his back with one hand while I methodically worked the dildo in with the other. I drove deep, pulled almost all the way out, the generous rhythm he used to like.

I was relieved Kai wasn't here to see this, though I knew he'd approve.

"I'd forgotten," Jonathan murmured. "There's something just so amazing about getting fucked."

"Don't talk," I said. "You always talk."

He laughed. "Am I ruining the mood?"

Just as he said that, the phone rang. "Oof. One thing I do *not* feel like, at the moment, is answering that," Jonathan said.

"The machine's on," I told him. "It's probably Kai."

"If it's Kai I'll talk to him."

311

Hey, world, we could hear Jonathan's recorded voice say, *you've reached Paradise. Leave a message for Stayton, Kai, Jonathan or any of the rest of the Opera Gang.*

But it wasn't Kai calling.

"Hello Jonathan," said a woman's voice. "It's Janine. Please call me back. It's very important. It's about your dad."

I had never flown before. In so many ways I'd traveled very far from the enclosure of my youth, but never by airplane. The thought of flying made me distinctly nervous, and the fact, it turned out, even more so. As the plane surged down the runway, faster and faster—it didn't seem possible to be moving so fast—I instinctively gripped Jonathan's hand and held tight. He laughed, caressed my hand, and I thought about what he had said about my fear of losing control. Consciously I willed myself to surrender to the elements.

When I worked up the nerve to look out the plane window, we were sailing amid magnificent summer thunderheads. It seemed impossible anything bad could happen to us. My dread about the next three days gave way to an utterly unwarranted exhilaration.

But Jonathan damped all that in no time. "For the record," he announced, "I feel just awful this afternoon. Once more you've been wonderful. I couldn't have gotten myself up here on my own. And I just want to tell you in advance that I think I know what all this is about." He sighed and looked out the window, rubbing his forefinger and thumb together the way he did when he was distracted.

"What all what's about?" I had to ask.

"Dad," he said. "What's going on with him. It's moon sickness."

"Moon sickness?"

"Janine told me about it. Seems something's happening to the astronauts. Depression, nervous breakdown. They've all gotten divorced, or turned into recluses, or they've fixated on these strange ideas. One of them started an institute to investigate paranormal phenomena. He claims something very weird happened to him when he was on the moon. Another one went to find Noah's Ark, because when *he* was on the moon, that's what God told him his real mission in life was. Go figure. And Dad—well, he's locked himself in the attic. I guess it's understandable. Once you've gone to the moon, what're you supposed to do with yourself?"

"I saw one of the astronauts," I said, "in a car ad on TV."

"See what I mean? It's something NASA never thought of. But it's something that's been coming for years. Since when I was a kid. Only nobody stopped to think. Oh well, I suppose my soothing wit and unorthodox style will iron everything out. In case you hadn't noticed, I just radiate healing sunbeams. At night I glow blue in the dark. Janine's always overestimating my therapeutic charms. You know, she actually used to think all they needed for the perfect marriage was to have me around the house."

"Well, it definitely worked for the Dempsey/Voegli household," I said. "Why not there?"

I was anxious to meet this father who'd fascinated me so many years before. I remembered that moon flight so clearly, how vulnerable Allen Cloud looked as he stood, shaky and unshaven, on the deck of that aircraft carrier after splashdown. All those weightless days, the atrophy of bones and muscle, the mysterious physiological changes space put one through—before I knew it I was remembering not Allen Cloud but my own father, who in conjunction with that charlatan Dr. Lennox never believed a word of those lunar exploits. A Pentagon boondoggle from start to finish, filmed in the Nevada desert and directed by Hollywood Jews, the same ones who faked the Holocaust.

It was a train of thought that led me to one startling vista after another. Jonathan's father hadn't needed to sell Vacu-Luxes on the side, he hadn't needed to show old slides of Africa or rant from a pulpit on Sunday mornings. He just said "terrific" in that tight-lipped way of his. He just stood there on deck of the USS *Ticonderoga*, calm and collected as if he'd done nothing at all. As if walking on the surface of the moon were the most natural thing in the world.

If I'd wanted to be Jonathan through all that fumbling, forbidden exploration on the Naugahyde sofa in his basement, my dire fascination with the places I could send him and was myself still afraid to go—then I had also wanted his father for my own. I had been in love with his father. In love with that calm authority and reason, that monolith of indisputable Science backing him up. I had been in love with him because I didn't love my own father, in whom I'd lost all my faith—

313

couldn't love my father, or wouldn't, or did love him and knew that all too well and was terrified of that love.

What a panic I could get myself in up here above the Earth. I hadn't thought of my father in years, not since that day I'd used a black man I was sure I loved to banish his persecuting image from the television screen in my apartment living room. Or else I thought of him continuously, day in and day out, never conscious of the fact but determined by it nonetheless. It could make my head reel. I looked out the window, the dizzying heights to which we'd climbed. There lay all that landscape of earth—fertile fields and meandering rivers and patches of wood. The captain had told us we would be flying, at some point, over Tennessee. That small city off in the distance could even be Minerva.

I'd give anything to go home, I realized, the way Jonathan was going home. But not yet. I still didn't dare look back to the father I'd fled, the mother about whom I simply never had a thought one way or another—as I never thought about any women, those intelligent creatures of a different species so oddly intermingled with our own. I'd destroyed all that world of home as carefully and assiduously as I knew how.

In order to build my new home. That strange, patched-together concoction in the Virginia woods. What I felt was nothing less than terror: how I'd thrown my lot in with such strangers. And for good, too—with no chance of ever turning back.

Terrible thoughts. I found myself trying to back out—the way, in a dream, you might back out of some ghastly room that fills you with inexplicable dread. But there are thoughts which, once thought, you can't really unthink.

"Janine's been very good for Dad all these years," Jonathan was saying, the kind of chatter he could keep up for hours. I realized I hadn't been listening. "I can't tell you how good," he went on. "And I suspect he's been pretty horrible to her, though that wouldn't ever occur to him. But Janine's tough. She's weathered him. She needs a lot of love, and she's been willing to work very hard for it. That counts. You know, I used to resent her like hell. And boy was I mean to her. But I definitely admire her now. What she's been through. All those years she worked so hard for what she believed in. In some way, this attic thing's probably a relief. Get all that craziness out in the open."

"Your dad's not crazy," I said defensively.

"He's craziness itself," he laughed. "My dictionary definition of it."

"You're the one I used to think was crazy," I accused him. "I used to tell myself that. It scared me about you."

"And I thought it was my spooky and ravenous asshole," he said.

"All part of the same thing," I told him. "And then when you came back from Turkey and we went to the Virginia property, and you got that mad gleam in your eye."

Jonathan seemed to enjoy hearing all this. There was a kind of glee in him I hadn't seen for weeks. He told me proudly, "My mom has a saying: When in doubt, do anything."

"So you got it from her."

"Exactly. I saw that property and I just plunged right in. . . . Not entirely true. The mountains outside Alanya are almost completely de-forested—did you know that? So I was thinking a lot about the planet. I knew this boy who asked me, was it true there were no trees left in America? And that we all lived in skyscrapers, or in the subways? I thought maybe we could do our part to help save things. Rescue mission. When I was a kid I used to help Mom dry the dishes. That was my job. And I had this fantasy, when I was putting those dried dishes away in the cupboard—if something happens right now, at least I'll have put this many away. Or when I was cutting the lawn, I'd think the same thing—at least I've got this much cut. And then go on to the next thing and start that process all over. I used to imagine I was a honeybee, like a human honeybee, and everything I saw or did, I was storing it away. Saving it. And I had to save as much as I could before time ran out."

I had to shake my head in grim wonder. "You continually amaze me."

"No," he said, in one of those leaps of subject that had become more common with him of late, "the only person who continually amazes me is my mom. Trust me. Did I tell you she's started the dig at DioCaesarea? Seizo-Diarrhea I used to call it, the time we went there. I was in agony. She kept telling me to eat yogurt. But this archaeologist she's hooked up with has all the financing in place and they're apparently at the site and set for the summer. I got this long letter from her. The things she said would stun an ox."

"Gee," I said, "your mom. Pardon me, but now there was a lunatic. There was somebody who completely freaked me out."

"Yeah," Jonathan said. "The one person who actually figured out how she wanted to meet the world, and then went ahead and did it. Head-on. That should freak all of us out. About how we're not living our lives, I mean."

"You've forgiven her," I said, "for yanking you out of your element. Taking you to the ends of the Earth."

"There's absolutely nothing to forgive," he said. "She's the one who showed me my element, you could say. Or let me find it out for myself."

"And your dad?"

"That's the tough one," he said. "My one piece of unfinished business. I'm like that honeybee again, trying to save things up. Mom and I had some great years. And Dad went to the moon. But I never had him. Not really. And I don't think it's selfish to want that too. Just as one last thing."

Was I jealous to hear that? Or just frightened? This whole conversation had left me exhausted, off-kilter. *You have us*, I might have wanted to say. Or wanted even more to say, *You have me*.

But that warm June afternoon, higher above the Earth than I'd ever been, I spoke none of those fears. With a shudder our plane moved into a patch of turbulence. The captain turned on the seatbelt sign. We had to be passing over Minerva, I thought. I shivered. My parents were down there. My father and mother. Their house that had never been my home. And I thought of what my mother used to say whenever I shivered for no reason: someone is walking over your grave.

Jonathan must have sensed there was some kind of trouble. He reached over and held my hand, and in five minutes the sky was calm once again. Nothing stood between us and Houston.

ARARAT

I ate my meal alone in the upstairs "family" room of a restaurant, a sixty-year-old American woman clearly eccentric, clearly lost, probably beyond rescuing at this point. Lentil soup, bread, tomato salad. Frugal but sufficient. From across the room she kept staring at me, a woman some ten years younger than myself. We two solitary women. From below came the hearty sounds of men at their meal. A television in the corner played an American western dubbed into Turkish, but all her attention was riveted on me alone. Never had anyone stared at me like that since Allen so many years ago, forty years in fact, at McCauley's Restaurant in Armistice the night before he went off to Korea. But this stare was different. This stare held me not like a falcon holds its prey but the way any question may be said to hold within itself the possibility of unforeseeable answers. And yet I was not afraid, I who had lived with so much fear. When she rose, walked slowly, almost cautiously, to my table, I nodded for her to sit beside me.

Excuse me, she said in perfect, a shade too-perfect English, but I have known you somewhere before, I think?

Her full face, full lips, black hair interrupted by a striking swatch of pure white—I could see it where her scarf was pulled back. Those dark birdlike eyes, and I knew where I had encountered them before—day after day, half sunk in the cistern's black waters. Those benign, mysterious, abandoned Medusas whose gaze had turned me not to stone but back to flesh and blood.

What was I doing in Silifke that afternoon? Fly-blown, forsaken town where gunfire rang out in the night and the hotel smelled of feces and death. In my restlessness I had ventured there, it seemed, precisely for this encounter.

Doctor Tansu Ergüliç, she introduced herself. Professor of archaeology at the University of Ankara, protegée of the famous, even legendary Doctor Ekrem Akurgal—I had not, I was sorry to say, ever heard of him—and herself author of *Principal Monuments of the Seleucid Dynasty of Southeastern Anatolia*.

And who was I?

Political exile, ever-recovering alcoholic, unorthodox mother, victim of the space race, loverless lover, traveler in lands real and imaginary. . . .

After lunch we walked. Affably she put her arm through mine. Our course took us, I presume by chance, to the old Byzantine cistern, what the locals call the striped granary. Roofless now, a great steep-sided pit. We stood on the edge gazing down at the litter of old stones and saplings forcing their tenacious rootholds. A couple of Turkish air force jets roared by overhead. She talked of her work, the excavations she proposed to undertake—bureaucratic obstacles aside—at an obscure but celebrated site not far from here, in the hills to the northeast. She named it and I told her, I've been there. Dio-Caesarea. My son and I, years ago. . . .

I knew, she said, when I first laid eyes on you. . . .

That was all we said. Everything else was somehow understood in the ellipses.

During the years we lived in Istanbul, Jonathan worked from time to time as an English language tour guide, and I once happened by accident upon one of his tours. I had made my morning pilgrimage to drop coins in the outstretched, red-tattoed palm of the old woman who kept inscrutable vigil on the grounds of the Shehzade mosque, and as I cut through the inner courtyard there stood Jonathan at the center of a crowd of brightly attired foreigners. Cameras dangled from their necks. The Dutch and the Ottomans, Jonathan was telling them, shared a common passion for tulips. You could see it in the famous tulip carpets of the time, and in the faience tiles from Iznik.

How he came by such arcane information I never knew, though it seemed not impossible he was regaling them with complete fabrications. I marveled at how, despite their general lack of interest, for the moment he held them all rapt—and the crazy American lady also, as she lurked in the shadows of the porphyry columns.

This mosque in whose inner courtyard they now found themselves, he told his small band, was called Shehzade, which meant "Prince," and one popular story held that Süleyman the Magnificent had it built in memory of his favorite son, Prince Mehmet, who died of smallpox when he was twenty-one. Süleyman was so heartbroken, he sat weeping beside Mehmet's body for three days. And when the Sultan recovered, he determined to commemorate the prince.

It was a touching story, the restless Dutch tourists were satisfied, but Jonathan wasn't content to end things there. Maybe it was true, that father grieving for his son. But he had his doubts. He spoke darkly. There was another version of the story, he intimated, and in that version it wasn't Mehmet who was prince but another one of Süleyman's sons, Mustafa. A talented boy, precocious and sweet and responsible, but because of the unfortunate detail that his mother wasn't Roxelana, the Sultan's favorite wife, but another member of the harem, and because Roxelana had sons of her own, and ambitions, she concocted a plot to get Mustafa out of the way.

But the tourists' attention had started to drift. Singly or in pairs they wandered off to gaze at the merchandise being hawked in the porticoes of the inner courtyard.

I know it all sounds complicated, he pleaded with them, but everything about the Ottomans was complicated.

Roxelana, he went on valiantly, the jealous mother, the favorite wife, told Süleyman that Mustafa was plotting to take over. Süleyman had no choice. He called his son back from the provinces, and when Mustafa went to meet his dad—boom! The eunuchs got him. Strangled him in the corridor with a bowstring because it was against the law to actually spill royal blood. Süleyman himself watched from behind a curtain.

Jonathan conjured it so vividly, but with each successive word, each convolution of his marvelous tale he was losing them and he knew it. And I had suddenly the most vivid recollection: how he used to chatter on to his father, and I could see Allen's attention revert to the television set he sat in a stupor before, no doubt exhausted by the ardors and anxieties of his week in the field, and Jonathan prattling on with renewed vigor, aware his father had slipped from him but unable to figure out how to win him back except through more and more of the same.

He listened to Mustafa cry out and did nothing, Jonathan shouted. A shout not so much of outrage as some strange exultation. I was shocked. Men washing themselves before prayer looked up from the fountain at this outburst. Nervous pigeons exploded into flight from their perches under the domes. *Süleyman was so upset with himself that he built this mosque out of pure remorse*, Jonathan concluded quietly.

He'd lost his whole flock except for an old bald-headed man in a loud flower-print shirt.

Please, may I take your picture? the Dutchman asked him mincingly, adoringly.

All the wind seemed to go out of Jonathan. *Sure*, he said, shifting his weight to one foot, putting his hand on his hip. Smiling beautifully for the camera.

Then he saw me and turned away, and the look on his face—it was a look I hadn't seen before. Embarrassment, sadness, revulsion? In any event I scurried away as if I'd witnessed something shameful.

You'll never meet him, Tansu, because he writes me he's dying.

He's lost weight, he tells me. He's skin and bones. He has lesions on his legs, his arms, the soles of his feet. He has half a dozen intestinal infections. He thinks he detects early symptoms of toxoplasmosis of the brain. I could fly to America to be with him, but I won't. He doesn't want me to, and I don't need to. *What you and I have*—he writes me—*is this bond nothing can break.*

Or what he told me in Alanya as he prepared his return to America: we've seen things, you and I, nobody else will ever believe. Been places. Like Marco Polo when he came back from China, and they threw him in prison for telling lies, but on his death bed he confessed he only told the things he thought people might have a chance of believing.

As for me, Jonathan said, my lips are sealed.

We shared, among other things, the love of ruins that has brought me here—something in our various upbringings, perhaps. Dio-Caesarea to the Romans, Olba to the Greeks, Uzanzuburç to the Turks: a city named and renamed many times, old fortunes risen and fallen more times than a person can count. We loved these destroyed places of habitation, last farflung vestiges of collapsed empires. Loved the way weeds and wildflowers sprung amidst the toppled columns, sprouted from tumble-down walls. Goats grazing in the rubble of magnificent baths, and here villagers have quarried a city gate, a triumphal arch, the seats of a theater for the stones of their humble houses.

Mom, he told me once with that occasional, uncanny seriousness of his, you're very old.

Don't I feel it, I told him. Every last century of it.

That's what I mean, hundreds and hundreds of years, he said. You're older than you realize.

Gee thanks, I told him. Though I know what you mean.

Old as in ancient, he said.

And I did know what he meant, somewhere deep and shivering in my ancient, exhausted soul.

I remember watching his glee that day we came to Dio-Caesarea: how he did a little manic dance in the sunlight as we stood amid the jumbled stones of the overgrown theater, and suddenly I saw him, this point of brightness, spectacular and futile as a shooting star, and if sometimes I had doubts—what on earth are we doing with ourselves here?—that day I was euphoric. Euphoric we stood in this dry wind and harsh light on a desolate plain where an empire had languished two thousand years ago to weeds and desolation (and America too would have its day), my son and I, improbable as all hell but for our brief sliver of time, alive.

I found my own life so strangely handed back to me.

I have been thinking about that ancient epitaph you showed me in the necropolis cut into the rock face down by the aqueduct. Two thousand years old but still legible, etched in the stone sarcophagus long ago plundered but still perched in its niche (though inside some old bones still molder):

NON FUI.

FUI.

NON SUM.
NON CURO.

You translated for me: I was not. I was. I am not. I don't care.

I wish Jonathan could have stood beside us as you made out those words. I can hear his approving laugh. The way he would have said, "All right!" I wish, my dear Tansu, that you had met my son. He would, no doubt, have discomfitted you—as he discomfitted all of us. You would not have approved, I think, of his importing carpets to America. You would not have cared much for Demir, or Shahin, or the other Turkish men he loved so passionately. But you would have risen to the challenge. And though he would have grown tired of your tireless enthusiasm for Atatürk, for the luminous future of the Tigris and Euphrates hydroelectric project, for Turkey's belated entry into the European Economic Community, he would have liked you back—fiercely, impulsively, as was his way.

Once I went far to the east, to Van, Doğubayazit, to Mount Ararat rising auspicious above the high pasturage of the yayla. In a village there—nameless, forsaken, a mere huddle of mud-brick buildings, their backs to the unforgiving world—I sat in the "Family Beer Garden," as it was called, and drank tiny glasses of powerful tea and overheard the latest news as it was talked about at the neighboring tables.

An expedition had been through. One of the land rovers had broken down outside the village, the party had stayed overnight, sleeping on generously offered rooftops. They had drunk beer in this very garden, and through their interpreters—Turks from the west—had told their stories.

They were headed, it seemed, to the Mountain—no need, in that emptiness, to speak the name of that looming presence. The expedition's leader was a slim, polite man who had walked on the surface of the moon. And there on the moon, he said, God had told him to return to Earth to seek for the Ark of Noah in its final resting place high in the snows of the Mountain. Had they heard tell, he inquired mildly (but there was divine madness in his blue eyes), of the Ark? Had their shepherds perhaps glimpsed its petrified remains in the translucent ice of a glacier? Seen its skeletal ribs lying exposed on a shelf of rock

322

beneath the eastern cliff face? Any rumors, old wives tales passed down generation after generation?

The men had stirred uneasily, their reaction a mix of hilarity, skepticism, superstition. They still stirred uneasily as they recounted among themselves for the tenth, twentieth time the strangely persistent inquiries of this man who claimed to have walked on the moon—though it was agreed no one, save perhaps the Prophet himself, had ever walked on the moon. The moon was water, everyone knew that.

In this village the women stayed out of sight, those children who were about wore pinned to their clothing the blue glass eye to ward off the covetous gaze of pale foreigners. Two boys peered bravely around a corner at me as I sat listening to the old men recount for one another. The hugest, strangest rooster I ever saw pecked vigorously at the bare-swept earth. Desperate music wailed from static-ridden speakers affixed above the door. Seeing the two boys, one of the men made a sharp hissing noise to warn them back. He gestured brusquely in my dangerous direction. This woman here, this stranger, foreigner, *yabanci*, *giaour*, unbeliever.

Beware her gaze.

Had I too, one of the men wanted to know, come to seek the Ark of Noah?

I laughed and said no. I was only a traveler. I was seeing the world.

Why? they asked. Why did I want to see the world? And in particular, why their village? They were not in the habit of traveling to America to look at my village.

It is an American sickness, I told them. A modern fever. At night when you cannot sleep.

There is much sickness in America, they told me.

Yes, I agreed. There is much sickness there.

As I made to leave, they gave me, holding them out solemnly in the palms of their hands, magic glass eyes to protect myself from the modern fever, the American sickness, that had brought me—us—here in the first place.

There is another mountain, they told me, just beyond Ararat. Much greater. Miles higher in fact. But invisible. Only seen rarely, glimpsed now and then down through time by saints, the pure of heart, men who have lost but then recovered their souls.

We speak of it, they said, only in the rumor tense.

A HOMECOMING

Janine has left a yellow Post-it note on the attic door. He finds it when he creeps out, sometime after dark. His stomach is growling something terrible. It feels hollow, like someone carved him out with a knife.

Evisceration, he thinks.

What did I do wrong? says the note. *When you feel like talking, please let me know.*

He admires, terribly, her restraint. She didn't call the fire department or the cops, didn't have Frank come bust down the door. And yet, for all she could have known, he might have lain passed out behind that locked door all day long. And yet he vaguely remembers talking— nonstop talking, hours and hours of it. His throat's in fact sore with all that talking. But to whom? Surely not to Janine, but to somebody. Why can't he remember?

There's a special feel to the house at night that he's come to savor these past few months. He prides himself on having perfected the ability to glide around its empty rooms and hallways noiselessly. Easing open the refrigerator, he stuffs himself ravenously—various lunch meats, individually wrapped slices of Velveeta, cottage cheese from the container, half a loaf of Wonder bread, dill pickles. He taps four eggs and greedily gulps down their contents. Drinks from the carton of milk. He feels like some magnificent hulking beast. He's never been so hungry, never felt his hunger so gloriously slaked.

In perfect silence he ventures from the house. By ghastly moonlight the sycamores are amputated hulks cut down to a height of about ten feet. Beyond saving, no matter what happens now.

Too late.

But not too late for some revenge. He thinks about taking a sledge hammer to the Mustang sleeping there beneath its shroud, forever safe from bird or sycamore droppings, but resists the temptation. Too loud, too messy. It would call an immediate end to things, and he's not at all ready for that.

Sugar in the gas tank. A punk's stunt, but effective enough. He creeps back in the house and finds a five-pound, practically untouched bag in the cabinet. At best Frank'll have to have the gas tank syphoned, the engine vacuum-cleaned. At worst, it'll slag the works.

Good.

Next morning the tribunal has resumed its inquiry. The Owl and the Amateur have divested themselves of some of their finery and settled into more casual attire. The Owl's in a pince-nez, a maroon velveteen dinner jacket. The Amateur wears a moth-eaten racoon coat and carries a collegiate pennant. A cigarette in its holder, à la FDR, juts rakishly from his lips. The scene has changed as well—to the Luna Lounge, one of Allen's old Canaveral haunts. He hasn't been here in years, though for a while, after Joan and before Janine, it was the site of some pretty dire nights.

Partynaut.

They sit on bar stools, their backs to the bar, facing the entrance. A banner hangs above the door: THE FUTURE BELONGS TO THE BRAVE.

The Owl spits out, discreetly, a bolus. Allen can't help watching it there on the floor: mummy of mouse bones, twigs, congealed mucus. The bolus sprouts legs like a spider and scurries under a bar stool. Appearing from nowhere, Fiona Root reaches down and plucks it up. Looking at Allen, a look both forlorn and seductive, she puts it in her mouth and swallows. She moans with pleasure.

The court is in session, bellows the Owl. Then coughs as if embarrassed by his outburst. The Amateur claps his hands together and the door is thrown open to reveal a landscape of launch towers, rockets venting fuel, spotlights combing an angry sky.

Allen is made to understand that the prosecution will continue with its presentation of exhibits, a procession of carnival floats and drastic merriment that seems endless. He closes his eyes tightly, but still they keep coming. He can see them through his shut eyelids.

Here is a tastefully conceived and executed diorama of the V-2 launch site at Peenemünde. Werner von Braun, dapper in a gray shark-skin suit and fedora, scans the horizon with binoculars. The sky is a dull gray, the winter wind is whipping in off the North Sea. He lights a cigarette. Cut-away of his brain to show a pandemonium of gadgetry. HE AIMED FOR THE STARS AND HIT LONDON INSTEAD! signals a pennant above the display.

Here is a scale model of the underground rocket factories, the earth honey-combed with tunnels, secret chambers. Like industrious honey-bees, workers generously lent from the camp at Dora toil in the blistering darkness. Collectively they dream of potatoes, bread leavened with brick dust, old shtetl songs, the watery ooze of vomit. Their death throes, mercifully, occur offstage.

Here is an empty stage. From the ceiling, on visible wires, is lowered, slowly, an unsteady crescent moon. It floats just above the stage floor like a ship, and into it scramble white-smocked scientists, undercover operatives, low-level SS officers. Von Braun is last aboard, smiling and waving farewell to the crowds that gather, weeping and tossing handkerchiefs and flowers and contraband cigarettes his way. By his side, ever loyal, stands Gerhardt Walter.

In gaudy lights the slogan OPERATION PAPER CLIP appears on the side of the crescent moon as slowly, slowly, sprouting an imaginative floral design of red, white, and blue swastikas, it rises toward the ceiling to the faint, nostalgic strains of Lili Marlene. THE CLASP OF ETERNAL FRIENDSHIP ACROSS THE WATERS.

Here is Gus Grissom, whom everyone used to call The Ghoul. The Bad Luck Kid. Gus losing his Mercury capsule in the choppy swells of the Pacific. Gus appearing to spontaneously combust inside the cramped Apollo 1 capsule, blue flames spreading from his heart, leaping forth from his mouth, his eye sockets, rising through his eustachian tubes to burst his eardrums with tympanic thunder. Here is brother fire peeling back Gus Grissom's face to reveal the grinning skull beneath the skin. And beneath the skull the reptilian face remembered from half a dozen Saturday afternoon sci-fi flicks.

The whole show is accompanied by music—a band, approaching but never arriving, that spews forth endless military marches, Sousa or Bavarian oompah or the shrill tintinnabulations of the Sultan's Janissaries.

Here is displayed the hole in the ozone over Antarctica. A graph shows the trajectory of rocket launches, the introduction into the high atmosphere of partially burned rocket propellants. A large red question mark over the graph. But Allen knows. In a glass box to the side of the graph, shrunk to the size of a doll or perhaps a small cat, sits Chuck Brittain. He is wizened, blackened like a mummy. His eyes glow. He takes off his head like a helmet and holds it in his arms. "In the back of our minds," he says in a low voice, "all along, we knew what we were doing but refused to ask ourselves what we knew. Those gaping wounds we punched with every flight in our last fragile film of defense. X-15, X-100. Atlas-Centaur. Saturn V. The mighty Energia. No one has even begun to study the effects of increased ultraviolet radiation on the mutation of terrestrial viruses or bacteria, but common sense tells us those effects must be staggering. The biggest story of all, my friends."

He spins his head like a globe, and suddenly it *is* a globe, the blue world itself floating like an eye in the blackness of space. Allen watches transfixed. There is now soft music, elevator music, "Raindrops Keep Falling on My Head."

"Jet travel," Chuck says in a perky voice, as if narrating a television commercial. "Bringing together the four corners of our world. Overnight to anywhere, you name it, Tokyo, Istanbul, Ulan Bator. The gorgeous and heretofore untouristed capitals of central Africa. Dar es Salaam! Kampala! Kinshasa! Brazzaville! Out of Africa, always something new. Cradle of Life. Step right up, pay your money and get your booty. It's the modern miracle of jet travel, shrinking space and time, no boundaries anymore, everything set free at last, ah yes, bringing the world together. Reuniting the species after fifty million years."

Suddenly his voice drops to a whisper, sepulchral: "Fifty years after Hernando de Soto and his soldiers hacked their way through the marshes of the Missippippi Valley, other explorers reported nothing but abandoned villages where the Spaniard had seen thriving populations, splendid cities, sacred mound cultures, beautiful bare-chested women and gold-bedecked warriors."

When Chuck replaces his head on his body, the burnt face isn't Chuck's at all. It belongs, grinningly, to Kite Baxter. Allen has only time to call out his boyhood friend's name before the scene shifts. Before him now is a painting he knows well. He's studied it often. On his desk he keeps a reproduction he tore from a magazine and taped to a piece of cardboard backing. Pieter Brueghel. But this is the painting like he never saw it: 3-D and animated, lit as if from within, and a din of noise accompanying it. In a landscape gone livid with flames, the armies of death, pestilence, chaos advance relentlessly on the beleaguered human populace. A feast has been interrupted: death drags away the victims. A skeleton uncovers, for a horrified diner, a skull and thigh bones on a platter while a masked figure pours out casks of wine onto the ground. Here a skeleton is cutting a man's throat, there a mangy dog is eating a woman's face. A ship manned by a skeleton crew casts live victims, millstones around their necks, into a black pond where bloated corpses float. Riding a gaunt, sallow roan, death with a sickle sweeps shrieking multitudes into a large opening marked with a cross—but this haven, this ark of refuge, unbeknownst to those fleeing souls, is in reality the maw of a huge black coffin. On the blossoming meadow that has sprung up on top of the coffin, a skeleton, with relentless gleeful energy, plays havoc on the drums.

The background is smoke of burning cities, twilight of the world. Singly, or in small groups, humans are executed by the legions of night. Their corpses spin slowly, bound on wheels hoisted atop slender poles and turning in the raven-thronged wind.

This apocalypse. He himself has brought it on, he knows. He has peered into things that, once seen, can never be unseen.

The hell of knowledge. How can he ever retreat from that?

Tell us, taunts Fiona Root, athwart a charger, removing her mask to reveal a face blotched with lesions.

Tell us, leers Charlie, space-suited but helmetless, his face grotesque in makeup and a wig.

Tell us, whispers his father, as vultures tear at his flesh.

Tell us, demands Joan, her forehead exploded by a bullet from an Air Force–issue Colt .45.

Tell us, begs Jonathan, bound on a wheel and turning slowly in the wind.

Pièce de la résistance: masked attendants wheel in a final immense cart, a juggernaut bearing a huge stone likeness, Soviet heroic style, of Victoria Ivleva. In one hand she holds Sputnik, in the other, Yuri Ga-

garin. A choir of brightly scarved babushkas—they all resemble his mother—proclaim Victoria Ivleva savior of the universe.

He should have been more like her. He should have lowered himself into the sarcophagus. He should have sent back pictures to the world. Should have told the truth. He has done none of this, he has been silent.

His son is dying. His world is dying. This is the end. This is the end. This is the end.

Downstairs—no, on the stairs, coming closer—he hears voices. Janine is talking to someone right outside the door. She is rapping lightly, insistently with her knuckles. There is another voice.

The sycamores are down, the Owl and the Amateur fled. That foolish tale that was no tale, but he spun it out anyway, sitting on his son's bed, so many years ago. Before anyone ever walked on the moon or came home to tell of it. They took refuge here, briefly, huddled in his brain, terrified, disappointed, grievously sad. That is what it was, he thinks—they were passing through him on their way elsewhere. They were forsaking this house they had watched over.

"Hey Dad," Jonathan says from the other side of the door, the other side of time and memory. "It's me. Remember me? Jonathan. Prodigal son. I've come to see you, Dad."

He's too terrified to open the door. He's already seen Jonathan all too clearly, the blue-black lesion festering on the tip of his nose. He can't face this. He won't even speak.

"Dad," Jonathan says again.

Allen slumps down to the floor, his back against the attic door. "No," he moans, a small miserable voice audible only to himself.

"You should come out of there," Jonathan coaxes, that musical, slightly mocking voice. "You must be starving. Come get something to eat. It's okay."

It's not okay. The feast has been interrupted: death drags away the victims.

"Dad," Jonathan says, "what can I say that'll make you come out?"

He's having none of it. He wills himself to implode, become invisible, bodiless. Wills himself out the attic window, in disembodied flight over the lawns and cul de sacs of Nassau Bay, out to the sunny Galveston Highway and down to the coast, the massive sheltering thunderheads that build in the open expanse of the Gulf.

But he doesn't fly. He creeps on hands and knees as far from the door as the attic will allow—all the way to the imprisoning glass of the window.

Crouched there, peering out, he sees Frank, hands in his pockets, amble out his back door. Frank whistles a tune, breaks mid-melody to sing Zippity doo da, then resumes his whistled tune as he saunters over to the Mustang.

Allen's heart sinks to recall his escapade of the night before, though a little fragment of that heart soars heavenward with malicious delight. He even rubs his hands together in gleeful anticipation. Is he actually seeing all this, or is it another hallucination?

How he hates Frank, his ease in the world, his clear, corrupt conscience. Frank opens the door, slides into the driver's seat. Allen holds his breath.

When Frank starts the motor, the sound is simply atrocious. The cacophony—clearly, satisfyingly expensive—pays back, in a single instant, all that murderous chain saw—though of course it doesn't bring the sycamores back. Nothing brings anything back.

Except his son. His son is back.

SCHEHERAZADE

See? Janine makes a gesture of helplessness with both hands. Quiver around the edges of her mouth, and I think she's going to cry but instead she keeps forcing that brave smile she's smiled so long it's etched in the wrinkles of her face.

We all three huddle at the top of the stairs. They both watch me, but I don't know what to do.

I feel a cramp in my gut. Sharp needle of pain.

Dad, I say again. Knock hard on the door. But it's like he's dead. Like I'm talking to him on the other side of the grave and he's not responding. Seance I did with Julian in Williamsburg: beeswax candles and antique mirrors, goofy evening. Julian trying to get in touch with his dead mother, but it wasn't working. Something to do with the barometric pressure. Claimed it worked most of the time. Claimed his mother was bossy as ever over there. Then why bother? I said, and he looked offended. His entourage of undergraduates looked offended.

There's nothing to do but wait. Siege of Constantinople. Wait and wait for the unguarded gate.

Hey Dad, I try one last time. I love you.

We all wince to hear me say it like that.

The backyard looks like some terrible battle's been waged up and down its length. Tree branches strewn everywhere like the hurricane that passed through when I was ten and I made a fort from downed limbs. And the MacLean's yard next door too. In the middle of all that carnage stands a black man with a chain saw. I can't believe my eyes. I pick my way through the litter and go right over to him.

He has no idea who I am. Looks at me funny, then shuts off the chain saw.

Still fit and wiry like I remember but getting older. Forty-five now? Lines in his face. A gold front tooth.

Hey Bill, I say. You don't remember me.

He sort of laughs, surprised, searching for that name, and then he finds it, pulls it up from the deep. Says, Jonathan, my man. What you been up to? It is Jonathan, I got that right, don't I?

He frowns. I hate the shock of it on people's faces. The look on Janine's face at the airport. I remember how he fucked me, first time ever, and have to wonder, What's he thinking now? How fixed on him I was? How I was trouble from the word go?

Oh man, he says, you don't look so good.

My lucky star must've quit on me, I tell him.

He says, Don't tell me that.

Too late, is all I can say.

But he touches my arm anyway. Tells me, You didn't know half the shit you was getting into. Somebody should of told you.

It's the breaks, I say.

Aw shit, man, he says. And they're telling people it's from Africa too. But that's one big lie. CIA did this to you. Fort Dietrick, Maryland. I know about this stuff. Germ warfare. I got a friend who can tell you all about it. Top Secret.

Sure.

What I say is, It's so great to see you again.

So great and so strange. So strange to be standing where those two big sycamores used to be and now it's empty sky, drenching sun. I feel it's something bad that those trees are down. Something I'm on the verge of remembering but then can't.

I'm spooked.

I shake myself out of it and ask him, So you're doing okay for yourself?

Doing real fine, he says. I got three boys. You should see them. Big strapping boys. I thought for sure your dad was going to hire me when you left, but he never did.

Takes a step closer to me, says confidentially, You know, I think I busted up some of the bushes his old lady put in. Your stepma, right? Out here for hours digging her flower beds, so I don't imagine she's too happy. Those big branches come crashing down, they don't look out for nobody but themselves.

I wouldn't worry, I tell him. She's got other things on her mind.

My bowels are churning, and I desperately need to get myself on the toilet.

Hey Bill, I say. Got to go. Hang in there for me.

Man, he says, you promise to take care of yourself now, you hear?

Excellent care, I tell him. Excellent care.

I don't make it even to the front door before I've shit myself. Can feel it running down my pants legs and I have to pass Stayton and Janine at the kitchen table to get to the bathroom and it's times like this I think, Can't we just go ahead and get this farce over with?

My fucked-over life, I mean.

Janine's turned my old bedroom into the guest room where she installs me and Stayton. All fumigated, exorcised, happily remodeled. Bright yellow paint on the walls, furry wall-to-wall carpet underfoot. Low-quality antiques she's stripped and refinished, doilies on the nightstand, the dresser top, a woodland watercolor over the bed. Too depressing. I'm vanished from this place—all my old clutter, the kid I was and the fun I had.

Gone without a trace. Except for me. *I'm* the trace, I think as I wander the house upstairs and down. Dad still in the attic—moving around up there, pacing back and forth, but he won't come down. Janine and Stayton still in the kitchen drinking iced tea and talking about I can't imagine what. I let myself out the side door into the garage, step into the old familiar smell of the place. Hardly any room between Dad's Lincoln and the Cadillac Janine picked us up from the airport in. The 'vette's no longer around. Smashed up, Janine tells me, on the Galveston Highway back in '81. Dad loved breaking speed limits. Some demon at his heels all the time. Broke a leg, couple of ribs, but he's always been the lucky one. Mom never needed to worry on that score.

Against the far wall, stacks of cardboard boxes I'm surprised Janine never rooted out. I have to smile. Go over, open one up and sure enough: *National Geographic*. Years and years of them, back to when I was thirteen, fourteen and everything turned me on. I page through an issue, but it's hard to believe any of that stuff could ever get me hard. Still, I shot so much come on the concrete floor—there should be a scald mark there, like a handprint or a memorial. Used to think it might eat through to China, and these days it probably would.

The kid whose scientist parents are raising him in the Amazon—that was my favorite, and I look for it but of course can't find it. Though I wonder where he is now, straw blond and butt-naked with a string around his waist and two daubs of blue paint on his cheeks. He was my age.

Hundreds of magazines, and I read somewhere how nobody ever throws out a *National Geographic*, that the accumulated weight of them on the earth's surface is more than the weight of the Egyptian pyramids.

Then I find the pistol wedged down between the side of a box and the stack of magazines. Strange place to hide a pistol.

I take it out, heft it in my hand. Feel the cool, dark metal, how it fits my palm. How somebody crafted it, with such care, to fit a palm like that. To have that particular weight. To be so lethal. Dad's .45 automatic from his Air Force days that I recognize from when he took it out of the dresser drawer in the bedroom to show me. Telling me, I don't ever want to catch you going in this drawer. This gun is strictly off limits. But telling me in the same breath, When you turn eighteen and graduate from high school, Jonathan old buddy, this beauty'll be yours.

I check the clip, rack the slide. Unloaded. Dad used to keep the bullets in a box in the off-limits dresser drawer I wasn't supposed to go in, but how could I resist?

Fourteen, fifteen. No one's home and I strip down, wander the house with my aching hard-on. Pretend I'm the Amazon boy exploring. Rummage through closets, chests, bookshelves, the fascinating book on Human Sexuality shelved backward. Clever. The drawer that holds Dad's monogrammed handkerchiefs, a cigar box full of loose change and stray buttons, Mom's jewel box with the purple velvet lining I love to touch.

And at the very bottom, bundled in a chamois cloth, the Colt that will be mine one day.

Wrap a towel around my waist and do a striptease in front of the big bedroom mirror. Shake out my long hair and dance, watch my half hard dick swing like a pendulum, slap against my thighs. Feel my loose nuts jiggle in their sac.

When I come, my eyes turn into slits and I make all the noise I know how. Animal groan commencing at the base of my spine and then that one moment of floating free when I don't care if I'm dead or alive I'm stretched so thin, just one fading instant, but I try to get myself there as often as I can.

Lap the sweet sticky off my fingers and imagine it's not mine but somebody, anybody else's. Some boy at school, the Amazon kid, Bill who mows the grass for the MacLeans next door.

So many ways I can turn myself on, slip out of my skin to go traveling past the far planets. I'm so in love with everything back then.

And still in love, only now it's harder. Now there's something out there doesn't want me to love, and it's the death of me.

On impulse I stick the gun in the waist of my jeans, ferry it upstairs to stash in my bag in the guest room that used to be mine.

Scheherazade is lying curled up asleep on the bed. But I left her with Marco in Virginia. Or did I? Suddenly I can't remember—there's a fog that comes up in my brain. I look again and she's just a black T-shirt I left wadded on the bed.

When I come back downstairs, Stayton and Janine are in the kitchen making dinner and talking about me. Catch myself right outside the door and eavesdrop. The voyeuring hour. Odd how they've hit it off—and Stayton always claims women make him nervous. Well, I guess not the venerable Janine.

She's singing the praises of crystal therapy. How a friend of hers with breast cancer wore clear purple amethyst for six months and the cancer was gone. Sucked right out of her body. You could see how it turned the crystal cloudy.

Positive energy is what Jonathan needs, she says. His body needs massive infusions of positive energy.

I'm really not up on this crystal stuff, Stayton says.

It's very scientific, Janine tells him. The molecular structure of crystals focuses cosmic rays. You know, that energy that's diffused throughout the galaxy. The crystal traps it and hoards it up and when it comes in contact with the human body's magnetic field it releases.

Good for her, I think. Still the same old Janine. Dad hasn't broken her.

Stayton sounds doubtful. I don't think Jonathan would go for that, he tells her. He's very stubborn. He won't even go see a doctor.

Well, Janine says, of course, you know him so much better than I do. But I always thought he seemed incredibly open to new ideas. I always thought that was so wonderful about him.

Unfortunately, Stayton tells her, I think he's in some kind of deep denial these days.

Hard to believe I've made conspirators out of these two. Still, I can only listen to so much. I cough once to alert them and come striding into the kitchen.

You must have read our minds, says Janine. The spaghetti's all ready. We were just going to call you.

I see they've been sharing a bottle of wine. Another glass with dinner and Stayton's loosened right up.

I like you, he tells Janine. Totally out of the blue, but I can see she's pleased. She reaches out, touches his hand. Covers it with hers.

You're lucky, she tells me. You've found such a wonderful person.

Then turning to Stayton: You're a very just person, she says. Very moral. I could tell even at the airport when I first saw you. You have this scrupulousness about you.

Even if he does think women evolved from sea lions, I say.

But clearly I've offended him.

I never said that, he protests. I just told you I read that somewhere. I thought it was bizarre, in fact.

I don't believe in evolution per se, Janine says. What I believe in is progressive reincarnation, which is different.

Progressive reincarnation? Stayton asks.

I haven't realized Scheherazade's with us at the table. She sits quietly, in the fourth chair. Stayton and Janine either don't notice, or think it's not worth mentioning. I decide we really did bring her along from Virginia after all.

There's only so much matter in the universe, Janine goes on. Star stuff. So it all gets recycled. We come back as different forms, and over time those forms change. So we were here as dinosaurs millions of years ago, and right now we're here as human beings, and a million years from now we'll be sitting at this table having this conversation only we won't be human beings anymore. We'll be some other life form that we can't even begin to imagine.

You're pulling my leg, Stayton says suspiciously. Scheherazade looks from Janine to Stayton and back again. Obviously very interested.

Oh no, Janine assures Stayton. I mean, it sounds strange, but it's not. The Hindus were saying all this stuff three thousand years ago. And now science is confirming it. Every twenty-six million years the earth goes through this period of mass extinctions. Most species on the planet disappear. But something fills the gap. New life forms. Where do they come from? My theory is, When you reach a certain stage, you come back as a totally new kind of life form that the world hasn't seen before. At first there're just a few, because some individuals are ahead of others on the journey, but then pretty soon everybody is coming back as that new life form and after a while there aren't any of the old life forms left.

Sort of like Christians and pagans, I say.

I can feel Stayton getting skittish, despite the wine. And what does your husband think of this? he asks.

Janine waves her hand in front of her face. She's had more wine than Stayton. Her face is flushed.

Oh, Allen, she says. He's off in his own world. As you can see.

And she gestures toward the ceiling.

In the instant before Scheherazade starts talking, I know that's what's going to happen. Completely unsurprising, like she simply refrained all this time but for no particular reason. Normal tone of voice though I can't quite understand what she's saying, a blur of sentences. Or I can pick out individual words but then I forget them when the next word comes along. There's a prickling sensation up and down my legs.

She's trying to tell us her real name, I think. Saying it very slowly, over and over, the way you'd talk to a little child. Only I can't understand.

Next thing I know, Stayton's apologizing. I didn't mean that about Mr. Cloud, he tells Janine. Just being cranky. Such a cheap drunk. Goes right to my head. Oh brother. I'm about to either pass out or fall asleep.

You've had such an exhausting day, she says. Both of you. You look wiped out, Jonathan.

I *am* pretty wiped out if I thought Scheherazade was here and talking to me.

Go on up to bed, you two, Janine says. I'll clean up down here.

I notice how gray her hair's gotten, how the skin of her face has coarsened with time. Putting my arm around her: you're terrific, I tell her. Then let Stayton drag me upstairs.

His hands are all over me helping me undress for bed.

I'm not a total invalid yet, I remind him. Though I'm hungry for his hands on me. Want him to hold me down, keep me from slipping off. The bed, the planet. He's very drunk. Don't, I tell him when he tries to kiss me. But he goes ahead anyway. Kisses my mouth, my chin, my third nipple. Kisses his way on down. Takes me in his mouth before I can stop him, and then I don't have the will to stop him. Suddenly he hops from the bed and bounds over to his bag.

Good boys of the nineties, he says with a flourish, always carry a condom.

What on earth are you thinking? I ask him. You're crazy.

Look who's talking, he says. Tears open the package with his teeth and rolls it down my cock.

Too astonishing.

Stayton, I say. But already he's clambering on top of me, already he's easing himself down on me. Already I'm inside him.

So surprised I come in about twenty-five seconds.

I never thought, I tell him in the vacuum after.

Well, yeah, he says. And you thought you knew me.

He hasn't come, that big dick of his still hard so he fetches another condom from his bag and I unroll it down his magnificent length. Lift my legs and bare my soul to heaven. Better even than the moment of coming, so fugitive, and this could go on and on, and in my dream I'm opening up like a blossom, the red petals of a rose, opening and opening, exfoliating I think the word is, capacious as time itself.

I keep watching that black T-shirt where he tossed it onto my bag. Keep waiting for it to turn into Scheherazade right before my eyes. But it's just a T-shirt.

Stayton's always a long time coming. A long hard time that's never long enough and when he does come it wipes me out completely.

So we've done this, I say. We certainly waited a long time for it.

Appointment with destiny, Stayton tells me. Now we've come full circle.

He has the same calm look on his face as when the cops in Washington drag him away.

Death by hanging. Death by drowning. Death by sleeping pills. Death by carbon monoxide asphyxiation. Death by falling from a great height. From a bridge, from a mountaintop, from an airplane.

Death by razor blade to the wrist, the jugular. Death by gunshot wound to the temple, the mouth, between the eyes.

Death by fire. Death by fasting. Death by purposeful contraction of the AIDS virus.

Pneumocystis carinii, Kaposi's sarcoma, lymphoma, cryptococcus, candidiasis, cytomegalovirus, toxoplasmosis.

I know too much.

Death by willed cessation of heartbeat.

Lying in bed I'm too restless. Stayton sound asleep, the whole house sound asleep. Air conditioner's on and that makes me cold. I slip on my boxer shorts, wrap a blanket around my shoulders. Pad quietly downstairs to the kitchen.

It's dark. There's someone sitting at the kitchen table.

IN THE MIDDLE OF THE NIGHT

He's possessed by the odd, confusing feeling he's gotten away with something. It's been hours. Frank hasn't come storming over, banged on the back door, threatened to call the police. Apparently he's made no connection between the fate of those sycamores and the swift, albeit somewhat sophomoric retribution Allen's visited upon him. With admirable docility he's phoned a wrecker to haul the Mustang off to the shop.

The failure to make connections, Allen's thought earlier as he watched the kid from the repair shop hook the Mustang to his truck: perfect symptom of his species's final fumblings toward a well-deserved extinction.

Sooner or later the shop'll have to report a load of sugar in the gas tank. But even then, what will Frank choose to believe? What neighborhood kids or disgruntled investors will he find to blame?

Even with their recent, gentlemanly estrangement two plus two could never equal Allen Cloud locked in the attic of his house and capable of anything.

That house now seems—at last—settled into quiet, and Allen can almost pretend they've all packed their bags and gone away. That's all he wants—to be left alone with his grief. His mortification. Not to have to face the shame.

But the shame of what?

He forces himself again and again, in the dark, to name it. To tear relentlessly at the wound. His dying son. His own undeniable culpability in everything, everything.

Tomorrow, or the next day, or the day after that: sooner or later this attic standoff will have to end. And what words of apology or explanation will he possibly come up with? It horrifies him to realize how far preferable he'd find it, how much easier, to simply slip away under cover of night, never again darken the city limits of Houston or this house he's made the mistake of calling home. Never darken the limits of the whole sorry planet.

And in the midst of it all, his stomach is once again growling non-stop. Charlie, no doubt, would've had some mordant comment on that: through thick and thin, the stomach speaketh its own mind.

Well, the simple fact is, Charlie's long dead and Allen's famished.

Carefully he makes his way down the stairs that creak. For a moment he hesitates at the back door, tempted by a break to freedom. But he moves on, into the darkened kitchen. There's no disappearing from any of this.

The refrigerator's been stocked with strange, unfamiliar foods. He handles them in their packages: tofu, seaweed, bean sprouts. Bottles of vitamins: mega, multi, C and E and B. It's as if he's got the wrong kitchen, or his own's been colonized by strangers.

He lets the fridge door swing shut and sits down heavily at the table. Jonathan's food. He remembers reading about the diets AIDS patients concoct in their attempt to stave off the inevitable—but nothing brings it home, so to speak, like this.

If only he were dreaming now, and not earlier amid those fantastic conjurations in the attic. Unconsciously he draws a slip of paper from his pocket, looks at it, then after a long-dawning moment recognizes his own scrawl there, words he's jotted down, phrases. He's forgotten he took notes up there. Points he had to be sure to remember.

Final report of findings, he has written. *Human species is the disease. AIDS is only the cure.* Flinching to read that secret message he's brought back from the tribunal, he shakes his head in wonder and crumples the piece of paper.

When he looks up, Jonathan is standing in the doorway.

If he'd glimpsed his son on the street, he wouldn't have recognized him at all. But here in his own house, standing in the kitchen doorway in the middle of the night, there's just no question. And how long has Jonathan been watching him there? Blood rushes to Allen's face, he feels his stomach knot, his bowels grip up.

He clears his throat. "Your mother," he says in a shaky voice, "never could keep a secret."

"She wrote to you," Jonathan says quietly.

"She wanted to hurt me. It just about did me in, Jonathan. She knew it would."

Jonathan draws the blanket he's draped himself in more tightly across his shoulders. He could be as much an apparition as anything else that's recently passed before Allen's eyes.

"I'm glad she told you," he goes on, as if the two of them talking like this is the most natural thing in the world. "I told her to write you if she thought she could. But she didn't want to hurt you, Dad. She never wanted to hurt you. She just wanted to be able to live."

"To live," Allen says. Once again he has to shake his head in wonder. "So this is what everything's come to," he bursts out. "The buck stops here. Kaput. I feel like the captain presiding over some shipwreck. Some disaster that's been going on for years. Tell me it's not true. Give me some reason to believe it's not true."

"Dad, I'm not the messenger."

"No," Allen says, "you're the message itself." But he's not exactly sure what that means. "Come," he gestures wearily. "Sit down. Want a drink?"

Jonathan shakes his head. "I was never much on drinking," he says as he glides over to seat himself at the table.

"Well," Allen tells him—he feels a little defensive—"your old dad feels like having a drink. If you don't mind."

He goes to the cupboard and pours himself a good inch of scotch. His hands are trembling, he notices, sweat's broken out under his arms, along his ribs. Jesus, he thinks, it never gets any better. He sits down across from Jonathan, but he can hardly look at this gaunt stranger.

"I didn't expect," Jonathan says, "to find anybody down here. Janine's been so worried about you. But I don't have to tell you that."

Janine's too much for Allen to think about. One thing at a time. "She called you, didn't she? She made you come down to Houston."

"I've been wanting to come back here for a long time." Jonathan says it in a voice Allen thinks, considering the circumstances, is almost too calm. "And I had to wonder," he goes on, "if maybe this was your way of getting me here."

Never for an instant has that possibility occurred to Allen, and he contemplates it only to reject it out of hand. Still: he feels himself—the only part of him that's real—curl into a little anguished ball deep inside. Hunkering down in desperation. "I can't explain," he says, "what's been happening to me. It's a passage I had to make. But it's over. I can feel it now. It's over." He takes several deep breaths as if to demonstrate. "You don't have to worry. I'm fit and fine."

"Don't make it worse," Jonathan tells him, "by grieving for me. If that's what you're doing."

Of course it's exactly what he's doing. But he's also grieving for himself. For his planet. How to say all that, and to the son he's never really known besides? Fishing in his pocket for the wadded up piece of paper: "I wrote this," he says. "I didn't know I wrote it, but I did. And I don't know why I wrote it. A message that was sent to me and I took it down."

Jonathan takes the wad of paper, flattens it out, tries in the dim light to make out the words. He should turn on a light, Allen thinks, though he doesn't because light on all this would be unbearable. Stealing a glance at his son's nose, he sees no lesion there like he'd so clearly imagined. An unblemished nose, even a beautiful nose. His mother's nose. So what was he thinking? And that image had been so horrendously vivid in his mind's eye, as vivid as any of the rest of those images. What if they'd all been just as false?

But then his eyes fall on Jonathan's left arm, and what he spots there *is* a lesion, no doubt about it—the size of a nipple, flat dull color of a worn penny.

Jonathan looks up from the slip of paper to catch Allen staring at his arm. "Well," he says, adjusting his blanket, handing back the paper, "That's one way of looking at it."

"I've had several days of remarkably clear thought," Allen confides. "Has that ever happened to you? You wake up one day and see just what a fog you've lived your whole life in."

"I think," Jonathan says—and Allen can hear the dryness in his tone—"you could say that's one of the benefits of achieving old age."

This conversation's rife with booby traps.

"What's the good of wisdom," Allen blurts out, "if it doesn't profit

343

the wise? I read that somewhere. But I think it's true."

Jonathan laughs. "You know what *I* read somewhere? In an interview with an astronaut? Some reporter asked, 'So what did you think about when you were sitting on top of that Saturn V rocket with all its millions of intricate precision parts and tons of highly explosive fuel?' " He waits a moment, as if trying to recollect the answer's particular wording, then says, " 'I thought about how everything went out to the lowest bidder.' Do you remember saying that, Dad? It was so funny when I read it, like you were there in the room with me. I could even hear the sound of your voice, the way you'd say something like that."

Allen's completely forgotten. He doesn't even think it sounds like anything he'd say. Charlie, maybe, but he personally never had that kind of sense of humor. He comes out with the first thing that occurs to him. "Did you know," he tells Jonathan, "if we wanted to send a man to the moon right now—say, for some reason, we *had* to—well, we couldn't do it. We've lost the technology. Oh, we still have the plans, the blueprints and the specs and all that, but so much of the rest of it was all in guys' heads. And those guys aren't around anymore. Moved on to other things. Retired. Some of them are dead. It'd take ten years at least to build another Saturn V. In fact, we probably couldn't do it even then. We'd be better off designing some new rocket from scratch. And the same with everything else. The command capsule, the lunar module. All that stuff's vanished without a trace.

"It was just the little accident of the Cold War that put men on the moon. It'll be fifty, a hundred years before we go back. If then. We were way premature. And for what reason? So we could set up a flag, strew a little garbage around? Say we were there? Well, that's been the whole problem all along. That we were there. Everywhere we've been, we've made it worse than it was. Fucked it up. Some day I hope the aliens get their act together to do away with us and turn this planet of ours into one big nature preserve."

"Whoa." Jonathan holds up his hand to stop this torrent of remorse. "You're sounding like my friend Stayton. He's always getting apocalyptic on me too, though he comes at it from a different angle. Maybe it's the weather these days. Or maybe, deep down, we all know."

Allen squirms in his seat, feels zapped by guilt over his ranting. What right does he have to say any of this? "Jonathan," he apologizes—so strange to say that name—"I shouldn't be talking that way to you. Jesus am I sorry."

He puts his head in his hands and then on blind impulse forges right ahead to the heart of the matter. "You really are dying, aren't you?" he says. "It's not just something your mother made up."

But Jonathan doesn't answer. He jumps up from his chair, paces back and forth. "Sometimes I feel such a terrific energy inside me," he exclaims. "I don't know how to say it. Like I can go anywhere, do anything. Burst right through the roof if I have to. All that energy's trapped inside me and ready to explode. Like one of these days my body's going to rip apart and I'll fly free. It's like fire inside me."

Without warning he strides over to the stove and turns on the burner. With a soft *whoosh*, the ring of gas ignites in a halo of blue flame. Its glow fills the room, turns their faces blue, their arms, as Jonathan hovers there, bathed in that light, his blanket slipped from his skeletal shoulders.

Then he flicks the knob and the fire disappears without a trace. They're in darkness again.

"If you haven't already," he says mildly, sitting himself back down, "you should get Janine to tell you some of her rather unusual ideas about reincarnation. They're pretty interesting."

"Oh please," Allen cries. "Why do I keep getting married to these women who're just plain crazy? Tell me that, will you?"

"Mom's not crazy," Jonathan says, "and I should know. And from what I see of her, Janine's not either. Maybe you just think anybody who loves you has got to be crazy."

He does a drum riff on the tabletop. "I'm sorry, Dad," he says. "I didn't mean to say that. This disease does strange things to a person. But you should be nice to Janine. She really does love you. It's hard to let yourself be loved. It's scary. But for somebody to love you, that counts for a lot."

"And I'm horrible to her," Allen says.

"Maybe," Jonathan agrees. "Sort of." Then throwing up his hands: "Well, yeah, probably you are."

In answer, Allen's belly emits a thunderous rumble. It's his turn, embarrassed, to laugh. "The only reason you found me down here," he confesses, "is because I was starving up there."

"And I don't blame you," Jonathan tells him.

"I took a look in the fridge. There's all this peculiar stuff in there. Yours, I presume."

"Well, Stayton's really. It's what he makes me eat these days. Strict regimen. No wonder I'm losing all this weight, right? Crazy stuff like amaranth flour and quinoa and spelt."

"Never even heard of them," Allen admits.

"Lucky you," Jonathan says. "Terrible stuff. You'd be better off dead. But I'll tell you what, you know what I long for right this instant?"

Allen's almost afraid to ask. He's still thinking about this Stayton character, wondering if he's Jonathan's . . . whatever the word is. Significant other. Life partner.

Boyfriend. He winces to imagine. All those old phobias rear their ugly hydra heads.

"Salmon croquettes," Jonathan says matter-of-factly.

Allen couldn't be more surprised. "Jeez," he says.

"You used to make the best salmon croquettes. Remember? Salmon croquettes. How does that sound? I'm starving too."

"It's three o'clock in the morning," Allen demures.

"And getting later all the time. C'mon," Jonathan coaxes as he starts to rummage in the cupboard. Triumphantly he pulls out a can of pink salmon. "See? We're all set. I'll make them. You just tell me how."

Allen tips back his scotch, finishes it off in a swallow. "*I'll* make them. There's nothing to it."

"Excellent." Jonathan plays delighted drums all along the countertop.

"Shh," Allen reminds him. "You'll wake the house."

He spoons a dollop of Crisco into a frying pan.

"Stayton," Jonathan observes, "would skin us both alive if he saw that." His blanket keeps slipping off, and he gathers it awkwardly around his shoulders. Allen can't bear to watch those skinny shoulders, the rail-thin arms and emaciated chest of a war prisoner.

"Go put some clothes on," he tells his son. "You'll catch a cold or something."

"The toga look's just not working," Jonathan admits—the old Jonathan who used to get so unaccountably on Allen's nerves, some melody there he didn't like. It's still the same. Allen doesn't watch him go.

He takes the opportunity to pour himself another finger of scotch and slug it down. The kitchen's lit only by the steady blue of the burner flame. Oddly soothing. He slices an onion, molds the patties of salmon in his palm. Dredges them in bread crumbs.

There's nothing like the satisfying sizzle when he eases them down into the hot Crisco. He's surprised that what he feels isn't panic or sorrow but the strangest sense of exhilaration. A keen anticipation—as if for the first time in months, maybe even years, some future stands wide open before him. But what future it is, precisely, other than this unimpeded shimmer of promise, he can't possibly say.

While he cooks alone in the dark, he feels a song come over him, finds himself singing, softly, the words of the refrain. Lord I'm one, he sings, Lord I'm two, Lord I'm three, Lord I'm four . . .

Lord I'm five hundred miles away from home.

Minor key, an old hobo's chant from the dark trough of the Depression. But why that song, and why now? It used to make him feel so lonely, so empty whenever he heard it, and he's not feeling lonely or empty just now. At least he doesn't think so.

Earlier, in the attic, when the world cracked open at midnight—*then* he felt so empty and lonely he thought he'd die. He even longed like fire to marry a woman he'd never met. Victoria Ivleva. How grotesque was that? But that's all fading, already he can barely even recall the wretched details.

Away from home, he continues to sing to himself, away from home, Lord I'm five hundred miles away from—

Jonathan's footsteps on the stairs cause him to turn around. His son stands paused in the doorway, barefoot but clothed in old jeans, a black T-shirt. In his hand he holds a pistol.

Allen can't help it. Everything goes smash inside him. His heart leaps into his mouth.

"What the fuck?" he yells.

But Jonathan's not pointing the pistol. He holds it by the barrel, peacefully offers Allen the handle.

"Didn't mean to go scaring you like that," he apologizes. "Sorry. Do you recognize it?"

"Jeez. Where in . . . ?" Allen has to say, because of course, taking it in his hand, he does recognize it. "I looked everywhere."

"Out in the garage," Jonathan tells him. "One of those boxes of *National Geographics* Mom saved. I was browsing around out there this afternoon. I was so surprised you never threw them out."

Allen checks the clip. "It's not loaded," Jonathan assures him.

He racks the slide just to be sure.

Jonathan's right. It's empty. Allen remembers emptying it himself. It must have been some twenty years ago that a single, startling bullet popped out onto the floor.

It's too strange for words. Another memory, vaguely shameful, overtakes him.

"I think," he says, "and correct me if I'm wrong, but I think I was planning to make you a present of this pistol. When you graduated from high school. Isn't that right?"

"I think you were," Jonathan says. "In fact I know you were."

And I didn't, Allen thinks, and the reason for it makes a pretty shabby story.

"That gun's been misplaced," he explains, "for I don't know how long. But now it certainly should be yours."

Jonathan, however, backs off. "Guns scare me," he says. "I'm one of those people who think only criminals should have guns."

"No," Allen insists. "I want you to have it. It was my old Air Force pistol. From Korea." But when Allen makes to hand it over, Jonathan wards him off. Waves his hands in front of his face and shakes his head. Then, with apparent alarm, he points.

"Hey," he says. "Behind you. Don't let those yummy croquettes burn."

Allen has just turned to check on them when he's hit with such enormous force, some large hurtling body flinging itself through space, that with a yelp he goes crashing into the stove, and the pistol, as if powered by a life of its own, flies from his hand.

SIGNIFICANT OTHERS

We sat drinking iced tea on the brick patio, Kai and Jonathan and I, while Scheherazade drowsed contentedly in Jonathan's lap. It was, I have to say, a beautiful patio. We'd salvaged the bricks from an eighteenth-century house in Norfolk that had been slated for demolition: weighty, irregular, time-darkened things. We'd loaded the pickup with as many as we could carry away, and during Kai's last extended visit back in the spring had laid them in a herringbone pattern.

"I don't know," Jonathan exclaimed. "This is getting just way too much afternoon sun." It was a comment out of the blue, completely interrupting the tale of our adventures with which he and I had been regaling Kai. "What we need," he proclaimed, "is a grape arbor."

He would do that from time to time. He'd be thinking a number of different things at once and forget which level he was on. I'd learned the art of rapid modulation.

"Think of it as a breakfast terrace," I suggested. "Or what they have in Chinese gardens: a moon viewing platform."

The moon in fact was out, pale and near full in the late afternoon sky.

"You don't think a nice grape arbor would do wonders?"

"It'll attract wasps," I told him.

"I love wasps," he said.

"Well, I hate wasps," Kai weighed in. "Now get back to the story. The plot thickens. You just heard this shout . . ."

"I heard this shout from downstairs," I resumed, "that woke me right up. And Jonathan wasn't there in bed beside me like he should have been. So I went out in the hall, and Janine was out in the hall too, and so we both went downstairs to where the commotion was. The kitchen was dark. But I could hear Jonathan talking. He was saying something about burning."

"We were cooking," Jonathan explained.

"It was the middle of the night and all the lights were off," I added. "And I saw Jonathan's father had a pistol."

"I thought all the lights were off," Kai said.

"The stove burner was on. Everything looked blue."

"Mood lighting," Jonathan said.

"And I think there was moonlight coming in through the window."

"Wrong," Jonathan interrupted. "No moon that night."

"So anyway," Kai hurried me along. "His dad had a pistol."

"I thought he was going to shoot. I went lunging for him. I was scared."

"The gun wasn't loaded," Jonathan explained. "It was my high school graduation present he was trying to give me."

"Much belated," Kai said.

"Much," agreed Jonathan.

I told them, "How was I supposed to know all that? I thought I was saving Jonathan's life."

"Fortunately," Jonathan laughed, "nobody got hurt. Only a little shook up."

"You shrieked," I told him.

"Of course I did."

"And Janine screaming her head off," I added.

"You got to like Janine," Jonathan reminded me—just as a fit of sneezing overtook him. In a single liquid motion Scheherazade spilled from his lap to sleekly prowl the perimeter of the patio. "You," he said to the cat. "I'm getting allergic to you. Don't do this to me."

"Janine and I got along fine," I said, "but I don't think your dad ever warmed up to me much."

"You did come on a little strong," Kai observed.

"I knocked him flat on the floor is what I did."

"You could've killed him," Kai said.

"I was ready for anything."

"Dad was dealing with a lot that weekend."

"He never was all that sure who I was supposed to be," I said. "Even afterward."

"Oh," Jonathan amended, "I made it quite clear."

"He actually asked me," I told Kai, "if I was Jonathan's significant other. Well, what was I to say? Jonathan has many significant others?"

Jonathan laughed. "You should have said, No, I'm his demon lover."

"You boys," Kai said, "had some time of it. I can just tell."

"We covered a lot of very important territory," Jonathan told him simply.

"So you'll see your dad again?" Kai said. "You'll be in touch?"

"After all these years," Jonathan said, "yes, I think there's finally something between us. I'd like to know my dad. I'd like for him to know me. We're both, you know, mortal."

The matter-of-fact way he said it was deeply shocking. We just sat there in silence—a moment, more than a moment, till the silence became difficult to breach with any ordinary conversation. I watched Jonathan carefully—as if, I thought, I were some honeybee trying to store him away. Oblivious, lost in his own momentary, indecipherable thoughts, he sat with his head bowed, hands clasped, elbows resting on his knees. Above us floated the moon. A couple of turkey vultures wheeled lazily in a thermal. He stared resolutely downward.

Finally I couldn't stand it. Some sense of alarm registered in me and I had to say, "Tell us what you're thinking."

He didn't lift his head. He rubbed his thumb and forefinger together.

"I'm thinking," he said, still staring at the ground beneath his feet, "that you guys did a really terrific job on this patio."

And with that he started sneezing again, so violently he had to get up and go inside. Scheherazade, as always, followed close behind.

Later that night, in bed, Kai and I talked more—and differently. "I'm not sure why," I mused aloud, "I went after his father like I did. What I saw there, in that instant, that made me think he was going to do Jonathan some kind of harm. Because I really do think he was going to try to hurt Jonathan. But as you saw, Jonathan feels differently. It was one of those embarrassing moments—you try to help, do what you think is right, and you fuck it up completely. Did things go well down there? I can't really tell you. His father seemed so wary around us. Around me anyway. But maybe it was just me—I certainly felt uncomfortable with *him*. Though things loosened up a bit toward the end. The night before we left, he cooked us steaks and shrimp. Told us a little about his legal troubles. There's a big lawsuit that's ninety-five percent certain to go against him and he seems resigned to that. He's got no friends. He looked terrible. He's this sad, lonely, baffled guy. It's odd. And I made such a hero out of him all those years."

"You have this real thing against fathers," Kai diagnosed. "This resentment or bitterness or I don't know what. You're always setting them up for a fall. And then you're very unforgiving."

"That's not true," I said. "I'm totally aware how painful things were for him. Seeing Jonathan and all. I think he took Jonathan's illness very, very hard. Almost like it was *his* fault."

"When really it's Jonathan's?" Kai said.

I was taken aback.

"No, of course not. I'm not saying that at all. I'd never say a thing like that."

"Or think it," Kai said with that same unexpected edge of aggression in his voice.

"Oh," I said, "do you think I think it?"

"I don't know what you think."

"I don't get it," I told him. "Are you trying to pick a fight with me?"

"No," Kai murmured dully, "I'm not trying to pick any kind of a fight with you."

He didn't say anything more, but I could tell there was more. I lay there a long time beside him waiting.

Finally he said, "I've met this guy. I thought I should tell you. It's been going on for a few weeks. About three months, actually. I thought you should know."

There was such sadness in his voice. I just lay there and took it in. It held no surprise, really—it was as if it was something I'd already known. I wondered how I'd already known it.

I felt, oddly enough, relieved.

"Are you with me on this?" Kai asked gently, since I hadn't said anything.

"Yeah," I told him. "I'm with you. You thought now was the time I should know."

"I didn't feel right about it anymore."

We lay there on our backs, side by side, not touching at all—universes apart, in fact, despite being so close together.

"So what does this mean?" I asked him.

"I don't know. I honestly don't know. He's from Detroit. Plays classical trumpet, but is mostly into jazz. One of the brothers."

"I see," I told him.

"You've been away from me so long," he said. "Not just down here. What I mean is, you have Jonathan."

"We both have Jonathan," I shot back, but then thought about it. "No," I said, "neither of us have him."

"We came such a long way for this," Kai said. "There're a whole lot of things you and I need to be thinking about in the next few weeks. Thinking about and talking about."

"Whatever," I said.

"It's not going to be easy, Stayton."

"Our mistake was to think it would be," I told him.

A shade of warning crept into his voice. "Don't give up," he said.

"No," I assured him, "don't worry about that." I turned away from him, onto my side. "Right now I'm tired and I just want to go to sleep," I said to the wall.

He reached out, put his hand on my shoulder, but I told him, "Don't."

Sometime just before dawn I woke. I was used to waking in that house at all hours of the night with the odd, indescribable feeling that someone was there. That someone was peering in—not through a window, but through the walls or the ceiling. It's hard to explain. I'd lie there trying to fall back asleep and listen to the insomniac whippoorwill that sang in the fields beyond the house.

Next to me, Kai was sound asleep. His face at rest was so beautiful. I studied him for a while, thinking complicated but not unkind thoughts. Then for some reason, restlessness I suppose, I got up and went downstairs.

A pale gray light suffused the house. The minute before I walked into the room we called the airlock, I knew.

Jonathan must have gotten up sometime in the night as well, unable for reasons of his own to sleep, and arranged the candles so that the room flicked warmly around him, and filled the tub with hot water

353

hoping a bath might soothe him. He lay there looking peaceful. The candles had burned down about halfway, so he'd been lying there a couple of hours. Scheherazade crouched compactly on a small table by the windows and watched him with her inscrutable gaze. Jonathan must have known it was his time. The water was lukewarm, not quite room temperature yet. It had shriveled his skin, blanched it white. His dark lesions stood out starkly.

His big brown eyes were wide open.

He'd said he'd never go into the hospital. This turned out to be so easy for you, I thought with bittersweet relief. It wasn't even as if he'd died. He'd just left. Given his body the slip. That was the strange but distinct impression I had, and I remembered him telling me once, when we were restless boys and the streets of Minerva could barely contain us, how the dinosaurs didn't die out. How they turned into birds in love with the ecstasy of flight. How they flew away.

It was selfish, but I wanted to be alone with him. I sat there on the side of the tub for a few minutes stroking his stubbled cheek, running my hand through his short-cropped hair before I went up to wake Kai.

I had known, of course, that Jonathan wasn't going to make it. That this disease was fatal. That even had he allowed it, there was no cure any doctors in the world could give him. But knowing all that is not the same as living it. What I felt most of all was a simple sense of the incompletion of everything. Everything just stopped here—and then resumed its course with the single exception of Jonathan's absence from it all.

His father and Janine flew up for the scattering of the ashes. Kai had been adamant about Jonathan's wishing to be cremated: "He said, Don't let them stick me in that damp earth. Remember how cold he used to feel all the time? He didn't want that. He wanted to burn like fire."

Julian came out with his undergraduate entourage in tow—well-scrubbed, beaming boys, the very bloom of Virginia aristocracy. Also on hand was the vague, ever-elusive Marco, as well as a goodly number of the crew who'd helped us build the place up. On that warm, breezy afternoon in early July we traipsed out to the little pond that was near the back edge of the property. Already it was starting to dry up, as it did every summer. There wasn't much to the ceremony. We put a tape of "Beim Schlafengehen" from the *Four Last Songs* in the boom box Jonathan had always had by his side when working on the roof. Kai and I had arranged to say, in unison, a few simple words. "Our brilliant companion," we intoned, holding the bowl containing his ashes between us as Elizabeth Schwarzkopf's inimitable voice resolved *tief und tausend-fach zu leben.* "Matches struck in darkness," we uttered as the orchestra broke over us with a sob, "this was one."

Jonathan would have loved it, I think.

Then people came forward, took a handful of him and flung him to the breeze. It was more awkward than anything else.

"Ooh," Julian shrieked, "they're blowing back in my face."

Everyone laughed—through tears—except for Jonathan's father who looked utterly miserable and apart from everything. Afterward he wandered around the house, tumbler of scotch in hand. He kept reaching out to touch the walls, the door frames, the triple panes of glass in the greenhouse. Thoughtfully he caressed the leaves of the thriving plants and let the chickens peck about his feet.

"He built all this," he said to me several times, shaking his head and looking for the confirmation he refused, quite, to believe. "It's like a damn spaceship," he said. "One day we'll go to the stars in something like this."

"I'm sorry," I told him, "it had to happen this way."

Painfully, he waved me into silence. Janine and I exchanged helpless looks. Jonathan and his father: this thing beyond us we'd both been caught up in.

"I loved him like my own son," Janine confessed to me later. We sat on the front steps and drank wine. "I carried him in my heart. And his father carried him in his heart too. It was just difficult."

"Jonathan never made it easy for anybody," I said.

"It's why we loved him so much," she told me.

I finished off my glass, poured myself some more.

"I'm not taking this very well," I admitted.

"No," she said. "I can see you aren't. But he was so ill, Stayton. So weak. I could see that in Houston. But I have to tell you this. His aura was very strong. I could hardly look at it, it blazed so bright around him."

"I wish," I told her, "I believed in all that."

"It's true whether you believe it or not. Jonathan believed it."

"I know," I said. "I was always afraid he might be a little goofy that way."

"Anyway," she said, clutching my arm so tightly it startled me, "it's not Jonathan I'm scared for, Stayton. It's Allen. His aura's the one that's sick. It's very meager. It's flickering in the wind like it's about to go out."

I wrote to Jonathan's mother in Turkey—I didn't know what else to do, how else to get in contact with her, and I didn't hear back till after the ceremony. I'm not sure what I had expected. The tone of her note was slightly formal, distant—as if the full import of the news hadn't yet sunk in. Or even more curiously, as if the news didn't particularly involve her. She expressed no regrets. She thanked me for having taken care of him in his illness. For having been his friend. "Wherever he was," she wrote, "he always loved his friends very much."

I would be less than frank were I not to admit that I had, somehow, wished for more from that indecipherable woman.

"This doesn't change anything," I confirmed to Kai.

"No," he told me sadly, "I don't think it does."

We cared for each other too much not to be gentle with each other. But it was also, we knew, the end.

"You should stay here," he told me. "You shouldn't leave. Not until you want to. Anyway, you were right about one thing. I'll never be able to sell the place. Especially not now. Who on earth would ever buy the hassle of it?"

"It's not that much of a hassle once you get used to it."

Kai had never been down long enough to acclimate himself to the various whims and demands of the greenhouse. "But I'd like to stay," I said, "at least for a while. If it's all right with you."

"And you were the skeptical one."

"I lost my capacity for faith a long time ago," I said.

"And you went and sacrificed your life for this place," Kai observed bluntly.

"No," I told him. "That's not true at all."

"You won't feel too isolated? You're kind of in the middle of nowhere here."

"There's always the prison next door," I joked. "And besides, I've got friends in Williamsburg. I'll manage just fine."

I have no evil words ever to say about Kai. He did what he could—all along, he had done what he could. But it was clear we couldn't go back. Couldn't go back to a time before that day when, in a gesture almost too good to be true, Jonathan tossed us tart windfall apples from the ground of Kai's inherited estate. Impossible to go back to a moment before the phone rang in our Washington apartment and I heard that voice I hadn't heard in years.

Impossible, for that matter, to go back before Dr. Lennox's biology class, or the night in the Travelers when I was sixteen years old and my heart seized up at the sight of that long-haired, mascara'd boy I first thought was a girl as he danced to the music on the jukebox.

A week or so after the ash-scattering ceremony, after everyone had left and I was alone, I sat one evening on the sofa with Scheherazade purring in my lap and made myself watch the Voegli Gospel Hour.

There they appeared, my whole family, waving to the crowd, on a set resembling what I suppose was meant to be an American living room—gaudier than ours back in Minerva, certainly, but still in some unsettling way familiar to me. Seating themselves on two long sofas angled to face both each other and the audience as well, while behind them a roaring fire filled the fireplace and a beneficent painting of Jesus hung over the mantel, they exuded the waxy sheen of fruit beginning to go rotten. My brothers, in their early thirties now and balding, still eerily resembled each other, as did their curiously placid wives and somewhat unruly brood of young. I hadn't known that either Keith or Kevin had gotten married, or that they had had children. But then I had known nothing about them at all in the past ten years or so. As they had known nothing about me. I could see, though, how they'd grown into minor versions of their father. Our father. How one day they would fill his shoes.

My mother looked ghastly. She'd gained much weight, and the garish costume she'd been decked out in flattered her not at all. She'd always been a bit shy in public, and now she seemed flustered, even belea-guered by the scrutinizing presence of the camera. She said little, in that respect following the lead of my brothers' more photogenic wives, and I felt for her a pang of sorrow sharper than anything I'd ever felt for her in my life.

There was some desultory singing by my brothers and their wives, then a plug for the family's appearance at various churches and revivals around the South in the upcoming weeks. I was relieved no one seemed to be hawking the Vacu-Lux with its incomparable body ash siphon. The family had clearly discovered, down through the years, other and better ways to generate income.

Finally my father began his sermon. He gripped the sides of the podium and stared uncompromisingly at the camera. I made myself meet that stare without flinching.

"I have come to talk to you today," he told his viewers, "about a grave and insidious danger. The so-called environmental movement. You've heard all about it. Friends of the Earth. Save the animals. Back to nature. And it all sounds lovely, doesn't it? But I want to tell you this. The so-called environmental movement is allied with nothing less than the forces of Satan. You say, What? Well, if this startles you, then maybe it should. Because the Good Book could not be more explicit on this subject." And for good measure he thumped the pulpit with his Good Book. "We are specifically enjoined not to worship the creation but the Creator.

"They talk about conserving natural resources," he shouted in one of those dramatic transitions that had always been his forte. "Conserv-ing them for *what*? The Bible tells us: this world shall perish. Time shall be no more. There's nothing we can do about it, and I would even go so far as to hazard this: to try to do something about it is to try to thwart the plan that God Almighty Himself has ordained. Don't you think He created precisely as much in this world as we need to get us to the Second Coming? Far from conserving the Earth, dear brothers and sisters, I say we are in fact meant to use it up. If, at the Second Coming, we have not used this world up, then we have sorely *misused* it. And God will deal with us accordingly."

I sat helplessly mesmerized. I remembered how, as a child, I had longed for his love. How instead I had felt only the chill and splendor of his rectitude—and the secret, desperate, bullying scramble merely to be *right* that all that rectitude really concealed.

Sitting there in front of the television set, Scheherazade sleeping peacefully in my lap, I spoke aloud, calmly and resolutely, to the empty room. "I renounce you," I told my father. "I renounce you utterly and forever."

If for a while I had thought I might be settled, I saw now that I was wrong. My difficult journey had still only begun.

Your old Protestant upbringing you'll never shake, Jonathan would say, shaking his head in disapproval. Always looking for the point. The direction of history, the arrow of time. The long, arduous story of salvation itself.

In his last months, he kept haranguing me with a poem he'd been reading. I'm sorry to say now, I had less than infinite patience. "*Look,*" he'd declaim when I'd be trying to concentrate on some important, meaningless task at hand, *Look, I'm living. On what? Neither my childhood nor my future is growing smaller. Being in excess*—and here he'd rap that manic drumroll of his on whatever surface was available, practically shouting the words—*Being in excess wells up in my heart.*

I wish I could forget those words. I wish I'd never heard them, or that I'd listened more closely. Because I think I can hear him there, crouched inside my memory of the sound of his voice: coiled there, really, taut and springlike, as if he might somehow—against all odds of magic or faith or science—be about to leap forth.

Scheherazade seems to spend a lot of time looking for him too. She sniffs at odd corners, scratches at doors as if she expects to find him secreted away somewhere she least expects. We're some pair, she and I. We wander the house together, late into the whippoorwill-haunted night, sometimes all the way till dawn. And there are moments when I think that, all alone from all the people he knew, that little black cat and I have embarked on Jonathan's space ark after all, and we're sailing through a splendid abyss of stars exactly as he promised—orchestra-powered, bristling with minarets and banners, Beethoven at the helm and Captain Nemo on drums. And yes, Esther Williams did come along:

she's in the library reading Persian love poems while a chorus of shoe-shine boys from the streets of Constantinople serenades a crescent moon.

And I always thought I hated cats.

WHAT I KNOW NOW

Non fui. Fui. Non sum. Non curo.

That tiny assertion of life amidst all those killing negations.

My epitaph for Jonathan would be: He moved through the world as if the world could never be an obstacle. As if the world had been divinely conceived for human joy.

That was his brilliant mistake. The rest is love.

On the flat rooftop across the way someone has set up poles, strung lines, trained a grapevine into an arbor, refuge from late afternoon's clear heat—and they sit up there, grandmother and brothers and cousins, sipping tea, playing backgammon, chatting in the quiet, dignified way of the Turks. They have hung a splendid old carpet still alive with color and design over the railing to air. Someone is stoking the charcoal brazier.

Two black-draped women make their way along the street. How Tansu rages—"they are stupid, ignorant women," she says. Atatürk, her beloved Atatürk, was right to outlaw the veil. (Beginning first from the minaret of the Orta Camii down the street, then half a minute later from the Kuyularönu Camii and the Yeni Camii, staggered, cacophonous, comes the call to prayer.)

I am not a part of any of that life, nor will I ever be. I am known around Olba, the village that sits astride Dio-Caesarea's ruins, as the loyal assistant to Professor Doctor Ergüliç, who cows the local laborers with her fierce commands and astonishes everyone with what she brings to light from the covetous earth. I am the foreign lady without a home in her native land. The crazy American lady who sleeps on the roof. But from my rooftop I watch and listen. I breathe deeply, content to be only that traveler who has stopped here, for a time, to rest. Stopped years, in fact, all too aware how my journey to this place very nearly did me in.

An empty lot next door is planted thick with fruit trees, roses, oleander—every available inch filled, and I remember the lawns of Houston, those empty expanses of green, the poisons we employed to keep them that way. I think of that garden I made forty years ago in the California hills above Edwards Air Force Base. Everything grew there too, but most especially unease, the loss of God that was absolute, irrevocable.

Everything, I think, has moved toward this moment. Now and now and now. In Konya I once met a holy man, a dervish, who told me, "Perhaps God is so great that He does not even need to exist." A kind of joy, lightninglike but invisible, can flash out any instant. From my perch I can see a grandmother in black as she sits out on her terrace. Down in the garden, unseen by her, concealed by the lush foliage but visible to my own benign, prying eyes, a young girl is pulling the cool white petals from an autumn-flowering bush. Carefully she fits a petal over each of her fingernails, so that now she holds up her hands to admire ten moon-white fingertips. She's pretending—but what? American images glimpsed from television, a magazine? She touches one hand to her breast, with the other she gestures elegantly, like a princess. She flutters her white-tipped hands, admires them back and front, poses—while just above her head, unaware of all that infectious glamour, her austere grandmother sits with bitter fixity.

This thing we have hammered out together, Tansu and I, beat thin as gold in the light between us. Something I do not wish words for. And it shimmers.

———

In the bright light of a September afternoon, working in the precincts of a third-century villa, we unearth a coin hoard, a stash of silver minted mostly in the troubled reigns of Gallus and Valerian. Indications are that the clay pot was buried at the foot of a large tree, perhaps part of a sacred grove, perhaps only a favorite tree.

A long-forgotten family fleeing some long-forgotten disaster. We will never know their story, only that they buried these coins hoping one day, when the troubles were over, to return, to dig them up, to use them to resume the old life or out of the ravages start another. But they never came back. What happened to them, what fate they met with, we will never know.

All we can know is that they never came back.

I am there when we lift the hoard from the earth. No one has touched these coins, no human hands since the hands that buried them, centuries ago, so anxiously or with such impossible hope.

ACROSS THE WIDE MISSOURI

No real surprise to me. I mean, that I'm standing here. Moving and not moving. Wide field, black overhead and through my fingers I can see stars, valleys, billions of birds, I can see footprints across the sky.

The families they left and the villages they grew up in. People come and go, conversations I can't really remember. Words out of my mouth like the world. Nonsense of one great kind or another. Get the distinct feeling I'm waiting here, momentary—but for what I don't know. Or no words for, no thoughts. But something more substantial than this—conversations, and slippery like I've not really got a hold. Though certain things carry through. Forgotten but they'll come back to me.

Sooner or later.

Seismic tremors run all through this slumber. Satellite's body caught in the branches of a tree. A serpent's orbit underground.

A firefall in the eye trailing off in silence.

I have the sense of everything too late. Think I find myself saying that to somebody. These feelings, this sense of continually going away like the touch of a hand or lips. Sitting with me, a bench of some kind, here or there.

Somebody.

Then he goes or I go, I think I get up and walk away but then I'm still here. Melody that goes underground. Like water poured in a funnel, and that has something to do with what it's hard to keep track of. Beginning over and over again in the same place, not sure if it's just a feeling or if I really am beginning over and over again in the same place. Because if I am.

Or I'm watching a fire kindle, watching where the fire touches the log or lives off some interchange going on right at that exact point back and forth between the fire and the log I can mimic with my hands but can't find the words. My blue hands. Flickering.

Or that's not it.

Gibberish moon and what it circles. Always and now. Which means raptor, bird of prey. Which means a cave, a mouth full of stars. A good swallow, deep breath, doves in the dome. Time and underwater and planet earth.

Forget all these things. Here we go again.

(my blue hands)

(third eye of darkness)

. . .

now begin

BON VOYAGE

There's the day he shambles over to Frank's next door to present him with a check for seven hundred dollars.

"You don't owe me a penny for anything," Frank tells him.

"Yes I do," Allen says. "I'm the one who messed with your Mustang."

"No," Frank says. "Impossible."

"Scout's honor," Allen tells him. "And I'm damned sorry for it too."

Frank takes a moment to consider. "What in hell were you thinking?" he says. "I should sue the bejesus out of you."

"You could," Allen tells him. "Only if anybody knows how broke I am these days, it should be you."

"Hit pretty hard, didn't it?" Frank murmurs. Even Allen can detect how embarrassed he is.

"I suppose you could always take the house," he tells Frank. "The shirt off my back."

"No, no, no." Frank moves to put a stop to all that. "Don't be ridiculous. I don't want a penny of your money. But I still want to know what got into you. I always thought you had a soft spot for that car of mine."

The bright September sun gleams off the Mustang's red hood. It sits, shroudless, in the sun-flooded drive.

"It's very hard to explain," Allen says. "I'd rather not go into it."

They'll never, he realizes, be friends again.

"I respect that," Frank tells him. "It's been hard going all around."

A vague terror seizes Allen and he turns, hurriedly, to go.

"How's Janine?" Frank asks behind him.

"Oh," he says, feeling himself stiffen. "Janine's just fine."

He waits for what he knows is coming next. And it does come.

"I read about your son," Frank says awkwardly. "I read the obituary in the paper. I was very sorry to hear."

"Janine put that in," Allen makes himself say.

Beloved son of Allen and Joan Cloud. Sorely missed by his loving parents, his stepmother, his many devoted friends. Allen rubs his thumb and forefinger together. Secret motion of calm.

"It's a damn shame," Frank says. "Tragic is what it is."

Allen doesn't trust himself to turn round to face Frank. His composure, these days, is all shot to hell.

Taking great care with each word, he tells Frank, "I'll tell Janine you asked about her. That'll mean a lot to her." And then he resumes his secret and headlong flight.

He has to make himself do small things. Normal things. He thinks, consciously, Now I'm doing this, now I'm doing that.

Now he's cooking steaks on the grill. As for himself, he's got no appetite these days at all. It's for Janine. It's the little things, he's told himself, that count. And these days he spends much of his time—it's what he's resolved to himself—trying to make the little things count.

This is their life, after all. The only one they'll have together. And never has it seemed so precious.

He always liked to cook, though he never, till recently, had the time to do much of it. In another life, maybe, he'd have been a chef.

In another life. It's a funny thought.

Beef, he's read, is one of those bad habits that's killing the planet. But he thinks, Well, what can you do? We're at the top of the food chain, after all.

As for all those dire newspaper clippings and magazine articles in the attic—he's gone and thrown those out. Even the Brueghel, which was a shame since it was such a handsome reproduction. But there'd been enough in there to drive a man nearly insane with a sense of his own helplessness and futility. As he well knows. And what's the end of that line of thinking anyway? That we should all go out and extinguish ourselves?

If he's going to survive, he has to reject all that. You can't start wondering, halfway through the flight, exactly what it is that's holding you up. And yet the thought nags him: we will not survive.

He thinks of Jonathan's ark—that attempt, wide-eyed and finally ridiculous, at some kind of right living. All those plants and chickens plus the nagging odor of ammonia and flying insects everywhere, even in the bedrooms—"beneficials," those two housemates of his kept calling them, as if it made any difference. That kid never grew up, did he?

He won't think those thoughts. He consciously attends to the steaks sizzling on the grill, the pungent aroma of charcoal smoke wafting up to his nostrils. The marbled texture of the meat. A fine cut from a butcher he trusts and respects.

A butcher, perhaps. He could have been a butcher. His mind, it seems, is doomed to wander.

He watches Janine out in the yard with the poacher's spade he bought her for her birthday back in June—geologic ages ago. She's been putting in azaleas to replace the ones the sycamores took out when they came crashing down. At the time he'd felt bad when she marched over to Frank's to demand reimbursement, and the car still a secret from everybody, a mystery—but Frank's gone and let him off the hook. As always, he's got his luck. And you can hardly tell, anymore, what a war zone the lawn looked like there for a while.

Her face set with grim determination, Janine spades the recalcitrant ground. He feels such love for her. Such inexpressible love. All through his life, the only kind of love he's ever felt has been inexpressible. Locked up, silenced, the key thrown away. What was he so damn scared of anyway?

His love for his father, for his second wife and his first one too, for his son. His love for Chuck Brittain and Kite Baxter. It never did any of them any good.

There, he's said that to himself. Now he can get on, he thinks, with the rest of his life.

But there's no getting on with anything. Because suddenly he has the clearest memory: in the Virginia woods, Stayton and that black man Kai holding Jonathan's ashes in a green bowl, and he thought, a moment of utter panic seizing him, That's my son they have in their hands—only to realize, stifling the cry that almost broke from him, They didn't take him from me. He put himself in their hands. He chose, freely, to go with them. To turn his back. These are the people my son chose to make his life with. Homosexuals. The word he always feared the most—of all words.

Homosexual. He says it now, almost murmurs it aloud. Nothing happens. The world does not splinter and fall. Somewhere in those woods a bird—perhaps a hawk—had uttered a single piercing cry. Music played. Music Jonathan loved, someone had said—lush, and a singer sang in German. Music Joan used to love too, when they were first married and he'd come home to find her listening to the classical station on the radio. Then at some point she stopped, she listened to other things, and when he asked her why, she said classical music made her too sad to listen to alone.

Of all of them, Janine's the only one left him.

"Janine," he calls out.

She pauses in her work, shades her eyes as she looks his way. The sun seems to enfold her in its radiance.

"You go get yourself cleaned up," he says. "Food'll be ready in a jiffy."

Gingerly he plucks the baking potatoes in their tin-foil from the grill, juggles them onto a plate. Too hot to handle, really. With a fork he pries their jackets open, savors the rising steam.

"The most remarkable thing," he tells his wife once they're seated at the picnic table.

"Yes?" she asks, peering at him curiously.

He's not sure what he wanted to say.

"I loved my son," he says simply.

A flicker of concern crosses Janine's face. He knows that look. They've never properly discussed the events of that strange weekend back in June.

"Of course you did," she assures him.

"But I disliked him," Allen goes on. "The things he let himself get involved with. Sordid things. He made me so nervous that way. And I was right to be nervous."

"Nobody could've known," Janine says.

"I'm not doing a very good job of explaining this," he tells her. "I thought he cast me in an unfavorable light."

Janine's stopped any pretense of eating. She's staring at him.

"What kind of unfavorable light?" she asks in a way that makes him squirm. He should never have started this conversation. What on earth was he thinking?

"Let's just let it go at that," he says.

She reaches across the table to touch his hand. He can almost feel a shock go through him at her touch.

"Honey," she says. "You don't have to tell me any of this. You know I'll listen to anything you say. But I already know. I already understand."

"I'm through talking," he says. "I just had to say what I said. For the record."

For the record. He takes a big bite of succulent steak, chews slowly, reflectively. Done rare, the way he likes it. Done, in fact, nearly to perfection. He didn't think he was in the least bit hungry, but as he's always said, "Put food in front of me and it'll disappear."

The area where the solar wind becomes so weak that it is overwhelmed by incoming particles from other stars is considered the real edge of the solar system, a boundary called the heliopause.

The newspapers are full, every day, of the fantastic exploits of his species. It thrills him to see. And who knows where, ultimately, they might be bound for?

Voyager 2, he reads, will cross the heliopause around the year 2012. After that, in 6,500 years, riding on its momentum it will near Barnard's Star, and in another 11,500 years Proxima Centauri. By that time, Voyager will still be closer to the Sun than to any other star: one light-year, the distance light travels in a year, 5.8 trillion miles.

When he looks up from his newspaper the sun's setting, a honeycomb of light spots the far wall—though what's being reflected, he can't quite tell. He remembers how Joan used to watch his flight from their cabin in the hills above Edwards. How by the time she could hear his sonic boom the test flight was over. How Jonathan devised a calendar of meteor storms to chart the days, weeks, months his father was away on business. Both extraordinary events in their way, so far receded from him now in time, and yet up close he missed those things. Too busy, going too fast, and missed them entirely.

Invisible miracles.

Casualties of progress.

In the year 26262, Voyager should enter the Oort Cloud, a region of comets orbiting the Sun. Eventually, in the year 296036, it will pass close to Sirius the Dog Star, brightest star visible from Earth. By then Voyager will be 14.64 light-years—nearly 85 trillion miles—away from home.

Facts and figures, the stuff you can hold on to. And yet, if he's not careful, it can make him want to cry.

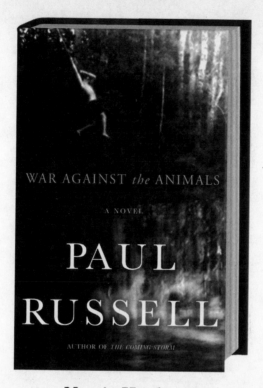